THE
MASTER
STROKE

Books by Elizabeth Gage

A Glimpse of Stocking
The Master Stroke
Pandora's Box

Published by POCKET BOOKS

THE MASTER STROKE

Elizabeth Gage

POCKET BOOKS

New York   London   Toronto   Sydney   Tokyo   Singapore

POCKET BOOKS, a division of Simon & Schuster Inc.
1230 Avenue of the Americas, New York, NY 10020

Gage, Elizabeth.
    The master stroke / Elizabeth Gage.
      p.   cm.
    ISBN 0-671-74815-7 : $21.00
    I. Title.
    PS3557.A327M37 1991
    813'.54—dc20   91-20762
                                                        CIP

First Pocket Books hardcover printing September 1991

10   9   8   7   6   5   4   3   2   1

To my parents

Acknowledgments

The author wishes to thank the following for their cooperation and advice in the preparation of this novel:

International Trade Administration, Department of Commerce
The Council for Exceptional Children (Educational Resources Information Center)
IBM Corporation
Apple Computer, Inc.
The New York City Historical Society
Childhelp U.S.A.
Ernst H. Huneck, M.D.

The background of this story includes several European capitals as well as a critical moment in the history of international finance and technology. I could never have successfully investigated such a complex subject without the help of experts in the field. In Paris, Mme. Marie-Claire Lalande offered indispensable assistance in opening administrative doors and procuring needed documentation. In London, Mr. Anthony MacAndrew was a patient and much-needed guide to the complexities of British finance. In Lausanne, Mme. Antoinette Vuillemin graciously shared her recollections of the postwar economic expansion and its effect on European business.

My heartfelt appreciation goes to Ms. Tina Gerrard and Mr. Jon Kirsh for their tireless and thorough assistance in my research. Thanks also to Mr. Bill Grose and Ms. Claire Zion, my editors at Pocket Books, for their invaluable advice and support. And last but never least, sincere thanks to Jay Garon, agent and friend.

Elizabeth Gage

Contents

The principle of all games is the same: a lesser power may defeat a superior power by placing it in such a position that its own strength works against it. In such a move or series of moves however, the lesser power runs the constant risk of being annihilated by its own gambit.

—*The Master's Book of Games,*
Leipzig, 1844

Prologue

The old man looked at the newspaper in his lap.

He was sitting up in his wheelchair, unable to turn the pages. The newspaper had been deposited on his knees a moment ago. All he could do was stare at the headline and the photograph beside it.

"This year's Businessman of the Year award has gone to a woman for the first time in the history of the award. Frances Bollinger, President and CEO of CompuTel, Inc., and acknowledged master of the computer field in business today, accepted the award at a banquet at the Waldorf-Astoria. Her husband was at her side."

The old man looked at the photo. It showed two attractive young people, the proud husband beside his beautiful wife. She was amazingly fresh and pretty, with clear milky skin and rich dark hair which fell to her shoulders. Her eyes glimmered with pride in her accomplishment and humility at the great honor being bestowed on her.

He wished he could crumple the newspaper with strong hands and tear it to shreds. Long ago, when he had had the chance, he should have strangled that girl. But his hands were useless to him now, inert and feelingless as two foreign pieces of pale meat in his lap. He could do nothing with them, not even turn the page to see what else was written in the article.

He could only sit here with her face dangled before him like a mocking curse.

"Shall I turn the page?"

An attractive young woman had come into the room. Unlike the tall brunette in the photograph, this one was small, fragile in her beauty, with silken blonde hair. He looked up into her eyes. The hatred and frustration he was feeling glistened in his coal-black irises. She noted it without comment and turned the page of the newspaper.

"I thought you'd want to see it," she said. "She has come a long way, after all. She deserves what she's got."

There was a brightness in her tone that was not without its hint of sadistic satisfaction. She knew what his predicament was. And she was enjoying it.

He said nothing. He could speak, of course—that was the only function left to his ruined body that obeyed his will. But he had found in his dealings with her that silence was the only way to retain what was left of his dignity—and indeed the only way to fight her.

Not that it really succeeded. For, even as she cared for his helpless body, washed and dressed him, she kept up a cool, superficially amiable conversation under which he always heard her rebellion and her triumph. She had him at her mercy.

He looked down at the newspaper. The article went on, describing the Bollinger girl's achievements, her marriage, her success. He closed his eyes, infuriated.

Seeing this, the girl returned and took the newspaper out of his lap.

"Well, maybe you'll want to look at it later," she said.

He was relieved. The brunette in the photograph and the pretty blonde in the room with him were like twin torturers. At least now he had only the blonde to worry about.

"It's time for your bath," she said.

With surprisingly strong arms she lifted him from the wheelchair and put him on the bed. Strong arms . . . or was it his withered body that made it so easy for her?

She undressed him, taking off the pajamas which were the only garments he wore these days.

Carefully she began to sponge him. He could not feel what she was doing. He knew that somewhere down there she was touching his sex, cleansing away the involuntary urine, and noticing as she did so that there was no response, no maleness there to find her strokes interesting.

What was worse was that his manhood had not died with his senses. Inside he was as alert as ever to her presence, to the perfume of her limbs, the blonde freshness of her body.

That was the exquisite essence of his torture. Though his virility was gone forever, his male instincts survived intact. And thus his obsession with her grew in proportion to his inability to do anything about it. He could only stew in his own juices as she teased him with her nearness.

And she knew this. How could she not? After all, she knew his needs and his hungers better than anyone else.

Her knowledge shone in the clothes she chose to wear, the colors she knew he had liked on her in the old days, the skirts, the blouses that hugged her small breasts. It stirred in her movements as she passed in front of him in the bedroom with its hospital bed. It sang in her voice when she hummed familiar melodies as she wheeled him to the solarium for his midday session with the newspapers and magazines, whose pages she had to turn for him.

She knew, all right. Even the delicacy of her attention to his needs was a way of twisting her private knife in his flesh.

She jealously kept him for her own. She would allow no one else near him, except his wife. Everyone said she was so devoted, so wonderful. He alone knew the real reason for her solicitude. He alone knew the revenge she was savoring slowly as she cared for him in his helplessness.

And today her triumph was at its peak, now that she could show him the image of the Bollinger girl's success, and taunt him with it.

Naked, he looked up at her as she bathed him. He felt his forgotten infancy stir within him, when his mother had cared for him in this way. That was seventy-five years ago.

Life had come full circle. In his time he had made presidents tremble, heads of state come to him on their knees, willful men cringe before his power.

And now it was all behind him, all banished by the face in the photograph, all eclipsed by the cool, smiling face of the girl cleaning his lifeless body.

"All right," she said. "Let's get you dressed now, and take you downstairs. You can watch some television."

He looked up at her as she lifted his pelvis to slip the pajama bottoms up. In her eyes, sidelong but glittering like a beacon, was the hatred she had owed him for so long, which she could now take out at her leisure.

"Are we ready?" she asked, smiling.

A single tear came to his eye and rolled down his wizened cheek.

"Not sad?" she asked, feigning concern. "There's nothing to be sad about. Cheer up. It's a beautiful day."

Worst of all, she knew that tear was not of sadness. It was of hatred, and of frustration. And she knew he was in her power now, forever.

"Come on," she said. "Let's go downstairs and read the papers. I'm sure you want to see the rest of that article."

Stifling the moan of rage that scalded his throat, he felt her push his wheelchair toward the next hellish hour of his destiny.

Book I
KING'S PAWN

$$=== 1 ===$$

New York City, six years earlier

To anyone interested in a career in business, Magnus Industries, Inc. was the only destination worth pursuing.

The corporation was not only a leader in all the financial and manufacturing fields it had chosen to explore in its decades of enormous growth; it also had a prestige rivaled only by General Motors, IBM, and a handful of similar corporations around the world. Its stock was blue-chip. Its financial rating had been A 1 for over thirty years, without a single quarter in the red, not even during the Depression.

The company was an aggressive innovator. It had pioneered new products and methods in engineering, manufacturing, and sales, and was the prototype of the multinational conglomerate, with subsidiaries in forty countries, each one a leader in the economy of its home base.

The corporation's headquarters was located in a seventy-story steel-and-glass structure on Sixth Avenue, designed by Wallace Harrison in 1931. The building was as forward-looking as the company it housed. From its glittering façade to its elegant lobby, the place bespoke prestige, quiet pride in achievement, and bold confidence.

Few visitors to that somewhat impersonal structure were unaware of the shadowy presence which gave the marching orders to all who worked within. Magnus Industries had been founded in 1921 by Anton Magnus, then a broad-shouldered, peasantlike immigrant from Switzerland, and built singlehandedly by him into an empire. Starting on a shoestring gained, it was rumored, from a series of shady stock deals made with someone else's money, he had used a combined elegance of strategy and ruthlessness of execution to conquer territory after territory, competitor after competitor, until by the mid-twenties Magnus Industries was one of the fastest-rising young corporations in New York.

But it was during the Depression that Anton Magnus made his fortune. Taking advantage of the bizarre business climate created by tight money, he had acquired dozens of bankrupt and debt-ridden companies, stewarded them through the lean years, and emerged in 1939 in control of a vast patchwork of financial influence.

He had seized control of all these companies by a mixture of urbane old-world charm and an iron fist which he brought out when it was least expected. He had a knack for gaining people's confidence while probing for their weak points, so that they were too dependent on him in one way or another, or too cowed by him, to refuse when he asked something difficult or unpleasant of them. Those weaker than himself he simply rolled over; those stronger he managed to outflank through clever manipulations until their strengths had been turned into weaknesses he could exploit.

A precocious chess master at age thirteen in the old country, Anton Magnus had not forgotten the lessons in strategy he had learned from his beloved game. He possessed the knack of seeing several moves ahead of his rivals, and for attacking without mercy when their defenses were down.

Anton Magnus played for keeps. More than one of his business enemies had been driven to suicide by the financial destruction he had suffered at the hands of Magnus. There were rumors that Magnus enjoyed humiliating people, and was not satisfied with his own success until he was certain that it had brought eternal punishment upon his rivals.

His single-handed conquest of the Great Depression was only the beginning. As a European émigré Magnus had seen the significance of the Nazi movement in Europe, and had foreseen the war. Long before Germany attacked Poland, Magnus had invaded the field of heavy industry which would, he foresaw, be responsible for building armaments for the U.S. armed forces. When the enormous government contracts came through, Magnus was ready.

By the end of the war Magnus Industries was a giant. When American knowhow was poured into the recovery of the defeated European nations, Magnus Industries was in the forefront of the rebuilding effort. Anton Magnus now acquired impoverished European companies for a song, just as he had bought American companies during the Depression. The vast European arm of the Magnus conglomerate dated from this period.

In short, Anton Magnus made as much money off postwar aid to the Axis Powers as he had by helping his adopted country to bomb them into destruction. And he made as much from the war as he had from the Depression. Out of the crises that ruined other businessmen, he had snatched success and power.

Magnus was a private man. He kept his personal life shrouded in as much mystery as the strategies that kept him a step ahead of his competitors. Though the photographic image of his impressive face, with piercing eyes, dark brows, and silver hair, was familiar to the public from dozens of handshake pictures with business leaders, governors, senators, and presidents, his private life was not the subject of public comment. Magnus had intended this.

Over the years he had had many mistresses, for his powerful personality and attractive, craggy features, combined with his fast-growing wealth and power, was too much for most women to resist.

In his thirties he had married the former Victoria Wetherell, heiress to the enormous manufacturing and shipping fortune. The marriage itself was an amazing coup for a foreigner like Magnus, with no lineage or breeding—the more so since Cartan Wetherell, Victoria's father, was a notorious snob, and had already betrothed his daughter to a young Boston man whose family had been a pillar of New England society for 150 years. No one among the Four Hundred of that day could imagine such a father countenancing the marriage of his adored daughter to an immigrant of peasant stock.

It was rumored that Anton Magnus had applied pressure to Cartan Wetherell in some subtle and not very legal ways in order to wrest his only daughter from him. Wetherell, who came from old money, was taken entirely by surprise when informed by his closest advisors that Magnus had infiltrated the Wetherell fortune so thoroughly as to be in a position to bankrupt his reluctant father-in-law if he wished. Once in possession of this frightening information, Cartan Wetherell had had no choice but to capitulate to the canny conglomerator.

In the years following their much-ballyhooed wedding Mr. and Mrs. Anton Magnus had three children. Gretchen, the oldest, was a mild-looking girl who became a well-known horsewoman before marrying into the Trowbridge family of Philadelphia.

Jack, a graduate of St. Paul's, Yale, and Harvard Business, had made his mark as an aggressive young executive at Magnus Industries, and was being groomed to take over the reins there when his father decided to retire.

At thirty-two Jack was a handsome and privileged figure. He had been romantically linked with beautiful women in show business and the arts as well as in society, and was considered the most eligible bachelor in New York.

The youngest child, Juliet, was more than a bit wild, and was the "problem" of the family—a problem whose existence was all but unsuspected by the world outside her own society, so adept was Anton Magnus at controlling the press's reporting about himself, his family, and his company.

They were a brilliant and successful family. Cartan Wetherell had gained far more than he had lost in marrying his only daughter to the then-unknown but powerful and intimidating Magnus. As the years passed the Magnuses gave parties which caught the eye of everyone in society, inviting artists, writers, and intellectuals in piquant combinations which soon put the rival New York society salons to shame.

The Magnus house, an extravagant marble mansion on Park Avenue which had once been owned by a decadent nephew of Cornelius Vanderbilt, was filled with furnishings befitting royalty. Added to the priceless antiques Anton Magnus had assembled were paintings, porcelains, and sculpture so magnificent that a privately printed catalog of the Magnus collection went into twelve editions.

Anton Magnus saw to it that his lavish parties were catered and decorated by the most forward-looking professionals in Manhattan. His summer entertainments at Southampton were even more gala, with hundreds of guests ambling languidly over the six-acre lawn of his country house. His daughters' coming-out parties, held at the Grosvenor Ball, were historic occasions.

There was not a hint of the *nouveau riche* about the Magnuses. Indeed, the family had such a cachet of elegance and originality that even the most discriminating of clubmen and society matrons could not resist coming to see what all the fuss was about. Victoria Magnus was deluged daily with visiting cards from the cream of society.

In a scant decade, through the sheer force of Anton Magnus's personality and ambition, the Magnus household became the most sought-after on the East Coast. Anton Magnus had overcome his humble roots and become an institution. Presidents, senators, governors joined with foreign heads of state to make an appearance at his balls. A famous story had it that Edward, Duke of Windsor, and his wife, the former Wallis Simpson, spent an entire evening at the Southampton house in 1939, being attentively squired from room to room by a Magnus hostess so as to avoid the British Ambassador, who was not speaking to the Duke or his wife. This clever choreography was rendered necessary by the fact that neither the Duke nor the Ambassador could bear to miss a Magnus party.

It was the beginning of a dynasty. Anyone in or out of society could see that. The Magnus family and empire glowed with a burnished elegance enjoyed by no comparable institution. The future of society as well as American finance and industry seemed to lie with the Magnuses.

They had come from nothing to become, in one short generation, the *crème de la crème*.

On this day in June, Magnus Industries' Manhattan headquarters was as busy as ever. The Personnel Office was crowded with hopeful young college graduates eager for the chance to find work in any capacity with the giant of American business.

Miss Althea Drake, Executive Assistant to the Vice-President in Charge of Personnel, occupied a position of considerably more power than her title indicated. Magnus insiders referred to her as the "Keeper of the Gates," since no applicant for a Magnus position could be screened for a job unless Althea Drake passed his or her file on with her personal recommendation.

She had achieved this position for several reasons. In the first place, she had been with the company since its inception. At fifty-five, a spinster, she had given her life to Anton Magnus and Magnus Industries. She neither missed nor desired a husband or family. She visited her married sister in Phoenix once a year, and that was that. In the early days of the company she had been Magnus's girl friday, working tirelessly from dawn until dark at whatever task he chose to assign her. Her loyalty was fanatic, her energy boundless.

Her personal limitations were obvious to Anton Magnus from the outset, of course. She lacked imagination and creativity. And her sex was against her, for Magnus had never dreamed of entrusting important executive responsibilities to a woman. So as the years passed he shifted her from one administrative post to another, always keeping a responsible officer above her, but always granting her sufficient power so that she could feel crucial to the company while not being able to do it harm.

At present the senior positions at Magnus were being filled by head-hunting at the highest level. Miss Drake took care of the entry-level posts. Here her expertise was valuable, for she knew the type of individual Anton Magnus was looking for—the young, bright, aggressive college graduate who could be counted on to make whatever sacrifices were necessary for the company. All such applicants she passed on to the personnel people. Anyone to whom she took a dislike, she summarily stopped at the front door.

Miss Drake was studying a file on her desk top. At length she looked up from it. Before her the subject of the file was seated.

Miss Drake could not help raising an eyebrow. The young woman across the desk was extraordinarily attractive. She was in her early twenties, with thick dark hair and limpid aquamarine eyes that shone with bright intelligence. She had a lovely complexion and a model's body. Small rounded breasts were outlined by her jacket. Her legs were long, her figure athletic and trim. Altogether she gave the impression of businesslike calm and readiness for hard work—just the impression an applicant for an important job wants to make.

Miss Drake looked at the file again. The girl's name was Frances Bollinger. She had graduated Phi Beta Kappa from the University of Pennsylvania in business, with a minor in foreign languages and mathematics. The file was full of excited recommendations from her college professors, as well as transcripts that showed her remarkable achievements as an undergraduate.

Clearly, the girl had everything. Perhaps a little too much of everything, Althea Drake thought as she looked from the file to the beautiful creature before her.

She closed the file and cleared her throat.

"Miss—Bollinger," she said. "Your qualifications are most impressive. Let me ask you, why have you chosen to apply to Magnus Industries?"

The girl smiled. "It's been my ambition to work for Magnus almost since I started college," she said. "One of my professors, Dr. Fiedler, had worked for your company during the war, when the Research Division helped the Navy develop the torpedo guidance system that was later used on D-Day. He inspired me a great deal. I've always thought there was no company as good as Magnus. It's simply the best, so I've had my heart set on working here for a long time."

Miss Drake nodded, glancing back at the file. Then she closed it and pushed it away from her across the desk top.

"We appreciate your feelings about us," she said. "But I'm afraid the company isn't hiring at the moment in your field. Things have been rather tight this year, and there's been a virtual freeze on new positions. You might try us next winter or spring. Things may have loosened up by then."

She did not try to soften the blow. It was obvious she was turning the girl down flat.

The girl's face registered frank disappointment for a moment. The beautiful features, so naturally energetic and sunny, shone with a touching melancholy. Then she brightened, as though aware that this business setting precluded any such show of emotion.

"Well," she said, "it never hurts to try. Thank you for considering my application."

She stood up and extended a hand. Althea Drake was impressed by her firm handshake, and by the quick, graceful strides with which she left the office, her long legs supple as those of a young racehorse as she moved.

When the girl was gone Althea Drake closed the door and sat looking out the window at the skyline of midtown Manhattan.

Of course, she could have sent the girl upstairs to Mr. Trask's office, thus passing her through the first barrier. Trask would have discussed her ambitions with her, and given her a battery of tests which the girl would no doubt have passed with flying colors. In twenty-four hours she would have had a job as a management or research trainee.

But the job market was in fact a bit tight. The company was not hiring just anybody right now, for its own situation in the marketplace demanded the right people in the right positions. And Althea Drake, understanding things as she did, felt that this was no time to take the chance of putting young girls in important jobs.

One could not trust them. They got married, got pregnant, demanded leaves of absence, left their jobs. They became emotional over work problems. They got involved with their supervisors. Magnus Industries needed people who could be trusted to give absolute commitment to their company over their personal lives. People who would not make waves.

And this girl, to judge by her looks, might be trouble.

Althea Drake squared her shoulders behind her desk. In her small way she had done her job to protect her company. She had kept it on the straight and narrow, where it belonged, and expunged from it a tiny cell which might have weakened the whole. She had eliminated the unexpected, and kept to the safe and predictable.

"Mary," she said into the intercom, "send in the next applicant."

Four weeks later the season was busier than ever. Althea Drake's head fairly spun from the work load, and from the new faces she saw at Headquarters, many of them recruited through her office.

She was more than a little taken aback when she saw one face that did not belong.

Miss Drake was in the lobby, coming to work on a hot Tuesday morning in July, when she saw Frances Bollinger, the girl whose application she had rejected, walking toward the elevators with two other girls who worked on the twenty-second floor.

She heard one of them call her Francie. The Bollinger girl smiled. She was carrying a briefcase, and was wearing a crisp skirt and jacket which hugged her magnificent body. A small purse hung from her shoulder. Her beauty was more obvious than ever as she stood out from her ordinary-looking friends, making them look like ugly ducklings next to a beauty queen.

It was clear she was not here on a visit. Her brisk posture, combined with her clothes, made it obvious she was coming to work.

Althea Drake hurried upstairs and checked Personnel's files for the girl's name. She found it easily. Sure enough, one of her assistants had processed the hiring of Frances Bollinger a week ago. She had been hired by Mr. Wilbur, of the Domestic Products Division, and the application put through without crossing Miss Drake's desk.

Althea Drake pursed her lips as she looked at the form. How had the girl done it?

Then she frowned. She recalled those fresh cheeks, the lush hair falling to the shoulders, the complex eyes, the nubile hips and long legs.

Mr. Wilbur was a married man, and a rather settled one into the bargain. But all men were suckers for a pretty face. Everyone knew that.

With a sigh Miss Drake closed the file.

2

It had not been as simple as all that.

Three weeks after Francie had been turned down by Althea Drake, Raymond Wilbur was sitting behind the executive desk in his office in Magnus Industries' Domestic Products Division, shaking his head despairingly.

Raymond Wilbur was a dedicated and hardworking division manager, if not the brightest light in the New York Magnus headquarters. He had been with the company for sixteen years, and had done his job well and dependably. He had a comfortable house in Westchester, a loving wife, and two young boys approaching college age.

Raymond Wilbur got along well on his Magnus salary. But college tuition was coming up for his two sons, so this was certainly no time for a change.

As luck would have it, however, trouble had come to Ray Wilbur despite his best efforts to avoid it.

Ray's Domestic Products Division had not shown a profit in seven quarters. Why this was so, no one seemed able to figure out. The market was strong, personnel was good and able, the products had long since been accepted by the public. The competition was not very aggressive.

Nevertheless, profits were off, and productivity had begun to take an alarming slide. Ray Wilbur had first noticed the problem after the initial losing quarter, and had held urgent meetings with his colleagues in an effort to turn things around.

But the meetings had not borne fruit. Since no one was able to understand the reason for the downturn in what had formerly been one of Magnus Industries' strongest divisions, no one could find a corresponding solution.

It fell to Ray Wilbur to report the sad quarterly news to his superiors, and even to the Board at a hellish meeting one Monday last spring. He had done his best to explain away his division's lack of performance, citing fluctuations in the marketplace, competition, problems in the economy. But the skeptical looks on the faces of the department heads had made it obvious his self-defense was impressing no one.

Meanwhile, each day at the office, he had to look at the smug face of Gordon Hiller, his chief assistant and the man most likely to succeed him as head of the division in the event of a shake-up. Gordon's pleasure in Ray's consternation was obvious. Gordon was simply biding his time and hoping that the higher-ups would soon decide to try to solve the problem in Domestic Products by changing the head man.

Ray Wilbur could feel his ulcer growing worse. He had not had a good night's sleep in months. He had not made love to his wife since last Christmas, so great was the worry wringing his insides. On weekends he drove his 1948 Ford aimlessly around the county, looking in supplication at the suburban landscape as though in search of an answer that would not come.

He knew his time was running out. At age forty-seven he would have deep trouble starting over at another company if Magnus dropped him.

His situation, once so secure, had gone from problematic to critical in one short year. He was skating on the thinnest ice of his career.

Now was the time for a miracle.

The miracle appeared, amazingly, in the form of a pretty young visitor to his office.

The secretary announced her as Frances Bollinger.

"She has no appointment, sir. She says it concerns the Domestic Materials Curve. She's . . . well, she's quite insistent, sir."

Sighing irritably, Ray Wilbur agreed to see the girl.

When she walked into his office and offered him a firm handshake he was startled by her beauty. She was tall, with an odd mixture of athletic trimness and girlish delicacy about her. Her eyes were clear and honest. There was a seductive, feminine warmth in her handshake.

"To what do I owe the pleasure?" he asked, suppressing the note of impatience that had been poised to sound in his voice. "My time is limited, Miss—what did you say your name was?"

"Bollinger," she smiled. "My friends call me Francie."

"Well, what can I do for you?" he asked, motioning her to the visitors' chair. She set her purse on the floor beside her and opened her briefcase.

"I'm trying to match up some problems in your area of expertise with some ideas of my own," she said ambiguously. "I'm something of a student of the Exchange Function problem. I'll only take a minute of your time."

Puzzled, Ray Wilbur gestured to her to go ahead.

She took a sheet of professional graph paper out of her briefcase, along with several charts, and handed them to him.

"The curve on the left represents the performance of your division over the last eight quarters," she said. "The second curve factors in the idea I've been working on, based on calculations using set theory and some high-level mathematical models."

She smiled. "I minored in math at the University of Pennsylvania," she said. "I'm sorry if I'm not being clear."

"What does it all mean?" Ray asked, peering at the complicated charts.

"It means," she smiled, "that the negative performance of your division over the last two years actually has its roots in a factor in the marketplace. You see, it's right here in the graph. Naturally, no one would think to look for it there, because on the surface the marketplace looks healthy, and the economy is up. But it's there nevertheless. The only way to reverse the downward trend is to take this factor into account and compensate for it."

"Compensate how?" Ray Wilbur asked skeptically.

"Well, in my opinion," the girl answered, her beautiful eyes focused on the paper before him, her fresh scent suffusing him as she leaned forward to point to the figures, "the correct procedure is to cut back on investment of manpower in the X quadrant, while increasing the commitment to the Y quadrant. At the same time the percentage of inventory as a function of sales on the upper side of the graph should be increased by at least thirty percent over a six-month period. The result will be a clear profit before the second quarter of next year."

Ray Wilbur looked at the graph, dumbfounded. What she was suggesting made no business sense that he had ever heard of.

"I know it sounds crazy," she said. "But the figures don't lie. You're overextended in X, and under half what you should be in Y. It's an old problem in set theory, but to my knowledge it hasn't been applied in economics yet, because conditions haven't called for it. But in the postwar economy, things have changed."

Raymond Wilbur sat back in his chair. He looked at the face of Francie Bollinger, framed by her lush black hair. Her expression had not changed. She was businesslike and respectful. But he could feel the intelligence behind those eyes, as well as her confidence in her figures and in her presentation. She knew what she was doing.

"How can you be so sure of all this?" he asked. "We have specialists working on the same problems. Not one of them has suggested anything along the lines you propose. To be frank, young lady, it flies in the face of every business principle I know."

She shrugged. Obviously she was not deterred in the slightest by his words.

"There's always room for new ideas, in any field," she said. "The whole history of Magnus Industries is a history of risk-taking in the interest of long-term growth. However, I don't see this procedure as a risk, really. It's more of a necessity."

He looked back down at the chart. The logic behind her figures was eccentric, but too compelling to deny without much closer consideration.

"Tell me something," he asked. "Where are you currently working?"

She smiled. "Nowhere," she said. "I'm looking for a job, as a matter of fact."

Ray Wilbur considered his situation. On the paper before him was perhaps the Ariadne's thread which could lead his division out of the miasma it had been in, save his job, and put Gordon Hiller back in his place forever.

This could be the light at the end of the frightening tunnel he had been crawling through for two awful years.

All he had to do was follow the trail.

But he could not do so on his own. Frances Bollinger, with her candid face, her bright optimism, and her stupendous command of the logic behind his division's problems, would be essential to him. He must not let her get away.

And no one else must know about her plan. She must be his alone.

"How would you feel about going to work for us?" he asked, doing his best to sound casual. "In my division, of course."

She smiled and stood up, her fine girlish body thrusting its youthful contours before him.

"I thought you'd never ask."

3

What Raymond Wilbur could not know was that the beautiful, convincing creature who had appeared without warning in his office was as much a surprise to herself as to him.

Even as she set about finding a way around the obstacle of Althea Drake's Personnel Office and getting herself a job at Magnus Industries by her own methods, Francie was astonished by her own cold determination. Never in her short lifetime had she distinguished herself as an aggressive or devious person. Yet now she was behaving like a veteran in business skulduggery.

She spent long hours at the New York Public Library and a variety of state and federal government information offices patiently searching for a weak link in the monolith that was Magnus Industries. This was not an easy task, for large corporations do not like to air their dirty linen in public, and are expert at covering up cash flow problems in one division with profits in another.

But Francie found her weak link. It showed itself on a rainy afternoon ten days after her interview with Althea Drake, only a few minutes before the Public Information Division of the Internal Revenue Service closed for the day. It was a profit-and-loss statement for Magnus Industries' Division of Domestic Products, available to the public under disclosure laws, but buried under a mountain of paperwork which Francie had spent three days burrowing through.

There was no doubt she had found what she was looking for. Raymond Wilbur's Domestic Products Division was the victim of a mysterious dropoff in profit and productivity. The division was an embarrassment to the corporation of which it was a part. And Raymond Wilbur himself was becoming an embarrassment to his demanding superiors.

Raymond Wilbur was a man in danger of losing his career. He was just the sort of man Francie was looking for.

Once in possession of this information, Francie had to analyze the problems affecting Wilbur's division and single-handedly discover a solution to them. This was in itself a challenge that would have dissuaded any other girl in Francie's position from pursuing her ambitious goal.

But it was, as luck would have it, a challenge which played to her own greatest strength.

Seventeen years before her encounter with Magnus Industries, Francie had been identified in kindergarten as a perky, mischievous five-year-old who happened to be a genius with numbers. Though she was in all other respects a normal child, her IQ was extraordinarily high. Her ability to solve technical and mathematical problems was approximately equal to that of a bright college student.

Her parents were at first unequipped to deal with the news of their daughter's amazing precocity. Marcus "Mac" Bollinger, a modest handyman and builder in the small Pennsylvania town of Francie's birth, knew nothing of mathematics. His wife, Helen, the daughter of local farmers, was as much in ignorance of how to handle a gifted child as he was.

The proud but befuddled parents sought the advice of Francie's teachers as well as experts in education for the gifted. They soon decided neither to burden the little girl with the knowledge that she was "special," nor to uproot her from her classmates and put her in a special school. Francie entered first grade on schedule and finished her public-school education at the same time as her friends from the neighboring towns and farm districts. The only thing that set her apart from her peers was her straight-A average in school, and the special math courses she took twice a week at a nearby experimental school staffed by professors from the state university.

Francie accepted her unique talent as a fact of life. Mathematics fascinated her. As a little girl she liked the shapes of numbers, and was superstitious about them. Her father had made her a gigantic 5 out of wood in his workshop. It stood against the wall in her bedroom, and she felt an uncanny vibration coming from it as it shadowed the room when she went to sleep at night.

Her affinity for the number 5 stayed with her, and was soon joined by a special feeling for other numbers—6, the number which signified peace and sleep for her; 7, the magic number of myth and superstition; 4, a grave and serious number full of secret wisdom; and 3, the number which mysteriously stood for herself.

Each of the ten single-digit numbers had its own unique personality. And the combinations of the numbers were like cosmic marriages. The marriage of 2 and 5 to make 25 was as personal to Francie as the mating of the family's two cats, a gold and a black, to make a tiger. Numbers were like playmates to her. They occupied her active mind, and were as familiar to her as her friends or parents.

The most difficult of math problems and calculations did not faze her at all. They were like games, brain teasers, and she enjoyed the challenge. Besides, she felt the numbers were her friends and would not conceal their secrets from her. Thus what other people saw as an astonishing genius on her part, Francie thought of as a hobby, and as a shield from her solitude—for as an only child she had to fill her own time, and make up her own games.

Helen Bollinger died after a painful illness when Francie was fourteen. The young girl was left alone with her father, who soon found a crusty Irish housekeeper named Mollie Maguire to help him look after Francie. Though her life at home with Mac Bollinger, a devoted and supportive parent, remained happy and warm, Francie found adolescence a trial. She blossomed early into a lissome and athletically gifted creature of rare beauty. Though she managed to retain close friendships with two girls from her own neighborhood, the other girls at school kept their distance. Whether this was because of her brains or her beauty, she never knew.

As for boys, they were hopelessly fascinated by her extraordinary looks—the long lush hair, the creamy complexion, and dazzling green eyes—but so daunted by her intellect that they dared not ask her out. Though she was humorous and welcoming in her treatment of them, and made friends with more than a few males who wished they could overcome their own shyness in her company, she never found herself in a romantic relationship.

This lack left its mark on Francie. She noticed how other girls, less gifted with physical beauty or personality than she, used a subtle female cunning to snare the males they were after. Francie soon realized that what the teachers called her "brain power" did not include this instinctive female intelligence that knew how to manipulate boys into jumping through hoops at one's command.

To her surprise Francie did not envy the other girls. She had no desire to dazzle the opposite sex with her beauty. She wanted to be loved for herself. She fantasized about the man who would someday own her heart, someone strong and kind and handsome, whose life would be joined to hers in an almost mystical conjunction similar to that of the numbers which fascinated her so. She decided that fate had not yet decided to bring a great love into her life.

So she concentrated on preparing herself for college—a rare achievement among the Bollinger relatives, but an experience her late mother had wanted for her, and a dream that Mac Bollinger intended to make real at all costs, despite his own poverty.

As it turned out, Mac's anticipated financial sacrifice was unnecessary. Thanks to her perfect academic record and sky-high test scores, Francie was offered a full scholarship to the University of Pennsylvania. There she decided not to major in math, for it was so much a part of her nature that she could not dream of making a career as a professor of mathematics. She wanted to get out into the real world, where the challenges were less abstract, more unexpected and thrilling.

So she chose business as her major, with mathematics and foreign languages as her twin minors. She had found early on that she could master a foreign language without effort in less than a year, and soon added German and Italian to the French and Spanish she knew from high school.

Unfortunately for Francie, who had by now grown into a ravishing beauty of eighteen, the young men who majored in mathematics at the university were as daunted by her intellectual gifts as the boys in high school had been. Few of them dared speak to her, much less ask her out.

As for the business majors—an all-male group—they were more aggressive, but in the end even less fun to be with. They invited Francie on dates, but showed themselves to be clumsy seducers whose hunger for her body was unaccompanied by any serious interest in her personality. She parried their advances with a smile, and managed to make platonic friendships with the handful of them who were not too unnerved by her intelligence to spend time in her company.

In both departments Francie came to be seen as a sort of magnificent freak, incomparable in her beauty as well as her intellect, but untouchable despite her welcoming personality. She was a popular figure, but no one knew how lonely she remained underneath her sunny surface. For she had yet to meet a young man who cared to know about the hopes and dreams and disappointments she might have wanted to share with him.

So Francie's solitude deepened. She hid it from her father when she went home on vacations, assuring him that she had lots of friends and activities at school. And she hid it from herself as well, concentrating her efforts on her demanding academic schedule while dreaming of the exciting business career ahead of her.

And a surprising new opportunity came along to fill her time even more fully.

It so happened that the Moore School of Electrical Engineering was located at the University of Pennsylvania, and it was there that the revolutionary new science of computers had had its explosive beginnings only a few years earlier, with the development of the now-legendary ENIAC by John Mauchly and J. Presper Eckert. Francie's roommate, a pretty young technical wizard named Dana Salinger, was taking courses at the Moore School, and convinced her to investigate it. Francie soon found herself enthralled by the notion of a thirty-ton machine full of numbers and limitless calculating ability.

As time passed Francie deepened her interest in computers, gaining experience on the increasingly sophisticated machines available at the university, and went on a field trip with some other Penn students to see UNIVAC, the commercial computer designed by Mauchly and Eckert in 1951. She heard lectures by the legendary John von Neumann at the Institute for Advanced Study, and read everything there was to read about computer hardware and the new field of programming.

By the time she graduated from the university Francie's fertile brain was teeming with new ideas about business, mathematics, and computer science which swirled together in kaleidoscopic colors. She also had a store of fantasies about her future in the exciting world of business, where she would not only find the professional fulfillment she had been preparing for all these years, but would no doubt encounter the long-awaited man of her dreams, the man who had eluded her when she was too young to be ready for him.

And, to go with her bright and active mind, she had a dossier full of gushing recommendations from admiring professors. Her business mentor, Professor George Fiedler, had written that she was "without a doubt the most brilliant student I have had the privilege of teaching during my twenty-five years in academia. She is destined for a great career at whatever she chooses."

This recommendation, whose text was unknown to Francie, might have garnered her an immediate executive-track position in any business in the country. But it had not impressed Althea Drake at Magnus Industries.

This had disappointed Francie, who had dreamed of working for Magnus Industries ever since the start of her business curriculum when she had learned of Magnus's brilliant record in research, its immaculate rating among companies, and its far-flung subsidiaries in exciting foreign countries which she had never seen, but whose languages she already spoke fluently.

Something seemed to snap inside Francie at the sight of Althea Drake closing her dossier with a cold smile and telling her that the doors of

Magnus Industries were closed to her. For nearly as long as she could remember, Francie had seen her sincere efforts as a student rewarded with high grades and approval from her teachers. But the world reflected in Althea Drake's unsympathetic eyes was a new and different world from the one Francie had known.

As though by magic, a new talent came from nowhere to join Francie's many natural gifts. Or perhaps it was not so much a talent as an inner fire that burst into life only now, after having smoldered unnoticed throughout her girlhood.

She simply was not going to take no for an answer from Magnus Industries. She sensed that Althea Drake's office was not a mere cubicle in a large building in Manhattan. It was the portal to a world in which good things did not happen unless one made them happen; in which obstacles did not get out of the way until one either broke them down or got around them through cunning and initiative.

This knowledge gave Francie her marching orders.

When she walked into Raymond Wilbur's office, dressed in a subtly sensual business dress bought for the occasion and armed with the charts and graphs which detailed the solution to Wilbur's problems, Francie felt like a new woman. Even the jitters she experienced at what she was doing were covered over by her breezy, efficient exterior. She was prepared to use every weapon in her arsenal to get what she wanted.

And for the first time in her young life she found herself mobilizing her feminine wiles in a piquant medley to make the right impression on a vulnerable male. She orchestrated her manner, her voice, and the subliminal movements of her body to add subtle messages of female attraction to the cool mathematical presentation she had prepared.

As though from outside herself she watched Raymond Wilbur fall under the combined spell of her physical presence and her undeniable expertise. Faced with the weapons she had sharpened so carefully before approaching him, he did what she wanted. He offered her a job.

And she was not surprised.

The old Francie would have been flabbergasted at this result, and at her own aggressiveness in bringing it about.

But the old Francie had ceased to exist. A new person, armed with unexpected talents, and perhaps subject to new dangers, had taken her place.

Francie felt the brief chill of this inner metamorphosis as she shook Raymond Wilbur's hand and accepted her new position. She sensed that the past had slipped out from under her as surely as the springboard from under a diver who plunges into thin air. The future was hers to create.

She called her father in Pennsylvania that first evening to tell him her good news. She could hear relief in his voice as he congratulated her.

"I'm so happy for you, Frannie," he said, calling her by the private nickname he had used since her childhood. "I always knew you'd make those New Yorkers sit up and take notice. I'm proud of you."

"Thanks, Daddy," she said, her excitement masking the unspoken truth. She had not told her father that Magnus Industries had turned her down flat when she first applied there. Nor could he know anything of the desperate gambit that had got her what she wanted.

"Don't let the big city get you down, now," he warned. "Take good care of yourself, and be happy." It was typical of Mac Bollinger to hide his worries and express only confidence in his conversations with Francie. She was all he had in the world since his wife's death, but he took pains to respect her independence and avoid hovering protectively over her.

"Don't worry about me, Daddy," she assured him. "I'll be fine. Everything is going according to plan."

As she hung up she could not help reflecting that the big city had made its first mark on her, after all. She had made her first phone call home not only to give Mac Bollinger her good news, but also to conceal from him the truth about how she had made it happen.

This was the first serious lie she had told her father in as long as she could remember.

Francie thought about this fact for a long time before going to bed that night. But when she woke up the next morning she had a lot of work to do, and much to learn. She forgot about her lie, and turned her attention to the demanding future before her.

$$=== 4 ===$$

At first things seemed to go well for Francie at Magnus Industries.

She went to work with a light heart and high hopes for the future. Ray Wilbur had put her in an office of her own, with the express order to schematize her fiscal reorganization plan so that he could present it to the Board at his earliest opportunity. He forbade her to talk about her work with the junior executives in the offices surrounding hers. He had her bring her work to him at the end of each day, so he could take it home with him and digest it before sharing it with his own superiors.

There was a cloak-and-dagger aura to her job that amused and stimulated Francie. She liked the feeling that she was working on something secret and important, something which qualified her for special treatment by the division head.

Her situation, however, brought with it a sense of isolation both within the division and within Magnus Industries as a whole. In her capacity as special assistant to the director, she was separate from the ordinary departments which bound the employees together in groups. She did her work alone, and reported only to one man, Raymond Wilbur. She had her own secretary, a friendly and down-to-earth girl named Marcia Bonner; but even Marcia seemed to treat her with a sort of awe, as though Francie were a creature neither fish nor fowl, to whom she did not know quite how to relate.

Magnus headquarters was a beautiful building, with sleek corridors, soft lighting to ease the pressure of work, and handsomely furnished offices. It was a silent place; one never heard voices being raised in anger, or saw faces distorted by emotion, as one passed through its premises.

But it only took Francie a short time to realize that this veneer of smooth-running efficiency hid a cold and impersonal company which did not welcome new employees with open arms.

The handful of Magnus executives Francie encountered during her first weeks at work were not friendly. They gave her alert, evaluative looks, and their polite pleasantries were without warmth.

She wondered if they knew about the somewhat unorthodox way in which she had been hired. Perhaps, she thought, they suspected she had got her job because of a romantic liaison with Mr. Wilbur. Perhaps her youth, combined with her high level of responsibility, made them uncomfortable. Whatever the case, they treated Francie as an outsider. She was left to her own devices in her little office, arriving early in the morning to work on her plan and leaving only after depositing her day's work with Mr. Wilbur or his secretary.

Four weeks went by in this manner, then eight. Francie was proud of her work and more sure than ever that it would bear fruit if and when it was implemented. But she did not feel at home at Magnus Industries, and she still could not put her finger on what it was about the place that made her so ill at ease.

Then the answer to all her questions came.

On September 15th, three months after Francie had come to work for him, Mr. Wilbur took her proposal to a board meeting and it was accepted. The financial reorganization of the Domestic Products Division was approved, and its implementation begun. Mr. Wilbur came to Francie's office himself to congratulate her.

"You did fine work," he said. "Keep it up. I'm very pleased." He wore a complacent look which suggested that those above him in the company had been impressed by Francie's accomplishment.

The only sour note in this was that when the company newsletter announced the reorganization and the research that had led up to it, Francie's name was not mentioned anywhere in the story. Her analysis and recommendation were described in considerable detail, but all the credit was given to Ray Wilbur and his "staff."

Francie was new to the company, and hesitated to make waves. But her stubborn nature would not allow her to keep silent about something that was bothering her. She told Mr. Wilbur of her feelings.

"I'm not saying that I should have been the star of the show," she said. "But it does seem to me that since the ideas and the work were all mine, my name might at least have been mentioned."

Ray Wilbur smiled.

"You'd better wake up to a few things about corporate life, Francie," he said. "Everything happens here by rank. The responsible officer gets credit for everything done under him. Who do you think is taking credit for this episode right now? The Vice-President for Finance, and above him, Anton Magnus. No one is thanking Ray Wilbur for a job well done. If you want to get along, you go along, Francie. That way, some day you'll be the executive in charge, and you'll be the one getting all the credit."

Francie looked him in the eye.

"I wouldn't want credit for work I didn't do," she said simply. "Not then, and not now."

Raymond Wilbur simply shrugged.

The next day, thanks to the gossiping of Ray Wilbur's secretaries, people in the company had got wind of Francie's little encounter with her boss.

"You were right to give him hell," said Marcia Bonner, warming up to Francie at last in the solitude of their office. "They're such a bunch of creeps. They wouldn't give a woman credit for anything around here . . ."

Francie was taken by surprise.

"Is that what was behind this?" she asked.

"What else?" said Marcia, bitterly amused by Francie's naiveté. "That's the name of the game at good old Magnus."

Francie was genuinely shocked. Somehow it had not occurred to her that what had been done could have had anything to do with her sex. She assumed it was rank alone, her lowly status within the company, that had determined her fate.

"How can you be sure?" she asked Marcia. "Wouldn't they have treated a man the same way?"

Marcia smiled sadly. "Francie, I can see you need to have your eyes opened," she said. "Tell me, how much are they paying you a year as Special Assistant to the Director?"

Francie told her the figure.

"Do you know how much an entry-level management trainee of the male sex makes here in his first year?" Marcia asked.

Francie shook her head. When Marcia told her the figure she turned pale with anger. It was nearly twice as much as Francie was earning.

"See what I mean?" Marcia said. "Magnus Industries doesn't place a high value on the abilities of the female sex. This corporation would no more give credit to a woman for executive initiative than it would promote one of the cleaning women to Vice-President. It's just the nature of the beast."

Marcia showed Francie a handful of articles in the same newsletter that had contained the story about Ray Wilbur and the reorganization plan. Sure enough, in more than one story the contributions of a junior male executive were acknowledged, while Francie's had not been.

In the wake of her conversation with Marcia, Francie took a hard look around her inside the company. She saw that there was not a single woman in a position of genuine executive responsibility. The only visible women were like Althea Drake, women with respectable titles, but in less sensitive areas of the company, and never in high enough authority to possess any executive clout—Assistant Vice-President for Public Relations, Executive Assistant for Consumer Relations, and so on.

As for Francie herself, she had an impressive-sounding title which concealed the fact that her pay was hardly more than that of a low-level executive secretary. And this in spite of an elaborate financial plan she had single-handedly devised, a plan that would revolutionize the financial structure of one of Magnus Industries' most important divisions.

Francie was quietly overwhelmed by the realization that her sex had had so profound an effect on her fate within Magnus Industries. The knowledge filled her with anger, for she felt as though her femininity were a taint that she was forced to carry with her wherever she went, a taint that branded her as less competent than the men around her.

Unable to bear her resentment any longer, she went to see Mr. Wilbur again. She expressed her doubts about the way she had been treated, and made bold to mention her salary.

"I've done work for this company that has made a difference," she said. "Can you explain to me why I'm making barely half the salary of an entry-level management trainee of the male sex?"

Ray Wilbur's face darkened. He spoke in a soft, warning voice.

"Francie," he said, "it took some doing for me to get you hired here without going through channels. Whether you know it or not, you're in a good situation at Magnus. No woman has done what you've done here in as long as I can remember. Now, if you start talking the way I just heard you talk, you're going to find yourself out of a job before you can turn around. Take my word for it, young lady: don't make waves. It will be your undoing."

With a new caution in his eyes, he watched her leave his office.

Raymond Wilbur hoped he had closed the door on the Francie Bollinger situation with his firm warning.

He never dreamed he was opening the door to one of the most dramatic episodes ever to befall Magnus Industries.

As for Francie, having seen the stone wall which greeted her complaint, she went disconsolately back to a work routine which was fast becoming unbearable.

She worked in solitude. Her only friends at Magnus were the handful of secretaries who served the executives in Mr. Wilbur's department. These young women seemed to pity her rather than resent her.

No one visited her office to say hello or pass the time of day. Now and then she would be approached in the cafeteria or the corridor by a condescending junior executive who treated her like a secretary and invited her on a date with the obvious in mind. When she refused, the puzzled male would turn his back on her with a shrug. After all, it was taken for granted within the corporation that the only chance a female employee had of gaining any advantage for herself was to be nice to the males who showed an interest in her.

Marcia Bonner commiserated with Francie, and told her horror stories of innocent young women who had succumbed to the attentions of such executives, which were often accompanied by promises of marriage. In most cases the girls ended up abandoned or worse. It soon became apparent to Francie that Marcia knew everything there was to know about the behind-the-scenes social world at Magnus, and was something of a mother hen to a lot of female employees whose affairs had led to unwanted pregnancies and other personal disasters.

Marcia did not need to warn Francie about the invitations she was receiving. In any case they soon ceased, for word of Francie's confrontation with Raymond Wilbur had now circulated through the incestuous grapevine of company gossip. Francie was no longer considered an eligible female, but rather a freak to be avoided. She was *persona non grata* as far as the executive force—an all-male body—was concerned.

Francie tried to forget her troubles by immersing herself in her work. But now that the reorganization in Domestic Products was being implemented by the accountants and managers, the creative aspect of her work for Raymond Wilbur was at an end. She had been told that there were other projects awaiting her attention, new challenges ahead of her. But when she asked Mr. Wilbur what they were, and when she could get started, he responded in evasive monosyllables and took his leave of her as fast as he could.

Francie could see the handwriting on the wall. The only thing she could look forward to was a virtually secretarial follow-up of her own work on the reorganization, and whatever busy work Ray Wilbur could find for her to do. Not only would she never get the official credit she deserved for her accomplishment, but she would also be denied the advancement that normally rewarded such an accomplishment.

Indeed, she might soon be laid off, given her behavior and her negative reputation within the company. She could almost feel the corporation turning its back on her. She had soured her career at Magnus Industries by making waves. Perhaps the higher-ups would fire her as soon as they had finished implementing the plan she had devised. Having used her up, they would throw her out.

Francie gave long and serious thought to her problem. She realized that her fantasies about Magnus Industries had turned out to be incorrect. The career she had dreamed of for herself was not to be.

Had she been another young woman she would have given up and accepted her situation, or looked for work elsewhere. But something about the injustice that had been done her by Magnus Industries had struck a nerve, the same nerve that had been struck by Althea Drake when she coldly told Francie the doors of Magnus were closed to her.

It was not in Francie to accept things as they were. Her most basic instinct was to fight them, to change them at all costs.

Yet there was no way out. She had already done her best to fight for her rights, and lost. Now she was a tiny cog in the enormous machinery of the corporation, forgotten and incapable of making a difference.

Or so it seemed.

5

Who's Who in Corporate America, *55th edition*

MAGNUS, Johan F. (Jack), son of Anton Magnus. Born 1923. Presently Vice-President in Charge of International Development, Magnus Industries. Educated St. Paul's, Yale B.S., Harvard M.B.A. Spent three years in Europe as manager of Magnus subsidiaries before returning to vice-presidency 1953. Considered a major force for innovation within the conglomerate founded by his father, though also being groomed for overall management responsibility. Most likely to succeed Anton Magnus as CEO and perhaps board chairman when the elder Magnus retires.

Considered a fair manager, but ambitious for the company above all. Rumors of a long-standing split with his father *re* company policy and expansion have not been confirmed. Close-mouthed to the press and even business colleagues about his ideas and plans, Jack Magnus is a company man in his actions.

The picture accompanying the item about Jack Magnus showed a handsome, dark-haired young man who bore an interesting resemblance to his father. Both men had a dark brow, penetrating eyes, and tanned skin. But where the elder Magnus was heavyset and virile without being handsome, the son was extremely good-looking and photogenic. He could have been a male model, so attractive was his chiseled masculinity.

Francie had spent a long time looking at that photograph.

She had also made it her business to learn everything she could about Jack Magnus from every possible source, within and outside Magnus Industries, Inc.

What she had learned both intrigued and puzzled her.

On the surface Jack Magnus seemed tailor-made to symbolize Magnus Industries in the future just as his father had in the past. He had been brought up within the company, and had made brilliant personal successes in it. He had proved himself an aggressive and hardworking manager, showing impressive profits and productivity in all the divisions he had headed since finishing graduate school.

Thanks to his encyclopedic knowledge of the corporation and his ability as a troubleshooter, he had been assigned to ever more challenging areas of company responsibility. He had traveled the world on his father's behalf, acting as liaison between Magnus Headquarters in New York and the many subsidiaries which the corporation was constantly acquiring. He spoke several languages fluently, and had made himself an expert on the ins and outs of Latin American as well as European business.

In this sense Jack was indeed a "company man," devoted to the corporation that bore his family name, a brilliant young executive who embodied Magnus's reputation for innovation, intelligence, and above all competitive aggressiveness. He would make a perfect successor to his father.

On the other hand, there were subtle signs that underneath, things between Jack Magnus and his father were not so smooth.

Within the corporation Jack had the reputation of a maverick. Whenever he was put in charge of something, he went his own way with it, often at the cost of bitter quarrels with his superiors, men who represented his father's wishes. These quarrels sometimes led to private altercations with

Anton Magnus which were too fiery to see the light of day within the company.

Jack seemed to take pleasure, so the rumor went, in achieving success on a given project by going outside channels, by flouting the established wisdom, by taking unusual risks. In his very first major managerial assignment, for instance, as head of a newly acquired consulting firm in Atlanta, he had fired the top people who had been approved by his father only two years before, and staffed the company with his own choices. This had caused a storm of dissension on the Board, but after another year the company in question had shown a 100 percent increase in productivity, and Jack was forgiven for his action.

It had been the same way ever since. Some observers thought that Jack deliberately went against the grain in order to show his independence from his father, and from the "Magnus style" of management. It was also rumored that Jack was possessive about the areas of his own responsibility, and did not take lightly to advice or interference from outside.

There were those who wondered whether Jack, so headstrong a son, would ever take over the reins of Magnus Industries. It was suspected that his need for independence was so consuming that he intended to start his own business elsewhere. But those who said this could not explain why, if such was the case, he had remained with Magnus this long. After all, he was in his early thirties now.

The question remained unanswered. But Jack's rebellion against his father had an additional foundation. It was widely known that Anton Magnus, ever the manipulative father, had picked out a bride for his son. With the interests of the corporation in his mind (as they had been in his own marriage to the Wetherell millions, and in his daughter Gretchen's marriage to the Trowbridge dynasty) he had chosen Belinda Devereaux for Jack, several years ago. The Devereaux oil empire, which was poised to branch out into communications, would be the single greatest coup that Magnus Industries, already a giant, could attain at this point in American business history.

But the marriage had not come to pass. Jack's betrothal to Belinda Devereaux, expected almost daily for the past six years, was still a question mark. Meanwhile Jack's widespread reputation as a ladies' man remained undiminished, leading many to believe that Jack had no intention of marrying Belinda Devereaux or anyone else any time soon.

Jack remained a hardworking, determined Magnus executive, who already had a place on the Board. But he would not publicly state that he intended to succeed his aging father as Chief Executive Officer of Magnus Industries.

Nor would he marry. Not yet, at least.

In studying Jack Magnus's life and work, Francie began to feel as though she knew him. Jack was a smart man, and a cautious one. He was learning everything he could from Magnus Industries, but keeping his options open, like a good businessman. He would perhaps take over Magnus Industries one day—if it suited him. He might marry Belinda Devereaux —if and when *he* decided to. He was consolidating ever more power, expertise, and influence, but would not allow others to dictate his actions. In this sense he was his father's son, stubborn, willful, creative. But these very qualities pitted him against his father.

One could only imagine Anton Magnus's frustration at the way his offspring had turned out. Jack was simply too much like his father to bend to the elder Magnus's will.

This was one of the two reasons why Francie was so interested in Jack Magnus now.

The other reason, more practical, was the fact that Jack was presently in charge of all Magnus subsidiaries in Europe.

Since the war Anton Magnus had made it a top priority to buy up as many struggling European companies as he could. His familiarity with Europe's economy, and the ever-expanding buying power of Magnus Industries, had allowed him to gain a foothold on a financial empire in Europe that could well make business history in the decades to come, decades which would show enormous growth as Europe recovered from the war.

Not surprisingly, Anton Magnus had put his trusted son in charge of liaison and cooperation among the ever-growing collection of European Magnus subsidiaries. For the last five years Jack had been pouring his energies into this task, shuttling back and forth across the Atlantic to report to the Board on his progress.

Jack was a brilliant manager and an even better troubleshooter. But, interestingly, not even his great skills could hide the fact that there was trouble in Europe.

The Magnus subsidiaries, many of them old companies with new personnel, or struggling young companies with inexperienced managers, were scattered over a dozen countries separated by different languages, different currencies, and different customs. Many of these countries had been on opposite sides during the war. Their executives did not trust each other, and this fact made effective communication and cooperation among them difficult, and sometimes impossible.

In the new Europe envisaged by the NATO powers, economic cooperation was to be a necessity. And Anton Magnus was determined to exploit the growth of Europe to his own corporation's advantage. But so far the Magnus companies in Europe were behaving more like strange bedfellows, not to say outright enemies, than like soldiers in a united corporate army. Their growth only seemed to increase their hostility to one another. Collectively they were losing money by not exploiting the opportunity to help each other with materials, information, and other elements that their lack of communication made unavailable.

The European companies were like a pack of competitive dogs whose leashes were hopelessly wrapped around the legs of the parent company.

This state of affairs, too chaotic to be covered up even in the optimistic Magnus reports to the stockholders, had come to Francie's attention at just the moment when she needed a new challenge badly.

Long a student of languages as well as principles of business, Francie felt that the confusion affecting the European companies was not a necessary evil. It could be reduced to manageable proportions if the right tools for analyzing and correcting it were discovered.

In the considerable spare time she now enjoyed in Ray Wilbur's division, Francie began searching for the practical solution which her sharp intellect had already identified in theory.

She spent long hours researching the European subsidiaries. She read every in-house memo and publication about the Magnus companies in France, Britain, Switzerland, Belgium, the Netherlands, West Germany, Italy, Spain, and Portugal. She studied their management, their productivity, their overhead, their tangled relations of competition and rudimentary cooperation. The subsidiaries included banks, manufacturers, accounting firms, mines, retailers, shipping firms, hotels, and even entertainment production companies. Together they made a crazy quilt which was like a picture in miniature of Europe's fast-growing but confused economy.

Francie's head spun from all the information she was taking in. But she was attracted by the challenge, and by her growing sense that her own intellectual background was offering her a solution to the problems in Europe.

And one essential feature of her education came unexpectedly to her aid now more than ever—computers.

It occurred to Francie that the problems facing the European companies could be solved by a computerized handling of their interrelationships. After all, computer language was not like ordinary human language. It formalized everything it touched, and made the information manageable in a new way. Differences in language or currency were not an obstacle to a computer as they were to an average person.

If the European companies could be linked up by computer technology, including payroll, profit-and-loss, materials, and even personnel, it might be possible to achieve in a few short months the sort of smooth-running cooperation across language and geographical barriers that would take long years of struggle in any other way.

Francie became more excited by her idea with each passing day. She devoted all her spare time at work to thinking about it, and spent her evening hours reading anything that might help her to put it into workable form.

Magnus Headquarters had recently acquired a powerful new UNIVAC computer which was installed on the forty-fifth floor. So far the new machine had gone relatively unused, for computer technology was so novel that management had not yet figured out ways to apply it effectively to the corporation.

Francie managed to get permission to use the new computer for her own purposes. She began experimenting with a special program designed to create an effective interface between the European subsidiaries. The work was painstaking and difficult, but it played right into the hands of her acute intelligence and innate stubbornness. After only a few weeks of work she was firmly convinced of the program's usefulness.

On fire with excitement by now, Francie set out to make of her secret project a firm proposal for change in Europe, just as she had done for the Domestic Products Division under Ray Wilbur. She drew charts and graphs which were ingeniously coordinated to account for the most disparate marketing and fiscal problems facing the European Division. Most importantly, she fine-tuned her master computer program and wrote a lengthy description of its internal logic and practical features.

Her aim was to create a presentation of her proposed system which would not only be easily comprehensible to the least technical of management minds, but would also make perfect business sense. She intended to present her scheme in such a manner as to win over whomever she showed it to.

And that meant, first and foremost, Jack Magnus.

Francie knew enough about Jack to expect that he would be skeptical. After all, he had been struggling with the European mess for five years now, and would not take kindly to an outsider, a beginner, telling him his business.

On the other hand, Jack Magnus's stock in trade for the last decade had been innovation. He was known for his tendency to take the least predictable, most unusual way to the solution of a problem. Whatever his irritation at being shown his business by an outsider, he would be intrigued by an original approach to a difficult situation.

Most important of all, Jack Magnus possessed great power within the corporation. If he took a liking to Francie's idea, he would be in a position to push it toward realization faster and more dramatically than anyone else at Magnus Industries.

This was the key to Francie's whole plan.

On the tenth of November Francie completed her detailed proposal for the computerized fiscal and managerial interface of the European Magnus subsidiaries.

There was only one way to proceed now. As a woman inside the Magnus hierarchy, Francie would never be listened to. If she tried to pass her suggestion through channels, it would certainly be ignored.

She needed to take her idea to Jack Magnus directly.

This was not an easy task. Jack was an exalted, almost bigger-than-life figure within the company, a figure with a mystique to match his father's. He was a member of the Board, and closeted at all times in meetings with men of the greatest power and influence.

Yet, if she wanted to better her own lowly position at Magnus, and get out of the rut she was in, Francie must find a way to get Jack Magnus's attention, and to make him listen to her idea.

After careful consideration of all her alternatives, Francie decided to begin with a low-key but direct approach. She addressed a memo to Jack Magnus, under her letterhead as special assistant to Raymond Wilbur in Domestic Products.

Dear Mr. Magnus, [it read]

For the past few months I've been working on the problem of a computerized interface between Magnus Industries' European subsidiaries. As you know, relations between these companies have been somewhat strained both from a fiscal and management perspective. My research has evolved into a concrete proposal for reorganization of the communications network linking the companies in question using computer technology.

The enclosed prospectus details the hardware needs and program specifications for the system I propose, as well as the procedure for implementation, and projected benefits for the next three fiscal years. I

would appreciate your giving this proposal your attention. If you find it of
interest, please don't hesitate to contact me.
Very truly yours,
Frances Bollinger, Special Assistant to the Director,
Domestic Product Division, 2235 B, Extension 415

Francie put her lengthy prospectus and memo into an interoffice
envelope and sent it to Jack Magnus's office.

Then, with a deep breath, she sat down to wait.

—— 6 ——

A week went by.

Then ten days, then two weeks.

Francie knew enough about corporate mechanics to realize that something was wrong.

She sent a second memo to Jack Magnus's office, asking about the fate of
the first. There was no answer.

Then she sent a third memo. Again there was no answer.

Finally she telephoned Jack Magnus's office directly.

"This is Frances Bollinger from Domestic Products," she told a preoccupied secretary. "I've had some communication with Mr. Magnus by memo
regarding a report I've prepared about relations among our European
subsidiaries. I'm having trouble getting through on this. Can you help
me?"

"What is your name again?" asked the secretary.

Francie had to spell her last name.

"Let me look into it," the secretary said. "I'll get back to you. What
department did you say you were in?"

"Mr. Wilbur's department," Francie said. "2235 B."

"2235 B, right," said the secretary. "I'll get back to you as soon as
possible."

"As soon as possible" turned out to be two more weeks, at the end of
which Francie received a one-line memo over the secretary's signature.

Your report will be duly considered, it read.

The tone did not inspire a great deal of hope.

Francie waited one more week before taking action.

At the end of that week she walked into Jack Magnus's office and asked the secretary at the front desk whom she might speak to about Interoffice Report No. 4756AA, which was the number assigned to her report.

There was a long delay as the secretary made several phone calls and left the room.

At last the secretary returned with a brittle smile.

"That would be Mr. Otis," she said. "He's down the corridor in Room 511."

"Thank you."

Francie went down the hall to Room 511, where she found a youthful, bespectacled management trainee who seemed confused and uninformed about her report.

"I'm sorry, Miss—what did you say your name was?" he asked.

"Bollinger," Francie said with a forced smile. "I'm with Mr. Wilbur's department."

The young man looked through a small file on his desk top.

"Ah, here it is," he said with an air of complacence. "Interoffice Report 4756AA, on Computerized Interface of European subsidiaries."

"That's it," Francie smiled.

"That's under review," said the young man. "You'll hear the results when the report has been fully studied."

"Who is studying it?" Francie asked.

"Er . . . well, I am," he said, looking a trifle sheepish.

"What do you think so far?" Francie asked, keeping her smile bright.

He looked flustered.

"Well, it would be premature to comment at this time . . . ," he said.

Francie looked at the cluttered shelves on the wall behind him. They were piled high with reports and ledgers.

"Tell me something, Mr. Otis," Francie said, more amused by the young man's innocence than frustrated by his uncommunicativeness. "Believe me, I won't be angry. Isn't it true that you're the only person responsible for reading my report? And isn't it true that you haven't gotten to it yet? And that you won't be getting around to it for the foreseeable future? Isn't that accurate?"

The young man turned cold, a real bureaucrat.

"No, that would not be accurate," he said. "You're wasting my time and yours, Miss—whatever your name is. And your report will be dealt with all the quicker if you leave this office and let us get on with our work."

Francie smiled and took her leave. She knew her report would never be read. It had been shuffled to an insignificant employee who obviously had no intention of giving it a serious study.

The corporate red tape of Magnus Industries, as it related to the office of Jack Magnus, had effectively buried Francie's report.

She had to start from square one.

"All right," she said to herself determinedly. "Two can play this game. You haven't heard the last of me yet, Mr. Jack Magnus."

Jack Magnus lived in an apartment on the thirtieth floor of a building on East 68th Street. It was one of the most desirable locations on the Upper East Side, with a magnificent corner view of midtown, Central Park, and the East River.

Its owner spent little time enjoying the view, however. Jack Magnus was a driven executive who took his work home with him every night after a long day at the office, and often spent entire evenings poring over reports, projections, and memos, barely taking time to brew another cup of coffee, until at last, sometime after midnight, he fell into a deep sleep which refreshed him for his next day's work.

Of course, these intimate facts were unknown to Francie as she journeyed to the building on a Monday evening, her proposal in her briefcase, her wool coat pulled close to protect her from the biting December wind.

When she reached the building she saw to her dismay that there was a doorman. He was inside the foyer behind the modern plate-glass windows, reading a magazine at his desk. The elevators were behind him.

Francie entered the foyer, a cold blast of outside air coming in with her.

"I'm here to see Mr. Magnus," she began. "He lives on the thirtieth floor."

"I know where he lives," said the doorman with a sour smile. "Is he expecting you?"

"Well, yes and no," Francie began. "You see . . ."

"Name, please?" he interrupted her.

"Bollinger. Frances Bollinger. I'm from Magnus Industries . . ."

The doorman had already turned away, and was speaking into the phone on the wall behind his desk. He managed to reduce his voice to so low a murmur that Francie could not make out a single word.

At length he hung up the instrument and turned back to her.

"You're not expected, so I can't let you in," he said. "Next time try calling first."

"But I . . ."

Before Francie could finish her sentence the phone on the wall rang, and the doorman turned to answer it.

He stood with his back to her. Again she heard him speak in muted monosyllables to whoever was calling. There was an obsequious tone to his voice.

He went on talking, not bothering to turn back and notice Francie. Perhaps he assumed she had already gone on her way.

Francie glanced at the elevators. The doorman's back was to them. She saw opportunity knocking, and seized it without a second's hesitation.

The first elevator, as luck would have it, was on the ground floor. The door opened and closed on her before the doorman could attempt to stop her. She pushed the button for Jack Magnus's floor, and the conveyance shot upward with a rush of pneumatic air.

She got out on an attractive landing furnished only with a large mirror. There was a window through which she saw a tiny sliver of New York skyline, the city thirty floors beneath her.

She walked slowly down the corridor. There were only four doors. The apartments behind them must be quite large, she mused.

Her destination was the first door she approached. It bore an engraved plate with a small knocker.

MAGNUS, J.

Francie stood looking at the enigmatic little plate. She was beginning to feel hot from the elevator and the warm corridor. She stood there, encumbered by her coat, her briefcase, and purse.

Then, on an impulse, she hurried back to the mirror by the elevator and looked at her image. The wind had tousled her hair. She smoothed it as best she could. Her cheeks were pink from the cold. She took a compact from her purse and dabbed at her face. At last, deciding that she looked as presentable as she needed to look, she went back down the corridor to the apartment door and gently tapped the knocker.

There was silence inside the apartment. Listening as carefully as she could, Francie heard absolutely nothing. Perhaps Jack Magnus had company. Perhaps he would not bother to answer a knock from an unannounced visitor.

Then she heard a muted sound of movement behind the door. She stood before the eyehole, wondering what she must look like from the other side.

She suddenly felt embarrassed and frightened. Jack Magnus was a famous man, and a powerful one. What had possessed her to come after him so brazenly?

She was on the point of beating a hasty retreat when the knob turned and the door slowly swung open.

Francie caught her breath.

Standing before her was the handsomest man she had ever seen in her life.

$$=== 7 ===$$

Jack Magnus was in shirtsleeves, his shirt open at the collar. He held a file folder open in his hand, and was squinting at his visitor, as though his eyes were still adjusting from the printed matter in the folder to the girl before him.

"Can I help you?" he asked, more than a trace of irritation in his voice.

"I'm sorry to bother you at home," she smiled. "I would never have dreamed of it. But your office has shown so much ingenuity in putting me off for over five weeks that I really didn't feel I could go on that way any longer."

"My office?" he said.

"Yes," she smiled eagerly. "I had worked out a plan for the computerized interface of the Magnus European subsidiaries, embodying a digital formalization of inventory, overhead, payroll, and most importantly a schematization of market position regardless of product or service. The plan would involve three mainframe medium-powered computers to be placed at central locations, say, Paris, London, and Lausanne, and a system of reporting and readout which I designed for the purpose. It's an experimental system, but I'm convinced it will work. So I passed it along to you through your office, but it was shunted off somewhere and I'm pretty sure it's never going to be read, so I decided to . . ."

"Hold it," he said, staring at her. "Slow down. What did you say your name was?"

"Francie," she said. "Francie Bollinger. I work in Mr. Wilbur's division. Domestic Products. As I say, I've been doing a lot of research on the European problem, and my specialty is computers and mathematical schematizations as applied to productivity. If I could have a couple of minutes of your time, I'm sure I could explain—"

"Will you slow down, for Christ's sake?" he said.

At last Francie fell silent. She studied the man before her. His pictures had not done him justice. He was tall and athletic, with the gracefulness of a matador. He had rich black hair and piercing dark eyes which were fixed appraisingly to her. She noticed his tanned complexion, and wondered whether he skied.

She could see dark hair on the chest beneath his shirt, and along the strong wrists emerging from his sleeves, one of which bore a Rolex watch. There was a hard readiness about him which impressed her.

"How did you get up here?" he asked. "How did you get past the doorman?"

She smiled again, a charming schoolgirl smile that touched him.

"He was busy on the telephone," she said, "so I sort of—well, showed myself up."

For a last long moment he stared at her. She wondered whether he was going to let her in, slam the door in her face, or have her arrested.

"I suppose you'd better come in," he said finally, stepping back to open the door.

She entered the apartment and stood staring at the beautiful view. Manhattan was spread out before her like a private spectacle. The city seemed to rise up and smile through the windows into the warm apartment. There was snow on the treetops in the park, and the lanes glimmered like dark silvery bands under the street lamps.

"Let me have your coat," Jack Magnus said.

She let him help her off with her coat. She felt the light touch of his fingers on her shoulders as the woolen garment came off. "Sit down," he said as he went to hang it up.

She sat on the deep leather couch and glanced at the apartment around her. His furnishings were simple—leather couches and chairs, abstract paintings, wide low tables, off-white walls, and lush carpeting in a soft indefinable tone which glowed warmly under the light from the lamps. The furnishings seemed to defer intentionally to the magnificent view from the two large windows.

Francie sat smiling at the restrained luxury around her, mentally comparing it to her cramped West Side apartment which faced onto a noisy, crowded street. Her office at Magnus Industries was an interior room, with no windows at all. She was not accustomed to views such as the one before her now.

At length Jack reappeared. She had to keep her eyes from opening wide at the sight of him. His handsomeness was almost bigger than life. Slacks and shirtsleeves looked more elegant on his hard body than a tuxedo on any other man.

As he came toward her she reflected that in the flesh his resemblance to his father was much less perceptible than in photographs. In fact, any shadow of the father was utterly eclipsed by Jack's amazing presence. He looked like his own man, resembling no one but himself in the perfection of his face and body.

"Something to drink?" he asked.

She shook her head.

He sat down on the chair opposite the couch and looked at her. She was holding her report in her hand. She felt his eyes move over her as he took in her blouse, her skirt, her legs, her high-heeled shoes. He was unhurried and cool in his examination of her.

"So," he said at length.

There was a silence. For a moment Francie could not find her words. She knew she had a lot to say, and only this one chance to say it.

He seemed to sense her disarray, and helped her.

"You work for Ray Wilbur, then," he said.

"Yes," she nodded. "I'm a specialist in marketing analysis. I did . . . I mean, I worked on Mr. Wilbur's schema for reorganizing the finances in Domestic Products."

"I know it," he said. "That was a brilliant plan. Frankly, we didn't expect something like that from Ray or his people."

"Oh. I didn't think—that is, it never occurred to me that you would know about that," she said.

"I sit on the Board that approved it," he said. "It was an easy decision. Ray's plan—or should I say, your department's plan," he added significantly, "was clearly the only way to go."

Francie smiled, encouraged. She could see that he was more interested in her now.

"What brings you to me?" he asked. "Why are you interested in the European subsidiaries? You already have a department of your own, don't you?"

Francie bit her lip thoughtfully. She had anticipated this question, but had no real answer for it.

"Well, I'm interested in problems of communication," she said. "You see, I did a lot of work in mathematics and computers at the University of Pennsylvania, and—"

"Europe is a long way from Domestic Products," he interrupted. "Do you have time on your hands in your own department?"

She hesitated. "Well, yes, in a way," she said. "Now that the reorganization is under way, I'm sort of between projects. Mr. Wilbur says—"

"Let me ask you something," he interrupted again. "How did you come to work for Ray Wilbur?"

"Well, I applied for the job—"

"What's your title?" he asked.

"Special Assistant to the Director," she said. "It doesn't mean much—"

"Did you answer an ad?" Jack Magnus asked. "Or were you referred by someone?"

She shook her head. "I went to Mr. Wilbur directly. I had some ideas about the division's fiscal problems, and I showed him the schematization I had worked out. Mr. Wilbur was kind enough to—"

"That's not the way Magnus Industries hires," he said, the ghost of a smile curling his lips. "We don't hire anybody except through Personnel or direct referrals."

"Well," Francie admitted, "I had been turned down by Personnel. But I thought Mr. Wilbur would be interested . . ."

"And he was," he finished for her.

"Well, yes."

He was looking at her more closely, his dark eyes narrowing. "And now you think I might be interested in this other plan you have," he said.

Francie nodded uncomfortably. His brief, curt interrogation had cut through all her camouflage and revealed just how aggressive she had been throughout her short career with Magnus Industries.

"You're a bit of a go-getter," he said.

She smiled as innocently as she could. "It was always my ambition to work for Magnus Industries, since I started college," she said. "When Personnel turned me down, I didn't want to take no for an answer. I thought the best way to go about things was to show I could do something for the company. I know it seems a little unusual . . ."

There was a silence. The sharp dark eyes were probing deeper as they studied her.

"I seem to recall the company newsletter's report about that reorganization," he said. "I have a good memory for names. Yours wasn't mentioned in that article, was it?"

After a reflective pause, Francie met his eyes.

"No, it wasn't," she said simply.

Again there was a silence, this time a longer one. He offered her a cigarette from the silver box on the table. When she shook her head he lit one for himself and sat looking at her. She wished she could see the train of thought going on behind those dark eyes.

"So," he said at last. "You want to tell me about a computerized interface for the European companies, involving—how did you put it?—digital formalization of inventory and schematization of market position irrespective of product or service."

She smiled. So he had taken in her every word at the door, despite his apparent irritation at being taken by surprise.

She nodded.

"All right," he said. "You've got my attention. You went to some length to get it, so you deserve to be heard out. Tell me how you expect to make this plan of yours work."

He put out his cigarette and sat back on the couch, his hands joined behind his neck. He looked very much at ease within himself, but also very alert and watchful.

Without looking at the printed proposal she had brought—for she knew its contents by heart—Francie cleared her throat and began to speak.

She talked for half an hour, but to her it seemed like only a couple of breathless moments. Jack Magnus did not move the whole time, but sat listening to her without comment, his eyes never leaving her own. At first she found it hard to meet his gaze, for fear it would break her concentration. But after a while she simply opened herself to the black irises fixed upon her, and let the words she had rehearsed for nearly two weeks pull her along in their irresistible flow. She could feel their logic and their truth, though Jack Magnus gave no sign as to whether she was convincing him.

When she had finished he sat looking at her for a long moment.

"You are remarkably beautiful," he said. The words were spoken coldly, like an observation by a scientist.

Francie frowned. "Does my appearance have something to do with the proposal I've just outlined?" she asked, an edge in her voice.

He smiled. "Magnus Industries does not encourage beautiful young women to draw attention to themselves as experts in marketing," he said. "Much less as specialists in mathematical formalizations and computer interfaces. You're going against the grain a little bit, aren't you, Miss Bollinger?"

Francie looked at him warily.

"I'm trying hard to do a good job at what I know best," she said. "To answer your question honestly, yes, it has been difficult for me to do that at Magnus Industries."

He nodded thoughtfully. Then the disarming smile brightened his face again.

"Well, I respect people who go against the grain," he said. "Our corporation could use a lot more of them."

She replied with a smile of her own.

He gestured to her report. "May I read that?" he asked.

"That's what I've been trying to get you to do for five weeks," she said, surprised by her own frankness.

"Well, you've succeeded," he said. "Let me look at it, and I'll get back to you. Did you put your office phone on the report?"

She nodded.

He looked at his watch. "Sure you don't want something to drink?" he asked. "Coffee?"

She shook her head. "I've taken up more than enough of your time," she said. "I appreciate your listening to me. You can keep this copy. I have another one."

He got up, left the room, and came back with her coat.

"Here," he said, holding it out for her to slip into.

For the second time she felt the touch of his hands on her shoulders, the only physical contact between them since she had appeared at the door. She smelled his clean male scent as he stood close to her. It was subtle, but very masculine, tinged with a bare hint of after-shave lotion and with the aroma of tobacco. She could feel the force of his will and of his intelligence coiled close to her. It made her knees feel weak, particularly after her long, desperate speech. He was not only the most attractive man she had ever encountered, but also by far the most powerful one.

"I apologize for the way my office treated you," he said. "I try to be open to new ideas, particularly from our own people. There's no excuse for the runaround you got."

"Oh, it doesn't matter." She smiled, turning to face him. "Since you . . ."

"Yes." He was looking down at her, a hint of affectionate understanding in his eyes.

"Well, I . . . ," she said, not sure how to take her leave of him.

"Until we meet again, then?" he asked, holding out a hand.

She watched her hand disappear into his large palm. The weakness in her knees got worse. She could feel the flush on her cheeks.

"Yes," she said. "Until we meet again."

"Thank you for coming," he said. "You'll be hearing from me."

He watched her into the elevator and then returned to the apartment. He picked up the phone and dialed the desk downstairs.

"Seth," he said to the doorman, "there's a young lady coming down. She's wearing a dark wool coat and carrying a briefcase. Put her in a cab to wherever she wants to go and pay the driver."

"Yes, sir," came the voice from downstairs, a touch of knowing humor in it.

"And Seth," said Jack Magnus. "Next time be more careful when you leave the desk to answer the phone. You never know who might slip in."

"Yes, sir." Now the voice on the intercom was chastened.

With a smile, Jack Magnus hung up the phone and stood looking out his window at the city below.

New York, he mused, was an interesting place after all.

—— 8 ——

Little did Francie suspect that her brief hour alone with Jack Magnus was to change her life.

After her visit to his apartment she settled down to the routine of work and to wait, not without skepticism, for him to evaluate her report and respond to her.

To her amazement, five days later she received a call from his executive secretary asking her to come to his office that afternoon.

Francie arrived to find the secretary waiting for her. The reception room of Jack's office was sleek and modern in its furnishings, with a lovely view of lower Manhattan outside the window.

"Miss Bollinger," said the secretary, apparently recognizing Francie despite the fact that she had never met her. "Mr. Magnus is expecting you."

A moment later Jack Magnus had appeared and ushered Francie into his private office. The room surprised her by its utter lack of outward show. The wall behind his desk was lined with deep shelves on which dozens of reports, prospectuses, and business publications lay, many of them dog-eared and filled with bookmarks. His desk top, on the other hand, was clean, bearing only a single manila folder, a calendar, and an ashtray.

He stood behind his desk watching her sit down in the visitors' chair. He was in shirtsleeves, as he had been at home, but now he wore a tie. He looked even more vital, somehow, with a touch of formality added to his aura of stinging male energy.

"I've read your report," he said. "There's a meeting of the Board tomorrow afternoon. I've managed to get you on the schedule."

Francie was taken aback.

"I . . . so soon?" she asked.

He smiled. "We've already kept you waiting for six weeks," he said. "Isn't that long enough?"

She was too shocked by his news to appreciate his joke.

"We'll meet at two," he said. "You'll describe your findings and your proposal, and the Board will consider it."

"I?" she said. "You mean me?"

Jack raised an eyebrow as he studied her across his desk.

"It's your work, isn't it?" he said. "You're closest to it. You're the logical person to explain it to the Board, and to answer any questions."

Francie turned pale. "But I haven't had any time to—to polish it. To prepare exhibits, projections."

He shook his head. "It's polished enough. The report you gave me is perfectly comprehensible and convincing. That's all they need."

"But won't they be—well, hostile to it? Me being a newcomer, and all?" she asked, thinking of those exalted people considering her drawing-board study of a terribly complicated problem.

He smiled. It was a private smile, as though something she had said amused him.

"If they're hostile," he said, "you'll win them over. That's your job, isn't it?"

Francie nodded uncertainly. "I—yes, I guess so."

"See you tomorrow," he said. "The boardroom is on the sixty-fifth floor. Just take the elevator. You can't miss it. Be there at two o'clock. My secretary is taking care of having copies of your report made for all the board members."

He had not sat down. His silence was her signal to thank him and leave. Francie felt paralyzed. Never in her wildest dreams had she imagined that her report would receive such fast action from a figure as remote as Jack Magnus.

She began to rise, but hesitated.

"I . . . ," she began. "Would you mind—I mean, I'd like to know what you thought of it yourself. My proposal, I mean."

He glanced at the folder on his desk top. "It's original," he said neutrally. "It's provocative. Whether it will work, I don't know. Let's see what the Board says."

His expression was inscrutable. Clearly he would say no more.

"Thank you, Mr. Magnus," she said hollowly. "I'll—I'll see you tomorrow, then."

And like that it was over. Francie was walking back down the hall to the elevators in a daze.

By the time she reached the twenty-second floor she had begun to recover her bearings. She would have charts and graphs blown up by a printing service tonight so that she could present the plan to the Board with its best face forward.

She looked at her watch. It was two-thirty.

There was still time to rush out and buy a new business suit for the occasion.

Her head spinning, Francie prepared for the biggest moment of her life.

The board meeting took place on schedule.

Francie appeared punctually at two, dressed in the new outfit she had bought. She had pinned her hair back and wore almost no makeup.

There were at least twenty board members present. They were intimidatingly old, staid-looking men, with gray hair, very expensive suits, and reading glasses which they dangled in their hands as they listened. Many smoked cigars. The room was expertly ventilated, so the atmosphere remained cool and pleasant.

There were no women. Even the secretary recording the minutes was a middle-aged man in an elegant three-piece suit.

At the head of the table, flanked by two men whose faces Francie remembered from a dozen photographs of the corporation's top executives, sat a figure whose stillness belied his obvious authority over everyone in the room. It was Anton Magnus. This was the first time Francie had ever seen him.

He was silent, and crouched rather low in his high-backed chair. He had iron-gray hair, jet-black eyebrows, and swarthy skin. He was dressed in a gray pinstriped suit. His hands were folded on the table before him. At first glance he seemed a fatherly figure, innocent and self-effacing. But on closer inspection she could see that this demeanor was only a camouflage for something else. The burning light in his black eyes betrayed the domination he exercised over the proceedings.

Francie looked away, intimidated. She listened as the minutes of the last meeting were read, and tried to avoid blushing as the agenda was announced, with her in second position.

"We'll start with Mr. MacNamara," said the presiding secretary, who sat at the end of the table opposite Anton Magnus.

"Thank you, Mr. Secretary," said a distinguished-looking man.

She listened carefully as he began a report on domestic policy, tax law, and the current fiscal situation. She only half-understood what he was talking about. She watched as the board members listened. She could almost feel the terrible power in their expressionless faces as the smoke drifted upward from their cigars and pipes. A few questions were asked.

Francie felt more out of her element with each passing moment. She was a raw newcomer to this enormous corporation, one of the most feared and respected firms on earth. And here she was making bold to communicate her computer plan to men who were accustomed to dealing in the multimillions of dollars. She felt like a child in the midst of a company of very serious adults.

Mr. MacNamara continued his presentation. Francie thought she could detect a trace of nervousness in his demeanor, as well as a rising tide of eloquence in his argument. Apparently the tax plan he was proposing represented the hopes of a lot of important people within the corporation.

She dared to glance again at Anton Magnus. His posture, if anything, had become even more self-effacing than before. He held a cigar in his fingers now, and he looked like a benevolent and rather tired old man. She could see no resemblance between him and his son. Anton Magnus represented Age in all its subtlety and complexity, while Jack, seated only a few feet away, was the very image of male attraction caught in the prime of youth and strength.

As luck would have it, Francie's eyes were on Anton Magnus when he gave a tiny sign to one of the men beside him. It was a brief sidelong flicker of his glance, combined with an almost invisible movement of his hand.

"That will do, Mr. MacNamara," the executive said suddenly, interrupting the speaker. "I think we've heard enough."

Everyone present understood this to mean that Mr. Magnus had heard enough.

"Call for a show of hands," came the secretary's voice.

To Francie's amazement, the vote was twenty to zero against the proposed plan. She could see from the manner of the vote, from the chastened demeanor of the victim, and from the almost audible sigh of relaxed tension in the room, that the proposal had never had a chance.

And somehow she knew that it was Anton Magnus who had killed it, with the silent authority of his sign language.

What chance do I have? she wondered, her heart sinking.

Now it was her turn.

"Miss Frances Bollinger, assistant to the director of Domestic Products, has been studying our principal European subsidiaries, and has outlined a plan for computerized coordination of these facilities. Miss Bollinger, your report, please."

Francie cleared her throat as she watched copies of her report being passed around the table. Her hands were cold. Somehow she managed to keep her fingers from trembling.

"Good afternoon, gentlemen," she said quietly. "I'm here to tell you about a plan I have devised for the computer networking of our European subsidiaries—"

"Can you speak up, please?" came a loud voice from somewhere. "The Board can't hear you."

Francie started over. She had to force herself to sound firm and confident in her presentation. She had spent long hours trying to soften the technical language of the report so that a reasonably well-informed executive could understand it without being a computer expert. Now her well-rehearsed words seemed weak and unconvincing to her.

She alternately spoke from notes and got up to point out figures on the charts she had brought. Her glance darted from one side of the table to the other, in search of eye contact with a friendly face. Some of the board members seemed uninterested, lost in thought. Others, however, were following her closely. It did not occur to her until much later that these were the executives more or less directly responsible for the European operation, and therefore concerned with the success or failure of her scheme.

When she had finished her report there was a silence. No one was smiling. No one seemed thrilled with her plan or with her. She did not dare look into the eyes of Anton Magnus, or even at Jack, who was sitting near his father, watching her without expression.

Suddenly one of the executives brandished his spectacles and spoke up.

"Central Electric, if memory serves, tried something like this and got burned," he said. He was not talking to Francie, but to his colleagues.

"They say the technology won't stand up under working conditions," another board member added, looking at the first. "Something about vacuum tubes . . . breakdowns. It's all a bit like science fiction, anyway."

"I'm concerned about making a bad situation worse," said a third executive. "The Europeans don't work well together at the best of times. What will happen if we get their inventory all mixed up on some electronic brain that none of them can understand? It will be a circus."

Francie could feel the tide of sentiment in the room going against her idea. What was worse, no one was asking her to defend herself. The board members were behaving as though she weren't even there.

As for Jack Magnus, he was not looking at her. But his eyes were alert as he glanced from one board member to another.

"There's also the question of overhead," said another executive. "These computers cost millions. We're pretty much overextended on the continent these days, anyway. How do we know a notion like this would be cost-effective?"

"John, what do you think?" asked another board member of one of his colleagues. "Haven't you had some experience in this area? We need some context here on costs."

At these words Francie flushed with anger. She could almost smell the condescension toward her from the assembled board members. Those who weren't looking at each other glanced interestedly at her body, and back to their notes.

Suddenly Francie understood the reason for their collective hostility. It was her sex. These men did not like being told their business by a woman.

"Excuse me, gentlemen," she said suddenly, her green eyes flashing. "If you'll turn to page seventy-seven of the prospectus, you'll find a detailed projection of start-up costs and long-term overhead. I think you'll find that all the variables, including hardware breakdowns, are taken into account. I have included an appendix on vacuum tube life expectancy and the current state of computer technology. I think I can summarize the issue in a few words . . ."

Francie quickly explained why the present state of the art in computer costs and performance militated in favor of her plan. She did not hesitate to use technical language to show that all the questions now being asked had already been taken into account in the body of her proposal. The lingering anger in her voice was eclipsed by a tone of brisk assurance. It was obvious she knew what she was talking about.

"I would not ask you gentlemen to consider a plan like the present one," she concluded, "unless I could prove it was an acceptable risk by any business standard you would care to apply. I believe this plan will increase productivity in Europe by twenty percent in a year or two. More importantly, there is the future to consider. Computer technology is going to revolutionize accounting and other procedures in the next decade. If we don't master this technology and use it for our own benefit, our competitors will. This could weaken our position not only in Europe, but around the world."

When she had finished there was a new silence, more ambiguous now. Francie could feel that the men around the table, although skeptical of her youth and her sex, had no alternative but to respect her expertise.

Jack Magnus had still said nothing. Neither had his father.

Francie's intuition told her that everyone in the room was acutely aware of the silent presence at the end of the table. None of them dared risk a definitive opinion until he had an idea of what the great Anton Magnus thought of Francie's plan.

And, at his end of the table, Anton Magnus was not saying.

At length the presiding secretary cleared his throat. He had apparently received a signal from somewhere to intervene.

"Miss Bollinger," he said, "thank you for your presentation. The board will consider the matter. You are excused."

"Thank you for your attention, gentlemen." Francie got up, gathered her papers, and turned to leave the room. She noticed that Jack cast her a brief sidelong glance, but he neither turned to meet her eyes nor got up to see her out. He was one of them now.

As the door to the boardroom closed behind her, Francie could almost feel the board members leaning forward to discuss her proposal.

Not until she was out in the corridor did it occur to her to wonder why they had not voted on it in her presence, as they had on the unfortunate Mr. MacNamara's tax plan.

She no longer cared what happened. She had exhausted what remained of her nerve in defending her plan to a blatantly hostile audience.

She just wanted to be alone.

She took the elevator downstairs to her office and sat in her chair, listening to the palpitating of her heart for a half hour, which seemed an eternity. Then she realized she had had nothing to eat all day. She wandered down to the cafeteria, got a sandwich which she was too nervous to eat, and went out onto Sixth Avenue for a walk in the cold December breeze. It did not refresh her. She felt as though she were about to faint.

Fleeing the busy traffic and hurrying pedestrians, she went back up to her office. She poured a cup of coffee and set it on her desk top, watching the steam rise from it without being able to make up her mind to take a sip. She was too paralyzed with dread to move.

She thought she was about to be fired. She thought someone on the

Board was up there pointing out a flaw in her plan, a fatal and humiliating proof of inexperience. She could almost hear the Board deciding to scrap the whole idea and get rid of its novice inventor. She imagined the executives joking about her temerity and her absurd proposal.

She struggled with tormenting ideas like these until four o'clock. Then there was a brusque knock at the door. Francie jumped at the sound, almost knocking over the now-cold coffee.

It was Jack Magnus. He entered the office without noticing its spare furnishings. He was still dressed in the silk suit he had worn to the board meeting. In his formal attire he was almost too perfect to be real. He looked literally as though he had just stepped off a wedding cake.

His expression, as usual, revealed nothing of his thoughts.

"Well?" she asked. "Don't keep me in suspense."

He stood before her, studying her. She could almost feel herself falling apart before his eyes. She wanted to grab him by his handsome shoulders and shake the terrible truth out of him.

At last he spoke. A slight smile curled his lips.

"You have a lot of work ahead of you," he said.

"What do you mean?"

"I mean they bought it," he said. "The whole thing. Just as you described it. Not more or less. And they want you to administer it. You'll have a new title—Assistant Vice-President in Charge of International Systems. You'll be setting up the computer network yourself. The Board has approved three mainframe computers for the European subsidiaries in Paris, London, and Lausanne. You'll have all the staff you need, and the budget you asked for. You have nine months to implement the system and get it operating before reporting back to the Board."

"You mean—you mean they liked it?" Francie asked, unable to take in so much good news at once.

He looked amused. "Don't say *like*," he said. "In business nobody likes anything—they buy it or they don't buy it. Believe me, buying is a lot more definite than liking. To answer your question, they liked it with their votes. You're in business, Miss Bollinger."

She leaped up from her desk and hugged him. She felt him pat her back. His touch was pleasant, impersonal. Yet it communicated a happiness he did not want to express too openly, and something like pride in her achievement. She sensed the warmth of his hard limbs behind the fabric of his jacket. She felt an impulse to lean on him for strength. She had not realized how terrified she was in anticipation of this board meeting.

Then she pulled back from him, embarrassed by her own susceptibility.

He was looking down at her curiously. His eyes seemed to darken at the sight of her own emotion.

"Drop in on me tomorrow morning," he said. "We'll go over some of the details. By the way, I understand you speak several European languages."

She nodded. "French, Spanish, Italian, German—and a little Portuguese."

"Learn Dutch," he said. "That ought to do it. You'll be leaving for Europe in two or three weeks. See you tomorrow."

With an inward gulp, Francie watched him go out the door.

At that moment, forty floors above her office, unbeknownst to Francie, the great Anton Magnus himself was thinking about her.

On his enormous walnut desk was her report. He paged through it absently, and then let it fall shut before him.

Anton Magnus had been in business for over fifty years. During that time he had made executive decisions involving countless millions of dollars and the professional lives of hundreds of brilliant and ambitious people. He had made a career out of sifting through the advice he was given by well-meaning subordinates and then making the difficult, lonely, and often brutal decision himself. He had learned to sacrifice all considerations, logical, financial, and personal, to one overriding concern: the welfare of his corporation.

Today, in allowing the Board to approve the Bollinger girl's plan, he had made such a decision.

But he had not made it rashly. He had made it in the full possession of his understanding of the marketplace and of the people around him.

Despite its surface cleverness, the girl's plan did not strike him as an acceptable risk. The idea was ahead of its time. It was too soon for a major corporation like Magnus to dirty its hands on so chancy a scheme. In a few years, perhaps, when enough smaller companies had had time to try out the idea, things might be different.

So Anton Magnus's first reaction, upon seeing the proposal rushed before the Board so precipitously, had been to veto it out of hand. The girl's youth and inexperience, combined with her lack of corporate position, only militated further against her proposal.

Yet something had stopped him. There was more to the plan than met the eye. In the first place, there was the very fact that the proposal had been rushed onto the schedule for today's board meeting—a rare occurrence. Secondly, by acutely observing the tenor of the Board's discussion and the first voice votes, Anton Magnus had been able to conclude without doubt that his son Jack was wholeheartedly behind the plan. Jack had obviously done some arm-twisting before the meeting to predispose a strong phalanx of board members in favor of the girl's work.

Jack was in direct charge of Europe. He must be convinced that the plan would work. And he had prepared the ground for it by lining up a majority of votes on the Board. Jack never did anything without a reason.

Or several reasons . . .

Anton Magnus wondered what those reasons might be.

This was why Anton Magnus had not exercised his power to veto the entire plan with one signal to his closest lieutenant on the Board. He had decided to let the Bollinger girl have her one chance to bring her plan to fruition—within a nine-month time limit.

Anton Magnus had spent his business lifetime combining a fisherman's patience with a chess master's sense of strategy to manipulate those around him, colleague and competitor alike, into doing what he wanted them to do. Certainly he had encountered no more canny or willful colleague than his own son, the man he himself had chosen to take his place at the helm of Magnus Industries. And Jack, a brilliant, determined, and ruthless executive, wanted this computer plan. He wanted it with the full extent of his power.

So Anton Magnus was going to let him have it. One day, perhaps soon, this little gift might empower him to seek a quid pro quo from his son that would make today's small sacrifice more than worthwhile. No one could predict the future. Today's sacrifice might be tomorrow's gain.

Indeed, there was always the outside chance, remote but real, that the system devised by Frances Bollinger might actually work. The technological and financial implications of such an event would be great, and might affect Anton Magnus, his son, and his corporation in unforeseeable ways. This was something to consider very carefully.

But at this moment Anton Magnus's thoughts were elsewhere.

He was not thinking about the Bollinger girl's plan, her eloquence and intelligence in selling it, or her ability to carry it out in her new position.

He was thinking about the slim, nubile body under those conservative clothes. She was a great beauty, and an unusual one. Her beauty sprung as much from her honesty and intelligence as from her flesh.

And he was remembering the way Jack had looked at her throughout the board meeting. Jack's expression had been worth a thousand words. He had been doing his best to look as neutral as possible. But a father knows his son.

Better, sometimes, than the son knows himself.

With the girl's image before his mind's eye Anton Magnus stood up and walked to the corner of the office beneath the tall windows where a small chessboard was kept. He looked down at the silent chessmen and smiled.

Frances Bollinger, a beautiful and innocent young woman, might make an ideal pawn.

Pawns, Anton Magnus reflected, were important pieces. Games could be won and lost depending on their moves.

But pawns must be sacrificed once they had served their purpose.

$$=== 9 ===$$

December 27, 1955

Francie was still recovering from the board meeting and rejoicing over its unexpected result when another event took place which was to have far-reaching consequences for her life. Jack telephoned her office, where she was embroiled in travel preparations, computer paraphernalia, and arrangements for a Dutch tutor, to invite her to a party at his parents' house on Park Avenue.

"The party has a dual purpose," he said. "My older sister Gretchen has just had a baby. It's my father's first grandchild, and he wants to celebrate that. Also, Magnus has just acquired a shipping subsidiary thanks to its relationship with Gretchen's in-laws, the Trowbridges. It's really a case of my father and Graham Trowbridge congratulating themselves over their two new babies."

Francie wondered briefly why Jack would think of her for such an occasion, but swallowed her second thoughts and agreed cheerfully to the invitation.

"There will be a lot of people there," Jack added casually. "Some of them are pretty well known. Don't let it intimidate you."

Francie was not to realize until the night of the party what an understatement Jack's words were.

The Magnus mansion on Park Avenue was an incredible sight. A six-story marvel of Grecian design in marble, it had been sold by the Vanderbilts to the city thirty years before, because not even the Vanderbilts could afford the taxes on such a piece of real estate. But Anton Magnus had bought it for himself when his corporation reached the number-three spot in the nation. By that time his personal assets had attained heights too astronomical to be made public.

He had restored the house to it all its former glory, and a lot more. All the fixtures, marble and parquet floors, paneling and trim had been imported from Europe. The paintings on the walls represented perhaps the finest private collection in America. Francie recognized the sculpture, the tapestries, the Aubusson and Oriental carpets, the china and furniture, from the catalog of the Magnus household collection which she had bought out of curiosity.

It was an amazing place, reflecting a dozen different styles and periods. Yet somehow, despite this diversity, it all bore the stamp of Anton Magnus's personality. This was difficult to explain. There was a peculiarly virile elegance about the place, which hid itself behind a veneer of old-world charm. The delicacy of the furnishings did not for a moment obscure the masculine will which had assembled them. One caught one's breath upon entering the house, for one could feel awesome power here, a power which did not have to flaunt itself, so sure was it of its own domination over all who came near it.

Francie was glad, in retrospect, that she had not come alone. Jack had insisted on being her escort for the evening. "You're going to need a companion," he said, "and I can't think of anyone I'd rather be with at my father's house. You'll understand what I mean when you get there."

When he picked her up he complimented her on her dress, a formal design with sinuous lines which hugged her shapely limbs.

"You're nice to take me under your wing this way," she said as they entered the mansion. The drive was crowded with limousines which made Francie feel like Cinderella at a ball where she did not belong.

"Not at all," Jack smiled. "It's you who's doing me a favor. I have selfish reasons. I try to avoid being under this roof whenever possible. Since there's no way to get out of it tonight, I wanted to be with someone I could respect. Believe it or not, that's a rare commodity around Magnus Industries."

Francie was flattered, but also perplexed by his words. They bespoke an unhappiness, not to say a loneliness, which seemed strange for a man of Jack Magnus's exalted reputation.

But she stopped wondering, and simply thanked her lucky stars for Jack's companionship, once she saw the guests who populated Anton Magnus's house that night.

They included dignitaries of all varieties, including delegates to the

United Nations, local and state politicians, both United States senators from New York, the Lieutenant Governor, and a representative of the President himself, bearing a congratulations gift for Gretchen marked with the presidential seal.

The cream of high society was also represented. These were people whom Francie was in no position to recognize, but Jack murmured enough descriptions to her in the course of her introductions for her to understand how important they were. They included members of the oldest and most socially admired families around the country, the Auchinclosses and Gouverneurs and Van Rensselaers from New York, the Converses and Biddles from Philadelphia, the Spreckels and Livermores from San Francisco, the Thayers and Endicotts and Wetherells from Boston, the McCormicks and Pulitzers and Ketterings from Chicago and the Midwest. And the looks on their faces made it clear they were not condescending to be here as a social obligation, but considered it a feather in their cap to be invited to a Magnus affair.

The array of exotic and famous human beings went on and on, almost unbelievable in its magnificence. Francie recognized great stars of Broadway and Hollywood, stars of the concert stage, painters, poets, novelists, publishers, filmmakers.

Among these rarefied species was another, a breed of man whom Francie was not sophisticated enough to recognize at first. But Jack pointed them out and told her who they were: they were presidents and CEOs of major corporations, corporations with names like IBM and General Electric and General Motors.

It was a stellar gathering which cut across every part of society, and represented only the best. Francie could hardly believe her eyes.

"Don't let them impress you too much," Jack said as he squired her through the elaborate salons, in which soft music played and thick carpets muffled the guests' already muted conversation. "They're just people, despite their names and their bank accounts. And I'll tell you a secret, Francie. Nine out of ten of them owe my father some sort of favor, or are afraid of what might happen if they made the mistake of refusing his invitation. Don't think you're looking at pure human status and achievement here. You're looking at power, and intimidation, mixed up in a lot of complicated ways. The more familiar with it you become, the less impressed you'll be—and the more disgusted."

Francie was surprised by the bitterness of his words. Yet she had to reflect that people at the top of society are no better than anyone else. Perhaps the ornate rooms of Anton Magnus's mansion were full of all the human weaknesses that one might expect from so large a gathering. And perhaps Jack knew enough about the peccadilloes behind these beautiful masks to find it all depressing.

Still, to Francie it was a fairyland, and she forgot her jitters as she enjoyed the famous hands she shook, the famous voices she heard, the faces she saw in person tonight after having seen them only in magazines and newspapers, or on movie screens, before.

What never occurred to her, in her excitement, was that she herself might be the object of the curiosity of more than a handful of Anton Magnus's guests tonight.

She could not help noticing the many eyes that followed her as Jack squired her among the guests. She had heard of his reputation as a great ladies' man, but had not given it much thought until now. She had not tried to imagine the invisible side of his life which existed outside her few meetings with him. She knew him only in those few fragmentary encounters, and they were more than enough to keep her mind occupied.

He led her through the crowded rooms to a salon decorated with ornate furnishings and French landscapes, where a small, gray-haired woman was chatting with a handful of contemporaries.

He introduced her as his mother. Francie did not know her by sight, but had heard through the rumor mill of her exalted past and her marriage to Anton Magnus. The former Victoria Wetherell, she had been a debutante and Vassar graduate on the verge of a successful marriage into the Bingham cosmetics family when, in 1920, Anton Magnus came from nowhere and literally swept her from her family's loving arms, overriding her father's objections and marrying her while she watched spellbound from the sidelines of the private battle between the two men.

The marriage, legendary by now, had catapulted Victoria Wetherell to a height of fame she had never imagined possible despite her privileged past—and this when her disapproving relatives had predicted it would be the ruin of her.

The battle against Anton Magnus had broken Cartan Wetherell's spirit, it was said, and he had died a drained man not long after his Victoria's wedding, for she had been his only daughter and his favorite child. Similarly, the violence of Anton Magnus's entry into her life had sapped what remained of Victoria's personal backbone, and ever since the dust had settled over her controversial marriage she had been a virtually enfeebled specimen of her sex, a timid little spirit haunting the rooms of their gigantic house as the family's rise to greatness swirled around her.

The births of her children seemed to complete the process of exhaustion that had begun with her marriage itself, and she claimed no authority over them, giving them over to nannies and tutors when they were little, and leaving it to Anton Magnus to discipline them when necessary and to direct the course of their lives. As the lady of the house she confined herself to insignificant social duties, a rather uncertain command of the servants, and long afternoons spent on the phone with her own mother or a handful of trusted Wetherell cousins, none of whom took her very seriously.

Like a hill of no intrinsic value which is captured in battle and then abandoned by the army which fought so hard to gain it, Victoria Magnus was an empty shell left over from the tug-of-war that had pitted her adored father against Anton Magnus. If she realized this—for she was an intelligent woman, in spite of everything—the knowledge only seemed to increase her helplessness.

Of all this Francie had an inkling before meeting the old lady. In making conversation with her now she realized that Victoria Magnus had shrunk to nothing in the shadow of her husband's awesome power, and was barely able to converse in her small voice. She was polite, being possessed of all the social graces engrained in a person of her background. But she seemed so frightened of everything and everyone around her that Francie felt sorry for her.

Francie could not help noticing that the old lady seemed alarmed by her own presence in particular, on Jack's arm. When she and Jack took their leave, Jack explaining that there were a lot of people Francie still had to meet, an odd light of worry, perhaps of disapproval, shone in his mother's eyes.

"Am I imagining things," Francie asked as they left the room, "or was your mother not very pleased to meet me?"

Jack did not answer right away. He was looking at the group of people they were approaching, near the grand staircase in the main ballroom.

"You're about to find out the answer to your question," he said. "I'm sorry you're being forced to learn so much about our lovely little family so soon, but please bear with me."

They came closer to a pretty young woman with chestnut hair and hazel eyes who detached herself from a group of guests and came forward to greet Jack and meet his companion.

Jack leaned forward to give the girl a kiss on her rosy cheek, and introduced her to Francie.

"Belinda Devereaux," he said, "I'd like you to meet Francie Bollinger. Francie is working with me on a project for the European Division."

He turned to Francie. "Belinda is one of our family's closest friends," he said a trifle uneasily.

He excused himself for a moment and left the two young women alone. Francie tried to make small talk with Belinda about the corporation and the guests at the party, but Belinda seemed uncomfortable and distracted, her eyes following Jack as he greeted some guests across the room. After three or four minutes Francie was relieved to see Jack return and take her away again. She could almost feel Belinda's eyes on her back as they moved through the doorway to the next room.

"She's very nice," Francie said.

Jack sighed. "Yes, I guess she is."

They walked in silence for a moment. Then Jack signaled to a passing waiter for two glasses of champagne, and squired Francie with astonishing expertise into a room that happened to be empty.

"They never use this room for parties," he said. "They say it's haunted. Some sort of family scene took place here during the Vanderbilt days. Anyway, it's kept unused. I used to play in here as a boy, when I wanted solitude."

He showed Francie to a loveseat and sat down opposite her, his champagne glass in his hands.

"I want you to have some idea of what's going on here," he said. "A long time ago my father decided I was going to take his place at Magnus when he retired. He also picked out Belinda Devereaux as the girl I was going to marry. Her family has more oil wells and copper mines than any other in the nation. Dad thought a match between me and Belinda would be just the thing for Magnus Industries. As you can see, he's accustomed to getting his way with other people."

He sighed, set down his glass, and ran a hand through his hair.

"I told him to go to hell," he said. "I also told him that I would not succeed him as head of Magnus. We had quite a row over it all. A series of rows, I should say. In the end I compromised on one point. I told him I would stay with the corporation until his seventieth birthday. That would give him plenty of time to find someone else to take over for him. I would go elsewhere, but continue to sit on the Board. And I would marry whomever I damn pleased—when I pleased."

Francie looked at him uneasily, as though wondering why he was telling her this.

"Well, that's where things have stayed," he concluded. "The old man is sixty-nine years old. He's waiting for me to change my mind. He's using his increasing age as leverage. You can't know how clever he is, Francie, how relentless, how inventive about getting his way." He smiled. "He's an old chess player from way back. He taught all his children to play. None of us could ever beat him. I came the closest . . ."

He sighed again. Clearly the subject was very uncomfortable for him.

"As for Belinda," he said, frowning, "I never see her, except at occasions like this. But she doesn't marry. She's waiting, you see. Waiting, like everybody else, to see if the old man will get his way after all. Everybody who knows the Magnuses is watching, like a bunch of spectators, because they find it incomprehensible that anyone could stand up to Anton Magnus."

Francie looked at him through her clear eyes.

"Why are you telling me all this?" she asked. "It's no business of mine, is it?"

He smiled sadly. "I just want you to understand some of the looks you've been seeing tonight. To understand what I've set you down in the middle of. People see me with a beautiful young woman like you, and tongues start wagging. My mother sees you, and she worries. Then Belinda turns up, and she gives you mysterious looks. I just want you to understand that none of this concerns you. It's the not-so-pretty private life of the Magnus family."

"Well," Francie said. "Thank you for clarifying things, but you really didn't have to. Your life is your own."

He sat forward.

"There's one more reason," he said. "You've done brilliant work for our company. Twice now you've shown that you're someone special, someone who deserves advancement and responsibility. Now, I'm the one who set you up for this European thing. The day will come, eventually—perhaps sooner rather than later—when I won't be at Magnus anymore, but you will. I don't want your association with me to work against you at that time. Corporate politics is a dangerous thing, Francie. More dangerous than you can realize. A little thing that happens today can come back to haunt you in five years, when a few individuals have switched positions. The people who don't like me have long memories."

Francie frowned.

"I don't live by worrying about things like that," she said. "If bad things happen, I'll deal with that fact. But I can't live my life under the shadow of potential enemies. All I can do is work hard and hope for the best. I'm not trying to harm anyone."

He smiled. "I admire you for that. It's a refreshing attitude. Not the safest one, perhaps, but at least it's honest."

Francie studied him, fascinated despite herself by his extraordinary looks. Now she could see the hint of his mother's heredity in his nose, his chin, his hair. But, like the Magnus features he had in common with his father, it was all eclipsed by his own special handsomeness, so that he seemed to have sprung from nowhere, a perfect man without a past, concerned only with the future he intended to dominate with his strong will and great talent.

"Your father is a powerful man," she said. "I get the impression that everyone here is afraid of him, except you. Can one person possibly be that powerful?"

Jack's smile disappeared. An expression of dead seriousness came into his eyes.

"You don't know how powerful," he said. "And how dangerous."

Francie said nothing, but studied the look in his eyes. It was a look of determination and of challenge, as though he knew who his adversary was and had made up his mind to get the better of him at any cost. He seemed to relish the battle.

Francie felt a little chill inside her at the sight of an emotion so dark and private.

At the same time she wondered why she had not yet crossed paths with Anton Magnus tonight.

At that moment, in a quiet office separated from the rest of the house, the Mayor of New York City sat meekly in an oversized leather chair, looking up at Anton Magnus.

For all the decorum of his posture, one could almost see the Mayor holding his hat in his hand. He looked unnerved, beseeching.

"Mr. Magnus," he said. "Anton . . ." He used his host's first name hesitantly. It was impossible to tell from the inscrutable look in the magnate's eyes what was pleasing or displeasing to him. The Mayor did not relish the role of supplicant, but he knew he had to play it to the hilt tonight.

"Anton," he said uneasily, "I'd like to think we have an agreement on this bond business. I'd like to be able to leave here tonight and know I can tell my people you're behind us. It would make a hell of a difference to all of us."

Magnus puffed at his cigar, intentionally looking away. His eyes had a strange, cold look, almost inhuman in their emptiness.

Behind those eyes Anton Magnus was thinking with utter clarity.

He knew that the poor Mayor was between a rock and a hard place. The city's balance of payments had been growing more and more unfavorable for the past five years, and the chaotic tax structure of the city and state, so poorly administered, so riddled with graft, had allowed things to get worse instead of better.

It was New York politics in a nutshell. They never changed. But in recent years the chips had been falling against the city.

Now Anton Magnus was cast in the role of savior. It was in his power to sway a large group of investors—all of them beholden to him in a variety of ways—to put several hundred million dollars into a special fund of bonds intended to bail out the city. All he had to do was say the word. But the bonds would not bring a return to the investors quite as large, in the short run, as some other properties available on Wall Street this season. It was purely a matter of good will and civic pride. And arm-twisting.

Anton Magnus had been looking forward to this moment for years.

Long ago, when the Mayor was merely an ambitious councilman garnering voters any way he could, he had taken it into his head to sling mud at the Magnus Corporation as a monster monopoly whose special tax breaks were bleeding the city dry. He had based his first campaign for Mayor on a pledge to crack down on corporate robber barons in the city. And he had won on that platform.

Naturally, once in office, his campaign promises had been forgotten as quickly as the canapés he used to eat before a big dinner at the Empire Room—the Mayor was a noted gourmand, a heavy man who liked his food and drink—and he had thought no more about them.

But Anton Magnus never forgot a slight, much less a bad turn. He knew that many of the mayor's supporters still considered him a defender against the evils of big business, and might put pressure on him at any time to enforce certain unpleasant anti-monopoly legislation more stringently.

So Anton Magnus had looked ahead. He had seen the city's financial troubles just off the horizon, long before any of the city's financial planners had. And he had slowly edged his corporation into a position from which it would exert the maximum influence at just the right moment.

Now that moment was here. The city was only a year or two away from complete insolvency, and the Mayor had come on his knees to ask for help. His own advisors had exhausted their limited imaginations in trying to explore alternative rescue plans. He had no one but Magnus to turn to.

So today, thanks to his careful planning over many years, Anton Magnus was in the driver's seat.

Which was where he had always intended to be.

"Mr. Mayor," he said with a respect as empty as the voice expressing it was full and mellifluous, "I quite understand your situation. And I'd like to help. But you must understand that I'll be asking my associates, who are shrewd investors, to put their money into something that will clearly give them a mediocre return on their investment. At this time in the country's economic history, that's asking a lot."

"Without your help, the city may go under," said the Mayor with a hint of irascibility. He was a fighter by nature, and did not appreciate being kept hanging this way. "Then we'll all be in the soup."

Anton Magnus darted a hard look into the Mayor's eye.

"Not all, Mr. Mayor," he said. "The tax laws are onerous enough in New York as it stands. I have offers from California to build Magnus Industries a skyscraper in downtown Los Angeles, and let us operate in it virtually rent-free. That's how badly our West Coast friends would like Magnus to move there."

The Mayor turned red.

"I hope you told them no," he said.

Magnus raised a dark eyebrow.

"Of course I told them no," he said. "But you know business, Mr. Mayor. Yesterday's 'no' is tomorrow's 'yes.'"

The Mayor took out a handkerchief and wiped his brow.

"Anton," he said. "What can I do to change your mind? What can I do to assure you of my friendship? You know how important Magnus Industries is to our city. I've tried over the years to let you know you have a friend in me."

"I didn't know you had friends among monopolists and robber barons," Anton Magnus said with quiet irony.

The Mayor turned redder. "You don't mean to say you believed any of that?" he said. "Anton, that was just politics. Surely you haven't held that against me?"

Magnus's eyes turned away coyly.

"What can I do? Please, Anton . . . ," the mayor asked.

Magnus cleared his throat. "My stockholders feel burdened by the tax laws as they're being enforced on our company," he said. "They don't feel we're doing as well in New York as we could and should be doing. The WR 52 State Capital Gains Tax, for instance . . ."

He did not need to say more. The Mayor had known from the start that tax would be a bone of contention. He had signed it into law a year ago, and it had brought millions of dollars to the city from Magnus and similar corporations. It was the first line of the city's defense against fiscal erosion.

"It's been good for the city, Anton," the Mayor said. "It's helped to slow our downhill slide."

Magnus nodded, raising an eyebrow.

"But I do understand your problem," the Mayor said. "Let me talk to my people. I'm sure something can be worked out."

"Before the end of this fiscal year?" Anton Magnus asked softly.

"Absolutely. I give you my personal word of honor," the Mayor said.

Anton Magnus stood up and held out his hand. He held it out regally, palm down, almost as though he expected the Mayor to kiss it. Gritting his teeth, the Mayor took the hand, turned it ninety degrees, and shook it warmly.

"Don't worry," he said. "Count on me, Anton. I can promise you a more reasonable approach on the part of the state tax people."

"I appreciate your understanding," Magnus said. "It means a lot. I'll meet with my corporate associates next week and see if we can't arrange something to help you out with the bonds."

"Thank you, Anton. Thank you so much. You'll never regret it, I promise you."

"There's one more thing," Anton Magnus said, as though on an afterthought. "My wife is curious to see Gracie Mansion. You know how women are."

"Why, of course, Anton!" The Mayor jumped at the chance to do a small favor. "If only I had known. Why, I'll invite you both immediately. When would it be convenient for you to come?"

"Not me," Magnus said. "Just my wife. Perhaps she could have lunch with your wife, Mr. Mayor. But you know how the press is. She might have to make a few remarks."

"Of course," the Mayor said. "I'll have the press secretary get right on it. I want the city to know how important you and Mrs. Magnus are to our very existence. It will be a great thrill."

"That's awfully kind of you," Magnus said. "You'll be present to welcome her, then?"

The Mayor gulped. "With all my heart," he said. "Leave all the arrangements to me. I'll have the newspapers alerted well in advance."

"Well, then," Anton Magnus said, rising. "I'm glad we have things straightened out." He gestured to the door. "I have a couple of phone calls to make before I join you outside," he said. "Why don't you greet your wife for me, and introduce her to Mrs. Magnus? I'll see you in a few minutes."

"Of course," the Mayor said, getting up to leave, though he knew this was an insult to his office and to his person, to let himself out while the great Anton Magnus remained standing behind his desk.

But he had no choice. As he closed the door he pondered the incredible power of the man he had just left. Anton Magnus possessed the influence to deliver a billion dollars to the city in a week, if he so desired. And to withhold it, if he deemed it inappropriate to extend his favor to the struggling metropolis.

The Mayor returned to the party, wiping his brow, and stopped the first waiter he saw. He picked up two martinis from the waiter's tray.

Almost before the waiter had turned away the Mayor had finished the first martini, and set down the empty glass on one of the inlaid George III walnut tables in the salon. The other drink he took with him as he went to find his wife and tell her the good news.

At a central spot in the main reception room, with its two curving staircases to the upstairs ballroom, stood Gretchen Magnus Trowbridge, greeting guests and receiving best wishes.

Jack introduced Francie to Gretchen, who was a pleasant young woman in her thirties, soft-spoken and surprisingly shy. Gretchen would have had a somewhat rumpled housewifely look were it not for the elaborate makeup, coiffure, and evening gown she wore, on which no expense had been spared. Her baby girl was asleep in a lavish little cradle by her side, quite oblivious to the gala goings-on around her.

Francie had already heard some stories about Jack's two sisters through the office grapevine. Gretchen, the older sister, had been the family's first-born, and naturally earmarked for a brilliant marriage.

Gretchen had been a quiet and well-behaved girl in her first youth, but had become troubled in her adolescence. She had been rebellious, had run away from home several times, and created such scenes with her parents that she had to be sent to a special girls' school which was little more than a reformatory for the very rich.

As a teenager she was quite pretty, with auburn hair, a milky complexion, and a lush figure. Her transgressions at school had led eventually to a family drama which took place the year before her debut.

She had met a young man while on a transatlantic crossing with her parents. He was the son of professional people who lived in Chicago. Gretchen had conceived an attraction for him, but had cannily kept it a secret from her family.

Using her considerable intelligence, she had moderated her troublesome behavior and managed to get herself moved to a fine girls' school in Lake Forest, north of Chicago. There she settled down, made friends, and got good grades. The Magnuses were so pleased that they were willing to let her finish out her education there. They knew many North Shore families who kept a distant eye on Gretchen, so they felt safe.

Then the blow fell. One weekend the girls' school telephoned to say that Gretchen was missing. Anton Magnus sent his force of private detectives to look for her, and she was eventually located in northern Wisconsin, near the Canadian border, where she was enjoying a forbidden honeymoon with the Chicago boy she had met on the ocean liner. They were married, having eloped by prearrangement just at the moment when Gretchen's absence would not be noticed at the school. Gretchen had fabricated a note from home saying she had to be away for ten days on a family matter.

Naturally Anton Magnus saw red when he heard all this. The marriage was quietly annulled with the consent of the boy's parents. Gretchen was taken out of the school immediately, for it was realized that she had only gone there in order to be near her beau. The entire affair was hushed up thanks to Magnus's influence with the press.

The only fly in the ointment was that Gretchen was now pregnant. This problem was solved by an abortion performed in Switzerland.

After that episode Gretchen's days of independence were behind her. She dutifully appeared at family gatherings, finished her education at Vassar, and married a boy chosen by her parents, Elliot Trowbridge. The marriage obviously had a corporate and social basis, for the Trowbridge fortune was legendary.

Gretchen became a docile young woman, a little on the plump side, pleasant to talk to but never "all there," to use the expression of her friends. She spent her time running insignificant errands and entertaining family and friends, and only showed some excitement about life on the day she found she was pregnant with her first legitimate child, the baby girl whose existence was the reason for the party tonight.

Gretchen had accomplished nothing since her marriage except fulfilling social obligations and attending scattered charity functions, but she took her housekeeping duties seriously, almost too seriously. Her house was so spic-and-span that no one felt very comfortable in it. She cleaned and recleaned, dusted over and over again. Her husband, a spoiled young man who drank too much and gambled, didn't seem to notice. Those who knew Gretchen best felt sorry for her. Her old intelligence shone through only in an occasional incisive remark about the latest Broadway opening. The letters she wrote to friends were as impersonal as corporate memos.

But she seemed thrilled with her baby. Friends and family thought this would bring her alive again. Hoped so, at least. Others, less charitable or optimistic, thought it was too late for that. They saw her mother's pusillanimity showing through in Gretchen. She seemed so afraid of life, so uninvolved. Sadly, as was the case with so many wealthy girls, Gretchen had had her chance to become a person in her own right, and had apparently expended her resources in her short-lived youthful rebellion. There was nothing left for her but to go through the motions of being a socially visible wife and mother.

Despite having heard of Gretchen's unhappy past, Francie took an instant liking to her. There was something down-to-earth and vulnerable about Gretchen that charmed her.

"You must be thrilled," Francie said, looking at the sleeping baby and feeling a twinge of envy for the proud mother.

"It's been a long wait," Gretchen said. "We've been trying for a long time with no success. I think I've had every fertility drug in existence. I'm relieved."

Gretchen warmed up quickly to Francie, and was soon regaling her with stories about the tribulations of caring for her first baby. But suddenly a shadow passed over her face. Involuntarily Francie turned to see what had caused it.

Anton Magnus had appeared from nowhere and was approaching his daughter.

"Hello, Dad," Jack said, interposing himself between his father and the two young women. "I'd like you to meet Francie Bollinger. Francie, Anton Magnus."

This was Francie's first close-up look at the great Anton Magnus. He was a man of average height and build, with a broad chest and gun-metal gray hair. He had thick black eyebrows and gleaming dark eyes. His skin was tanned. He held himself with the same impressive stillness she had noticed at the board meeting.

"I've heard a lot about you," he said to Francie. "Your report before the Board was excellent. We're looking forward to great things from you. Good luck with those computers of yours."

He was already turning his attention back to Gretchen, but in the brief instant that he held Francie's hand she felt an astonishing penetration in his look, as though his eyes were boring into her soul, asking a very blunt and powerful question to which she herself did not know the answer.

"Gretch," he said to his daughter, "how are you feeling? Party not tiring you too much, I hope?"

Gretchen's response to his inquiry was astonishing. She somehow managed to communicate her polite no without either looking at her father or speaking to him. She simply stared straight ahead, her features expressionless. This was an amazing performance which impressed Francie.

"Baby sleeping soundly?" Anton Magnus asked with a glance into the cradle.

Again Gretchen gave her strange, mute response, giving him the information he needed without acknowledging his existence. She kept her eyes fixed on a point somewhere beyond their little circle, out among the throng of guests circulating before her.

Anton Magnus turned to Francie. "My first grandchild. I can't stay away from her for long."

The tension between father and daughter could be cut with a knife. Gretchen had not once met her father's eyes, Francie noticed, or addressed a single word to him. There was something desperate and stubborn in her manner, a painful thing to behold.

Yet Anton Magnus's veneer of fatherly solicitude never faltered.

"I'd like to hold her for a moment, if I may," he said.

Gretchen turned pale as a ghost, but did not move as he stooped to pick up the slumbering baby, whose little hands clenched and unclenched as she was held against her grandfather's chest. The silence in the little group was deafening. Magnus cooed a few inaudible words to the infant, smiled, and put her back in her cradle. Then he turned to Jack.

"May I talk to you for a moment, son?" he asked.

A look passed between the father and son which was no less remarkable than that between Magnus and Gretchen, though far different. It was a look of serious entente from man to man, as though both were aware of some important state of affairs which joined them, whether they liked it or not. A look that was not without hostility, perhaps, but still a look of involvement, as of uneasy bedfellows embarked on a mission too important for them to indulge their dislike of each other.

Francie stored this impression away and spent a pleasant ten minutes talking to Gretchen, who relaxed palpably when her father had departed. The more Gretchen unwound, the more she showed herself to be a troubled but highly intelligent and warm young woman. She and Francie were well on the way to becoming friends when Jack returned.

"I've got some people I want you to meet," he said to Francie. "See you later, Gretch."

So that's the immortal Anton Magnus at home, Francie thought. She had now had two occasions to see Anton Magnus—the remote, silent man at the board meeting, coolly smoking his cigar as his nervous minions gathered around him, and now the gentle paterfamilias of whom his married daughter seemed inordinately frightened.

Francie could feel Gretchen watching them from behind, looking from Jack to herself with the same air of inquiry that was in so many other people's eyes tonight. Francie did not know how to feel about it. She was flattered to be the guest of so attractive and eligible a young man; but something about the Magnus household, added to her impressions of the corporation and the famous people here tonight, made her intensely ill at ease. She thought of her hometown in Pennsylvania, and briefly wished she were back on the old front porch with her father, where everything was so familiar, and the warmth of his love made her feel so easy and comfortable.

Jack led Francie smoothly upstairs and past a series of salons in which guests were chatting and drinking champagne.

"What do you think so far?" he asked.

"You have a lovely family," Francie said diplomatically.

"They're all terrified of the old man," Jack said with a shrug. "With Gretchen it's almost a parody. He picked out her husband, as you can imagine. That's what we're celebrating tonight: the fruit of his matchmaking. Poor Gretch hasn't seen Elliot Trowbridge since the day the baby was born. He's on the Riviera. He's a gambler. It's sad—Gretch is a nice girl at heart. She'll turn out like Mother, I'm afraid. Women are no match for a man like Dad."

"Well, I liked them, anyway," Francie said with a smile.

"The best is yet to come," he said. "Or the worst, depending on how you look at it."

He took her exploring through what seemed an endless maze of salons, drawing rooms, reading rooms, all of which were filled with handsomely dressed people amid equally handsome furnishings. He seemed to be looking for something. Along the way he regaled Francie with whispered stories about some of the famous guests present, and their relationships with the Magnuses over the years.

He touched her elbow when they entered a room in which a beautiful young woman with sleek blonde hair pulled back by a diamond clip was chatting, smoking a cigarette, with two or three young men captivated by her beauty and personality. She was holding a fluted champagne glass in her slender hand, but did not drink from it.

Francie almost smiled her admiration. Never before had she seen the very figure of the upper-class girl, who had all the advantages and all the graces.

Julie Magnus—for Francie recognized her from pictures she had seen in the press—was almost too lovely to be true. She was a small woman, delicate, with a perfect figure. She wore a Dior dress that showed off her tiny waist and slim arms. Her feet were bare, for she had kicked off her shoes. She had a porcelain complexion and limpid blue eyes. There was a languor about her, a stillness almost, as she made cool conversation with the three beaux who were in virtual silence, hypnotized by her.

It was like seeing a princess with her consorts. Julie was clearly accustomed to the utter command decreed by her beauty and her position in life, and she played the role without a false step. Just as Jack sometimes looked as though he had stepped off a wedding cake, Julie looked as though she had leapt gracefully from the cover of *Vogue* into this quiet drawing room.

But there was something else, hard to define. It was a sort of alarmed electricity in the air, as though the handsome young men in attendance upon Julie realized that under her tranquil surface lurked something dangerous. Their air was one of expectancy, even of awe.

Seeing Jack and his companion, Julie excused herself and came to meet them.

"Brother dear," she said. "Long time, no see." She patted Jack familiarly on his handsome cheek, a touch of irony in her manner. Then her intelligent eyes met Francie's, and she looked her over curiously.

"Julie, this is the girl I was telling you about," Jack said with a note of pride in his voice. "Francie Bollinger, my sister Juliet."

"Don't call me that," she chided him. And to Francie, "He likes to tease me with that ghastly name they picked out for me when I was too little to defend myself. Actually, I think the Magnuses suspected that I would grow up to marry a Montague and spoil their plans for me. Anyway, I'm delighted to meet you," she said, breaking into a friendly smile as she extended a hand. "My brother has told me of your achievements. To hear him talk, you're the greatest thing to hit the company in memory."

"Oh, I doubt that," Francie said, feeling the small hand in hers. "But it's nice to meet you. I've heard so much about you . . ."

Her voice trailed off, for a significant smile lit the other girl's pretty lips. Neither needed to say the obvious—that whatever Francie might have heard could only have been bad.

Juliet Baker Magnus, according to rumors which had gotten out of hand too long ago to be silenced now, was the quintessential wild young rich girl, only more so. She had been kicked out of as many finishing schools as her parents could send her to. She had been involved with as many unsavory boyfriends as she could get her hands on. She was currently between colleges, having been quietly asked to leave Smith after having an affair with a professor of French who could not resist her beautiful little body and sinister charms.

Since the age of nine or ten she had been involved in every type of mischief known to rich girls. She had been caught shoplifting. She had been arrested for public mischief. She had been disciplined for violent pranks at her schools, including the time she set fire to the headmistress's collection of wigs at Miss Compton's Academy for Girls.

As soon as she got her driver's license she began cracking up the Magnus family's cars, doing expensive damage to a collection of Bentleys, Rolls-Royces, Ferraris, and Mercedes too long to list. Once she had seriously injured a pedestrian when driving drunk. There had been a lawsuit against the family, but Anton Magnus's high-priced attorneys had managed to quietly settle and hush the whole matter up.

By the time Julie reached her teens, alcohol had become an integral part of her exploits. She appeared drunk in public, created disturbances which attracted the police, and then abused the officers verbally and even physically. It was rumored she had experimented with dangerous drugs, including cocaine and Benzedrine, which was so easily available by prescription to weight-conscious women, and was to be found in the medicine cabinet of everyone she knew.

Julie's misbehavior was relentless and almost calculated. She never made a serious effort to escape detection in her escapades. In fact, she was something of a genius at getting caught. Her more respectable, or at least punishment-conscious, friends at school had long since given up associating themselves with her pranks, for she was sure to get caught, and they with her. The result was that her companions became of a lower and lower stripe—troubled girls like herself, or girls too stupid to know better than to join her. Promiscuous, self-destructive girls, natural outlaws like herself.

Now that she was older she led a double life as far as the opposite sex was concerned. She often dated young men of the best families who could not resist the combination of her beauty and the exalted Magnus name, and was considered, despite her wildness, an excellent match for whoever had the courage to try to handle her. At the same time she surrounded herself with gigolos, society hangers-on, and the dregs of the upper crust as companions for her more unsavory adventures.

Her activities outside the staid Magnus mansion were almost too wayward for description in polite conversation. She was on a downward course, though she had no police yellow sheet despite her dozens of arrests, thanks to her father's influence with the New York City Police.

The only thing she had managed to elude was getting pregnant. Whether this was the result of birth control, a physical peculiarity, or dumb luck, no one knew.

With all these rumors at the back of her mind, Francie was amazed at the composure and politeness of the young girl before her. The most salient feature of Julie Magnus, outside her beauty, was her very obvious intelligence. Jack having excused himself to greet some guests, Julie took a brief stroll with Francie, leaving her three beaux in their thrall behind her, and asked Francie about her work.

To Francie's astonishment, Julie knew about the Moore School, and had more than a nodding acquaintance with computer science, having studied it at Smith with a young professor who thought computers were the wave of the future. More yet, she was very sympathetic. She had a way of listening seriously to whatever Francie said, and of responding with an understanding which showed that, however wrapped up she was in her own troubled life, she was truly listening to Francie, and truly cared.

When she asked Francie how she liked working at Magnus, Julie was sympathetic as Francie skirted the subject of the corporation's coldness of spirit and meanness toward women.

"You have courage," Julie said. "It's a jungle where the men have all the weapons. Use those brains of yours to see you through. The corporate animal is ambitious, and ruthless, but one thing he isn't is smart. That will work for you."

She pointed to the priceless paintings lining the hallway with its side tables and lowboys.

"You notice our portraits," she said with a wry smile. "They don't look much like us, do they? That's because they're all Wetherells. We can't show portraits of the Magnuses, because they're all dead peasants, buried who knows where. You see, we have everything that goes with breeding here, except the breeding itself. That's what my father would like the world to forget."

"One would never think that, to look at you," Francie said. "You're such—well, such distinguished-looking people."

At this an odd look came into Julie's eyes, flickered there for a second, and then disappeared.

"Well, we come from a long line of bandits and killers," she said. "Or at least that's the way I imagine us. There must have been something of the murderer in my father's veins to get us as far as he has."

Again something odd lurked in her ice-blue irises, like a cat's paw. It was a deep, abiding resentment of her family, her father, combined with a reluctant admiration. As though the very edifice she hated was so big, so daunting, that she could not help respecting its power.

"We're all proud of Gretchen for managing to conceive a child with that husband of hers," she concluded. "But Anton Magnus still doesn't have a male grandchild to carry on his name, does he? That little job is up to my handsome brother."

She asked Francie about her own life, and seemed surprisingly avid to learn more about it. Francie told the skeleton of the story about her mother's death, her father's quiet existence, her devotion to him, her years at the university—and she found Julie listening with a sort of silent passion.

"Well, it's not a very interesting life," Francie laughed, ill at ease with the other woman's inordinate interest.

"On the contrary," Julie said. "It's the most interesting kind of life—and the most unusual. A happy life. That's a rare thing, Francie—may I call you Francie?—rarer than you know."

"Of course, call me Francie."

"Perhaps we could have lunch some time . . . ," Julie began to say.

Francie was about to answer when she saw her companion's expression change, so abruptly that it completely erased what she had been saying. Julie looked alert, on the defensive, and somehow frightened. The friendly mood that had joined the two young women vanished.

Francie turned to follow the direction of her gaze. Behind her she saw Anton Magnus and Jack approaching. The father, a good six inches shorter than the son, had his hand on Jack's shoulder and was steering him toward the two girls. One could sense the power of Anton Magnus's presence as he held his son, though Jack, so tall, so athletic and proud, seemed to be allowing himself to be led merely from respect rather than from intimidation.

And as they came, Francie could see, washing like a brief wave over a sand drawing which it erodes to nothingness, Jack's resemblance to his father, barely visible but there nonetheless. In that instant the Magnus heredity joined the two men like a secret bond. Yet Jack seemed to erase the similarity through a trick of his bearing, as though it were a taint he wanted to banish from his flesh.

Jack was smiling at Francie. "What's this?" he asked. "They've left you all alone? I can't have that."

Surprised, Francie turned to speak to Julie.

But there was no one there. At the approach of her father, Julie Magnus had simply vanished.

The rest of the evening passed in a pleasant glow of champagne, distant music, and quiet conversation. Jack was such a perfect host that Francie felt truly at her ease. She began to feel closer to him, though their opportunities for private conversation were limited by the countless famous and important people he introduced her to.

The only sour note that occurred during the rest of the party came as a complete surprise to Francie.

She and Jack were moving through the upper hallway past a large drawing room when they sensed a disturbance going on inside. Jack touched Francie's arm to hold her back.

"Let me take care of this," he said. "Just wait for me."

He disappeared into the salon, where one could hear that shocked silence which always follows a scene. Francie stood in the hallway, wondering what could possibly be going on.

A moment later Jack appeared with his sister Julie in his arms. He carried her toward the staircase leading to the bedrooms. Two of the three young men Julie had been with earlier were watching in fascinated dismay as the third of their number accompanied Jack toward the staircase.

Francie watched in astonishment and chagrin. Julie had not passed out, but her body was entirely inert. She looked paralyzed. Yet one could somehow sense a will and an obscure intention behind her limp posture.

Francie met Julie's eyes as Jack carried her past. The pale irises were blank. There was not the slightest hint of recognition. Julie might have been looking at a total stranger. The transformation was amazing and uncanny. Jack held a virtual robot in his arms, a corpse.

"Is she ill?" Francie asked one of the two young men.

"No, just drunk," he said. "She might have added a pill or two to the recipe earlier in the evening. That doesn't help."

Francie was silent. It seemed only moments ago that she had been conversing with an alert and very charming Julie Magnus.

"Does this . . . happen often?" she asked the young man.

He shrugged. "Every time there's a party here," he said. "She goes under right on schedule, at approximately the stroke of midnight. Her parents have learned to get the more sensitive guests out of the way before the witching hour."

He noticed Francie's stricken look.

"Don't worry about it," he said. "She'll be fine in the morning, after a Bloody Mary and a few aspirin. This is Julie's way of having a good time."

Francie managed a smile. It occurred to her that the inert form of Julie Magnus was a deliberate embarrassment to her parents, who were even now entertaining guests only a room or two away. This thought was psychologically interesting, but the sight of Julie in her drugged stupor had shaken Francie. It was a glimpse of the willful disintegration of a lovely and talented girl. Francie would have trouble getting it out of her mind.

After a few minutes Jack returned.

"I apologize for my sister," he said. "Let's get ourselves a safe distance away from the scene of the crime."

He took her arm and steered her away from the still-crowded corridor where she had waited for him. He led her toward a quieter part of the house. She thought of asking him about Julie's sudden collapse, but he did not seem to want to talk about it.

"Here," he said. "Let me show you one of my secret places."

He took her through a complicated series of rooms, including a bedroom, a large storage closet, and a sort of attic. She followed obediently, awed by the house's seemingly endless recesses.

They came out on a tiny landing behind a round porthole window which overlooked the main ballroom. They could see all the guests circulating, with Anton Magnus now at the center, chatting amiably with a man who appeared to be an ambassador of some sort.

"Quite a sight, isn't it?" he asked. "Anton Magnus and his world." He shrugged. "Appearances can fool you. This is the biggest charade you'll ever see."

"You don't like your father very much, do you?" Francie asked quietly.

Suddenly he looked very serious, almost severe. He took both her hands.

"Take my advice, Francie. Don't ever get within striking distance of him. No one deals with my father without getting hurt. It's the law of the jungle. Always remember that."

The look on his face was strange, filled with something between hatred and grudging respect.

Then it softened as he turned to her.

"I'm afraid we disgust you," he said. "The decadent rich, and all that."

Francie shook her head in the shadows. "Unhappiness makes me unhappy," she said. "I don't like to think of you being where you don't want to be."

He looked down at the crowd. "It won't be for long, anyway," he murmured.

Suddenly his face lit up. "I've been thinking," he said. "When I leave, perhaps you could come with me. If I make it worth your while, I mean. I'm going to need all the brilliant people I can lay my hands on when the time comes. Perhaps I can lure you away."

Francie smiled. She could think of no response.

"You see, I don't want you to be unhappy, either," he said. "You don't belong in the same world with Anton Magnus."

She said nothing.

He looked down at the guests.

"When I was a boy," he said, "I was the first to find this place. Gretch never knew about it. I don't think my parents did. Nobody but the architect did, and perhaps some old Vanderbilt folks who were children once. I used to come up here and spy on the adults when they were having their parties. God, they looked like royalty to me then. The balls, the orchestras, the women's beautiful dresses, the music wafting up here all full of echoes. I thought their world was magic, in those days."

He looked thoughtful. The pain in his face was obvious. He turned to Francie.

"I wish you had been here then," he said. His words saddened her. All at once she realized how lonely a life a boy could have in this Magnus world.

He was looking deep into her eyes now.

"Wishing isn't much of a remedy, I guess," he said.

She touched his cheek in a reflexive gesture of sympathy.

She felt his hand on her shoulder, the fingers grazing her neck softly. A strange languor came over her, gentle and seductive. Then all at once, as though by a magnetism whose existence she had never suspected before, she was in his arms, pulled close to him, her lips opened to receive the deepest kiss she had ever felt in her life.

Her own arms found their way around his waist, and they came closer and closer together, his kiss filling her with waves of flame as the hardness of his body pressed more and more urgently against her. Spasms of weakness hurried up her legs and through the quick of her. In that instant she felt his protective manner turned to the essence of male need, and she had no defenses against him, for her body had been awaiting this moment since she first saw him in the doorway of his apartment, two weeks ago. She had been dreaming of his kiss in all her senses without her conscious mind ever realizing it.

She did not try to resist or pull away, even though forbidden rhythms of female wanting were making her stir against him. Her fingers had found their way to his hair and were buried delightedly in it as he held her closer.

She began to realize that her passion was more dangerous than she had suspected. She wanted to let him go, even to force him away. But her body had managed somehow to touch him in all the crucial places, thighs against thighs, breasts pressed to his chest, hips caressing him, speaking in their own language of the soft skin under the fabrics covering her, and of the warm waiting female essence deeper still.

Suddenly his hands were beneath her waist, pulling her to the center of him with a terrible hunger. The flame inside him leapt quickly under her skin, and all at once, like a spasm of primordial power, the moan of her ecstasy came from her lips, an irresistible song of delight, dying against his chest as her body trembled in his embrace. Shocked at herself, she held him close to keep him from seeing her face. Her halting breaths were the only sound between them.

At last he released her. She saw his face coalesce before her like a ghost in the darkness, visible now but no more easy to comprehend than it had been before that fatal and marvelous kiss.

He let her go, but kept his hands on her shoulders.

"I'm sorry," he said. "I shouldn't have done that. You barely know me."

"No—you have nothing to apologize for," she said. "I'm the one who should apologize. I'm—well, I'm an old-fashioned girl. Don't think I make a habit of throwing myself at men. It won't happen again."

She looked away, but he touched her chin to tip her head toward him. His smile was so understanding that she managed to return it. Her hand, with a shy will of its own, traveled from his shoulder to the nape of his neck, and caressed it familiarly. She straightened his tie.

"You have lipstick on your lips," she observed.

"Do I?" he asked, as though delighted by the information.

She took the handkerchief from his pocket and wiped his lips. Even this contact seemed distressingly intimate. Before she could fold the handkerchief and put it back in his pocket he grasped both her wrists, held her immobile, and kissed her again, more chastely this time, but no less seductively.

When it was over she looked into his eyes.

"We should be getting back," she said. "Your parents will wonder where we are."

He frowned. "I guess you're right."

"Am I a mess?" she asked. "Do I need to go to the powder room?"

"You don't need anything," he said. "You're perfect."

He looked at her. He seemed intrigued, curious. Yet something of his earlier expression of youthful sadness remained. He touched a finger to her cheek, and ran it through her hair, making her eyes close in pleasure. Then he released her.

She felt unsteady on her legs as they moved from the landing. She had seen more of the Magnus world than she had bargained for, and in the form of handsome Jack Magnus, it had already touched her where she had not intended to be touched.

As Jack saw her home she felt relieved to be leaving that world behind. But when he kissed her goodnight, she wondered whether she had left it behind at all. For it seemed to have taken up residence in a part of her too intimate, too vulnerable, to thrust it away again.

As she fell into a fitful sleep, the aroma and taste of Jack Magnus all over her, Francie felt that for the first time in her life she knew what it meant to live dangerously.

═══ 10 ═══

At two-thirty that morning Julie Magnus heard a quiet knock at her door.

She knew the party was over. She had heard the last of the guests leaving, for she had awakened about an hour after Jack deposited her on her bed. The champagne never stayed with her long. She seemed to get high as a kite, just long enough to cause some sort of trouble—and then the drunkenness disappeared, leaving her drained and headachy in her bed.

Tonight had been like all the other nights. When she awoke she took a few aspirin and put on her pajamas. Then she got into bed and waited for sleep, dazed but unable to drift off. She heard the house grow quieter around her as the servants cleaned up after the party. She thought of the people she had seen tonight, and the embarrassment she had caused, and she stared into space, not knowing what to think about anything, but waiting for the coy hand of slumber to come to her, which might take hours.

The soft knock at the door made her stiffen. She said nothing.

Slowly, hesitantly, the door opened. A figure entered the room and closed the door with a tiny click. She thought she heard the lock turn shut.

"Juliet . . ."

It was the same old voice, full of apology for disturbing her, full of timid reproach, concern for her welfare, and above all sadness at the pass things had come to.

She did not say a word.

Her father came forward and sat on the edge of the bed.

"Juliet," he said, "how are you feeling?"

She felt his fingers encircle her hand. She stiffened, but said nothing.

"Your brother made your apologies," he said. "I don't think anyone blames you."

She would not speak. Silence spread embarrassingly between them.

"You know," he said, "everyone likes you, Juliet. All our friends. You don't have to make a spectacle of yourself. Everyone respects you. You're a fine person. We all know that. If only you respected yourself more . . ."

She gazed at his silhouette in the darkness. She smelled the familiar aroma of brandy, expensive cologne, and fine cigars, which used to fascinate her when she was a little girl sitting on his knee as he read the newspaper.

"When you were a little girl," he said, apparently reading her thoughts, "we were so proud. I couldn't believe my eyes. Gretch was a big girl already, and Jack was in school. And here came this little packet of blond loveliness . . . Why, you were like a magic little fairy in our midst."

He fell silent. He did not let go of her hand. Her palm was sweaty, but his was dry, dry and calm as always. She listened to his speech in a sort of pained fascination. She had heard it many times before.

"Try to pull yourself together, Juliet," he said. "Try to be the girl you deserve to be. We don't hold past actions against you. The important thing is to put the past behind, and think of the future. You can do anything you want to do, be anything you want to be. Won't you think about that?"

He was too tactful to tell her she was ruining her life with the worthless, promiscuous young men she chose for companions. In fact, when she brought them home he was courtly and polite to them, concealing his distaste manfully. Anton Magnus was the soul of tact. And even when his daughter pushed him to the outer limits of his patience, he kept his calm.

"Your mother thinks you need a change of scenery," he said. "Why don't you go to Biarritz for a couple of weeks? Take longer if you like. Take a friend with you. I might be able to find time to bring Mother along on a weekend. We miss you when you're gone too long."

She stiffened at these words, but left her hand in his, watching it lie there, with eyes he could not see in the darkness.

"Well, I'll let you think about it," he said. "We want you to be happy, Juliet. Just remember that. You're our beautiful girl, and we want only the best for you."

He touched the covers at her neck, and pulled them back slowly. Her pajama top came into view, a blue glow in the shadows. It was an old-fashioned pair of pajamas, flannel, almost like those of a little girl.

"Say you'll try," he cajoled.

She said nothing.

He reached for the top button of the pajama top and undid it. Then, slowly, he loosened the other buttons. She watched in silence as her breasts were bared to him.

"Juliet," he said. "My lovely Juliet."

Her eyes were open wide, gazing emptily into the darkness. She did not move as he bent to kiss her nipple.

$$=== 11 ===$$

In the living room of the small rural house there were three people. The mother sat in an old straight-backed Amish chair, knitting. The daughter, a slim fourteen-year-old, lay on her stomach on the braided rug, chewing her pencil as she read her history book, her bare feet protruding from her jeans, her calves waving languidly in the air as she concentrated on the notes she was taking.

The father sat in his work clothes on the couch, ignoring the murmuring radio as he looked at his family. Neither the wife nor the daughter looked up to see the drained look in his gray eyes.

He was a big man, impressive in his height and bearing. From a distance people thought he was physically intimidating. But when they got close they immediately felt his dreamy introspection, and they knew that the last thing in the world Mac Bollinger could ever be to anyone else was an enemy.

In fact, around the county he had been thought of since his adolescence as a bit "touched," a man whose thoughts were not quite of this world. There was something odd, even eccentric, about his intimacy with objects, his feeling for wood, his poetic sense of structure. It was thanks to this quality that he solved carpentry and construction problems with ingenious inventions which made him a sought-after workman.

Mac was a sort of poet of wood and stone, a handyman of the spirit. And, like all poets, he was a dreamer. He was a bit peculiar in the way he got things done and in the time in which he did them. The county people understood and accepted this, and were rather protective of him because of it.

But it was not as a dreamer that Mac Bollinger looked at his little family today. It was as a man brought brutally face-to-face with a reality he could not bear to contemplate.

Helen glanced from her knitting to Francie, and back into her lap. Her eyes met

Mac's for a split second, and the tired irises seemed to smile. Then she resumed her work.

How innocent the moment appeared! Wife and daughter busy at their everyday work while the husband, returned from his day of carpentry and handywork, sat here in the home he had built with his own hands in the town of his birth. A domestic and peaceful scene.

Yet fate had changed everything. Helen was knitting that sweater in a size too large for Francie. The girl was still growing, and at the moment she had plenty of clothes. Helen was knitting this sweater for a larger Francie—a Francie she herself would not live to see.

For Helen would die soon. They all knew it. This would be her last summer with her husband and daughter. She was knitting this sweater as a frail link to the future she would not share, and as a wry protest against the illness consuming her.

That was typical of Helen. Though soft-spoken, she had a backbone of steel and a sharp, somewhat dark sense of humor about the cruel absurdities of the world. It was like her to sit here calmly creating a garment which would not be used until after her death.

The mother and daughter resembled each other in a curious way that was not physical. Helen's wispy brown hair and tawny eyes had not been passed down to Francie, who was a striking brunette with flashing green irises. Nor had Helen's oval face and somewhat sallow skin been transferred to her daughter, who took her features—if not her extraordinary beauty—from Mac's side of the family.

No, the resemblance was more subtle, almost spiritual. It was Helen's character that had left its imprint on Francie. Helen's quietly determined way of approaching the world, Helen's refusal to let the world get her down, were clearly qualities that Francie had inherited.

But where Helen's strength was alloyed with a brittle private edge, a veering into sadness, Francie's personality was all sunshine and smiles. And while Francie had inherited Mac's creativeness—everyone said her genius with numbers and equations smacked of Mac's own talent as an inventor of gadgets and a designer of useful modifications to homes and farms—she had escaped his tendency to lethargy. Mac was a dreamer who liked to sit back and watch the world go by. Francie built her own happiness from constant energetic activity. In this she was her mother's daughter—brisk, determined, indomitable.

Perhaps, Mac sometimes mused in his fatherly pride, Francie had got the best of both her parents, and been spared their weaknesses.

It was optimistic thoughts like this that kept Mac from despair when he looked at his wife and daughter nowadays. Helen was growing thinner all the time—the morning ritual of putting her on the scale had become a nightmare which nearly destroyed his courage to face the rest of the day—and weaker. Each week her eyes showed more pain, a pain she would not show in words, a pain that came more *from her grief at seeing her family slip away than from the physical agony she endured so courageously.*

It was only by fixing his mind's eye on Francie, and by assuring himself of her strength—a strength which increased as time and the struggle with impending grief tempered her—that Mac could watch Helen go, and feel that he himself could bear to survive her and finish bringing Francie up.

He looked at his daughter now. In her silence on the rug she seemed to sense his scrutiny. Her shapely limbs stirring, she looked up and smiled. With an effort he gave her the tiny wink which had always been the sign of his humor and good-fellowship toward her.

He admired her as much as he did Helen. But he could not help worrying for her. Despite her smiles and her energy, she was a vulnerable girl. Though a genius with numbers, she possessed no natural armor against the cruelty of others or the unfairness of the world. Her shy, solitary status in the socially competitive world of high school proved that.

Nor could her introspection, which bore the trace of Mac's dreamy inner world, protect her from the cunning of which willful men were capable. Indeed, her beauty might expose her to painful struggles which Mac could not even imagine.

He could not bear to think of Francie being hurt. And Francie had sensed this in him over the years, and developed an extra smile, a reassuring and almost maternal element in her personality, to calm his fears.

But now she was about to be hurt as she had never been hurt before. And Mac could do nothing to stop it, nothing to protect her. For his own world was to be brought crashing down about him when Helen left.

He looked from the dying mother to the growing daughter, who was still only the embryo of an adult woman. How would Francie fare after Helen was gone? What would become of her when the natural link from daughter to mother was severed by death? Would she hide her hurts and disappointments behind her bright smiles, as Helen had hidden them behind her own less sunny surface? Or would she retreat into the private domain of her intellect, as Mac had hidden in the shadowy world of his dreams?

Who could tell what would happen to her as she trod the perilous path of young adulthood? Mac could not know, could not predict. Could not protect.

On the other hand she was adaptable and courageous. Her natural stubbornness had armed her more than once to bounce back from pain and disappointment, and to face difficult challenges with a confidence that neither her father nor her mother had ever really felt.

She was born to be happy. And she seemed to know this, and to be prepared to fight off unhappiness with all the resources of her sharp mind and resilient personality. Perhaps in her inventiveness she would find her own solution to the fearful dilemma of living in the world.

Despite this hopeful thought Mac Bollinger's heart was heavy with foreboding. The only place on earth that had ever been his natural habitat—this home, and Helen's heart—was about to be taken from him. He wondered if he alone could be a family for Francie after Helen was gone. It was a challenge he had never expected to face.

He resolved to find a resource within himself to help Francie cope with the future. Just as the sweater Helen knitted now would be waiting for Francie when she grew big enough to wear it, so would the last and best of Mac's strength be waiting as a refuge for his daughter and a proof of his love.

Helen looked up from her knitting once more, and saw what was in her husband's face as he gazed at his daughter. She smiled. He met her eyes, and knew she understood. His worry eased for a precious instant as their love joined them to each other and to Francie. Then Helen's pain bore her away once more, and she went back to her knitting.

As for the girl reading on the floor between her parents, she had noticed nothing. Youth and hope sang their eternal song in her soft young body. And her father looked on, hope and despair fighting a prolonged battle in his heart as he watched her.

On January 12th Francie left for Europe.

An office had been set up for her in Paris, at the headquarters of Magnus-France, the largest Magnus subsidiary in Europe and itself a powerful conglomerate. From her command post in Paris she would personally supervise the work of setting up the main computers there and in Lausanne and London. It would be her responsibility to procure the computers, hire and train operators, and make the entire network functional before next fall's deadline.

As awesome as this responsibility was, Francie was anxious for it to begin. She wanted to get out of New York as quickly as possible.

Out of New York, and away from Jack Magnus.

The two weeks since Anton Magnus's party for Gretchen had passed as in a dream. Francie had worked long hours every day, dividing her time between preliminary correspondence with her European contacts, and trips to Armonk, New York, where she met with IBM executives to discuss the specifications of the three central computers that were to be installed in Europe within the next few months.

Francie's days were filled with a thousand details which saturated her mind, leaving no room in it for thoughts of anything but the enormous challenge facing her.

But her nights were a torment. Because each evening, as she lay in bed and felt the preoccupations of the day slip away from her, one by one, they were eclipsed by the image of Jack Magnus, hovering before her mind's eye and making slumber an impossibility.

She seemed to remember each word Jack had said at the party, every smile and gesture. She recalled his odd, bitter sincerity when he talked about his family, his almost paternal tenderness to Gretchen, though Gretchen was his older sister, and his solicitude toward Julie, who had come apart at the seams practically before Francie's eyes.

She could still see the elegant suit he had worn that night, his tanned face, the smiles he had used to introduce her to the various guests and to the members of his family, the quiet sidelong looks he had cast her throughout the evening. It all stood out in memory with an unnatural sharpness.

And all these images led inescapably to the sudden, unexpected moment of intimacy she had experienced in Jack's arms, high above the assembled guests at the party, hidden from sight in the tiny cubbyhole where he had played long ago as a mischievous young boy.

The memory of that kiss haunted Francie. She had never experienced anything like it before. As the glittering world of Anton Magnus spread itself out beneath the two of them like a nocturnal terrain viewed in the flash of a bolt of lightning, it had seemed as though all that power was coursing through Jack's hard limbs, through his knowing lips and tongue and fingers, directly to the quick of her, setting her on fire. She had felt she was losing herself, losing control, in a way that she had never dreamed possible.

Even now she could still taste him, feel the hardness of his flesh, and the male urgency of the hands pulling her closer, closer, as the song of her ecstasy moaned in her throat. The memory made her feel faint and woozy.

And there was no denying that her body had given him the paroxysm of its pleasure in no uncertain terms. She herself had been taken almost entirely by surprise, like a girl who discovers her womanhood before she is ready. And that womanhood had given itself to Jack before she could measure it and try to rein it in.

She looked back on her frightened, shamed words—"I'm an old-fashioned girl"—and cursed their callow innocence no less than her hot physical abandon in Jack's arms. What must he think of her now? Was he smiling over the memory of her unbridled sensuality and her candid allusion to her own virtue?

This thought filled Francie with chagrin. She was a proud young woman, and from the outset at Magnus had wanted to be her own person. Though grateful for the helping hand she had received from Jack with the Board, she desperately wanted to carry her own load, to be judged on the merits of what she could accomplish rather than to be sponsored by anyone else. She could not bear the thought that Jack might interpret her forwardness as a symbolic repayment of her debt to him, or as a girlish infatuation with his power.

After all, she told herself, what had happened was no more nor less than a kiss between adults. It had meant nothing. Less than nothing.

Francie thought of charming, diffident Belinda Devereaux, whom she had met and conversed with at the party. To all intents and purposes, Belinda was Jack's future wife. This alone proved that his life was his own, and that Francie had no part in it.

And if, as rumor had it, there was a conflict between Jack and his father over the idea of marriage to Belinda, this was none of Francie's affair. No more, for instance, than the other secret conflicts that seemed to lurk beneath the dignified surface of the Magnus family.

All this, she firmly told herself, was none of her business. Indeed, it only made it more compelling for her to attach no importance to what had happened with Jack, to put it behind her and get on with the difficult job at hand.

With these thoughts in mind Francie had avoided Jack for the past two weeks, communicating with him only by memo about her preparations for Europe. And, to her surprise, and to her involuntary disappointment, he kept the unspoken bargain, and did not get in touch with her.

Throughout her lonely evenings at home, Francie could not stop herself from watching the phone. And when it did not ring, she cursed its stubborn silence as well as her own childish waiting.

She longed to get on with her trip. Ironically, even the unknown continent of Europe would be a more solid ground now than Magnus Headquarters, where Jack was only a few floors or a phone call away, and where the clamor of her fantasies about him was a constant upset to her already tightly strung nerves.

So Francie made her hurried preparations to leave. But even as her better judgment urged her to get on that plane as fast as her legs could carry her, her woman's flesh longed for her to pick up the phone, hear Jack's voice, find a way to see him, to get him alone, seduce him somehow into the clutches of her wanting so that his own could come to join it . . .

There was not a minute to lose.

Francie took the ten-hour flight to Paris, her baggage weighted down with paperwork. She was far too pent-up to sleep on the plane, so she spent the whole trip studying her Dutch grammar book and poring over the subtleties of her master computer program.

By the time the plane landed in Paris, at six in the morning, Francie was exhausted, but too excited by the new challenge ahead of her and the glitter of Europe to feel fatigue.

She was waiting in the baggage claim area for her suitcases and the boxes containing her computer materials when an oddly familiar voice spoke to her in French.

"Mlle. Bollinger? Vous permettez . . ."

She turned to see a handsome Frenchman immaculately dressed in a business suit and overcoat, holding out a hand in greeting as he smiled at her.

"I— How did you recognize me?" she asked.

"My spies in New York alerted me that you were very beautiful," he said in English. "Allow me to introduce myself. Roland de Leaumes."

"I . . . oh! It's you," Francie said, smiling. She had been communicating with Roland de Leaumes by letter since Jack put her in touch with Magnus-France. He was a Vice-President of the French corporation, and he had been her most valuable contact in advance orientation to the new environment awaiting her.

Now she understood why his voice sounded familiar. She had heard it twice, on overseas telephone calls, when she phoned Magnus-France to confirm the details of her arrival.

In the flesh Roland de Leaumes was everything an American girl expects a romantic Frenchman to be. Tanned, elegant in his silk suit, youthful and athletic at forty-five, he had dark hair with a touch of gray at the temples, and dark eyes which had a sleepy sensuality as well as great warmth and intelligence. He spoke perfect English with only the subtlest trace of an accent, and treated Francie with a delicacy and aplomb born of generations of breeding.

Roland de Leaumes took Francie in a company Citroën to the attractive Left Bank apartment, in the Rue du Cherche-Midi, where she would live during her stay in Europe. The building was charming and very old, with a courtyard behind coach doors, a concierge's loge, and a small space of lawn in which a curious statue of a female sphinx sat crouched atop a stone base.

The apartment was on the top floor. The elevator was tiny, and Roland had to make two trips to get all of Francie's baggage upstairs. But the apartment itself was a wonder. A former artist's studio, it had windows twelve feet tall behind which Francie saw the Paris rooftops, with their little chimneys, and a couple of blocks away, the twin cupolas of the Saint-Sulpice church. It was a delightful view, and seemed to capture something of the essence of Paris.

When all Francie's bags were safely deposited in the living room Roland de Leaumes prepared to take his leave.

"I am so glad you have arrived safely," he said.

"You were kind to pick me up," Francie said. "I didn't mean to get you up so early in the morning."

"It was a pleasure," he said. "Now perhaps you will wish to get some rest. I could call you later in the day?"

Francie shook her head. "I'd like to get to work right away," she said. "I'm not tired at all."

"Are you quite sure?" he asked. "The time difference on international flights can be very exhausting."

"I'm sure," Francie insisted.

"Very well, then," he replied. "I will invite my colleagues to meet you for lunch today. Say, one o'clock? I'll pick you up here myself."

"That sounds wonderful."

Francie spent the next three hours going over the materials she had brought with her and wondering how to put her best foot forward with the French executives. She took a shower, brushed her hair carefully, and put on the conservative skirt and blouse she had picked out three weeks ago for this occasion.

Roland picked her up punctually at one.

"Do not be alarmed if some of my colleagues have trouble warming up to you at first," he warned her as they approached the restaurant where the lunch was to take place. "You must remember that our country is still recovering from a lot of things, and we are not yet as intrepid as you Americans in developing new business methods." He smiled as he opened the car door for Francie. "In any case, you will quickly charm them out of their misgivings," he concluded.

This was not as easily accomplished as he had suggested, Francie soon realized when she sat down to lunch with eight very wary Frenchmen whose polite greetings betrayed more than a hint of suspicion at her intrusion into their world.

"Mademoiselle," they greeted her, one after the other, rising to shake her hand but not smiling.

"Très content . . ."

"Enchanté . . ."

Then, without further ado, the ordeal began.

To her surprise Francie found herself faced with objections to her computer plan even more strenuous than those expressed by the Board back home in New York. To make matters worse, these questions were being put to her in fast, idiomatic French by foreigners who seemed bent on testing her mettle.

"*Si Mademoiselle avait bien voulu se renseigner sur les besoins de l'Europe . . .*" said one of the executives in a condescending tone.

"*Il faudrait quand même considérer les convenances . . .*" said another.

"*L'ordinateur est une machine infernale, entièrement inouïe dans le commerce,*" insisted a third, blowing smoke from his Gitane as he frowned at Francie.

Clearly the Magnus-France executives were wary of the new computer plan to be imposed on them by the feared parent corporation, and even more suspicious of the young and inexperienced girl who had been given charge of so enormous a responsibility.

Francie struggled to meet their objections with calmly reasoned reassurances about her system, the new convenience it would offer them, and the minimal changes it would entail in their work routine. She realized that tact was of the essence in her comportment toward them, so she tried to be as friendly and cooperative as possible.

She discovered to her dismay that her fluent French did not include some of the technical expressions required for an understandable description of computer technology. More than once, in the course of her explanations, she found herself at a loss for words. The fatigue of her overnight flight seemed to drag her physically downward as she struggled to find responses in the unfamiliar language. The heavy smoke from the French cigarettes hurt her eyes, and the close atmosphere of the restaurant began to take on a hazy unreality.

Luckily for Francie, Roland de Leaumes came to her aid. He possessed all the basic vocabulary concerning what the French called *les ordinateurs*, and rescued her not only with needed technical terms but with explanations of his own which were designed to reassure and calm his excitable colleagues.

By the meeting's end a sort of stalemate had been reached. Francie had managed to impress the French executives with her expertise and friendliness, but they were obviously adopting a wait-and-see attitude, loath to believe in computerization until she could prove its practical effectiveness.

At last they took their leave with handshakes all around. Francie was complimented eight times over on her perfect French, a fact which surprised her, since she had felt as though her mouth was full of marbles all afternoon. She smiled her thanks and promised to meet with them all again soon.

"Thank you for stepping in when I needed you," she told Roland on the way back to her apartment. "It was stupid of me not to have mastered my own technical jargon in French."

"On the contrary," he said, smiling. "Your French is magnificent. And your few problems with the technical words only added to your charm. Believe me, my colleagues now understand how serious you are. You did wonderfully. But now I think you must rest." His handsome face betrayed a hint of concern for her exhausted condition.

"I'll see you tomorrow at the office," Francie smiled as he dropped her off at her door in the Rue du Cherche-Midi.

"I will look forward to it," he said, making sure the concierge had let her in through the coach doors before waving goodbye and driving off in the silent Citroën that had brought them.

Francie went upstairs and sat down on her bed. Her blood was tingling from the afternoon's exertions. Despite her fatigue it still seemed impossible to sleep.

She stood looking out her window at the rooftops. In the waning sunlight of late afternoon the Left Bank looked gloriously foreign and inviting. On an impulse she decided she did not need to rest, but would go out exploring. According to her guidebook she was only a few blocks' walk from the Boulevard Saint Germain and the Latin Quarter. She would finish out the afternoon with a relaxed stroll, go to bed later after a light dinner, and sleep through until tomorrow.

She took off the business suit she had worn to lunch and put on slacks and a sweater. She got out her large purse, put her camera in it, and prepared to go out.

Then the strange languor she had felt during lunch came back, a bit stronger now, dragging at all her senses and making it hard for her to decide to leave the room. She lay down on her bed for a moment to rest before going out.

She closed her eyes, feeling the warm air of the room caressing her cheeks. For an instant she saw her private genie, the face of Jack Magnus, floating before her mind's eye. But it seemed far away, and less daunting now that she had put an ocean between herself and Jack.

Nevertheless his lips came closer, his arms were around her, and the pungent male aroma that had set her on fire the night of the party was back in her senses, and the hard feel of his embrace all over her body . . .

With the prohibited image penetrating every corner of her dreams, Francie fell into a heavy, exhausted sleep.

When she awoke it was after midnight. The streets outside were silent and empty. The neighborhood was asleep around her.

For a long moment Francie lay as though drugged, powerless to move. She realized that her dreams had all been of Jack, and that three thousand miles of distance were not sufficient to banish him from her thoughts.

At last she sat up and tried to get her bearings. She still felt cottony and a bit dizzy, but wide awake now and unable to sleep. Her body's inner clock was still a long way from adjusting itself to Paris time.

So she went to work. She took out some of her paperwork and set about putting it in order. She began drafting a memo in French to send to her colleagues tomorrow. She thought over the challenge of assembling a new team to work with her.

She worked all night, trying unsuccessfully to catnap as she realized that the new day would surely bring more fatigue with it.

At eight o'clock sharp she was at Magnus-France's headquarters on the Boulevard du Montparnasse, getting things in order in her new office.

Her secretary, an attractive young Frenchwoman named Antoinette, greeted her warmly and showed her around the building.

"Will there be anything else?" she asked as Francie prepared to get down to work.

"One thing, yes, Antoinette," Francie said. "I'd like you to go over to the Sorbonne and get me French translations of the following articles on computer science." She handed the girl a long list which she had written down overnight. "You'll find that most, if not all, are readily available in the technical publications. I've also listed some periodicals in Dutch, Spanish, German, Italian, and Portuguese. Try to find me translations in those languages as well. Take all the time you need. I won't need you back here until mid-afternoon."

"*Oui, mademoiselle,*" said the astonished girl.

Francie smiled as she sat down at her desk.

So much for computer jargon in foreign languages, she thought.

After that first crazy afternoon in Paris Francie never really regained her sleep patterns of old. Her inner timetable was permanently upset by the newness of Europe and by the pressure of the work she took on herself.

But, a soldier in her essence, Francie used this dislocation to her own advantage. She worked during the late hours when the Europeans were asleep. She accomplished mountains of work when no one else was up and around. She slept when fatigue overtook her, and spent her odd hours working.

In no time she had set up an efficiently working computer coordination office at the Paris headquarters. It was here that the first IBM 650 was set up, with Francie personally supervising the installers and the operators who had been eagerly awaiting the machine.

Then she set off for Lausanne and London to set up the two additional mainframes, and made lengthy visits to Rome, Madrid, Lisbon, and The Hague to meet the heads of the other Magnus subsidiaries and to brief them on her system while selling them on its advantages.

During her long absences from Paris Roland de Leaumes oversaw the running of the office on her behalf. She quickly realized that he was a lifesaver for her. Though he had his own high executive responsibilities within Magnus-France, he was the most conversant of the French with computer technology, so he made time to meet with her people and see that her orders were carried out efficiently when she was away.

Francie found herself telephoning him nearly every day to report her progress and to hear his reports on the situation in Paris. Before long she realized that she looked forward to the gentle, euphonious sound of his deep voice for moral support as well as for hard facts. He had almost by instinct become her confidant and protector.

"*Tenez bon*," he would joke with her when she told him about a problem she had encountered with one or another of the European groups. "What is it you Americans say? *Keep a stiff upper lip*. Don't worry, you'll win them over in no time."

Francie needed all the encouragement she could get. As she had feared, it was not easy to make the Europeans understand that computerizing the communications between their companies would make life easier instead of more difficult for them. Most of the executives looked upon computers as futuristic electronic brains filled with sinister and unreliable circuitry.

The same executives were not without mistrust for Magnus Industries, their far-off parent company, and they quickly transferred this emotion to the brilliant, efficient young woman who explained her innovation to them in their own language. More than once Francie got the impression that they considered her too young, too pretty, and too foreign to be taken seriously.

But far worse than their suspicion of her, which seemed to dissipate with increasing familiarity, was their more rigid mistrust of each other.

In Rome, where she was taken on a gala tour of the Vatican, the Coliseum, and the Galleria Nazionale d'Arte Antica, she was told over a festive dinner at Andrea how impossible the Spaniards were.

In Spain, where she was shown the priceless Velázquez collection in the Prado, the fabulous Escorial, and the ancient town of Aranjuez on the Castilian Plain, she was told that the English were barbarians who knew nothing about modern business.

In London, where she spent three glorious days exploring the elegant Mayfair district, the British Museum, and the gardens in Regent's Park, she was told by polite British employees of Magnus Britain, Ltd., how hopeless it was to be forced to have business dealings with the French (with whom, except for the past few decades, the English had been at war more or less constantly for the past six hundred years).

And back home in Paris she was shown the Latin Quarter, the broad leafy *allées* of the Bois de Boulogne, the charming Ile de la Cité and Ile St. Louis, and the picturesque heights of Montmartre, while learning from her colleagues how impossible it was for them to deal with the Italians, who controlled three huge Magnus mining firms and were an uncivilized band of crooks and brigands.

By the end of her first whirlwind tour of the European subsidiaries Francie realized just how bad were the divisions between the Europeans. Though geographically located more or less as close to each other as American states back home, they were worlds apart in attitude, and looked upon each other with a wariness based on centuries of conflict.

Yet the very depth of this mistrust confirmed Francie in her belief that the computer network she had devised for Europe was a crucial innovation, capable of revolutionizing the way the Magnus subsidiaries did business with each other, and increasing profits and productivity for them all.

Even the most skeptical of the Europeans to whom she explained her plan had to admit that the computers she would use cared nothing for their currency problems, their difference in language—computer language being a thing unto itself, understood by all programmers—and least of all their differences in temperament and culture.

Gradually, through patience and tact, Francie won more and more converts to her cause. No doubt her fluency in the European languages helped in this, as did the fact that her explanations came from a pair of sensual lips beneath limpid green eyes full of a femininity as daunting as was Francie's great intellect.

The only chink in the smooth-running mechanism of her new life came from a direction she had not anticipated.

The Europeans, to a man, knew Jack Magnus and held him in high regard. It was only thanks to Jack's expertise, indefatigable energy, and diplomacy that the feuding Europeans had been able to function as well as they had over the past five years. More yet, it was only because they knew Francie was here under Jack's imprimatur that they were willing to listen to her at all.

As a result, Jack's name was always on the lips of the people Francie worked with. They covered him with praise, asked her for news of him, and asked when he would be coming to Europe next.

The thought of seeing Jack again filled Francie with mixed feelings. Part of her was not at all afraid of having him come to Europe to see her new system when it was in place. She welcomed his judgmental eye, and the challenge of creating something that would please and impress him.

But her very eagerness had a double edge. It betrayed her desire to see him again, to be close to him, and perhaps to find herself in a situation in which his desire for her could overwhelm his natural restraint as it had the night of his father's party for Gretchen.

Her own longings infuriated Francie. Not a day went by without her body reminding her a dozen times that its secret places were hungering for him more treacherously than ever. Her nights were haunted by his image and the memory of his embrace.

She wondered what he thought about when news of her doings reached him back in New York. Did he recall their kiss? Did the memory make him smile, or perhaps stir an instant's need in his own senses?

Francie fought to banish these ideas from her mind. She told herself that she was an independent individual, self-determining, and that no man could reduce her to a bundle of hapless fantasies with a single kiss.

Nevertheless, she knew that someday Jack would come to Europe to see the results of her work. And that imaginary day lingered before her mind's eye like a sunlit dream of excitement and guilty pleasure.

Forcing the alarming image from her consciousness with a spasm of resolve, Francie threw herself into her work, harder than ever.

12

New York, January 13, 1956

Juliet Baker Magnus, dressed in a strapless sheath by Chanel which was just simple enough to pass for an ordinary dress in the eyes of the uninitiated, though immediately recognizable as a priceless original by those in the know, entered a lounge on Third Avenue which bore the unusual name of *Ophelia's.*

Julie was alone, and unencumbered for the evening. She had spent the afternoon alone in her room, reading a copy of *A Farewell to Arms*, and enjoying the silence of the house. Her mother was too afraid to approach her, for if she got too close Julie might recreate the scene she had played last week, a bitter quarrel in which Julie used barracks language and broke a Wedgwood vase, and after which Julie had disappeared from the house and not been seen for two whole days and nights.

Father was at work, of course. Julie had pondered the notion of going over to Gretchen's to see the baby, but had decided against it. She was never comfortable with Gretchen, at the best of times. And the baby, so small and defenseless, made her nervous.

So she had pored over the Hemingway in the silence of her room, alternately smiling at the writer's self-conscious mannerisms, and frowning in concentration when she saw the serious kernel of what he was trying to write about. She had smoked cigarette after cigarette, sipped at a cold cup of tea, and opened her window to let the smoke out, noticing the passersby on Park Avenue.

At four she had closed the book and begun to pace the room nervously. She had had all the distraction she could take. The tension building up inside her all afternoon was at the breaking point. She must move, must do something.

She put on a brilliant act of fatigue and relative good humor through dinner. Mother and Father barely noticed her, making small talk with each other about Gretchen and the family. Julie had caught one sidelong look from her father, who was only half-listening to his wife's complaints about some of her relatives on the Wetherell side.

When dinner was over Julie had gone to her room, put on this dress, chosen earrings, necklace, and bracelet at random, and gone out the side entrance without so much as a goodnight to anyone. She had walked to the corner of 65th Street, hailed a cab, and told the driver to take her downtown. She had him drive her around until they reached this rather seedy section of Third Avenue, and then stopped at a popular-looking lounge.

Now she sat at the bar, drinking a dry martini and watching the patrons in the mirror above the bar.

Julie was playing a game she had invented only recently. She studied the patrons, trying to determine from the mirror image of their demeanor, and from the snatches of their conversation, which one would have the courage to approach her first. She had deliberately selected clothes which would put ordinary men ill at ease. She had arranged herself as bait, bait for not just anyone but for a man with a streak of bravado or of desperation which would embolden him to come to her.

Only someone a little special, or a little crazy, would detach himself from that crowd and meet her halfway. So Julie sat gazing coolly in the mirror, waiting for her Prince Charming to emerge from the shadows.

She saw him coming from a dozen feet away. He had surprised her by emerging from a corner she could not see in the mirror. But she knew from his pace and the look in his eye that he was her man.

"Buy you a drink?" he said in a confident, deep voice with a Brooklyn accent, a mellifluous voice in which something dangerous stirred.

She turned to look at him. He was young, and very handsome. A man in his twenties, with carefully styled hair a bit on the long side. He wore a shirt open at the neck with a sport jacket thrown over his shoulder. He had a deep chest, and strong arms. She suspected he worked out with weights.

A chain bracelet was about his wrist. She thought she saw a tattoo on his forearm. His eyes were very dark, smoldering. There was a glow of arrogance in them. He had long, beautiful lashes, so long that they added something mysteriously childlike to his tanned face, though this only served to accentuate his somewhat excessive masculinity.

Intrigued by the pantherlike readiness of him, Julie met his eyes.

"I already have a drink," she said.

A smile curled his sensual lips. The black eyes were appraising her now. He crossed his arms over his chest. She could see how tight his slacks were. The outline of his manhood was obvious; it was clear he liked to advertise it.

"A walk, then," he said, not at all put off by her answer.

"Where would we go?" she asked, raising an eyebrow as her eyes slid over him.

"Your place. My place." He smiled. "Doesn't matter."

"You have a pretty high opinion of yourself, don't you?" Julie asked, sipping at her martini.

"I believe in giving credit where credit is due," he said.

Clearly he was a match for her in repartee. He was intelligent behind his crude exterior. The look in his eyes left no doubt of that.

Intelligent, but uneducated. Smooth, sexy, but not refined.

He had not made an error of grammar yet. She could see already that he prided himself on his elegance of manner. Though his costume was designed to show himself off to women a dozen classes below her own, and though it betrayed the limitations of his horizons and his ambition, it revealed a magnificent male body and an ego to match its charms.

"What makes you think I'm looking for company?" she asked.

"Oh, a little bird told me that," he said.

She thought for a moment. Then she turned and looked into his eyes. "You trust your instincts, don't you?" she asked.

"Don't you?" he retorted ambiguously.

"Marcel Proust once wrote," she said, "that life is a perpetual mistake."

He laughed. Then he leaned close to her ear and spoke in a conspiratorial voice.

"Is he here?" he asked, winking.

The literary reference had not fazed him a bit. Instead, it seemed to have amused him.

Despite herself Julie smiled. He watched her lips curl, admiring her pretty face and expensive scent.

"Anyway," he said, "you're not a mistake. You came to the right place."

She could see the hair on his chest beneath the open collar of his shirt, and smell his fragrance, which was pungent, but clean and attractive. She could almost feel the force coiled in his hard body. She wondered if the goods matched the window dressing.

She decided to find out.

"My place is out," she said.

He laughed. "It always is, honey," he said. "But don't you worry about that. The world is full of homey little places."

He helped her off the stool. His grip was firm, masculine. Being touched by him on the elbow was somehow more intimate than being taken to bed by most of the young men she had known in her life.

She paused as they approached the door.

"I don't know your name," she said.

"Johnny." He held out a hand. "Johnny Marrante. At your service." Again he seemed to mock her with his assurance. Oh, he was a smart one, all right.

"What's yours?" he asked, still holding her hand.

She hesitated.

He smiled. "Never mind, babe," he said. "Don't tire yourself out making up names for my sake. You've got more important business tonight."

"Call me Julie," she said, a trifle ashamed of her own timidity.

"That's a nice name," he said with a smile, as though he did not believe her. "Well, come on, Cinderella." He opened the door for her. "We've only got two hours until the coach turns into a pumpkin."

Somehow that word, *pumpkin*, on his lips, told her the last thing she needed to know. He was going to be good. Very good.

* * *

He did not disappoint her.

He took her to his apartment, a short ride away from the lounge, in his own car. The place was gaudily decorated, with paintings of nudes on the walls and an aura to the furnishings that suggested he was a serious lady-killer. There was a living room, a small kitchen, and a large bedroom with a king-sized bed.

She did not see much of the living room, for he turned off the lights almost as soon as he had closed the door. He curled an arm around her, just below the breasts, and held her with her hips against his sex, nuzzling softly at the back of her neck.

What a strange embrace that was, Julie thought. He was behind her, the powerful forearm immobilizing her as he kissed the soft skin beneath her cheek. Now his free hand came to slide over her hip, and she smelled the sweet tang of the bourbon and tobacco on his breath. The hand traveled smoothly, with a sort of delicate triumph, over the small rounded hip, and the hard male sex rested against the soft line between her buttocks, not pushing, not grinding, but simply resting there to tell her of its presence and its purpose.

Despite herself her eyes closed, a sigh escaped her lips, and she felt a yielding in her senses which was already far deeper than anything she had intended to feel tonight.

He knew he had got under her skin already, and he began to enjoy his advantage. He walked her to the bedroom, his hand on her shoulder, and carefully took off her clothes, folding her dress almost daintily over a chair, then touching contentedly at her undergarments as they came off.

Before she knew it she was naked, again with her back to him, her eyes unseeing as she gazed out the window to the dark street. She felt his hands slip down her arms, over her fingers, down her thighs, and back up to her waist, measuring the smallness of her—for at five feet two and a hundred and five pounds Julie was a very tiny girl, with a porcelain delicacy about her.

Then she heard a zipper, and a rustle of clothes, and her breath came short as she realized he was stripping himself too.

She turned to see their naked bodies in the mirror. He stood behind her. She could see the proud man's sex standing erect between his legs. It was very large. Something about the tense expectancy of the organ looked obscenely melodramatic. Yet it was all the more sexy for this impression.

The warm hands came to rest on her shoulders, softly massaging her. And this time his lips touched her earlobe at the same instant that the tip of his sex grazed her loins.

"Come on, Cinderella," came his whisper in her ear. "Time for the ball."

For the first time in years Julie Magnus was surprised by a man. Johnny was an expert seducer. Unlike the clumsy, drunken young society boys who had fumbled for her in the back seats of cars, unlike the sleazy gigolos she had surrounded herself with to embarrass her family, Johnny was an artist of the highest order at bringing a woman to orgasm.

He was thorough in his caresses, firm and masculine. His hunger for every part of her was insatiable. But he was slow and smooth in exploring her, making sure that he was owning her in each forbidden place, making sure she accepted him there and even clamored for him, before giving her her pleasure and taking his own.

Every inch of him was so hard, so smooth, that before long she could not distinguish any part of him, or indeed his entire being, from the huge male member between his legs. For he was entirely given over to this slow, exciting probing into each corner of her flesh. He accepted her little sighs and moans with a strange familiarity, as though he had known her inside and out all her life.

He spread her legs and penetrated her carefully, tight and triumphant, feeling her thighs curl delightedly around his waist as he stroked her deeper and deeper. She began to shudder almost immediately, for he seemed to find the hot center of her orgasm almost before she knew it was coming.

And each movement, even the most tiny, was in its own way a ravishment, perhaps a defilement—for he knew how high a society she came from, he knew she was slumming with him, and he intended to teach her a lesson.

He did not ask her to touch him, never once guided her hand or her lips to him. He was the master, she the slave, and she was all given over to her yielding and her moaned little entreaties for more, more, more.

How long it went on that way she did not know, for she was lost in the pleasure he was giving her. But her excitement rose and rose, fueling itself from each orgasm, until, when she felt him push deep into her for the final thrusts, still slow, still atrociously knowing, she was beside herself.

"Oh, God," she moaned, her pelvis trembling madly against him, her hands grasping his hips to pull him deeper inside her. "Oh, God . . ."

"Easy, baby," he murmured, smiling down upon her as he ground smoothly into her. "Easy, honey." And those words, so full of mocking pity and intimate knowledge, sent the final shock through her, so hot that she cried out her ecstasy as her hands fluttered against his flesh.

"Oh," she murmured against his chest, her breaths still coming short, long after it was over. "Oh . . ."

"What is it?" he asked.

"I've never felt so . . ." She searched for a delicate word, and could not find one. "So completely fucked."

"That's what I'm here for, babe," he murmured against her brow.

"You're good," she sighed. "Very good."

"Like I say," he reverted to his ironic crudeness of speech, "I believe in giving credit where credit is due."

She purred, and reached between his legs to take him in her hand.

Suddenly, for the first time in her memory, she herself felt inadequate.

"Was I . . . ?" she asked.

He laughed to hear her diffidence. Now he knew he had her where he wanted her, for he had worked his way through all her pride to the trembling maiden at the core of her, and she was all aglow with the newfound innocence that his flesh had given her.

"You're a sweet little thing," he said. "You just needed to be laid by a real man, that's all."

As these words sank in he smiled and kissed her cheek. "Take it easy, Cinderella," he said. "Just leave me your glass slipper, and I'll be back for more."

"I hope so," she said with the candor of a virgin.

She had never felt this way before. She recalled his handsome face in the mirror at the bar as he approached her. She had expected someone a bit more bold than the others, perhaps a bit more crazy.

But she had got much more than she bargained for.

Like Cinderella, she was far from her familiar world now, in a place where intoxicating new pleasures awaited her, as well as, perhaps, dangers she could not foresee.

But the danger of Johnny Marrante was precisely what made him so sexy.

=== 13 ===

Paris, July 15, 1956

The great day was here at last.

The main computers in Paris, Lausanne, and London were ready and staffed by operators personally chosen by Francie. These operators had spent the last two weeks priming the computers and pumping in information from every corner of the European subsidiaries, each of which now possessed a small office dedicated especially to the reporting of data by teletype to the computer bases.

It was now time to "turn the system on," and see if it worked.

Francie was with Roland de Leaumes and a dozen or so observers in the computer center in Paris. She knew that similar onlookers were present at the other two main locations, eager to find out what was to happen. Top Magnus executives throughout Europe were watching skeptically, as were their competitors, to see if the eccentric new idea of large-scale computerization could possibly succeed.

Francie was smiling, but her heart was in her mouth. She was acutely aware that this entire operation had been conceived and designed by herself. The buck stopped with her. If the system did not operate efficiently, there was no one to blame but herself, for she was the author of the master program that must make it work.

She was also aware that New York was awaiting today's result. Word had filtered through the Magnus grapevine that the Board was watching with particular interest, and not only because the vote that had granted Francie her mission had been a close and hotly contested one. The success or failure of the system would reflect importantly on Jack as its sponsor, far more importantly than on the mere fate of Francie Bollinger.

And there was something more vast to consider. If Francie's system really operated as intended, it would have an enormous impact on the whole concept of business communications. It could trigger a revolution in business worldwide, and the financial and practical consequences would be incalculable.

So today was a watershed.

Francie stood beside Roland de Leaumes in the computer center. There were teletype lines open to London and Lausanne. When Francie gave the word, all three computers would begin running the program, and the chief operator here in Paris would ask the computer its first question. The question had already been decided on. It would be a simple one, in computer language, asking for a comparison of the inventory for two Magnus divisions, one in Italy and the other in Portugal. The answer should take no more than two seconds to appear on the printout.

Francie looked at Roland, who smiled supportively. He was his familiar self this morning, calm and balanced. His handsome dark eyes shone with confidence in her. She was glad he was here to help her through this crucial moment. In recent months she had become a regular visitor at his lovely house in Passy, and made friends with his wife and daughters. The Leaumes family was the closest thing Francie had to a family of her own in Paris, and Roland her best friend. She needed him now more than ever.

"London is ready and waiting," said a secretary with a phone at her ear, smiling to Francie.

"Lausanne is ready also," said a second secretary.

"All right, then," Francie smiled, crossing her fingers. "Let's go."

As she watched, the secretaries spoke into their phones. The chief operator at the mainframe threw a sequence of switches and gave instructions to the computer through a keyboard.

There was a silence. The lights on the various power displays blinked briefly. The magnetic tape inputs moved as the typewritten query was translated into machine language. After a few seconds the printout chattered briefly, and was silent.

The operator got up from his seat to look at it, and then turned to Francie. She hurried to his side and looked at the sheet, with its computer symbols and rudimentary snatches of ordinary language.

There was only one sentence.

DATA UNAVAILABLE, said the printout. CHECK COMMAND.

Francie frowned in perplexity. "What does London say?" she asked the secretary.

The secretary spoke into the phone, and then looked up at Francie.

"There is no function," she said.

Francie looked at the other secretary. The look on her face made it plain that the answer from Lausanne was the same.

"Let's run the command again," Francie said. "I'll do it myself."

She sat down at the keyboard and very carefully instructed the computer to perform the simple task which was to be its first accomplishment.

The result was the same.

DATA UNAVAILABLE, replied the machine without hesitation. CHECK COMMAND.

Again the secretaries spoke to London and Lausanne, and shook their heads to indicate that the computers had not functioned.

For the third time Francie ran the instruction through the machine. It was an absurdly simple command, so basic that it was unthinkable the computer would not respond instantly.

Again the answer was the same. DATA UNAVAILABLE. CHECK COMMAND.

Francie flushed. She glanced at the onlookers in the room. Most of them seemed perplexed. But there was also ill-concealed triumph in more than a few of the faces of those present. They were secretly delighted that the grandiose scheme on which so much time and money had been spent was crumbling before their eyes—and that its ambitious, confident mistress was suffering a humiliation richly deserved by her inexperience and the arrogance of her project.

She had wanted to revolutionize business for forty companies in foreign countries she had never even visited until a few months ago! She was going to tell everyone how to run his business! She was going to change the world . . .

Well, so much for the computer revolution.

Francie could feel this snide and complacent thought all around her.

Fighting back the tremors in her nerves, she turned to those around her. She opened her mouth to speak, but no words came out. The entire French language seemed to have abandoned her as surely as the computer on which she had placed all her hopes.

It was Roland de Leaumes who stepped in to rescue her.

"*Allez, les enfants,*" he said authoritatively to the others. "*Au boulot.* Get back to your work. You've seen accidents happen before. This is nothing to gape at. We'll let you know when we get the system running properly."

With sidelong smiles and a few ironic murmurs, the observers left the computer center.

Roland was looking at Francie. Concern was visible in his dark eyes.

"Can I help?" he asked.

"No, thanks," Francie said, mustering as much calm as she could. "Just let me work on it for the rest of the afternoon. I'll see if I can find out what's the matter."

"You're sure?" he asked, touching her elbow gently. "Perhaps I could offer some moral support?"

She shook her head. "It would only bore you," she said.

"You mean I'd be in the way." He laughed. "But you're too nice to say it. All right, I can take a hint. But don't overdo it. Promise?"

"I promise," she said. "I'll quit before seven."

"Good," Roland smiled. "And don't worry. You'll find the trouble soon enough."

A moment later he was gone with everyone else. Francie dismissed the two operators and went to work on the computer herself. She was glad no one was there to see her hands shake as she approached the machine.

The rest of the day was a silent agony for Francie, and a murmured revel for those within Magnus-France who had viewed her innovation with skepticism from the start, and looked upon her with suspicion as an attractive but untried representative of the parent corporation across the Atlantic.

Francie worked alone at the computer, typing in commands, studying the program's reaction, and telephoning instructions to London and Lausanne. She could almost hear the whispers going on throughout the building about her system's failure and her spectacular embarrassment, but she managed to put them out of her mind.

Within an hour she had realized where the trouble lay. It was in the program's schematization of certain information relays, and in the crucial fact that the computer had not properly understood the logic behind this schematization.

But locating the problem was not the same as eliminating it. To her chagrin Francie realized that today's fiasco was no accident, but came from a flaw in the core of the program itself. Worst of all, nothing in Francie's experience as a student of computer science suggested a solution to the problem. She would have to improvise boldly in order to solve it. If it could be solved at all, that is.

In her absorption in her work she lost all track of time. She was still working frantically at the machine, darting from one display to the next, and making fevered notes on a large yellow pad, when she glanced at the clock on the wall.

It was nearly midnight.

With a sudden rush Francie's nervous energy abandoned her, and she collapsed into the swivel chair before the computer's control panel. She realized she had pushed herself much too far for one day. The job ahead of her was an arduous one. She would need to pace herself and keep her strength up, perhaps for many weeks, if she was to succeed.

She left the computer center and walked along the silent hallway to the elevator, which she took to the seventh floor, where her own office was located. She used her key to open the door, went past Antoinette's desk to the inner office, and turned on the lights from the wall switch.

To her surprise there was a large bunch of flowers on her desk top.

There was a note attached to the bouquet. It was in French handwriting, but the message was in English.

Happy Birthday, it read. *Many happy returns.*

It was signed *Jack.*

Francie's breath caught in her throat. She had completely forgotten about her birthday. She would be twenty-three years old next week at this time. How could Jack have known about this? Why would he go to the trouble to congratulate her from a continent away?

Francie blushed as she saw the remainder of the note.

P.S. I intend to spend it with you, if you haven't any other plans. See you next Thursday.

The note trembled in Francie's hand. Jack was coming here to see her! She sat down in her desk chair and stared numbly at the flowers.

Jack coming here!

It was not simply his coming that came as such a shock—she had known or suspected that at some point he would come here, since Europe was his province, and since her own operation was under his authority.

It was the fact that he was coming now, at the very moment when her professional life was at its worst crisis.

When he arrived she would have to explain the spectacular failure of her system, a system which had been built and implemented under his aegis. It was a failure that affected all the European companies whose welfare was Jack's responsibility. Therefore it must have an impact on his own standing within the parent corporation.

Francie's own shame would thus extend to the very man to whom she owed the only good fortune that had come her way at Magnus Industries.

The man about whom she had not stopped dreaming for a second since leaving New York six months ago.

And all because of one unforgettable kiss that had occurred at Anton Magnus's party for Gretchen and her newborn child, a kiss Jack had perhaps forgotten, but which still glowed like a burning ember in all Francie's senses, hotter if anything because of the passage of time and the deepening of her obsession.

Now Jack was coming here. When he arrived she would have to try to convince him that she could still make her system work, and that her high-sounding promises about computerization were not mere pipe dreams. More yet, she would have to make him forget somehow that the girl he had gratified with his confidence and his attentions six months ago was now the author of a grandiose failure that was the talk of Magnus-France.

It would be the performance of a lifetime. Francie was an accomplished mathematician, but she was not an accomplished actress. She did not know whether she could bring this off.

It all depended on Jack.

With that thought, her hands shaking, she put the note back in its little envelope and closed it in her desk drawer.

But the tremors in her fingers were radiating through all her limbs, and finding their way to the very quick of her.

Jack coming here to Paris! To help her celebrate her twenty-third birthday. And, certainly, to check on the progress of her computer system.

But perhaps, she mused, there was more to his coming than this alone. Perhaps he himself had not forgotten their evening together, and was coming to her, at least in part, as a man, and not just an employer.

This was the most daunting and delicious thought of all.

Tearing herself away from it was perhaps the most difficult thing she had ever done.

Let him come, then, she thought as she got up to leave the office. What will be will be.

Leaving the note in the desk behind her, she went home to get some sleep, so that tomorrow she could return to search for the weakness programmed into her system.

$=\!\!=\!\!= 14 =\!\!=\!\!=$

Francie did not see Jack until, unexpectedly, he appeared at the door of her office.

It was Wednesday afternoon, the day before her birthday. She had expected to meet him at tomorrow morning's TWA flight from New York.

But here he was, dressed in a gray silk suit, his complexion tanned as always, his hard limbs outlined by the fabric covering them, his dark eyes sparkling as he smiled at her.

"What are you doing here?" she asked, gulping her admiration for the picture he made in the doorway. "I wasn't expecting you until tomorrow."

"I got an earlier flight," he said without further explanation. "How are you, Francie?"

The sound of her name on his lips almost made her eyes close in pleasure. She forced herself to her feet and moved to shake his hand.

"Very well, thanks," she said with a brittle smile. "And you?"

"Fine. How are things going?"

She felt her façade of confidence crumble. He had got directly to the point.

"Not very well at the moment," she said, deciding to tell him the unadorned truth. He was not the sort of man who appreciates false reassurances.

"Really? Problems?" he asked.

"I'd like to show you, if I may," she said. "Are you tired from your flight, or can you listen to what I have to say?"

"I'm good at sleeping on airplanes," he said. "Let's go."

She took him to the computer center and laid out the program for him, explaining as clearly and succinctly as she could that there was a serious "bug" which had not yet been identified, and that she had her work cut out for her.

When she had finished she stood back and faced him.

"There, I've said it," she said. "I'm sorry about this, Mr. Magnus. I had thought the system was ready last week. There's nothing for it but to examine the elements, one by one, and then rewrite the program so it works." She paused. "What happened came as quite a shock to me . . ."

He was looking at her carefully.

"Do you think you can get the whole thing working before the deadline?" he asked.

She forced herself to meet his eyes.

"I don't know," she said. "All I can do is try."

He looked from her to the computer, and back again. "You seem upset about this," he said.

She smiled, a brief, phony smile full of obvious dread.

"I am—upset," she said. She started to add something, but the words would not come. She felt like a child admitting a mistake to a stern and respected teacher.

Now there was something appraising in his look. "Too upset to get the job done?" he asked.

Tears had started to come to her eyes, but she fought them back bravely.

If there was one thing she would never do, it was to show her feelings to Jack Magnus. He had hired her. She must make him respect her. No matter what.

"No," she said firmly. "You don't have to worry about that."

He gestured to the program. "Is it your considered judgment that this thing is going to work out?"

She followed the direction of his gaze to the stack of papers and notebooks in which she had invested so much, and which concealed a crucial flaw she had not rectified.

She took a deep breath.

"In my judgment," she said, "there's nothing wrong with the system. I committed an oversight somewhere in the mechanics, but that can be corrected. I feel sure of it."

This was not entirely true, and Francie knew it. The flaw in her program was so deep-seated as to threaten the very concept on which her system was based. There were no rules or guidelines in existing program logic to lead her out of her dilemma. Another programmer would have already given up on the entire plan.

But Francie felt a visceral certainty that the answer she needed was right in front of her—albeit like a needle in a haystack. The mathematical intellect that had never let her down since her childhood was telling her that she could solve this problem, if she simply approached it with an open and inventive mind. Creativity, not mechanics, was the key now. She could not give up until she had found out where she had made her mistake.

But she was lying to Jack in assuring him of something which was in fact not at all sure. She knew that all of Europe was Jack's responsibility. He must make the decision whether to invest additional time and money in this project, or to scrap it and try to forget the wasted effort it had cost.

He had not stopped looking at her. She could almost feel him trying to measure the trustworthiness of her explanation. A man in his position must be trained by hard experience to see through the false reassurances of those beneath him.

"All right," he said at last. "That's good enough for me."

Surprised, Francie looked up into his eyes.

"You mean . . . ," she said. "You mean you're not going to . . . ?"

Suddenly he laughed. "Fire you? Chop your head off? Get somebody else, or start from scratch? I can tell you don't know a lot about management, Francie. A good manager knows how to acquire the best people and let them do their best work. He doesn't push the panic button when delays or problems occur. If he did, he'd never get anything accomplished at all."

He touched the program. "What you're doing here is very complex, and very important. It was almost inevitable that there would be problems," he said. "Just stick with it. It will all work out. I'm sure of that."

She measured the impact of his words.

"Well, I—I appreciate your confidence," she said.

"You wouldn't be here unless you deserved it." His voice was calm and controlled.

There was a pause. He looked at the clock on the wall.

"I'll let you get on with your work," he said. "I have to touch base with a few people this afternoon. Can you have dinner tonight?"

"I—of course," she said.

"I'll pick you up at eight," he said.

She nodded. "Do you know where . . . ?"

"Your secretary gave me the address," he said. "I know the Left Bank pretty well. I won't have trouble finding you."

Again there was a pause. A little smile of nervous admiration played over Francie's lips despite herself as she contemplated his astonishing ease and indescribable handsomeness.

"Well, then, I'll see you later," he said.

"Yes." She stood up with him. He was smiling at her with a composite expression, at once businesslike and personal. She could not tell what it meant.

Then, with a last nod, he was gone.

Alone with the computer, Francie let out a deep breath.

Could it really be? In one stroke Jack Magnus had appeared at her threshold, washed away her sins, given her a new lease on life, and, most of all, turned her dread into a joy she had not felt since the last time she saw him.

Shaken, Francie contemplated her relief and her happiness.

And the fact that tonight she was to see Jack again.

He picked her up at the appointed hour and took her to Lasserre for dinner. She was awed by the plush Louis XVI décor of the legendary restaurant, the liveried waiters, captains, and sommeliers, and asked him why he had brought her to so elegant a place.

"It's an important night," he said. "Surely you haven't forgotten?"

She looked at him in perplexity.

"Your birthday, remember?" he said.

"Oh! That." She laughed. "What in the world made you remember my birthday?"

"Let's just say I'm a born busybody." He smiled. "I probably know more about my colleagues than is good for me. Anyway, I'm here."

He raised his glass of champagne and touched it to hers. She blushed despite herself as she returned his smile.

Dinner passed quietly, punctuated by company gossip and small talk which did nothing to abate the rising storm in Francie's senses. Her feeling of relief over Jack's positive judgment of her work had given way to a strange excitement which was increased by being at close quarters with him in this elegant, intimate place.

She was glad when dinner was over and they got outside in the fresh air. Jack had brought a Magnus-France company car, and he drove around the Place de la Concorde, glancing with Francie along the magnificent route of the Champs Elysées to the Arc de Triomphe, before heading across the Pont de l'Alma into the narrow streets of the Left Bank.

There were no parking spaces near her building, so Jack drove around at a leisurely pace until he found a spot in the picturesque Rue du Dragon, a narrow street full of antique shops. Together they walked to the corner of the Boulevard Saint-Germain for a brief glance at the busy night life of the area, then back to the Carrefour de la Croix Rouge, with its scattering of small shops, and finally to the darkened Rue du Cherche-Midi.

"Would you like to see where I live?" Francie asked a bit nervously. "It's a lovely little apartment. Roland de Leaumes rented it for me for as long as I'm here."

A look flickered in Jack's eyes at the mention of Roland, and disappeared at once. Francie did not know what it meant. The look that succeeded it was entirely neutral, inscrutable.

"I don't know that I have much to offer you in the way of a nightcap," she said. "You certainly deserve one, after that magnificent dinner."

"I don't want to tire you," he said. "You seem to have been working awfully hard. You're too thin."

"Oh, don't mind that," she said with an odd little shrug.

They had passed the concierge's loge and the courtyard with its little crouched sphinx, and were standing before the elevator in the rear foyer. The glow of the *minuterie,* the time-limited hallway lights of all French apartment buildings, cast an odd light on Jack's face. Everything was mellow and golden.

"Perhaps I'd better let you get your sleep," he said.

She said nothing, but smiled at him suddenly, a smile that seemed to cast its shadow like magic over his handsome features.

She had just touched the elevator button when the lights went out.

The little foyer was in total darkness. Somewhere on the wall nearby, Francie knew, was the switch to turn the lights back on.

She never reached it, for before she could turn to find it she was in Jack's arms.

There was no time to wonder whether it was she who had made the first move, or whether those long male arms had curled around her of their own accord. She only knew that the kiss which had changed her life in Anton Magnus's mansion was upon her again, hotter if anything, and more intimate, sending shocks through the quick of her like a comet in whose trail were the hundreds of private moments she had spent dreaming of Jack since that first kiss.

A voice inside her warned that she was taking a step she could not retrace. But it was silenced by the power of his kiss. She held him close, felt her body shudder against his, and heard the strange female moan in her throat as the darkness bound them together.

Then, somehow, they were inside the elevator. The tiny enclosure seemed to force them closer together, and the heat inside Francie's senses erupted faster as the conveyance slid up the shaft. Her eyes were closed, but her hands, with a knowledge all their own, were caressing him and encouraging him. They found their way under his jacket to the hard ribcage under his deep chest, and gloried in the firmness of his flesh.

His kiss deepened as the elevator pushed them higher and higher, and she felt his hands close about her waist. Their touch seemed to make her go crazy. She moved against him, a weird rhythm of sinuous female limbs singing seduction to every part of him. Somehow the slim hips shuddering in his arms told him he might touch her more intimately, even now, and the firm hands slipped beneath her waist to pull her harder against him. Her tongue greeted his own, teasing it with subtle little strokes that made a groan stir in his throat.

Later she would wonder how they had got from the elevator into the apartment, how she found her keys to unlock the door. She would never remember, for passion had stripped her consciousness of everything but Jack.

The only memory she would retain was their shared darkness, the feel of his caress on her shoulders, her breasts, her thighs, and the almost painful clamoring of her skin to be naked for him. The only sound in the apartment was their breathing, made short by desire, and the slow whisper of their hands as they explored each other.

Francie knew that something awesome and long-awaited was going to happen. She would have been consumed by stage fright were it not for the unsuspected wisdom of her body, which had been preparing for this moment all along, and now knew exactly what to do.

She slipped her fingers up his chest and under the shoulders of his jacket, which came off easily. She kissed him again, and now the buttons of his shirt were coming undone. She could feel her dress coming loose in its turn. All the garments separating them were falling off with a will of their own, like petals from flowers born to fecundate each other.

She led him slowly to the bedroom, pausing over and over again to kiss and touch him. By the time she lay down on her bed she was naked. She watched him rear up before her, silhouetted against the Paris night, an erect male god as he shrugged out of his clothes and looked down at her.

She held out her arms to him.

He came to cover her with himself, and the sweetness of his tongue entered her mouth at the same instant that the hardness between his legs grazed the soft portal to the core of her.

A sort of slow wildness overcame her, so that her body, helpless with pleasure, was nevertheless knowing and bold in its movements. She could feel his own excitement rising quickly to a fever pitch, and even the sharp urgency of male need did not surprise her, for her body knew just what to do with him.

She held him by his hips, guiding him slowly as her own kiss deepened inside his mouth. A long series of smooth undulations joined them, sensual and slow, bringing him inevitably closer, so that the hot tip of him probed at the flesh of her secret place, already opening the waiting door, a bit more and a bit more. Then, with a shudder, she felt him enter her.

Even the flash of pain she felt at his coming was pleasure to her, and ecstasy. She heard the groan stir in his throat, and her little cries of delight came to caress it as she gave herself more completely, hips arching to pull him deeper, fingers grazing his hard thighs, breasts standing out to feel the crisp hair of his chest against her nipples.

Then everything seemed to explode. The Jack she had dreamed about for so long was lost in the storm erupting inside her, and all her thoughts about herself were burned by the hot thrill surging through every sinew of her. She did not know who she was or what anything meant, but she did not care. Her body no longer belonged to her.

She could not see what Jack saw as she lay beneath him: a lovely slender nymph transformed by pleasure, her flesh undulating seductively, the hot little nipples dancing under his thrusts, sweet woman's hands resting lovingly on his hips to help him own her the more completely, long creamy thighs caressing him in rhythms ever more sensual, more irresistible.

But she realized that her surrender was kindling a terrible fire within him for he surged and flamed inside her with an inhuman power, over and over again, deeper and tighter and more intimate with each stroke, his passion rising to greater and greater heights, until even her cries of ecstasy were lost in the tumult of it all.

As the fire grew hotter and hotter she no longer knew whether her own abandon was making him this way, or whether he himself had lost control, taken leave of his own real world to join her in this mad slipping of flesh upon flesh, this triumph of pleasure over sanity.

She thought it would never end. Yet his final strokes took her by surprise, upraising her to a mad height she had never dreamed of in her guiltiest fantasies. He came deeper and deeper, and a great spasm of her body opened the last door to him.

She heard a low scalded groan in his throat. A sweet hot stream came to flood within her all at once, and a sudden quiver of her most intimate sinews strained to receive it. Then it was over.

She lay limp and drained in his arms.

A kiss touched her forehead, then another and another, softly grazing her eyelids and cheeks. She curled her arms about his neck and held him closer.

Now she knew what she had been waiting for all her life.

The night passed in a dream. How many times they made love she did not know. She only knew that each time was different, and that each time, in a different way, she gave all of herself. It was as though the miracle of his touch brought countless new selves into being inside her, each of them unsuspected before now, and created to belong to him, to excite him and pleasure him in ways she had never dreamed herself capable of.

It was a long, beautiful process of losing herself. And to the Francie who had lived by her own strong will for twenty-three years, it would have been a frightening experience, for it was surrender in the most total sense of the word. But she had Jack to hold her close, and he banished her second thoughts again and again with the beauty of his body. He was as insatiable as she, and something in him, she felt, was surrendering too in the face of this wild chemistry of desire that was pulling them together.

When it was over a delicious fatigue overcame them both. Pale moonlight was coming in the window, and she lay beside him, watching it bathe his handsome features. Asleep he looked even more mysterious and attractive than awake. There was something enigmatic and almost child-like in his slumber.

She saw him stir as a dream troubled his face. In awe she watched his arm reach out to curl around her, to draw her to him. She dared to kiss his cheek, his lips. He held her close, and she wished she could join him in his dream, so that in thought they could be as united as they had been by pleasure all night long.

She wondered if he sensed the revolution he had wrought in her. She knew she would never be the same after tonight.

And she was glad it had been this man, the most beautiful of all, who had taken her maidenhood and made her a woman.

What it all meant, and where it was leading, she knew not. She only knew that the past was banished forever, and the future stretched before her like a limitless ocean of pure pleasure.

With that thought Francie fell into a beautiful, dreamless sleep.

When she awoke she was alone in the bed.

Alarmed, she sat up and looked around her. The clock showed seven o'clock.

She felt dazed and disoriented. Could last night have been a dream? Could she have come back here alone and descended into some sort of insane solitary fantasy, alone in her bed?

But the glow inside her body reminded her that it had all been real.

She came awake slowly, feeling the sheets caress her nakedness. She listened for any sound of Jack in the apartment. There was none.

She got up and went into the bathroom. She looked at her face in the mirror. Her hair was awry. Her features bore the traces of passion. The naked shoulders and breasts in the mirror were her own, and yet she looked like a stranger to herself.

A gnawing fear came over Francie, taking root in the lingering throb of her senses and echoing through all the corners of her mind. She knew that what she had done with Jack was irremediable. And now he was gone. She was left alone to ponder what had happened between them.

She lingered for a moment, staring at her reflection in the mirror. Now the face truly unnerved her, for it belonged to a heedless creature who had led Francie into actions she could not undo, and emotions she had no right to feel.

Turning away from the glass, she stepped into the shower and turned on the water. She felt the stream of droplets cleanse her, hot and stinging. But it could not cleanse away her memories. And she knew that, wherever Jack was now, he knew her for what she really was.

By the time she emerged, wearing a terrycloth robe with a white towel wrapped around her hair, she was convinced that she had committed the greatest mistake of her life. She could never face Jack Magnus again with the same confidence she had had before.

When she entered the tiny kitchen she almost cried out despite herself. Jack was sitting at the table, looking up at her.

He smiled.

"Fancy meeting you here," he said.

Francie stared at him in surprise. "I thought . . . ," she stammered. "I thought you . . ."

He said nothing. Her eyes darted over his body. He was dressed in the slacks he had worn last night. His shirt was open at the neck, revealing the deep chest she had covered with her kisses. The black eyes gazing up at her were full of knowledge. She could almost see the reckless nymph she had been last night reflected in their depths.

"I . . . ," she began embarrassedly. "I mean . . ."

He saw her disarray and stood up. She was trembling all over, unable to control herself. He put his hands on her shoulders and drew her to him. She could feel his warm body through the terrycloth of her robe. Almost at once desire came to add itself to the pain in her emotions, and she was torn unendurably.

She would have begged him to leave her now, to forget her, had not something unexpected happened.

He took her in his arms, lifted her as easily as though she were a child, and carried her gently back into the bedroom. He placed her on her bed, looked down at her as she lay gazing up at him, and smiled at her.

Then he reached down with a tanned hand and touched delicately at her cheek, her brow, her wet hair. His caress seemed to calm her. The look in his eyes was filled with a mixture of gentle melancholy and happiness which hypnotized her.

He went on that way, soothing her with his caresses as the look in his eyes penetrated deeper and deeper into her feelings. Though his own mystery did not abate in that extraordinary look, she knew that the most private part of him was gazing down at her now.

He took both her hands and held them softly. His lips parted. She wondered what he could possibly say to lessen the upset in her mind. Perhaps he was merely searching for tactful words with which to salve her chagrin before escaping her.

The words he spoke took her utterly by surprise.

"I love you," he said.

Francie's eyes opened wide. She could not believe what she was hearing.

"Will you marry me?" he asked, clasping her hands tighter.

Francie was in a daze. The words sounded as though they had come from another planet, another life. Were it not for his hands holding her so firmly, she would have feared he was about to disappear as abruptly as Cinderella's coach and horses at the stroke of midnight.

"You're not going to say no, are you?" he asked. "Because if you do, I'm finished."

He was looking at her expectantly. A kaleidoscope of expressions lit her beautiful face, from shock and alarm to a growing, irresistible happiness.

The smile that ended it all was as candid as that of a child, and the light in her green eyes like the dawn of a new season.

"Oh, Jack," she said. "Oh, my God . . ."

Suddenly he pulled her to him, and the large hands were around her back. Her face was against his chest. She could feel his heart beating fast.

"Say it," he murmured, a harsh sound in his throat. "Whatever it is, please say it. I've got to know. I love you, Francie. I've loved you since the first moment I saw you, in that corridor outside my apartment. It was as though I couldn't breathe. And every day it gets worse. I couldn't bring myself to tell you back then, because we had just met, and you were so new to the corporation. I didn't want to confuse you, to tear you . . . But I can't wait any longer. It's killing me. Please, Francie . . ."

"Yes," she said. The word slipped out with a will of its own, as certain of itself as the passion of her body last night, a word that easily bypassed her tortured mind, carrying with it secrets she had tried to hide from herself all this time, but that could no longer be denied.

"Yes, you'll marry me?" he asked. "Yes, you love me?"

"Yes, yes, yes," she replied, exultation singing in her voice. "Oh, Jack . . ."

He hugged her closer, rocking her back and forth in his arms. It seemed as though the earth was collapsing under her like the thinnest of ice. Yet she felt that he himself was the ground she would walk on from now on, Jack and only Jack, forever.

Their embrace grew tighter and tighter. The glory inside Francie's mind left her unable to breathe. The same seemed true of her lover, whose heart was beating against her breast. The revelation that had just passed between them was almost too intense to bear.

Slowly he lowered her to the sheets. She lay looking up at him, her eyes alive with a strange intensity. He looked into them as though hypnotized.

Then his hands opened the terrycloth robe, softly, and he looked down at her naked body. There was awe in his eyes, and infinite admiration.

For a last instant Francie contemplated this whirling of fate which had torn her from her own life in one short night and set her down in an alien place worlds removed from the dreams that had seen her through her whole lifetime. Losing herself that way would have killed her, were it not for the eyes looking down at her now, eyes which promised a new life and new dreams so beautiful that for their sake she could gladly sacrifice everything she had been before.

And so, saying goodbye to the past she knew so well and hello to a future of which she could know nothing but a pleasure beyond words, Francie gathered Jack Magnus to her breast.

=== 15 ===

New York, July 27, 1956

Belinda Devereaux sat at the dinner table in her parents' Sutton Place duplex, looking at her mother and Victoria Magnus, who were engaged in conversation.

A moment ago Anton Magnus and Brent Devereaux, Belinda's father, had brusquely absented themselves from the table to have a cigar and a glass of port in Mr. Devereaux's library. That left the women to linger over dessert and eventually to repair to the drawing room, where their gossip would continue while Sarah Devereaux crocheted a sweater for her niece and Victoria Magnus paged through a magazine.

It was the same routine every time the Magnuses came over. Even though Brent Devereaux and Anton Magnus were hugely powerful men, and their wives much sought after in the highest society in the land, the two couples behaved for all the world like elderly middle-class people accustomed to creature comforts and boredom.

The gatherings were always here, unless the Magnuses took Belinda and her parents to the Plaza or the Pierre for dinner. Somehow it was too embarrassing to have Belinda to the Park Avenue house without Jack there, and when Juliet might make a scene at any time. The whole thing felt safer here.

And Belinda had to endure it, feeling like an atrocious and ungainly fifth wheel, and dreaming all the while of Jack. For Jack was the unspoken raison d'être of these insufferable little dinners, the silent ghost behind them, as well as the one human being who never in a million years would have graced them with his presence.

Jack was in Paris tonight, troubleshooting a new computer system being set up by Magnus-France. But even if he had been in New York, he would not be here. He always found excuses for avoiding these gatherings. He would not leave his independent life to come to an obligatory dinner with his prospective in-laws just because Anton Magnus had told him he must come.

No, the essence of Jack's willful personality decreed that he would not allow such an imposition on his freedom. Ironically enough, Belinda respected him for this, and even admired it in him.

If only she had that kind of courage herself! Who could tell where such a quality might have led her in life?

But since she did not—since she was unable to detach herself from the slim hope that Jack would somehow choose her in the end no matter what, since she was the slave of the future that Anton Magnus and Brent Devereaux had mapped out for her—she had to go on enduring this interminable ritual.

Tonight had been like all the other dinners. Polite cocktails, the men dominating the conversation. Friendly greetings from Mrs. Magnus—a creature so terrified of everything and everybody that she seemed like a bird trembling in a gilded cage—and a paternal kiss on the cheek from Anton Magnus, his eyes meeting Belinda's with sympathy and with a sort of significant knowledge, as though to say, "You and I are the most important people here. You and I have unfinished business, and I'm here to see that we carry it to a successful conclusion."

Cocktail conversation, a magnificent dinner prepared by the Devereaux' cook, and finally the men beginning to fall into bored silence as the wives' gossip took over the conversation. Then the men abruptly disappearing to talk of male business, while Mother and Mrs. Magnus exchanged rumors about the hundreds of friends they had in common, and relatives as well, since the Devereaux were connected by marriage to the Trowbridges, Gretchen Magnus's family.

"Gay Swinerton and Rollie are getting a divorce," said Mother. "Can you believe it, after all this time?"

"My goodness, but I thought they were so wrapped up in each other," said Mrs. Magnus. "I saw them only last month, at Newport. And their children looked so sweet."

"Well, you know how Lea Widener is. When she sets her sights on a man, he doesn't stand a chance. Not even a poor kind fellow like Rollie. It's such a shame."

"Personally, I don't know how she does it. She's showing her age, you know. Even her face lifts have face lifts."

Belinda could not bring herself to join in this feckless, empty chatter. She was not a gossip by nature, but a studious, quiet girl who craved intellectual stimulation.

She had a degree in English from Swarthmore, and for the past four years had been taking courses toward a Doctorate at Columbia. She had the vague idea of becoming an English professor, and teaching the literature she loved—romantic literature above all, including the Brontës, George Sand, Byron—in the event that that became necessary.

Belinda was in a bind that was squeezing her a bit more cruelly each day. For she had no real desire to be a professor. All she wanted was Jack Magnus.

But she could not avoid knowing that she would only marry Jack Magnus in the event that his father won a battle over Jack which Jack was even now fighting with the essence of his pride and his stubbornness. If Jack lost that battle, she would no longer have to think about being an English professor. But she would have to worry about being married to a husband who did not want her. And that would open the door to unimagined heartache.

On the other hand, if Jack did not marry her after all, then she would finish her degree and get a teaching job. She would spend her life communicating to her students the flights of romance that had captivated her in the works of her favorite authors. This would be a lonely life, certainly, but not a useless one. It would be a consolation of sorts for what she had lost.

Both dénouements had their perils. It was hard to say which would be worse. The safe, lonely way, without Jack, or the more dangerous course of becoming his wife against his wishes.

So Belinda remained on this fragile perch, flanked by two abysses, while she listened to the idiotic empty prattle of her mother and Mrs. Magnus, and wondered how she had got herself into this mess.

Belinda had been a healthy, normal child, if a bit retiring. She was by far the most intelligent of the Devereaux children—her two sisters were much older, and had married into wealthy families long ago—and also the most isolated. As a child she had learned to play by herself, invent her own games, decorate her own room, choose her own books, lose herself in her fantasies without interference from the outside world. Loneliness brought a kind of independence.

By age thirteen she had become a shy but self-sufficient girl, not without pride in herself, not without confidence in the future.

Then Jack had come along. He was already twenty by then, and a brilliant, dashing university student. He had been invited with his parents to the wedding of Simone, Belinda's older sister, and introduced to Belinda on the lawn at the Devereaux' Southampton house.

Belinda would never forget that day, for it had brought both the joy and the curse that were to hang over her life forever afterward.

Jack Magnus at twenty was the most handsome man Belinda had ever seen. He was perfection incarnated in male flesh, a Michelangelo sculpture of youth and masculinity brought to life. Her maiden's heart, not very sensitive to men before that moment, had awakened with a start and given itself utterly to Jack. There is only one first love, and Jack was Belinda's.

Nervously she had convinced him to let her show him around the Southampton house. He had seemed happy to get away from the wedding guests. He was curious about her schoolwork, her interests. With childish candor she showed him her room. On the desk was a paper she had written for her English class, entitled, "What Poetry Means to Me." He read it with interest, and asked her a respectful question or two about the ideas she had expressed in it. He seemed to like her. He even went so far as to tease her a little. She blushed to the roots of her hair at his attention.

She felt a timid veil of intimacy fall delicately over them both. As they left her bedroom and toured the house, she felt she wanted to know him, to be his friend, more than anything else in the world.

Then the blow fell. They went back to the lawn, where Anton Magnus and Belinda's father were waiting for them. Both men were wearing sly matchmakers' smiles as they stood in their formal dress watching the young couple approach them. Jack saw the look in their eyes and turned to Belinda. Gone was his friendly banter, gone was his smile. The look on his handsome face was suddenly cold.

Jack did not say another word to Belinda after that. He seemed to know something she did not, something that had changed all his thoughts about her.

He left the party early, without saying goodbye to her.

It was only later, through a series of murmured remarks from her mother, and then a phone call from one of her girl friends at school, that Belinda learned the truth. A deal had been struck between her father and Anton Magnus at that wedding party. His youngest daughter was to be reserved for Jack Magnus. This would be the greatest plum yet for Brent Devereaux, who had already made advantageous marriages for Simone and Valerie, his older daughters. The Magnuses, it was said, were delighted with the plan.

It was all arranged.

However, after that first day Jack Magnus never showed Belinda Devereaux anything but the most unwilling attention. Gone forever was the charming intimacy with which he had read her paper, the gentle mocking eyes, the deep but respectful voice, his curiosity about her and—heartbreaking irony!—the fact that he liked her.

Never again would Jack take her seriously, or bestow the smile of his interest upon her. For it was not Jack himself but his father who had chosen her.

She had become a pawn in a battle between two men determined to get the best of each other, two men who would never give up.

And she had remained in that position ever since.

That one fateful day had lifted Belinda's heart to a height she had never imagined, and then plunged it to a depth more suffocating than she had ever dreamed possible at her tender age.

For a long time after that day she wondered how she was going to cope with the burden she had to bear. But as she grew into her adolescence, and was forced to meet Jack over and over again on a hundred social occasions, seeing in his eyes the same indifference even as she recalled that initial afternoon when he had been so kind to her—as these things happened Belinda found the only solution she could for her problem.

She kept her love safe for Jack Magnus, never allowing it to flow outward to any young man she met. And she kept her body for him as well.

The fact that she knew Jack did not want her love, cared nothing for her, only increased the nobility of her cause. It was with an almost monastic self-sacrifice that she cherished her love and felt it grow inside her, not needing for him to requite it, but devoting herself to it unstintingly.

It seemed to Belinda in her romantic heart that if she made this final sacrifice for him, giving up everything, allowing nothing but him to occupy her heart, fate might some day reward her by bringing them together after all.

And, she reasoned more cunningly, if Anton Magnus won out in the end and managed to force Jack into marriage with her, then the power and the purity of her love would slowly triumph over Jack's indifference.

Belinda had read stories of people from countries where marriages were arranged by parents. She had felt a seductive warmth inside her when wives and husbands told of being paired up as children by powers beyond themselves, but found as time passed that they had grown to love each other as much as if they had chosen each other in the first place.

Belinda cherished this dream for herself and Jack. She did not know whether it would ever come true, but she was keeping herself pure for it, and for Jack. Each day her love grew, and the very fact that this love must grow in secret, unfelt by the man who was its object, gave Belinda courage. If and when Jack accepted her, she would bring him a great love, a love strong enough to melt his armor of rebellion against his father.

As to whether that day would ever come, Belinda could only wait and see. And in the interim she knew she was only half a person, not at all the complete individual she could have grown into in other circumstances. But she made this sacrifice for Jack as well.

So tonight she sat here, feeling like a fifth wheel as always, knowing that her loneliness and humiliation were visible for all to see, knowing that the wives' gossip was meant to cover her predicament, knowing that the men had retreated to the library so as to escape her shame—and she accepted all this, because she loved Jack, and because that love could see her through the worst of trials.

But tonight was a worse trial than usual. For tonight Jack was in Paris, where, Belinda knew, the beautiful Magnus employee named Francie Bollinger was now working.

Francie, the beautiful, bright, sensual girl who had been on Jack's arm the night of Gretchen's party, the sight of whom had nearly broken Belinda's heart. For they made so perfect a couple, Jack and Francie. Both so tall and energetic and intelligent. People made to fly through an exciting life together, people made for each other—if they had the freedom to choose each other.

Belinda had felt like a leper that night. Not only because Francie was so beautiful, and because of the glow Belinda noticed in Jack's eyes when he looked at Francie—but because Belinda knew that her own taint, the taint of being unwanted, had been on her face like a scarlet letter for all to see, for all to witness as Jack introduced her to Francie.

She had ended the conversation as fast as she could and slunk away from their company. That party had opened a wound in her heart that had hurt with unbearable intensity for weeks afterward, and never really healed.

And tonight—everyone knew it—Jack was in Paris, while Belinda was here alone, acting as companion for a quartet of aging, worried, hopeful parents for whom she was a shy and quiet burden which they must cover over with their conversation and their false levity.

But even this Belinda would endure. Even this most exquisite of humiliations she would bear, for Jack's sake.

At last it was time for the Magnuses to leave. Anton Magnus came out of the library looking calm and self-possessed. Belinda's father, as always, seemed intimidated by Magnus, though Brent Devereaux was much taller than his guest. The eager smile of solicitude and obsequiousness lingered on her father's face as he kissed Victoria Magnus and shook Anton Magnus's hand.

"We'll see you soon again," they were all saying. "Call me next week. A lovely dinner . . . Thank you . . . Thank you . . ."

Anton Magnus detached himself from the group and came to take his leave of Belinda. He took her hand and kissed her softly on her cheek.

"You're looking so lovely, my dear," he said, "as always."

And, bending closer to her so as not to be overheard by the others, he added, "Courage, my child. Everything is going to work out for the best. I promise you."

She nodded with a weak smile. He chucked her under the chin like a little girl and murmured with a smile, "All is arranged. Trust me."

16

Paris, August 20, 1956

Dear Dad,

I have wonderful news. It's wonderful to me, anyway, and I think you'll be happy to hear it.

The computer system I've been working on for the past few months has finally clicked. It was a long haul, and I had my problems with it along the way, but they've all been ironed out now, and we'll be giving the system its final trial run in a couple of weeks.

I've missed you a lot all this time. So often I look out my window at the Paris rooftops, when it's evening, and think about you, and the way we always used to rock together on the front porch at the end of the day. Paris is an exciting and wonderful place, but it isn't home. Nothing can be, I guess, but home itself.

I can hardly wait to get things implemented here so I can come home and see you again. Thanks for your letters (I know you're not the writing type, so thanks all the more). And thanks for the pictures you sent. They made me homesick, but happy, too.

Much love always,
Francie

Francie sealed the letter to her father and mailed it before she told anyone else of her breakthrough. Somehow she wanted him to be the first to know her good news.

Three days ago, working alone in the Magnus-France computer center on the labyrinthine intricacies of her program, she had found the missing logical link which had caused the breakdown in the system. The problem had been much more serious than even Francie had realized. She had had to devise a whole new concept in stored-program language in order to solve it. Nothing in her entire computer education had prepared her either for the challenge she faced or the inspiration that had allowed her to meet it.

Her own inventiveness had surprised her, and she would have been proud of her work were it not for the withering thought of how close she had come to complete disaster before finding the solution.

She had never told her father about the alarming false start that had made her feel so humiliated before her French colleagues, and made her wonder whether she was really capable of making the system work. It was a lot easier, she found, to tell Dad things were running smoothly and well than to admit to him how rocky her existence had been since coming to Magnus.

By the same token, she had not told Dad about Jack. This, if anything, made her even more uncomfortable in writing him her news, and she could only wonder whether her subterfuge showed through in her letters.

Jack had sworn Francie to total secrecy about her engagement to him. He wanted her to complete her system before the world knew of their marriage plans.

"My father won't take lightly to my going my own way on this," he said. "I want to present my marriage to him as a fait accompli. I don't intend to get into a battle with him, using you as the weapon. I want to keep you out of it. But it's essential that you finish your system before we get married. I want you to have that accomplishment for yourself and for your own career. You did this, and you deserve the credit."

"I haven't done it yet," she had protested, smiling.

"But you will. I have no doubt of that. Nothing must stand in your way. We have to present my father with two things he can't do anything about—first, that you've done a brilliant thing for his company, and second, that you're my wife."

Francie had accepted these conditions.

Thus, now that she had made her breakthrough, it had two joyous meanings for her. In the first place, her great challenge was about to become a reality. There was no longer the slightest doubt in her mind that the system would work for all Europe. She knew as an engineer that she had found the solution.

She also knew that now nothing stood in the way of her marriage to Jack.

At his own insistence Jack had returned to Europe twice since the fateful night of his first visit to Francie. She had tried to argue him out of it, reasoning that it would look suspicious to his colleagues if he spent too much time in Europe, but he had shrugged off her scruples.

"No one at Magnus tells me what to do," he said. "I come and go as I please. Besides," he added with a smile, "I can't be away from you any longer. I'll go crazy."

Each time Francie saw him was more magical than the last. His visits were short, but their brevity only increased the extraordinary intimacy which joined him to Francie. They gloried in each other's bodies with a hunger that was almost desperate. So overwhelming was the physical side of their closeness that it seemed to banish all thought.

Something inside Francie warned her that being swept off her feet this way was dangerous. But she could not help it. The sound of Jack's voice on the phone, the sight of his handwriting in one of the brief notes he sent her, sufficed to paralyze her will. And when she saw him in the flesh and felt his arms around her, the entire world seemed banished by his touch.

When they were separated she dreamed of him all night long and coveted her memory of him throughout her work days, lingering over each detail of his face and body. But when she saw him she found that her mental image of him never seemed to correspond precisely to the awesome reality of his arms, his kisses, his caresses. So this was what it was like, she mused, to lose one's heart to a man. It was like a dizzying downward flight, increasing in speed until it took one's breath away.

And when they made love she could feel his own obsession with her body and her passion, as she had felt the first night they were together. There was something insatiable in his lovemaking. He seemed to drink her in with all his senses, as though he had been incomplete all his life, and had only awakened to the secret of his own manhood through meeting her.

During their quiet nocturnal conversations she learned more about him. She came to know his opinions, his dreams, his hopes for his own future as an independent entrepreneur.

And she learned about the difficult childhood in which he had grown up in his father's shadow, and his battle to find himself as a man despite Anton Magnus's strong will and manipulative personality. Jack was the only member of his family who had dared to stand up to his father. He felt a combination of protectiveness and pity toward his mother and sisters, who remained entirely within Anton Magnus's orbit. Jack's position in the family was a lonely one.

Francie learned all this and much more about Jack Magnus. Yet even as she grew closer to him, his mystery seemed to deepen. He was a private man, accustomed to keeping his own counsel, a man of action who did not find it easy to express the essence of himself in words. Only in the fire of his lovemaking did Francie feel she touched him at his core.

So that she felt she knew him very well, almost too well, and not at all. And this lingering enigma only increased her passion to be his wife, so she could know the rest and love every bit of him. She understood how deeply he had been hurt by a lifetime in the world of the Magnuses. She wanted to help him heal his wounds, and to leave that world behind him.

The great day was not far away now. Soon she would belong to him completely, and forever.

As she went downstairs to the concierge's loge to mail her letter to her father, she felt once more the pang that had gone through her each time she had written him since accepting Jack's proposal. She wondered if Mac Bollinger, an intuitive man who knew her almost as well as she knew herself, could sense from her letters that she was in love. She had tried to make the letters as breezy and relaxed as possible, but the joy inside her was so consuming that perhaps it sang in her every word.

Her discomfort was the worse because she longed to share her news with Mac more than with anyone on earth. She needed to feel his support in this great new step she was taking.

And she felt guilty about hiding the truth from him. She had inherited her old-fashioned ways from Mac himself. She knew that in his heart of hearts Mac would want to meet her young man, to get to know him, to feel sure his only daughter was loved, and to formally give her away. In the best of all possible worlds Francie would have taken Jack home to Pennsylvania and let him ask Mac Bollinger for her hand himself.

But she must keep silent for Jack's sake. Powerful obstacles stood between her and actually being married to him. She must wait until the marriage was an accomplished fact before telling anyone.

With these thoughts in her mind Francie called Jack in New York as soon as she had mailed the letter to her father.

The timing was perfect. It was four o'clock in Paris, ten in the morning in New York. Jack was in his office.

"Darling," Francie told him. "I've done it. It's going to work. I'm sure of it."

"Wonderful." Jack's voice sounded unnaturally clear. "That's great news. I have to confess, though, that I'm not entirely surprised. I kind of figured you'd prevail sooner or later."

"And there's one more thing," she added.

"What's that?"

"I love you."

She heard his low laugh on the line.

"I hope nobody's listening in," he said.

"I don't care who knows it," she cried, beside herself at feeling so close to him. "I love you, I love you, I love you!"

"Same here," he said rather cautiously. She wondered whether his secretary was in his office. "That goes double," he added, a smile in his voice.

"I've set up a new trial run for next week," she said. "If it works, we'll start up the whole system as soon as possible."

"I want to be there," Jack said. "This means as much to me as it does to you."

"Yes," she laughed, a hectic exultation in her voice. "I want you with me when it works. Darling, darling . . ."

"Take it easy," he laughed. "Take good care of yourself, and keep in close touch. I'll talk to you soon."

They said goodbye. For a long moment Francie held the phone in her hand, savoring the magic of the voice that had just come out of it.

Then she came back to earth and dialed Roland de Leaumes' office to tell him her good news.

"Everything is go again," she said. "I want you to notify everybody that we'll try again a week from today."

"I'm on my way," Roland promised.

Francie thanked her lucky stars for Roland. It was he who constantly reassured the Magnus subsidiary heads all over Europe that despite its false start, Francie's plan was sure to be a great success. Thanks to his tireless public relations efforts, the Europeans believed computerization was a genuine part of their companies' future. With the exception of Jack himself, Roland was Francie's only true ally within the corporation.

On fire with excitement, Francie closed the program and went home to sleep. She had not slept more than five hours a night for a month, and was exhausted. Her senses tingling with her intellectual breakthrough as well as her anticipation of marriage and the honeymoon in the Greek Islands which she and Jack had planned, she went home and fell into a deep sleep.

It never occurred to her to lock up the program.

$$=== 17 ===$$

New York, August 24, 1956

In an office inside Magnus Industries' Sixth Avenue headquarters, two men sat across from each other at a large executive desk.

On the desk top between them was a file that had been brought by special messenger from Paris four days ago.

The visitor in the leather armchair before the desk was looking from the file to the man opposite him. He was waiting for the question he knew was coming, the question which was the reason for his being here.

It came without further delay.

"What do you think?" the man behind the desk asked. "What are we talking about here?"

The visitor cleared his throat. "We're talking about something much more important than you thought," he said.

There was a silence.

"How important?" the man behind the desk asked, his eyes narrowing.

The visitor stirred in his chair. He was a bit awed to be in the presence of such power, and yet he was not unconscious of his own importance.

His name was Alexander Caulfield, and he was Vice-President in Charge of Research and Development for one of the largest computer manufacturers in the world. He had been brought here because he was the best in his field. No man alive had a better knowledge of computers and their applications. Few men anywhere had analyzed the future uses of computers as he had in his professional work and in the handful of abstruse technical articles he had published in scientific journals.

He had been given the file to read, and paid what was to him an enormous sum of money to keep both his study of the file and his opinion an absolute secret.

With a slight gesture to the file on the desk top, he spoke carefully.

"In order to understand the importance of a thing like this," he said, "you have to realize that the computer field is young. It's young, but it's on the verge of taking off. Today computers are freaks, curiosities. In ten or fifteen years they'll be as commonplace as television sets are now. What that means in terms of money can hardly be estimated."

He paused, searching for the right words to express his thoughts. The man behind the desk had said nothing, but was simply gazing at him through those penetrating dark eyes.

"We're all aware of what the patent for the picture tube of an ordinary television set is worth today," Alexander Caulfield said. "Everyone who builds one has to pay a royalty for it. Now, what you've shown me is a similar item. On the surface, of course, it's a system with a specific purpose—the interfacing of some European companies. But the program itself contains some logical secrets which are, to my knowledge, absolutely new in computer technology. No one has thought of them before— though it would have made an enormous difference if someone had."

He joined his hands meditatively. "In a few years there will be dozens of communications systems, not only in business but in education, government, the military, banking, and so on—and they will all have to embody this logical linkage which we see here. Since we assume that this program will be protected by patent law or trade secret law, its author will have to be paid a royalty each and every time the system or one of its analogues is used."

The man across the desk cleared his throat.

"How much?" he asked.

"You mean, how much is it worth?" Alexander Caulfield asked.

His interlocutor nodded quietly.

Caulfield shrugged, raising his eyebrows as he glanced out the windows at the midtown skyline.

"Tens of millions, at the very least," he said. "Possibly hundreds of millions. It depends on how quickly the growth of computers proceeds, and how well the product is protected."

He sat back and let his words sink in.

There was a pause which seemed interminable to Caulfield. The man behind the desk had not stopped staring at him.

At last the man gestured to the file.

"What is your opinion," he asked, "of the person who created this?"

Caulfield smiled.

"That's easy," he said. "He's a genius—whoever he is. I don't know if he realizes what he's achieved. I do know I'd give a great deal to meet him someday."

You mean "her."

The man behind the desk did not say these words.

A moment later Alexander Caulfield had taken his leave. The man at the desk sat alone, looking out at the Manhattan skyline.

Hundreds of millions . . .

How he had underestimated her!

But all's well that ends well, he decided.

He picked up the phone on his desk.

"Yes, sir?" came the secretary's voice.

"Have John Dorrance from our patent department come to my office this afternoon," he said. "No later than three o'clock."

"Yes, sir."

"There's something else," he went on. "I want you to make a payment from my personal account," he said. "There is to be no record of it within the company. Is that clear?"

"Yes, sir. To whom shall I make it out?"

"Roland de Leaumes. Magnus-France, Paris. His home address is in your files. Have it delivered confidentially. Not through company channels."

"And how much, sir?"

"Twenty-five thousand dollars."

"Very well, sir."

He hung up the phone. He sat thinking for several minutes. Everything was changed now. There were so many new things to weigh. Things that had not been in the balance an hour ago. Things that could make all the difference.

He picked up the phone again.

"One more thing," he said.

"Yes, sir?"

"Make me a lunch date with Belinda Devereaux," he said. "Tell her it's important. Make it as soon as possible. Tomorrow, if you can."

"Yes, sir."

With a sigh of relief he hung up the phone and closed his eyes.

Belinda, he thought. *Of course.*

She would need to be told. If Alexander Caulfield had been the first step, then Belinda was the second.

=== 18 ===

Paris, September 2, 1956

Two days remained before the official start-up of Francie's system.

The second test of the computers had been a resounding success. Every element of the master program had functioned perfectly, thus confirming Francie's triumph over the logical and mathematical difficulties she had faced. Now it was time to put the whole operation into action, and begin a new era of efficient, cost-saving communication among the Magnus European subsidiaries.

Francie was almost too excited to work. She had slept little in the past week, spending all her waking hours either poring over her program or telephoning the far-flung Magnus technicians who would be responsible for managing the system when it was in place.

And when she was not thinking about the program, she was thinking about Jack.

She expected to hear from him at any moment about his plans to arrive in Paris. She knew that what Jack wanted was first to see her system go into formal operation, and then steal her away from Paris headquarters for a brief honeymoon in the Greek Islands. Their getaway would be shrouded in complete secrecy. No one would know they were married until they returned.

That was what Jack wanted. He insisted it was the only safe way, and also the most romantic way. It would allow him to preempt any objection his father might have against his marriage, and at the same time give him total privacy and freedom with Francie.

"I don't want to marry you in St. Bartholomew's Church in New York," he said, "with all the Magnus and Wetherell relatives on hand, along with everyone else in high society who thinks our marriage is his or her business. That's no way for us to start our life together."

Jack wanted his marriage to Francie to be his final and definitive step outside the world of the Magnuses. Francie had no objection to this, for she knew how deeply he needed permanent independence from his family, and especially his father.

Besides, Francie wanted Jack to herself.

And now their long wait was over. Her dream, and Jack's, was about to become a reality.

As she was hard at work in her office Francie was brought a telegram from New York. It read:

RETURN TO MAGNUS HEADQUARTERS NEW YORK IMMEDIATELY STOP
SUSPEND ALL OPERATIONAL PLANS UNTIL AFTER CONSULTATION STOP

It was signed by Sanford Ewell, Senior Vice-President in Charge of Internal Relations and, as everyone knew, Anton Magnus's chief executive assistant and right-hand man on the Board.

Francie tried telephoning the corporation long-distance to tell Mr. Ewell that this was a most inconvenient time for her to leave Paris. But his secretary told her he was unavailable and had left instructions that she was to return to New York immediately, no matter what.

Perplexed, Francie tried calling Jack. But he also could not be reached. So she booked a flight, packed a small bag, told Roland to have her programmers and operators keep the system on hold until he heard from her, and left for New York.

The flight was long and tiring, made worse by Francie's restlessness and her wonderings about what was afoot in New York. Perhaps, she mused, some sort of high-level decision had been made about Europe, and it had affected the timetable for her system. Perhaps the Board required a last-minute report from her before giving its final approval for implementation.

She arrived dazed and exhausted at five o'clock in the afternoon, and immediately called Magnus headquarters. But all the offices were closed. She had just missed them.

Francie went to her apartment on the West Side. Under the influence of her long trip across time lines the place looked strange. She had not seen it in eight months, and it felt alien and almost macabre.

She tried calling Jack at his apartment, but there was no answer. She went out to buy a few groceries, put them in the refrigerator, and took a hot shower. She made herself a simple dinner, and then called Jack again. Still there was no answer.

Francie sat down before the television set in her living room. She turned on the early evening shows, but they seemed bizarre and surrealistic to her. At length she realized that she was experiencing the shock of traveling from one culture to another without warning. Last night she had been in a charming apartment on the Left Bank in Paris, listening to Mozart on the radio and hearing the news of Paris weather and politics in the suave tones of a French announcer.

Now she was seeing Lucille Ball and Desi Arnaz creating rollicking comedy before a shrieking studio audience.

It was too much for Francie. She turned off the television, got into bed, and turned off all the lights.

New York hummed around her with an intensity of sirens, car horns, and rumbling tires a world away from the peace and quiet of the Rue du Cherche-Midi. She felt out of her element, alone and disoriented.

If only Jack were here! He could explain everything, put her mind at rest, ease her nerves.

And take her in his arms . . .

After two more fruitless calls to his apartment, Francie gave up. Her energy was gone. She closed her eyes and fell into a heavy sleep full of troubled dreams.

The next morning, early, she went to Magnus Headquarters.

She showed her identification at the security gate downstairs and, surprisingly, was asked to wait. A few moments later a man she had never seen before appeared from the elevators and held out a hand.

"Howard Aldrich," he said. "I'm representing the Corporation, Miss Bollinger. I need to have a word with you before you see anyone else. Why don't we step into my office?"

He led her to an empty office on the ground floor, only a few steps from the security desk. There he motioned her to a hard wooden chair.

His face was serious.

"Miss Bollinger," he said, "I won't beat around the bush. Magnus Industries, Inc. is terminating your employment as of this moment. I am here to assist you in this transition and to see that things run smoothly. Believe me, your comportment in leaving this building today can and will have incalculable effects on your future in your profession."

Francie's face registered disbelief. She simply could not take in what he was telling her.

He produced a piece of paper.

"I want you to read this," he said. "It's a recommendation, signed by the Vice-President in Charge of Personnel."

Francie took the paper and tried to focus her eyes on the text.

> This is to certify to whom it may concern that Frances Bollinger was employed by Magnus Industries, Inc. from June 25, 1955, to September 3, 1956. During this time Miss Bollinger's work for the corporation was exemplary. She showed herself to be a tireless and dedicated employee, serving the best interests of the Corporation with great energy and effectiveness.
>
> We highly recommend Miss Bollinger for work in any capacity she chooses to pursue, and will ratify this recommendation by phone upon request.

Francie was too stunned by what was happening to notice that the glowing recommendation omitted all reference to computers or to the special project she had worked on for the Corporation.

She looked up at the stranger.

"I don't understand," she said. "If they feel this way about me, why are they firing me?" There was no sarcasm in her voice. She was genuinely amazed.

He smiled. "No one can read the mind of a great corporation," he said. "Let's just say you didn't fit into their plans."

Francie thought of Paris.

"I left a very complicated operation behind me in Europe," she said, forgetting her own emotions. "We're implementing an important new system tomorrow. I delayed it in order to come here today. It's a difficult thing to manage. I'm not sure the people there will know what to do in case of a problem."

The cool smile on the stranger's face—she had forgotten his name by now—made her begin to understand her situation.

"That will all be taken care of," he said. "You don't need to worry about it."

She sighed. "Well," she said, "I guess I'd better clear out my office."

He shook his head. "That's already been done. Your things have been packed and will be delivered to your home, or wherever you say, when you give us the word."

Francie turned a shade paler as she looked into his eyes.

"I have a lot of business and personal things in Paris . . . ," she began.

"Those items are being gathered together at this moment," he said, a glint of ill-concealed sadism in his dark eyes. "They will be forwarded to you here. The Paris apartment will revert to the Corporation. I might add that your security clearance has been revoked in Paris and the other European cities as well as here. That's no reflection on your honesty, of course. It's a routine precaution."

Francie understood. She was *persona non grata* at Magnus from now on. She could no more return to her computer center in Paris than she could go upstairs in this building. To Jack's office, for instance . . .

"All right," she said, clinging to the thought of Jack as she looked into the soulless eyes of the stranger before her. She just wanted to get out of here as fast as possible. Jack would know what was behind all this. She had to talk to him right away.

The stranger led her to the door and held it open for her as she went out onto the sidewalk by Sixth Avenue.

Francie was too stunned to say goodbye to him. She had been brought home from Europe to be summarily fired, and physically escorted out of the building.

She hailed a cab and gave the driver her address.

The minute she was home she picked up the phone. She dialed Magnus Industries. When the receptionist answered she asked for Jack Magnus.

There was a click, and then several rings.

"Mr. Magnus's office."

"Hello. I—is Mr. Magnus in the office at the moment?" Francie asked.

"Whom shall I say is calling?"

"Frances Bollinger."

There was a pause, oddly significant.

"Well, Miss Bollinger," the secretary said, her voice cold now, "I'm afraid Mr. Magnus is unavailable."

"It's really very urgent," Francie said quickly. "I've just been called home suddenly from Europe. It concerns the new computer system we've developed under Jack's—under Mr. Magnus's direction. Really, I must speak to him right away."

"I'm afraid I can't help you, Miss Bollinger. You see, Mr. Magnus is out of the country. He can't be reached."

Francie's hand shook as she held the receiver. "It's really terribly important," she said. "Could you give me an address where I can contact him?"

"No, I can't do that," the secretary said. "He's—not taking any calls."

There was a silence.

"To be honest," the secretary added, "he's—well, he's on his honeymoon."

Francie's blood ran cold.

The secretary was saying something, but it was gibberish to her. After a moment Francie simply hung up the phone.

She turned to look through the window at the city street outside. Nothing looked familiar, nothing welcomed her. She had never really lived here. Events at Magnus had moved too fast to let her settle in.

Now it looked like another world.

She did not know how long she sat there, watching the day pass. Fatigue combined with shock to make her confused. The thoughts flowing crazily through her mind were as meaningless as the objects she saw around her.

The phone rang. Francie picked it up anxiously, hoping that somehow help was on the line. But it was only the storage company that had been hired to hold her things. She was asked when it would be convenient to have them delivered to the apartment. In a daze she said this afternoon would be fine.

An hour later the delivery men brought the boxes containing her few books, pamphlets, and stationery from her office at Magnus Industries, an office she had not seen in eight months. There was a brutal efficiency to everything that was happening. Francie signed for the things, watched the delivery men leave, and sat in a daze, looking at the boxes piled on her living room floor.

At length she noticed that there was a small stack of mail included with her things. Most of it consisted of office memos and junk mail. But she found a note in familiar handwriting, undated.

With trembling fingers she opened it.

Dear Francie,

I am writing to tell you the most important thing I have ever told anyone in my life.

I once tried to warn you about the dangers facing you as well as me at Magnus Industries. Now, too late, I realize I underestimated them.

My father is a powerful man. More powerful than either of us thought. That, and only that, is why things worked out as they have.

Things are not what they seem. My marriage to Belinda is not worthy of the name. One day I will be free of it. When that day comes I will seek you out and try to win your forgiveness and your love.

Until that time I don't have the right to complicate your life with my presence in it.

I don't ask you to forgive me, but only to keep your mind and heart open to the idea that what has happened is not real, not as we were and are real.

And to tell you that I still love you, and will always love you more than myself, more than my life.

Jack

Francie stared down at the note. It was wet with her tears. Then she crumpled it, held it to her breast for a long time, and threw it in the wastebasket.

She sat back down and watched the afternoon crawl by. The passing minutes seemed like so many knives plunged into the wound opening wider inside her heart. Dazed, she no longer even noticed the apartment around her.

When evening was a dark shadow creeping into the room, she got up, picked up the note, uncrumpled it and placed it between two pages of one of her favorite books on her shelf. She closed the book and put it back in its place. Something told her she must not let the note out of her possession.

She watched her little apartment grow darker. Even in the heart of her grief her mind continued working.

There was a lesson in that note. More importantly, there was a lesson in what had happened to her. She realized she was too young, too innocent, too naive to see it yet.

In time, perhaps, she would understand it.

For she had plenty of time on her hands now.

Or did she?

The one thing Jack Magnus could not have known when he wrote that note came into Francie's consciousness with a crash.

She was pregnant.

===== 19 =====

Western Union, September 4, 1956

FROM: Anton Magnus, New York City
TO: Jack Magnus, aboard *M.S. Kungsholm*, en route to Athens

DEAR JACK

CONGRATULATIONS STOP ENJOY YOUR HONEYMOON STOP NO HARD FEELINGS I HOPE STOP

DAD

FROM: Jack Magnus, aboard *M.S. Kungsholm*
TO: Anton Magnus, New York City

DEAR DAD

NO HARD FEELINGS STOP BUSINESS IS BUSINESS STOP BELINDA VERY HAPPY STOP SEE YOU WHEN I GET HOME STOP

LOVE JACK

Book II

QUEEN'S GAMBIT

$$=== 20 ===$$

The Wall Street Journal, *September 10, 1956*

Magnus Computer Breakthrough Announced

Spokesmen for Magnus Industries' European Division have announced a revolutionary computer link-up of the corporation's European subsidiaries using state-of-the-art technology in a way never contemplated before.

Robert A. Bach, Vice-President in Charge of International Systems, made the announcement yesterday at a news conference here. According to Bach, Magnus computer specialists here and in Paris, London, and Lausanne used the IBM 650 computer in modified form, with programs developed by Magnus's computer division, to link up the European facilities' marketing, materials, and fiscal inventories, cutting across language and currency barriers.

"We expect the entire European operation to gain at least 20 percent in productivity in the next three quarters, and possibly much, much more," said Bach. "We feel that Magnus's computer people have made an epoch-making breakthrough here, and one that will affect the entire future of business everywhere."

Francie sat alone in her apartment, gazing numbly at the *Journal* article.

She pondered the odd fact that Jack Magnus's name was mentioned nowhere in the article. That was a fine irony, since Jack was at the center of the entire story—as was, of course, Francie herself.

Her world was whirling around her, crystallizing in forms she had never dreamed of before. All the rules were changed. All her assumptions about herself, about her past, her future, her purpose in life, were shattered. In their place was something new and exquisitely painful, like a cracked mirror whose distorted image is the only truth.

And the heart of that truth was betrayal.

Alongside the *Journal* article she had put the announcement of Jack's wedding to Belinda Devereaux from the *Times*. It had been published nearly a week ago, but she had had plenty of leisure to go to the public library and get a copy of it.

The wedding announcement was brief. It included pictures of the bride and groom, a mention of their famous families, and of course a few words about Jack's distinguished career at Magnus Industries. No mention was made of the couple's long informal engagement. Not even a reader who knew them intimately could know the whole story behind their long-delayed marriage.

Did Francie know it herself?

With this thought in her mind she got up, went to her bookshelf, took down the book in which she had saved Jack's note, and removed the wrinkled piece of paper. Though the feel of it in her hands made her sick to her stomach, she forced herself to reread it.

Almost immediately she found the line she was looking for.

Things are not what they seem.

Francie pondered the line for a long time, and then mentally factored it with the *Journal* item, the *Times* wedding announcement, and the pictures of Jack and Belinda, almost as though these were elements of a theorem which she could comprehend only by putting them all together.

As she looked at the face of Jack Magnus in the photo—the *Times* had used the same picture that was used in the Magnus directory—she realized that Jack's resemblance to his father was really quite astonishing. She wondered how she had failed to see it before. Something about the look in their dark eyes joined father and son, far more than the mere resemblance of their features. They were creatures of the same flesh, after all.

And as Francie studied the pictures, her gaze grown cold as the inside of her heart, she heard the echo of Jack's voice, in Paris, swearing her to silence about their affair and their wedding plans.

Let's keep our plans a secret, he had said.

Francie smiled at her own naiveté. The almost biblical injunction, "nothing is what it seems," was perfectly tailored to punish her own stupidity and her own shame.

Now she understood why Jack had sworn her to secrecy about their affair. She understood why there had been no ring, no solid token to prove that marriage was Jack's real intention. He had never intended to marry her at all.

What, then, had he intended?

I want you to finish your system before we announce our plans.

For the first time since she met Jack, Francie's logical mind turned away from his handsome face and focused itself on his actions and their consequences. Everything was clear now. One only had to look at the end results of her affair with Jack to understand his motives from the beginning. Magnus Industries had its revolutionary computer system, thanks to the programming secret Francie had worked so hard to discover.

And Jack was married to Belinda.

Therefore Jack had intended that Francie complete the computer system for Magnus Industries before he married Belinda. And he had wanted to take his pleasure from Francie's body and her passionate lovemaking as long as he could before the inevitable moment when he betrayed her.

This was the unavoidable, almost mathematical conclusion that must be drawn from the events that had cost Francie her livelihood and broken her heart.

And Jack had done it all.

Francie had been as blind as a child in her dealings with Jack Magnus. Well, she was a child no longer.

It had been two weeks since she had returned from Europe. In those two weeks she had eaten practically nothing, and had barely slept, preferring to spend her nocturnal hours sifting and resifting the terrible facts about herself, about Jack, and about Magnus Industries.

She had never in her sheltered life dreamed of a depth of evil such as she had now encountered. But, having once encountered it, the scales were peeled from her eyes. She felt a new lucidity growing in her with each passing moment.

She knew she had to survive this episode somehow, and go on with her life. She knew that she was made of stronger stuff than the total despair engulfing her now. She was still young. Her whole life was ahead of her. The most important thing was not to allow what Jack had done to destroy her. She must survive.

This she saw with absolute clarity, as though from outside herself.

But she also saw something else, something more terrible and more immediate.

She could not begin to live until she had first destroyed what Jack had done to her. For in stealing her heart, in order to break it, he had planted his seed inside her.

And that seed must be expunged before she could go on with her life.

* * *

On September 20th Marcia Bonner, who still had her job as secretary in Raymond Wilbur's Domestic Products Division at Magnus Industries, received a telephone call from a familiar voice.

"Marcia, this is Francie."

"Francie! How great to . . . I mean, it's wonderful to hear from you." Marcia did her best to hide the catch in her voice. "How are you doing?"

There was a pause on the line.

"Marcia," Francie said in a cold, even tone, "you once told me that if I needed anything in New York, I could ask you. Remember?"

"I—sure, Francie." It had been a long time ago, when Francie was still a newcomer to New York as well as to Magnus Industries, that Marcia had offered to share her streetwise familiarity with the ins and outs of the big city in any way she could. Now that Francie's rapid rise and fall at Magnus were accomplished facts, Marcia was frankly surprised to hear from her old friend.

"Anything I can do," she said. "Really. It will be a pleasure."

Again there was a silence between the two young women. When Francie spoke at last, her voice had a hollowness which made Marcia suspect what the purpose of her call was.

"This won't be a pleasure for either of us," Francie said. "Can I meet you at your place tonight? Say, around eight?"

"Of course, Francie," Marcia replied nervously. "Just take it easy until then, all right?"

"Don't worry about me," Francie said. "See you at eight."

Ten days after her phone call to Marcia Bonner, Francie appeared at the office of Dr. Eugene Brandt, the internist she had consulted a year and a half ago for a routine physical. The young, attractive doctor greeted her warmly, recalling the hopeless crush he had conceived for her on her first visit. But his smile faded when he saw the look in her eyes, and realized how emaciated she was.

"Everything all right?" he asked guardedly. "No physical problems?"

"I'd just like you to examine me," Francie said, her voice neutral.

Within minutes the doctor saw evidence of what she had had done to herself, and understood why this healthy young woman was back in his office.

"What happened?" he asked in a concerned voice.

The look in her eyes amazed him. It was the coldest look he had ever seen. Already knowing Francie as a bright, friendly young woman, Dr. Brandt could hardly believe his eyes. It was as though she had transformed herself overnight into another person.

"An accident," she said quietly.

She refused to answer any further questions. Dr. Brandt examined her thoroughly and found to his relief that the abortion that had been performed on her was competent, and that there was no evidence of infection. He referred her to a gynecologist who practiced in the same West Side building as he, and then ordered her to rest in bed for ten days and return for a follow-up visit.

She returned as instructed, and the doctor found that she was healing well. But her demeanor still disturbed him. There was a tranquillity about her that was almost inhuman. She looked incredibly beautiful in her pallor, but also haunting, witchlike, as though she had been through an ordeal too terrible to reveal.

The doctor could not know that Francie, a young woman brought up to believe that abortion was an unforgivable crime, had survived the previous week by focusing the infinite hatred inside her on everything that was done to her body and to the unborn child inside it. The ordeal had changed her in a way that she herself could not fathom. She knew she had lost her trusting, innocent self forever. But she could not know what kind of person would come to replace it. She could only look to the future to show her what sort of identity would allow her to survive.

For she intended to survive. She had unfinished business to attend to.

The young doctor, not yet married, had been half in love with Francie from the first moment she walked into his office a year and a half ago. Now his heart went out to her even more than before, but he could not help feeling afraid of her. The intensity behind those limpid green eyes alarmed him. It seemed to betoken an extraordinary capacity for love, but also for hate.

The doctor decided against reporting what was obviously an illegal abortion to anyone else. He almost dreaded Francie's follow-up visits to his office. He was glad he knew no more of her story than he did.

When at last he pronounced her entirely healthy, she thanked him politely, shook his hand, and came no more. He continued to dream about her during his lonely nights at home. But now his fantasies about her beauty were overcome by sympathy for her suffering, and awe before the cold determination that had replaced her formerly cheerful personality.

Francie took good care of herself in the weeks that followed. She ate well, took vitamins, and when she was able, began to exercise. She took long walks around Manhattan, enjoying the fall breezes and getting as much sun as she could.

Then she called her father. She told him she had been brought home from Paris because of a serious infection, but was already on the mend. The Paris computer operation, she said, was to be handled by others while she recuperated. She told him this was a perfect opportunity for her to come home for a visit. Delighted at the prospect of seeing her, he agreed.

Mac Bollinger met her at the train station. If he could see how profoundly altered she was by the past month, he managed to hide his emotion. He took her home, got her settled into her old room, which had been kept unchanged for her, and helped her make dinner.

For ten days they lived in the intimacy which had once been their life together. They shopped together, Francie did some sewing for Mac, and they drove around the county. They passed Amish families moving slowly along the country roads in their carriages. The fall colors glowed in the Pennsylvania trees, and the pungent smells of autumn, a season of death and invisible rebirth, were everywhere. Thick stands of pines and birches bordered the pastures like calm sentinels.

In the evening Francie and her father sat on the porch rocking and talking about all the news they had not been able to catch up on during these past months.

In her weakened condition Francie found it difficult to lie to her father. Yet her every word about her experience at Magnus Industries was a lie. The lie she had told when she first hid the truth about how she had got the job at Magnus seemed now to have spread to limitless dimensions. She described a happy work routine in Paris, friends there and in other countries, and the sudden illness that had put her in a French hospital before she came home. She told Mac about the success of her computer plan, and managed somehow to tell him that her promising career at Magnus would resume in New York after her visit with him.

The inventiveness required for so many lies drained Francie, and for the first few days it seemed that she was growing weaker rather than stronger as she puttered around the old house and cooked meals for her father.

Then she began to feel better.

Mac Bollinger could not know that her newfound energy was coming from new ideas growing inside her fertile brain.

Francie was beginning to make plans.

The heady flow of events which had stolen her balance from her during the past year was behind her now. She could take stock of her scars and of her strengths. Already a blueprint for bold action was taking shape inside her mind.

She left Mac Bollinger after ten days, telling him she had to get back to work in New York. She made sure to tell him her work phone would be different now, that he must wait for her to get in touch. Of course her apartment address remained the same.

Sad to leave her father, but delighted to be free of the web of lies she was forced to tell him, Francie returned to Manhattan.

When she got there she began studying the want ads. She shopped for new clothes, and ate as much as she could in an effort to gain weight and look healthy. Then she began applying for jobs at major companies.

Francie was offered jobs at nearly all the firms she approached. But she did not accept them.

She clearly saw that the same prejudice against women which was so integral a part of Magnus Industries also affected the other major companies. She could readily find work in any one of them, but her rank and salary would be far below that of any entry-level male employee. The struggle for advancement and recognition would be a slow and frustrating one at any of these companies. It would be like starting all over again.

This realization forced Francie to rethink her plans. The timetable she had in mind could not tolerate so gradual a progress.

She would have to try another way.

On a windy day in November, eight weeks after the loss of her child, two and a half months after the betrayal that had changed her life, Francie walked confidently into the Manhattan Chamber of Commerce. She was dressed in a business suit, her hair brushed out so that it shone like a lush mane under the pale lights of the office.

"I'd like to find out how to start a business of my own in Manhattan," she told the clerk.

"All right," he said. "Let me get you some information booklets."

She smiled as she accepted the materials. The clerk was too fascinated by her beauty to realize that it was not his own face she was seeing as she thanked him.

It was the face of Jack Magnus.

And behind it, like the image hidden behind a palimpsest, was the face of Anton Magnus.

$$\equiv 21 \equiv$$

Anton Magnus was buried alive.

The coffin was tighter than he had ever imagined. It was impossible to move or breathe. The satin, fetid and noisome, hemmed him in on all sides.

He could not defend himself, not cry out, not move so much as a finger to tear his way out of this foul prison. Yet he was alive!

It was a mistake, an enormous mistake. An innocent accident had occurred, a trifling physical spell or attack. It had left him alive, though in a state of paralysis. But the idiot doctors had consulted with their spectacles and their stethoscopes, murmured to each other in low tones, worried tones—for he was an important man, and they knew that his death was an important event—and in their collective incompetence had pronounced him dead and allowed him to be put into this coffin.

He had spent a lifetime learning to trust no one but himself, for all men, he knew, were weak and confused creatures. Yet now, by a cruel twist of fate, his very life had been placed in the hands of such men, and in their fearful stupidity they had consigned him to this agony.

He was an important man, the most important of men. And thus the coffin was of priceless wood and metal, the finest money could buy. It had been custom made at the request of the bereaved relatives. And now the victim was inside it, helpless, speechless—but alive.

Once under the ground, the fancy box with its polished trim and fine materials was no match for the slow attack of the earth's creatures, the earth's corrosive gases and bacteria and fungi. The box was rotting, no longer a protection, but only a prison.

The odor inside it was unlike anything he had ever smelled in his worst days on the earth. Worse than anything smelled in the war, in the poverty of his youth, in the most ghastly of nightmares. It was sweetish, ripe, and incredibly penetrating. It crept deep inside him and enveloped him like a shroud.

Now he realized why it was so intimate, that cruel stench. It was the stink of his own decay. The slow collapse of his own cells, the rotting of his sinews. The silent, horrid decomposition of his very self.

He would have wept his rage, roared out his very lungs in his panic and agony, were it not for the silence and the immobility, which were the essence of this punishment. He could not move, could not so much as whimper. Yet his nerves were at the point of explosion. His entire being was in the final panicked spasm of flight, when the organism knows that its worst fear has come true, that the predator is upon it at last in hideous triumph.

Yet all he could do was lie here and experience that final, screaming paroxysm of terror as a slow, drawn-out, infinitely spreading instant, devouring him like a silently gnawing worm.

And now the true horror of his situation came to him. For the worm was not a mere idea. It was a reality. A long, undulating, slimy worm of the earth, burrowing its way with infinite patience toward him, slowly displacing the rotting timbers of the box, finding its way through the interstices, chewing easily through the quilted satin until it reached his defenseless, immobile flesh.

And it was not one worm. It was hundreds, thousands. All converging on his prison now, coming closer, closer, moving on tiny rings of flesh, squirming through the earth, the wood, the satin with minuscule but clearly audible sounds of stirring, brushing, gnawing.

For worms have teeth, strong little teeth that tear and grind, and potent digestive juices that corrode and ravage. They are not weak animals, but powerful destroyers, powerful eaters of carrion.

And they were coming closer and closer. The first one was coming up his chest, reaching his neck, his cheek, and crawling, with horrid undulations, along his nose, with unerring patience and precision, toward his eye . . .

Anton Magnus awoke with a start.

For a long moment he looked about him through unseeing eyes, still blinded by the nightmare which was so terrifying and yet so familiar.

Then, his breath still coming short in his throat, he became aware of his surroundings. He was in his study at home, seated in the comfortable armchair before his chessboard. He must have dozed off after dinner while playing over the 1939 Buenos Aires tournament game between Capablanca and Czerniak.

He looked at the clock. Midnight. He had slept for an hour and a half, then. Of course no one had knocked at the door. He left strict orders that when he went into his study alone he was not to be disturbed for anything unless specific orders to that effect were given.

Evenings like this, alone at the chessboard, were Anton Magnus's way of sifting the thousands of details that demanded his attention, and allowing them to simmer in the hot cauldron of his judgment, so that tomorrow, or the next day, or next week, he would be ready to make the decision that might affect thousands of people and millions of dollars.

He liked to sit with an aged calvados—the spicy apple brandy reminding him of his youth on the farm—and slowly replay the great chess matches, matches whose moves he knew by heart. He liked the cool stillness of the chessmen, allied as it was with the brute power and force of their position on the board.

Chess was a cruel game, despite its surface elegance. Through the infinitesimal moves of inanimate men on a checkered board, one could twist the rope around the opponent's throat and squeeze the life out of him.

The real world was no different. Chess had long since taught Anton Magnus how to make his enemies' power into a detriment, how to turn their own force against them, how to make them fall over their own initiative and intellect, so that it was always Magnus who won, Magnus who twisted the fatal knife, pulled the cord tighter, and ended up taking home the winnings.

Anton Magnus sighed now at the sight of his beloved chessmen. The set had been hand made for him by the finest sculptors in Italy. The men were made of turquoise, jade, onyx, and other precious stones. The board was made of marble. A special set of lamps had been installed in the ceiling so as to throw light on the beautiful pieces, bringing out their facets and colors without tiring the eyes.

It was almost as great an esthetic pleasure to gaze upon the men as it was a strategic one to play the game. Anton Magnus relaxed. His nightmare was fading, he was safe at home in his own study, and, as always, master of all he surveyed.

He studied the board. It was the scene of a vicious, silent struggle. At the heart of the middle-game Czerniak had fought off Capablanca's attack with a series of desperate moves, and seemed on the verge of evening the battle. But Capablanca, ever alert to the subtle weaknesses behind his opponent's strategies, stopped him short with a single move of his knight and finished him thirteen moves later.

It was a great game, a masterpiece of logic and strategy. And it had taught Anton Magnus a lot over the years. It was like an old friend. But as he grew older, it seemed less an ideal to be imitated than a reflection of his own life, a sort of monument to his own genius.

For Anton Magnus was, in his way, a genius.

He closed his eyes now, knowing he was safe from the nightmare, and recalled the very first move, the one that had started him on his way in business and sown the seeds of Magnus Industries.

It had been so simple! At the time Magnus had been a twenty-four-year-old immigrant whose life's savings were not enough to buy a Model T Ford. His opponent was one James Q. FitzGerald, a cunning and greedy Chicago businessman out for a quick buck.

FitzGerald owned a lucrative chain of retail stores in the Chicago Loop. He had hired Magnus to be the manager of a new branch store on State Street. In return for his generosity he expected Magnus to contribute three hundred dollars to the firm—a sum which exhausted Magnus's paltry savings. Magnus was to be repaid as soon as the branch proved itself solvent.

FitzGerald intended to pocket the money, of course. After a decent interval he would fire Magnus and find a new victim, another unsuspecting immigrant, to handle the job and pay for the privilege. It was tactics such as this that had made FitzGerald's small fortune.

But Magnus had seen through the plan. And he had one of his own.

James FitzGerald was enamored of a pretty Catholic waitress named Mary O'Shea. He had been paying her court for some time, but she had refused his advances, reminding him of his wife and three sons on one hand, and on the other alluding delicately to her virginity, which she was saving for the Prince Charming she expected to marry one day. But the flickering light in her eyes and the subtle signs of her body in FitzGerald's presence gave him hope, and kept his desire at the boiling point.

Anton Magnus found out about the girl, and spent an evening alone with her. He used a special kind of charm on her, and a special kind of leverage, that were worlds away from the crude blandishments of James Q. FitzGerald.

By that evening's end the plan was set. The next time FitzGerald saw Mary O'Shea she agreed to spend the following Wednesday night with him in a posh hotel on Michigan Avenue. FitzGerald, beside himself with joy, forgot to wonder about what had caused the girl's sudden change of heart. The delight he experienced in her arms during their tryst more than justified his long wait for her. She was a coy and knowing lover, and gave herself to him in inventive ways which left him faint with pleasure.

The morning after their meeting FitzGerald discovered that the key to his business office next door to the Stock Exchange was missing from his key ring. He got a locksmith to let him into his own premises, and immediately discovered that several thousand dollars' worth of negotiable securities had been stolen during the night.

FitzGerald instantly suspected Mary O'Shea of having purloined his precious key. But he could not have her arrested without having word of his intimate relationship with her come out. Not only would FitzGerald's wife learn the truth—a fact of no great importance—but his mother and father, in the Old Country, would hear of it as well. And the good opinion of his parents and the extended family was something James FitzGerald could not live without.

So FitzGerald went himself to the young lady's furnished room, intending to intimidate her into returning the securities in exchange for a promise not to prosecute.

But Mary O'Shea had left her lodgings, and given no forwarding address.

James FitzGerald had no choice but to shrug off the loss and go back to his business.

While FitzGerald was cursing his bad luck, Anton Magnus was cleverly investing the stolen securities on the Stock Exchange and turning James FitzGerald's few thousand dollars into a hundred thousand.

Now it was time for the master move.

Anton Magnus went to FitzGerald and openly admitted his theft. Citing his poverty and his desire to rise in the world, he told FitzGerald of the investments he had made, and returned to him the borrowed securities.

FitzGerald's greed now carried him away. He demanded that Magnus turn over 90 percent of the capital realized on the theft, in return for which he, FitzGerald, agreed not to turn Magnus over to the authorities.

Anton Magnus's lips curled in the smile that was destined to make powerful men cringe in the future. His black eyes bored into James FitzGerald as he made a quiet counteroffer. He, Magnus, would buy out FitzGerald and become sole owner of the entire chain of retail stores, for the sum of fifty thousand dollars—a price approximately one-fourth the value of the chain.

Predictably, FitzGerald laughed in the arrogant immigrant's face.

He stopped laughing when he saw Anton Magnus's hole card.

It was an envelope containing photographs documenting the passionate evening FitzGerald had spent in the arms of pretty Mary O'Shea. All the parts of the couple's naked bodies, and the various positions of their rapture, had been lovingly captured by the camera.

Along with the photographs was a contract providing for the transfer of ownership of the FitzGerald retail empire to Anton Magnus.

Magnus let it be known to James FitzGerald that he had two minutes to sign the contract. If he refused, copies of the damning photographs would be published in tomorrow morning's Chicago *Tribune,* along with a lengthy interview in which Mary O'Shea confessed that she had been seduced by the powerful businessman into a "love nest" relationship.

FitzGerald's signature was on the contract in one minute.

Anton Magnus was now the sole proprietor of a lucrative chain of retail stores, and the possessor of fifty thousand dollars, the remaining half of the money he had earned on the stock market with the certificates borrowed from James FitzGerald.

In the next year Magnus turned his fifty thousand dollars into a million on the bullish stock exchange. Within five years he had turned his lucrative chain of stores into a retailing and manufacturing empire which spread throughout the Midwest. Soon he added a silver mine in Nevada to his holdings, and two apparently dry Texas oil wells which came in not long after his acquisition of them.

By the end of the decade Magnus Industries—for that was by now the name of Magnus's patchwork empire of companies—was worth thirty million dollars.

At about this time, unnoticed by the business world which had long since forgotten him, James FitzGerald, a ruined man who had gambled away his savings and taken to drink, quietly committed suicide by putting his head in the oven in his Chicago kitchen and turning on the gas.

Thus Anton Magnus had used both the greed and the sexual weakness of his victim against him. He had done his research well. He knew all about FitzGerald's business practices, his method of using poor immigrants to line his pockets. And he knew about FitzGerald's marriage and his concern for his family's good opinion of him, before making his first move.

Moreover, Magnus's initial conversation with Mary O'Shea had revealed that her virginity had long since been sacrificed to the exigencies of life in the big city.

After the FitzGerald episode Anton Magnus went on to greater and greater things. But he remained faithful to his initial strategy: he never dealt with an opponent without firm intelligence as to the opponent's weaknesses. And he never took prisoners. In the first ten years of his business life he sent at least a dozen men to their deaths, for he would not compromise where money was at stake. He wanted it all.

Today, forty years later, Anton Magnus had many enemies. But they

ELIZABETH GAGE

could only lick the wounds he had caused them, for his power was too enormous to allow them to contemplate revenge. Magnus had accomplished the greatest feat possible for a man of business: everyone feared him. And since fear breeds submission, no one dared say no to him.

The years had been kind to Anton Magnus. He had a wife from one of the best families in the nation—a special kind of arm-twisting had been required to get her away from her father—and he had a brilliant son and two lovely daughters. He was on top of the world.

He had enjoyed life to the fullest. He had had all the women he wanted, all the pleasures. But none of these matched the chess game of life itself. Great men like Anton Magnus never live for mere enjoyment. They live for challenge, and fulfill themselves by piling achievement on achievement. It is their very insatiability for accomplishment that makes them great, while lesser men, easily satisfied by brute pleasures, leave no mark upon the world.

Anton Magnus was a success.

Of course, his recurring nightmare of being buried alive had come along, many years ago, sometime during his first decade in America. And since then it had tightened its hold on his sleep. But he lived with this discomfort, because each time he awoke from the awful clutches of the dream he recalled that it was only a dream, and that in his real life he was free to do as he pleased.

On the other hand, the years were passing now. Too many had passed, in a silent flow he could not stem. Like all men of enormous power, Anton Magnus had to live with the cruel irony that his influence over the world did not extend to his own body, or to the passage of time which progressively weakened it.

And thus his familiar nightmare had more power to frighten him, to remind him of the fate that awaited him when death came.

Because of the dream, he had long ago decided that he would be cremated when he died. He had left strict instructions as to the medical examinations to be performed upon him after the last illness or accident, and even named the physicians to be called in. He updated this clause of his will constantly. The clause specified that he was to be cremated within one hour of the certification of death.

This certainty that the fate of the dream would be avoided gave Anton Magnus the measure of comfort he needed. He was ashamed of the fearful emotion that motivated him, but he reasoned that every man had a right to fear death.

THE MASTER STROKE

For as long as he retained breath and mind, he would dominate the world around him. Such was his power that after death, too, he would leave his indelible mark upon the world and upon the people in it. And for those who had wronged him or attracted his anger, he would reserve a lingering revenge through various plans worked into his business empire. He had left standing instructions with many of his lieutenants, instructions which would enforce the continuing punishment of those he had decided to hound into permanent penury.

Alive or dead, Anton Magnus was a force to be reckoned with.

He looked from the chessboard to the antique clock on the bookshelf. A quarter past twelve.

Across town, exhausted from taking care of her baby, Gretchen must be fast asleep. Magnus wondered if her worthless husband was at home. Probably not. He was probably out screwing some starlet, or gambling somewhere. That marriage was a failure. But it had served its purpose financially.

As for Jack, he was either at home with Belinda, or at the office working. No one worked harder than Jack.

That was because no one knew better than Jack how important business was. He had learned this from his father, and never forgotten it.

Anton Magnus was proud of his son. But this did not mean he trusted him. He knew perfectly well that Jack had given up his flirtation with that pretty Bollinger girl, and married Belinda after all, because he knew this was no time to displease his father. It was a strategic and necessary move on his part.

Jack was playing a waiting game. He did what his father wanted, gracefully, for he knew it was up to Anton to pass the reins of the greatest corporate power in the nation into his son's hands when the inevitable time for retirement came.

Jack believed, rightly enough, that time was on his side. If he kept his father happy for the short run, the reins of Magnus Industries would fall to him when Anton Magnus was forced by age and infirmity to relinquish them. Then he would go his own way, without a thought for the father's wishes. In his heart of hearts—like Anton before him—Jack cared only for himself.

This arrangement suited Anton, for he wanted the corporation to stay in the family, and wanted someone at its helm whom he knew and whose actions he could predict.

It was an interesting chess match between a father whose powers were inevitably limited by time, but whose intellect and cunning were undiminished—and a clever son who believed he had only to wait for the keys to the kingdom to pass into his hands.

Anton Magnus intended to win this game, age notwithstanding. He admired Jack's ability, and intended to use him to the hilt. He had plans for Jack, and for Magnus Industries, that extended far beyond his own retirement. As a chess master he owed it to himself to pull the strings, even if he was no longer personally in charge.

Jack, of course, had different ideas. He could hardly wait to get rid of his father and go his own way.

But Jack, whatever his qualities, was not half the man his father was.

And where was Juliet at this moment?

Out tomcatting somewhere. She was no doubt drunk with one lothario or another, perhaps drugging herself, and getting into as much trouble as she dared.

But before long she would come home.

Anton Magnus decided he would visit her tonight.

He allowed his thoughts to travel over the earlier years of his marriage, when he had long since lost any attraction he might have once felt for his wife, and when his many easy conquests of hungry, ambitious young women had begun to bore him.

It was then that he had found himself fascinated by little Gretchen.

She was a proper child, an intelligent and somewhat prim creature. Perhaps that was what had attracted him to her, along with the odd sight of her spindly little nine-year-old legs, her delicate hands, her odd childish aroma.

He had toyed with the idea of having sex with her, but had second thoughts. She was his own flesh and blood, after all. A defenseless child . . .

Then, as much to silence his own scruples as to enjoy her body, he had gone to her room late one night, awakened her from her sleep, and seduced her.

She had given in to him pliantly, her eyes full of awe, wordlessly accepting his warning never to tell anyone of what had passed between them. And the pleasure he took from her flesh was small compared to the excitement of breaking the mysterious law against incest.

Later Gretchen grew troubled, and he knew it was because of what he had done to her. But this did not stop him. And when Juliet was six, infinitely more pretty than Gretch had ever been, and infinitely more mercurial, he had done it to her as well.

With Julie the piquant sense of sin and danger had been even greater, for behind the awe and terror in her eyes there was something wild which excited him. As she grew up that wildness became self-destructive and extremely violent. Even tonight it was directing her steps, wherever she was, and perhaps leading her into deep trouble.

And that was because of Anton Magnus, too.

As his girls got older—Gretchen permanently cowed and passive, now, and Julie wayward and uncontrollable—he sometimes asked himself whether he would eventually suffer some punishment for what he had done. After all, incest was a mortal sin. Even a man as arrogant as Anton Magnus could not help feeling awed by the thought that he had gone against nature, and caused incalculable harm.

But this very thought flattered his pride.

He reflected that in many societies, and even in Christian society only a few hundred years ago, incest with daughters was looked on as a man's right, when a man was king of his own castle. It was only in modern times that the prohibition had become consecrated by usage, so that incest was thought of as an unspeakable crime. Anton Magnus considered himself a throwback to the days when it was permitted for a strong man to have his way with his chattel, with all those females under his roof.

In this way Anton Magnus justified himself. He was different from ordinary men, and thus did not have to obey ordinary rules. So he took his pleasure from Gretchen, and then Julie, without losing sleep over it.

After all, he sometimes told himself, they were only females. It was not as though either was a male heir. It was not as though either of them was Jack.

This thought was in his mind now as he got up to take a shower, and then to read in bed until he heard Juliet come home.

With a satisfied sigh Anton Magnus turned out the light over his chessboard. The pawns were precisely where he wanted them. He had put them there—and there they would stay, until he chose to move them again.

He was master of his world.

=== 22 ===

While Anton Magnus was yawning before his chessboard, his daughter Julie was lying on her stomach amid tumbled bedclothes, stifled gasps of ecstasy escaping her lips to die against the pillow.

Johnny was inside her, buried so deep that it seemed he had taken possession of her very flesh. His slow thrusts overwhelmed her with their force and intimacy, so that her little cries were a sensual mingling of agony and delight.

He worked smoothly at her, not merely pumping as another man might have ineffectually pumped at her small loins, but probing, exploring, setting each sinew afire, proving with each stroke that she was his thing, his slave, that none of those secret places would ever forget his touch or cease clamoring for it.

She heard him murmur, "Come on, babe." He ground himself deeper into her, so deep and so tight that she thought she would burst.

"Oh, God," she cried into the pillow. "Oh, God . . ." But her moans were not complaints, really. They were cries of rapture, the rapture of a proud girl who does not like to surrender the tiniest portion of her freedom to any man, and whose surrender is therefore the hotter and the more piquant to the rare man who can force it from her.

"Baby," he cajoled, knowing she was on the edge of her final paroxysm, and enjoying the suspense. "Come on. Give it to Daddy."

His words were the final taunt. Weeping her pleasure into the sheets, she gave him her last frantic groan, and collapsed in helpless orgasm, tears streaming from her eyes.

Only now did he slowly push himself the last inch and, holding her steady and calm with his large hands, let the white river of his pleasure inundate her.

"Oh, God," she repeated, beside herself. "Oh, God . . ."

For a long moment they stayed that way, his hands on her haunches, his sex throbbing to the hilt inside her, not ebbing in the slightest. He enjoyed knowing how completely he filled her, and how completely he owned her.

He looked down and watched her little hands clench and unclench in the sheets. He studied the smooth shape of her back, her fragile spine, her slender shoulders, and the pretty girlish globes between which he was buried. How delightful she was! Such a creamy and yielding creature in his arms, but with so strong a will behind those cool blue eyes of hers. A will he enjoyed breaking. And so sharp an intelligence as well—an intelligence he could reduce to heaving animal surrender at his whim.

But it was not so simple as that.

Now that he knew Julie better he found himself needing her in a way he was not familiar with needing women. Something about her smallness, her smooth porcelain skin, fascinated him. And he was impressed by the perverse way she welcomed him in all the forbidden places.

She was someone special, not only in her own hothouse world, but also to a man like Johnny, who came from outside it. A rare and exciting flower.

"I haven't seen you in a while, Princess," he said. "What have you been up to?"

She sighed, turning over on her back and putting a hand behind her head. She purred like a kitten satisfied with its bowl of milk.

"Not much," she responded.

It was a non-response, and it bothered Johnny. He had noticed how rigorously she kept her own life separate from her trysts with him. She had told him about her famous family, describing it in few words, words tinged with contempt. But he had been aware that her brevity was not merely a result of hatred for her family. It also signified a desire to keep him away from her life.

At first this attitude had suited him perfectly. He enjoyed knowing how much more intimate was his contact with her than any of the society faggots she hung around with. Her behavior in bed left no doubt of that.

But now he was not so sure of his feelings on this score. True, she was sharing a part of herself with him that no other man knew. But the rest of her remained walled off from him.

And this invisible part was troubling.

"Not much, eh?" he said. "I find that hard to believe."

She said nothing. She was looking into his eyes, not without concern, but certainly without fear.

"Well?" he asked.

Her lovely brow knitted in a look of irritation.

"Do I interrogate you about your private life?" she asked. "You're not jealous already, are you, lover? Just because we've done a little fucking in an out-of-the-way place?"

Johnny frowned. Her tone was condescending.

He studied her. How different she was from the ordinary, common girls he screwed in the course of his days. There was a delicate sculptural elegance about her that he had never seen in a woman before. And underneath it was the brittle, scarified edge that gave such tang to her words, her little smiles, her movements. She was a complex creature. She had been hurt, that was easy to see. She was sensitive underneath her cynical exterior. And that sensitivity made his heart go out to her. But she never shared it with him through her words.

And for this there was a reason. Julie was a proud girl, a girl of her exalted class. Johnny was acutely aware that she was sharing herself with him as an outsider, as someone who could never belong to that society, who would never even once see it from inside.

More yet, he knew she belonged to that society in every sinew of her body and in every cranny of her soul. It had formed her, and she was its creature. And from the point of view of her society—however much she loathed it and rebelled against it—he himself was a low, cheap, even outlandish figure, a man from the gutter.

This, he suspected, was part and parcel of the pleasure she took with him—slumming. She understood that none of the cream-puff men of her social class could ever satisfy her in bed the way he could. But this fact, and even the panting, weeping surrender that went with it, still indicated that in her mind he was a freak, a sort of stallion born of another breed from her own, a creature whose sexual gifts were all of a piece with his Brooklyn accent, his cheap cologne, his mind unpolished by education.

And thus, though he might pleasure her, dominate her even, she would never dream for an instant of giving him her respect as she gave it to the men of her society. Much less her troubled heart . . .

And when the time came, it would be one of those other men, those smooth, empty, cold-eyed society faggots, that she would marry, and whose children she would bear.

These thoughts filled Johnny with frustration and disgust. He loathed his own sensitivity, and resented Julie for filling him with confused feelings.

So now he released her, sat back, lit a cigarette, and leaned against the headboard of his own bed, feeling moody.

She sensed his upset. She sat up, naked, and lit a cigarette of her own. How pretty she was in her small blond beauty! Even now his seed nestled between her legs, as the satisfaction in her lovely features made clear.

But the look in her eyes was troubled. She had felt through her feminine

radar that he had withdrawn from her. She sat smoking, and looking at
him.

"You're a long way off," she said. "Penny for your thoughts."

He said nothing, but watched the smoke from his cigarette hover like a
screen between himself and the naked girl.

"Come on, lover," she said, reaching to graze his knee. "You were
dynamite, as always. What's got you down?"

He looked at her. He could not find words to express what he was
feeling. The hurt inside him was upsetting, for he lived only by his pride,
and he could not admit to any kind of weakness or emotion.

Suddenly he said, "Tell me about your father."

She looked perplexed. "My father?"

"Yeah," Johnny said. "What's he like, anyway?"

She looked at him through pained, almost angry eyes. He sensed that
the subject was taboo. That must be why she had never spoken of it before.
Perhaps that was why he had brought it up now—to squeeze her, to make
her ill at ease.

"Why do you care?" she asked cautiously.

"I want to know," he said, a bit stubborn now.

Julie sighed.

"He's an asshole," she said. "Does that answer your question?"

There was a silence.

Slowly Johnny shook his head. "Not quite, babe. What kind of asshole?"

She sighed again. Clearly she was uncomfortable. "The worst kind. The
worst in the world . . . Jesus Christ, Johnny, why did you have to bring
him up?"

He smiled, determined. "He's your father. I'm your man. Your only
man. I have a right to ask you about him."

He could see her flush with anger in the shadows.

"A right?" she asked.

He could feel her strong will rising up against him. He already knew,
from various small hints dropped in the past, that she hated and feared her
father, and was in awe of him. Johnny could understand this, since Anton
Magnus was such a remote and daunting figure. Perhaps, again, this was
why Johnny had chosen this moment to bring the old man up. Because he
knew the old man meant something special to Julie, had a special place in
her thoughts. And Johnny wanted to share those thoughts as he had
already shared her flesh.

He saw that she was angry and upset. So he decided to push harder.

"A right, yeah." He looked at her. "I'm part of your life. I've got a right
to know a little something."

His talk of rights over her had irritated her. She shot him an angry look.

"That's where you're wrong, stud," she said with palpable venom. "You're a great lay, but that doesn't give you rights."

"What's that supposed to mean?" he asked.

Her lips curled in a twisted smirk.

"I've got a great stallion over at Forest Hills Stables," she said. "He can give me a terrific ride, better than any horse in the county. But that doesn't mean I have heart-to-heart talks with him about my problems, Johnny. Think about that."

The last words sank into his flesh like a knife. She had made the mistake of denigrating his intelligence. He had never allowed that, and never would.

He reached out slowly, caressed her shoulder, and caught her by the hair. He pulled her face downward on the bed, so violently that she cried out. She was doubled over, her face pushed down between her spread thighs, crying out in pain.

"Listen, pussy," he said through clenched teeth. "I'm no stallion. In case you think that's what I am, you're in for more trouble than you know."

He let go of her hair and, before she could react, slapped her hard across the face. His large palm caught her ear, her cheek, and her lips. He was surprised to see blood starting out at the corner of her mouth. He had not realized he had hit her so hard. And she was so small, so fragile . . . Her eyes had filled with tears. His heart went out to her at the sight of her vulnerability.

But she was looking at him through eyes in which fear mingled with something infinitely more wounding to him. She was stunned by the power of the blow, and by his anger. But she was measuring him across that terrible distance, almost condescendingly, the way a white mistress must have looked in awe and contemptuous terror at a large Negro slave on the selling block a century ago. Her fear included no respect. Her concern betrayed no real consideration. She was looking at him from within the ivory tower of her class, a tower he could never penetrate as he penetrated her soft body so easily.

"Well?" he asked, his hands dangerously poised to seize her again.

"That's the first time you've hit me," she said.

"Probably not the last," he said. "You knew what you bargained for, Cinderella. This is real life, too, you know."

"What's that supposed to mean?" she asked.

He looked at her appraisingly. A sort of bravado came into his eyes.

"He can't be as tough as all that," he said. "What can it take to be able to con a lot of people out of their money, and to keep a bunch of company slobs afraid of him? Not that much, I bet."

He felt her bristle at these words. But she remained silent.

"Maybe I'll meet him sometime," he said. Then, having measured her silence, he added, "Maybe I'll make it my business to meet him sometime."

"You'd never get close enough to shout hello across Times Square," Julie said. "And if you did, he'd squash you like a bug."

She regretted her words almost immediately. She realized there had been something innocent and boyish about his bravado. All she had had to do was deflect his anger, his hurt pride, and assure him he meant more to her than Anton Magnus ever had. But her words had slipped out with a will of their own. And now it was too late.

Johnny reached out with one strong hand and pulled her naked to his lap. The grip of his hand on her arm was painful, and she cried out. She knew he could break the arm with one twist of his wrist. He buried the other fist in her hair and pulled hard. She winced, and a childlike whine of pain escaped her lips.

He raised a hand to strike her. He would teach her a lesson.

But he looked down at her, a helpless, angry little nymph with her soft body and the sweet place between her legs. The terror and pain in her eyes touched him.

He pulled her face close to his. The blood was still trickling out at the corner of her mouth. Slowly, holding her by her hair, he pulled her closer, and licked at the blood. It tasted hot and pungent and strange. Like a cat he licked at it, cleaning it from the wound he had caused.

Her eyes went dim. A sigh escaped her lips. Then her little tongue came to join his, to lick at the slick male member which was cleansing her of her blood. The tongues played with each other for a moment, and a little moan stirred in her throat, a moan he knew all too well.

He kissed her more deeply, and pushed her down into the sheets. Her anger and hurt were still all over her face, but eclipsed now by desire, just as the trickle of blood was eclipsed by the slick wash of his own saliva.

He reached to touch her nipples, gently, and watched the flicker of response in her eyes. He ran a finger down her stomach and gently ringed her belly button, softly so as not to startle her, but so sensually that he felt a shudder run through her loins.

He smiled. The finger paused, grazing the downy hair on her stomach, and then crept downward, caressing the sweet smooth skin beneath the navel until it reached the golden tuft between her legs. Holding her with his gaze, he let the finger travel further down, until it found the moist essence of her, hot and ready for him. He watched her eyes half-close.

"Now what?" he asked softly.

"Please, Johnny," she begged. "I'm sorry I made you mad. Come on. Don't tease me."

The finger was probing delicately at the tender sex eager for his touch. He felt her back arch, saw the pert little breasts tremble, and noticed a tiny drop of new blood at the corner of her mouth.

His lips reached that little spot, and he licked it carefully, at the same instant his sex found the other, hidden lips, and slid smoothly between them to its hilt.

The moan in her throat was almost desperate.

"Oh," she murmured. "Oh, God, Johnny. Oh, please."

Sure of her submission now, he placed his strong hands under the smooth globes beneath her waist, raised her up like a doll to position her for his strokes, and began to hump her carefully. She trembled and cried and sang her surrender, jerking and squirming in his grasp. Her orgasm was coming faster, because of the violence that had joined them. This was their reconciliation, this hot coupling.

And somehow the pain and the rebellion of this girl made his own pleasure rise quickly within him, for he wanted and needed to give it to her, and to taste hers in return. She had got under his skin now, she was no longer the rich society girl he had bragged to his friends about. She mattered, in her flesh and her anger and her hurt.

And for the hundredth time, as he teased her with his power over her, and her female sinews trembled with her inexhaustible need for him, he felt that tiny part of her recede, the one part he could not touch for good or for ill.

He thought of her father. Somewhere in those depths where Julie kept herself hidden, the father, a remote figure in countless photographs, dressed in thousand-dollar suits and entertaining crowned heads and politicians, the father dwelt, and owned her. The look in her eyes just now had confirmed it, even as the tremors of her body proved the dominion Johnny had over it.

Johnny would not forget this. It had passed between them almost by accident tonight, bringing with it the first rift between them. But he would never forget it now. It was too late.

The anger he felt toward her was inseparable from the prohibited tenderness thrilling dangerously through him, a tenderness which wanted not merely physical possession, but love.

So it was that the knife of his jealousy twisted sharply inside him at the same instant that his seed came forward to give itself to Julie. And as the final spasm burst, Johnny was shaken as never before. Having cared too much, he had given too much. And the creature in his arms, more enigma than woman, stole his seed while withholding her soul.

What a thrill it was to feel her soft body in his embrace! But the rage that had made him strike her, moments ago, came to take up hidden residence in the arms that held her to him now. It could be banished no more. It was here for good.

With this troubling thought at the back of his mind, Johnny pulled Julie closer and kissed her lips.

23

New York, January 25, 1957

Eight weeks had passed.

It was a cold and windy Monday morning. The city seemed hunched on itself under a bleak sky, preparing to endure the first real onslaught of winter.

In a tiny midtown storefront on 40th Street not far from Seventh Avenue, Francie sat alone at the beat-up, used desk which was her place of work.

There was nothing in the one-room storefront except this desk, her swivel chair, a file cabinet, a wooden visitors' chair with standing ashtray, a work table, and a couple of posters on the walls advertising IBM computers.

On the storefront window was a sign, painstakingly designed and painted by Francie herself:

COMPUTEL, INC.
Business Computer Consultants

Francie had just managed the rent on the place with her savings from her year's work at Magnus Industries. She knew she could not survive in business for more than a couple of months without a contract of some sort.

After setting up the storefront, she had placed tiny ads in the business papers and sat down to wait for responses. Unable to bear the tension of her inactivity, she immersed herself in every technical journal and scientific publication having anything to do with computers. She did her homework, learning everything she could about state-of-the-art advances in computer technology and programming. She knew her livelihood might depend on her being in command of all the facts available.

She also knew that, in the happy event anyone came to her for consulting help, she would have to be able to devise a program in a minimal amount of time to handle the inventory and fiscal needs of a midsize business in an affordable way. Already her fertile brain had managed to devise concepts, loosely derived from her work at Magnus, which could do the job.

There was still the question of hardware. Francie of course possessed no computer of her own, and would be lucky to be approached by a firm that did. She had made inquiries about gaining access to local mainframe computers, and had found that time could be bought on them, but only at high rates. She would have no choice but to pass this considerable expense along to her customers—when and if they came. It would make her work much less affordable than she had hoped.

This was a problem that not even Francie's considerable intellect could solve.

Still, she intended to stick it out until she could find a way to get her company off the ground. She knew that computers were the wave of the future in American business. She intended to stay at the forefront of computer development, come what might. She would survive until the right thing came along.

She wondered, though, whether her new business would fold before ever having served its first customer.

She had managed through an effort of will to keep up her courage in the face of the fact that not a single customer appeared at her door in the first two weeks of operation. Her only visitor was the mailman, who brought the phone bill and some junk mail. Her only phone calls were wrong numbers or salesmen who tried to sell her office equipment.

Her days were a torment, alone in the office listening to the indifferent traffic go by outside the windows. Her nights were spent in restless somnolence, filled with images of a past she could not bear to ponder and a future which was inscrutable as a dark crystal.

She knew that her greatest enemy was hopelessness. And to combat hopelessness she looked at the clippings she had put on her bulletin board, clippings from the business press describing Magnus Industries' ground-breaking computer link-up system.

She knew it was her invention, the fruit of her own intellect. She had set it up single-handedly for Magnus; she would do the same for other companies. The talent was hers, as was the idea.

I am valuable, she told herself over and over. *I am worth something. I have something to contribute.*

She repeated it, but she had more and more trouble believing it.

On this day she was seated at her desk, teeth gritted as usual, watching the passersby outside out of the corner of her eye as she tried to concentrate on the technical journal in her hands.

To her surprise, one of the faceless pedestrian figures paused in front of the shop, staring at the sign. He was a young man in his twenties, dressed in jeans and a leather jacket. He looked rather rumpled and unkempt under the bright sun.

He looked at the sign and then peered through the window. He seemed doubtful. But after an interval he opened the creaky door and came in. The bell jingled hollowly to announce his arrival.

Francie looked up at him and smiled.

"Can I help you?" she asked.

He looked at the posters on the walls and the old furniture.

"Maybe not," he said. "From your ad in the papers, I thought you might have a bigger operation."

Francie raised an eyebrow.

"We're big enough for what we do," she said, mustering a confident smile.

He came toward her desk and stood looking at her, resting his hands on the back of the visitors' chair without sitting down.

"And what is that?" he asked.

"I beg your pardon," Francie said.

"What sort of consulting do you do?" he asked. There was skepticism in his expression, but no real disrespect.

Francie cleared her throat, preparing to lie as best she could.

"I—I mean we—" she began, "we design computer systems for businesses. Whatever your needs are, we'll tailor a program to handle them. We rent hardware here in the city, unless you have your own."

He stood gazing down at her, apparently not at all impressed by her carefully wrought lie.

Then he asked the question she dreaded most.

"Who have you done work for?"

Francie cleared her throat. Then she gave the only answer she could. It was not entirely truthful, but it was not a complete lie, either.

"We did some work for Magnus Industries," she said. "You may have heard about it. An interface system for their European subsidiaries. We did most of the set-up and all the idea work on that."

A doubtful look came over his face.

"I didn't know a company like Magnus used outsiders," he said.

"They did this time." Francie tried to control her blush.

Luckily for her, he changed the subject.

"How many people do you employ?" he asked.

"Uh, seven—counting myself," she said, not meeting his eyes.

He pulled the chair back and sat down. As he did so she realized that he was slightly overweight, a fact which added to his rumpled look. His hair was a nondescript sandy color. His eyes were tawny brown, and lazily intelligent. They were looking at her more closely now.

"You wouldn't be telling me a white lie, would you?" he asked.

"I'm sure I don't know what you mean," she said.

"You wouldn't be all alone here, would you?" he asked.

"I'm the only one here today," she said bravely. "Everyone is out working. Someone has to stay in the store."

"Ah." There was a twinkle of amusement in his eyes. "Well, I'm glad to hear you're doing so well. I don't think I came to the right place, though."

"Really?" Francie asked, trying to conceal her disappointment. "Are you sure we can't help you?"

"Not unless you've got a job for me," he said. "The fact is, I'm looking for work. I saw your ad in the papers and thought you might need help."

Francie's face fell.

"Oh," she said. "In that case, I guess you're right. We're not, uh, hiring. Not right now."

He looked at her appraisingly. The same glint of humor was in his eyes, and playing subtly over all his features. He took out a cigarette and lit it, never taking his eyes off her. The smoke curled toward the ceiling in the stale air of the office.

"I'd be interested to hear about this job you did for Magnus," he said. "I understand it was a rather involved job."

Francie said nothing. She wondered why he had not left.

He looked around him. "Am I wasting your time?" he asked. "Did you have something else to do?"

"I—no," she said. "Well, the Magnus job was a programming problem above all. We got the hardware from IBM, and I—we—wrote the programs to link up the subsidiaries."

"What kind of automatic coding did you use?" he asked.

Francie raised an eyebrow. "A variation on the 422," she said, "with an algebraic compiler we designed ourselves."

She went on with her description, not hesitating to make the language technical, for she wanted to show him that she knew her field, and that her work was genuine.

He interrupted her with another question, then another, both of which went straight to the heart of what she had done for Magnus. His language was as technical as hers, and she had to do some fast mental shuffling to keep up with him. It was a sort of intellectual jousting which alarmed and stimulated her at the same time. By the time it was over she knew he was a computer expert in his own right. She also knew that he now took her seriously.

He stubbed out his cigarette.

"They didn't give you credit for it in the press, did they?" he asked.

She hesitated. "Well, that's a long story," she said. "It needn't concern you."

He gave her another probing look.

"Well," he said, glancing around the beat-up storefront, "the important thing is that you're doing well for yourself."

Francie nodded, a wan smile on her face.

"But," he said, standing up, "if you're not hiring, you're not hiring. Thanks for talking to me." He turned to leave.

Francie stood up to walk him to the door. As she did so she noticed the oddity of his appearance. Though he was tanned as a construction worker, and looked like one in his shabby jeans and ancient leather jacket, there was also something gentle and languid about him. It took root in those dreamy brown eyes and seemed to radiate through his body. He was hardly a matinée idol. But he carried himself with an ease that was masculine in a way she had never seen before.

Somehow she was loath to see him leave. She had enjoyed ventilating her bottled-up reminiscences about the Magnus job, and had been pleased to see how impressed he was by her knowledge of her field.

Perhaps reading her mind, he stopped at the door and turned to her.

"Tell you what," he said. "If you won't hire me, how about having dinner with me?"

Francie hesitated, looking into his eyes.

"It'll make me feel better," he said. "If you've ever pounded the pavement before, you know what job-hunting is like."

He glanced at the office behind her. "I see you have to hold the fort until your colleagues get back," he said. "Why not meet me for dinner later? Say, around seven?"

Francie looked at her watch. "I guess I could get away," she said. "Where did you have in mind?"

"The Automat on Forty-second and Third," he said.

She looked at him uncertainly.

"Us job-hunters have to watch our pocketbooks," he added with a grin.

The look in his eyes was still tinged with irony, but also with a calm self-possession which intrigued Francie. His conversation about computers had impressed her. This, and the mention of the Automat, were enough to make up her mind.

"It's a date," she said.

Three hours later Francie was seated at one of the chipped Formica tables at the Automat, having watched Sam Carpenter—for that was his name—eat a large plate of spaghetti and a slice of apple pie while she managed a cheese sandwich. Now she was sipping her coffee and watching him light up his third cigarette of the evening.

"You smoke too much," she said.

He nodded lazily, the smoke curling up over his tanned face. She noticed that his hands looked rough, almost like those of a workman.

"You don't eat enough," he rejoined.

They both smiled.

Their dinner conversation had been sparse so far, concentrating on the weather and the expense of life in New York.

"Tell me about yourself," Francie said.

He shrugged.

"Not much to tell," he said. "I grew up in upstate New York. Ithaca, by Cayuga Lake. I went to Northwestern's Tech Institute. I married a girl there. A girl from the Midwest. Then I dropped out when they drafted me after Korea started."

He paused to puff at his cigarette, a Lucky Strike.

"In the army I worked on the trajectory boards for the ground-to-ground missiles," he said. "They were computerized. That's how I got into computers. When I got home my wife was waiting with the divorce papers. She said that time had come between us. Words to that effect. I didn't make a stink. The look in her eyes made it clear she had another fellow."

Again he paused.

"No children?" Francie asked.

He shook his head. From a sidelong light in his eyes Francie guessed that this was a subject of considerable regret for him.

"Anyway," he said, "I had a lot of computer experience under my belt by that time. So I decided to forget about Northwestern and look for work. I got a job at one of the big companies here, and did fairly well for a couple of years. Then I began to realize that the jungles over here are about as bad as the ones over there. Worse, in a way. In the war you knew who your enemies were. In a big corporation, you begin to wonder whether you have any friends at all."

Francie had to suppress her bitter smile at these words. How well they described her own experience!

"So I quit," he said. "I hung out here and there, did a little free-lance work, and tried a couple of other big companies. Then I dropped out. Went home, spent some time doing odd jobs around my hometown, and did a lot of fishing. Now I'm back looking again."

His eyes turned to Francie.

"What about you?" he asked.

She cleared her throat. She did not want to tell him the whole truth, certainly not about Magnus. And she suspected that he had told her only an outline of his own experience.

"Well," she said, "I was born in a small town in Pennsylvania, in the Amish country. My father was a local handyman and builder. He's still at it, as a matter of fact. He's a sort of tinkerer, and a dreamer. I bet you'd like him," she added, looking at Sam's lazy eyes, and imagining the two men fishing together. "He's not terribly practical, though. He likes to work with his hands, and doesn't understand much about money. My mother handled that end, until she died. He would have been off swapping stories with farmers all day if she hadn't kept him on the straight and narrow."

"When did she die?" Sam asked.

"When I was fourteen," Francie said, not concealing the sadness that came over her face. "That was ten years ago. It seems like more."

She felt his nod. There was a silence.

"My story is more conventional than yours," she went on. "I went to Penn, and then straight to Magnus. I had a fairly productive year there . . ."

"Who was your boss at Magnus?" Sam asked suddenly.

Francie blushed.

"I—I beg your pardon?" she asked.

"I mean, who got you started on the European plan? That must have cost money."

Francie tried to hide the evasion in her eyes. She did not want to talk about Magnus. On the other hand, Sam's question required a simple answer, and she could not very well refuse to give it.

"Jack Magnus, I suppose," she said with studied indifference. "His people got the credit for it in the end, anyway. But it was my idea. As you say," she added with a frown, "corporations are jungles . . ."

She fell silent for a moment. She wanted desperately to change the subject.

"Isn't he the boss's son?" Sam asked. "I think I've read about him in the press."

Francie nodded. Her blush had deepened despite herself.

"Anyway," she concluded, "they let me go, so I sat around for a while wondering what to do, and then I decided to start CompuTel."

She met Sam's eyes. Though his look of languid curiosity had not changed, she could feel his sharp mind evaluating what she had said, and perhaps drawing conclusions she did not want him to draw. She realized she had revealed more than she had intended, and already undone some of the lies she had told him earlier at the office.

Yet he said nothing. There was a pause while he watched his stubbed-out cigarette smolder in the cheap metal ashtray.

"Well, you're different from me," he said. "In your place, I would have gone home to Pennsylvania and wasted a year or two fishing. You've jumped right back into the fray."

She pondered his words. He had put his finger on something about her that she had never quite faced before. She was, indeed, a driven individual. She lacked her father's dreamy accommodation to reality. She was not made to rock on a front porch or sit in a fishing boat, watching the world go by. She seemed to have inherited her mother's hardheaded determination to keep things under control, but with a large dose of ambition thrown in.

Looking across the table at Sam, who possessed the curious combination of great intelligence with a lazy refusal to let the world force him into its rat race, she thought she saw a youthful image of her own father. She envied him his unflappable repose.

"Do you have brothers and sisters?" she asked.

He shook his head. "You?"

Francie shook her head.

There was another silence. The spell between them seemed to deepen. It was as though each had now said enough. Their few words had brought them to a strange closeness. Though she hardly knew him, Francie felt less alone now that she had met him. He seemed to share her solitude without intruding on it. The feeling was pleasant. The Automat, so unromantic, was perhaps the ideal setting for such a relationship.

Francie looked at the cold coffee in her cup. She felt a grip of pain. She realized how lonely she had been for the last three months—and, indeed, before that as well.

He looked up at her. His face was serious, but very kind.

"There aren't any other people working with you, are there?" he asked. "You did tell me a little white lie, didn't you?"

Francie hesitated. Part of her wanted to get up and get away from this man as fast as possible. She had already revealed far too much, stumbled too quickly over the traps he had laid for her.

But the sympathy in his eyes took away her courage.

"There's no one else," she said.

He nodded, and looked around at the tired patrons of the Automat who were either chewing mechanically at their food or staring into space.

Then he sat forward.

"Are you in a hurry to get home?" he asked.

Francie looked at her watch. It was eight-thirty.

"Well . . . what did you have in mind?" she asked.

"If you have time to take a subway ride with me down to Spring Street, there's something I'd like to show you," he said.

"I—is that where you live?" she could not help asking.

"Yes, but it's not what you're thinking." He smiled. "It's not my etchings I want to show you."

There was a pause.

"What, then?" Francie asked.

"It's a computer."

For the first time since she had met him she saw a look of almost childlike excitement in the eyes of Sam Carpenter.

A half hour later Francie stood in a large, chilly loft with frosted windows beyond which the factories and tenements of the Lower West Side loomed in the darkness.

The loft was enormous and cluttered, reflecting in its disorder the preoccupied personality of its tenant. At its center, sprawled over seventy or more square feet, was something that looked only vaguely like a computer. It was a series of boxes, cables, electrical control boards, and other equipment, thrown together like the garage invention of a boy.

"Is this what you wanted me to see?" Francie asked.

Sam nodded. "I call him 9292," he said. "I named him after my old address in Ithaca. He's a fully operational high-powered computer. I modified him from about a dozen outmoded high-level analyzers from here and Boston and New Jersey. He doesn't look like much, but he can do everything an advanced IBM or UNIVAC can do—and, I think, a bit more."

Francie looked at the machine in fascination.

"Magnetic drum, I assume?" she asked.

"Two thousand words of magnetic core memory," he nodded. "He'll do a multiplication in two milliseconds."

Francie was fascinated by now. The sheer size of the machine impressed her, as did the confidence of its creator.

"Does it break down often?" she asked.

"Now and then," he nodded. "He's about fifty percent vacuum tubes, and the rest solid state. He goes down when the tubes get weak. But I fix him. We understand each other."

Francie looked at the enormous, seemingly jerry-built machine.

"He's certainly large enough," she said, unconsciously accepting Sam's humanizing view of the machine.

"You should have seen him four or five months ago," Sam said proudly. "He was nearly twice this size. I've been doing some experimenting on him with solid-state circuitry. It's incredible how many functions you can squeeze into a small fraction of the space required by vacuum tubes. And I've only begun. In a year 9292 will probably be no bigger than a Ford Fairlane—or at least a Lincoln Continental," he added, smiling.

Francie was even more taken now by the implications of what she was looking at.

"In Europe," Francie said, "we were using three IBM 650s, with magnetic input and teletype. We needed a lot of memory."

He nodded, taking out a cigarette. "9292 could do that for you," he said with complete confidence.

"Of course," she added, "what I have in mind for local businesses is much less ambitious. What I want to do is make it possible for a medium-sized businessman to computerize his inventory and billing without having to own a machine of his own. I thought a centrally located computer, with the customer reporting figures . . . But, of course, the rent on such a machine would be enormous."

Sam was smiling.

"I was never much of a programmer," he said. "Machine capability, hardware, is my game. But I see what you're getting at. With your programs, and 9292 here . . ."

Francie's mind was working at triple speed. But even as she thought, she realized that Sam Carpenter was a step ahead of her. In this room was the hardware she had been looking for all this time.

She looked up at him. He was coolly smoking his cigarette, and gazing at her. How much at home he looked here, among all these wires and dim lights! He was in his element.

"Are you thinking what I'm thinking?" he asked.

"Perhaps," she said. "The customers I'm looking for certainly can't afford to rent or lease mainframe computers. But if I could provide the hardware as well as the program, and give them service for a monthly fee . . ."

"You'd have matched up supply and demand," he concluded for her.

She looked at 9292. "But this is yours," she said. "I couldn't ask you to—"

"Think of it this way," he said. "You need a computer, and I need a job. Shouldn't that be enough to bring us together?"

"Do you think it would work out?" she asked hesitantly.

"Why don't we find out?" he smiled. "You like adventure, don't you?"

She stared at him. He was leaning against a battered table, the cigarette burning in his fingers, looking as placid and relaxed as he had the first moment she set eyes on him. And he was asking her to change her life only five hours after meeting him.

But his logic was inescapable.

"You smoke too much," she said with a little smile.

He shrugged. "I could cut down," he said. "Maybe you'd be a good influence on me."

Despite herself she grinned back at him. His humor was disarming.

"Have we got a deal?" he asked.

I hardly know him, she thought to herself.

But somehow she felt she already knew Sam Carpenter well enough to take a chance on him. Besides, her own prospects were so slim that she should be grateful he wanted to join forces with her.

She crossed the room to shake his hand.

"If you're willing to take a chance on me," she said, "I'll put my money on the two of us, and on 9292."

"Sounds good." He shook her hand.

It was the first time he had touched her. His palm was warm and dry, his handshake firm but gentle. The calm brown eyes that had impressed her from the first moment she saw him were focused on her now, full of the same intelligence, and of another quality which she could not name. Perhaps it was humor, or perhaps simple kindness.

Francie felt she had found a friend. She decided to gamble on this intuition.

24

Johnny Marrante released his grip on the naked shoulders beneath him and arched his back slowly.

The only contact between him and the girl was his penis, buried to the hilt inside her.

He listened to her sigh as he ground the hard shaft deeper into her with a corkscrew motion. She smelled of rather cheap perfume, along with the musky aroma of a female in heat, which always turned him on.

She had ratty teased hair, she wore too much makeup, and her shape was less than perfect in the hips, but she had big beautiful breasts with nipples like rosebuds, and he always enjoyed sucking her until she moaned for him to enter her.

Her name was Angela, and she came from a neighborhood in Brooklyn not far from where he was born. She was a good lay, but a crude one. She hungered for sex in an animal way, almost too urgently. He came to her when he needed the slippery pungency of female desire at its most blunt and feral.

But tonight, even as the undulations of her flesh found their way to the need rising inside him, he was dissatisfied. He was no longer hearing the girl's husky cries, no longer looking down at her slightly flabby stomach or the brown thighs spread beneath him.

He was thinking of Julie.

He had not seen her since their angry quarrel about her father—a quarrel that had ended in a bloody, intimate lovemaking that still left its mark in all his senses.

Ever since their fight he had gone back to Ophelia's every night in the hope of seeing Julie. But she had not appeared.

He suspected that what had happened had angered her more than he had realized, or perhaps shamed her. He wanted to make things up with her.

At last, almost desperate with need for her, he had dared to call her at home.

"Miss Magnus is not at home at present," said the crisp English voice of the housekeeper. "May I ask who is calling?"

The first time the question had so flustered him that he had hung up. But later he had decided he must not be daunted by a mere housekeeper. So he had called back and left his last name only. Mr. Marrante.

Julie had not returned his call.

He had called again, and the English housekeeper had assured him that his first message had been transmitted.

"Miss Magnus has your message, Mr. Marran-tee," she said, mispronouncing his name with a touch of condescension. "And I'll certainly pass along this call to her."

After that he had tried several times to reach her. There was no response. Obviously she was not at home to him.

This upset Johnny considerably. He realized Julie had a separate existence which she guarded determinedly against any incursion on his part. She was hiding behind the ramparts of that life, using them to keep him from her.

This bothered him a bit more each day. For he missed Julie badly.

And now, as Angela's hungry loins sucked and squeezed at his throbbing sex, it was not Angela at all who excited him. It was Julie. Her soft blond image had entirely eclipsed that of the common creature in his arms, and it was for her, for the fantasy, that he was grinding and working and pushing, and feeling a terrible fire leaping through his loins.

"Baby doll," whimpered Angela. "Give it to me. Please, baby. Oh!"

He looked down at her indifferently, seeing her naked female flesh as a poor substitute for the golden image which had stirred the sudden and unexpected fire inside him.

All at once, surprising himself, he came with a great burst inside Angela. The huge tremor of his orgasm left her limp and moaning, and he listened irritably to her cries and whimpers, his eyes closed now, his inner attention entirely given over to the image of Julie.

He had called her Cinderella, only in fun at first. But was there not after all something magical about her, something of a fairy-tale creature whose attractiveness came from the fact that she was not quite real, not rooted in the common world of ordinary women like poor Angela?

And hence she was unforgettable, and haunting, like the storybook Cinderella whose charms forced the prince to search for her among all the common women of the kingdom.

Johnny waited a decent interval, withdrew from Angela, and lit a cigarette. She cuddled up against him, a tall girl with strong limbs, and he smelled the somewhat tacky aroma of her hair. He patted her shoulder absently and touched her breast.

"Honey," she murmured. "Thank you. You're the greatest."

"Don't thank me, babe," he sighed, puffing at his cigarette. "You were dynamite."

"I hope so, hon. I want to be dynamite for you. Always."

Her submission annoyed him. She was so shallow and unsophisticated. There was no real backbone inside her, no real character. She was just another guinea girl from Brooklyn, a fast girl who was loose enough to depart from the strict sexual codes of her family and her society, and whose body, once she had sacrificed it to his desire, was no longer a prize.

She was of his own society. They were as alike as two peas in a pod. It would be a woman like her that he would marry some day—but a virginal one, a woman who saves her prize for the marriage bed before dedicating herself to a life of submission to her man.

A woman with olive flesh, ungrammatical English, cheap clothes, cheap tastes, and a storehouse of Italian beliefs, myths, and habits as predictable as the greasy smell of pavement, engine smoke, and the restaurants that filled the streets of the old neighborhood.

This was Johnny's destiny. This was what was waiting for him.

Perhaps that was why something in him rebelled tonight, not only against the familiar flesh of the girl in his embrace, but against the whole world she represented, past and future.

And perhaps that was why the image of Julie, who had given him her body with a mixture of awe, of rebellion, and perhaps of self-destructiveness—a girl so full of secrets—had come to own his lust tonight.

For Julie did not come from his world. The night he met her he had realized that she was adventuring fearlessly outside her own element, that something crazy inside her had put her on the make. This had excited him almost as much as her sweet little body.

He had wanted to give her a good lay, one she would not forget. And he had succeeded, and been proud of his prowess. But Julie, even in her physical surrender, had got under his skin somehow. For she did not surrender her difference as she did her flesh. She remained exotic and somehow unapproachable even in the tightest of his embraces.

And now Johnny reflected that if she had not found him that first night, she would have found another man like him to give her what she wanted. It had not been Johnny himself she was searching for. It had been any man who was well enough endowed, and perhaps far enough beneath her, to make one night in the sack interesting for her.

And now she was gone, immured safely behind the walls of her castle keep on Park Avenue.

So that, like the Cinderella of the fairy tale, she had taken the prince's heart with her when she disappeared into the night. And now it fell to him, like the prince, to scour the kingdom with her glass slipper in hand, trying to find her.

But was not this metaphor too flattering to himself? Was it not rather Johnny himself who, like Cinderella, had been ennobled for a few charmed nights, each time only to see his bubble burst at midnight, so that he was thrown back into his tacky, greasy world, hoping against hope that *she* would come to find *him* when it suited her?

Yes, she was the princess, hidden behind the granite ramparts of her castle, and he the pauper who could not scale those walls.

And now she was angry with him. Not for his physical cruelty, which she had enjoyed, but for his curiosity about her father.

She had shut him out. She was off in her fancy world with her handsome wealthy beaux, and he was exiled here in his sleazy existence with Angela and other girls like her.

Puffing on his cigarette, reaching for the beer on his bedside table, Johnny made a resolution.

He would break down those walls, and get through to her. He was not as easily shut out as she thought.

Johnny Marrante was nobody's stallion. He was a human being.

It was time to teach her who was boss.

25

For the first few weeks it seemed that the working combination of Francie and Sam Carpenter was no more effective than Francie alone.

There were no customers, and there was no more money to advertise CompuTel as a new and rising business. The idea of computerization was so new and untried that businessmen looked at it askance. Computers were thought of as multi-million-dollar "electronic brains" which were a science-fiction threat to wipe out present-day society, rather than as useful tools to make everyday jobs easier.

Francie and Sam tried everything they could to attract customers. They canvassed businesses, large, medium, and small, throughout the metropolitan area. They put flyers in thousands of mailboxes advertising CompuTel's unique and affordable service. They spent hours working up a convincing sales pitch which would disarm the average businessman's suspicions of computers. They took turns manning the office, and walked their feet off trying to find a chink in the indifference of the city to their wares.

Nothing worked. It seemed as though CompuTel was to be stillborn as a company. It was an idea too far ahead of its time to survive in the present-day business world.

Then a break came.

On a Monday in mid-March Sam came into the office with an excited look on his face. He carried an issue of *The New York Times* folded under his arm.

"Look at this," he said.

He opened the issue to the ad pages and showed Francie a full-page layout which she recognized as the weekly advertisement for the chain of drugstores called Discount Drugs. It was a dense pageful of weekly bargains on items from household tools to toys to over-the-counter drugs, with a large banner advertising discount prices on prescription drugs as well.

"Why are you showing me this?" Francie asked. "Everybody knows Discount Drugs. I buy my cosmetics from them."

"Two reasons," Sam said. "In the first place, think for a minute of the inventory problems a chain like Discount Drugs must have. Fifty stores in the metropolitan area alone. Thousands of different kinds of items in each store, not to mention a huge inventory of drugs. Can you imagine a more ideal customer for computerization than this business?"

Francie nodded. "I see what you mean," she said. "They're perfect for us. If we could attract an account like that, we'd have taken a big step forward."

Sam was smiling at her.

"Well?" she asked. "What was the second reason?"

"They're already on the hook," he said. "I had an interview with Sol Saperstein over the weekend. He's the owner of the whole chain. I approached him on a whim. It turned out he was easy to see. He's a nice guy, very down-to-earth. I found him working Saturday in one of his

Manhattan outlets. I think I've got him interested. But we need to tip the scales in our favor."

"How?" Francie asked.

"That's where you come in," Sam said with a grin.

Sol Saperstein had been in the pharmacy business for thirty years, and for nearly fifteen had been at the top of his profession.

He had put three sons through college, married a daughter to one of the most prominent Jewish families in the city, and paid a fortune taking care of his own extended family and that of his wife, including nursing home bills for his parents, until the death of his mother four years ago.

Sol had been a good husband, faithful to his wife, and perhaps more under her thumb than was good for him. She personally handled the accounting for the entire chain of Discount Drugs stores, and worked hand in hand with him in keeping the business at its high competitive level.

Her name was Irene, and she was a small, energetic woman who had been very beautiful in her youth, and who, in middle age, had become extraordinarily meticulous in her clothes and her grooming as her beauty inevitably faded. She was the buyer for the many beauty products sold by Discount Drugs. As a matter of fact it was Discount Drugs' lavish line of cosmetics which kept it a step ahead of its chief competitor, Potamkin Pharmacies, a Manhattan chain which had been inexorably expanding over the past ten years to a position almost equal to that of Discount Drugs.

Sol knew he owed everything he had to Irene. She was his soulmate and his working partner. But she was also a stern and demanding wife who drove him mercilessly. And Sol was a tired man. The war to build Discount Drugs from nothing had taken the best out of him. The second war, to keep a step ahead of Potamkin Pharmacies and its aggressive owner, Phil Potamkin, had sapped Sol's energies.

Sol was a man in need of a rest.

Sam Carpenter had gleaned most of this information from a single hurried interview with Sol Saperstein, for Sol was a complainer by nature.

"Look at this," he had said, waving a hand at the enormous floor space of the midtown pharmacy where Sam had met him. "Thirty employees, a million dollars' worth of stock right before our eyes, a rent that goes up every month, and a shoplifter around every corner. How is a man supposed to keep his sanity in a madhouse like this?"

Sam had taken the opportunity to acquaint Sol Saperstein with the benefits of CompuTel.

"You can computerize all your inventory and your accounts as well,"

Sam explained. "Once that's done all the necessary information for reordering, back-ordering, etc. will be at your fingertips. Your accounting will take less than half the time it does now, and your store managers will be free to concentrate on service to their customers instead of constantly taking inventory. And best of all, you can link up the overhead and costs for all your branches in one system. You'll know exactly how each branch is doing for each product. Reordering will be a snap."

"And how much is this supposed to cost me?" the canny entrepreneur asked.

At this point Sam had an inspiration.

"I should let my colleague Frances go over that with you," he said. "Frances is the one who does the business end."

"When can I meet with this Francis?" Sol Saperstein had asked.

"Name a time," Sam had said. "We pride ourselves on being available. That's what got us where we are today."

"All right," Sol Saperstein said. "Have him meet me here after lunch next Thursday. It can't kill me to hear your pitch."

Flipping a mental coin, Sam decided not to tell Sol Saperstein that he had the wrong sex for "Francis."

It would be best to let that come as a surprise.

The following Thursday Sol Saperstein was taken aback when a beautiful young woman in a bright business suit, wearing a sensual perfume and a friendly smile, came to his office at the appointed time and introduced herself as Frances Bollinger.

"I don't get it," he said. "You mean—you mean *you're* Frances?"

"Call me Francie," she said, shaking his hand. "All my friends do."

"I, ah—sure. Sure, Francie," Sol Saperstein managed to blurt out. "Come on in my office and tell me all about CompuTel."

Sol Saperstein was prepared to be seduced by the stunning looks of the girl who had come to keep the appointment with him. He was not prepared to be overwhelmed by the most irresistible sales pitch he had ever heard before.

The service CompuTel offered to Discount Drugs was a revolutionary one, and virtually guaranteed to reduce Sol Saperstein's overhead by 20 percent in the first year. Moreover, the service would be surprisingly inexpensive, an easy write-off for Sol, as Francie explained, showing tables of facts and figures to support her convincing argument.

Sol Saperstein was impressed. Nevertheless, he could not help shrinking from the idea of committing so much of his business to a computer. Like most people, Sol was terrified of "electronic brains." He had no concept of computers as what they really were—simple calculators, although on a high level of performance. He thought they were abstruse technological monstrosities intended to do the thinking for people and to run things on their own.

But Francie disabused him of these prejudices even as she charmed him with her sweet, down-to-earth manner and impressed him with her amazing grasp of his business problems. By the end of their hour together he was more than a little in love with her, and at least half-convinced that no other solution but CompuTel would free him from the ulcers his business was giving him.

But half was not all. Sol Saperstein was a cautious man.

"It's too big a risk for me to take alone," he said. "Let me talk to Irene about it. She handles the accounting. If she thinks it's all right, we'll give it a try."

Francie had reached the stumbling block that had been waiting for her all along. Sol Saperstein never made a serious decision without consulting his wife.

It was all up to Irene now.

As luck would have it, Irene was visiting her ailing mother in Miami and would not be back for a week. A dinner was arranged for her return, with Francie to lay out her whole proposition.

Francie used the interim wisely. Not only did she prepare an elaborate printed version of her proposal, tailored specifically to the needs of Discount Drugs. She also did a bit of private investigating on the side, about which she did not breathe a word even to Sam.

On March 27th Irene Saperstein returned from Florida. Two days later Sol took her to dinner with Francie and Sam at a quiet midtown restaurant not far from the branch of Discount Drugs where Sam had first met him.

The four talked over CompuTel's proposition for an hour. Irene, a small and fastidious woman whose blue eyes sparkled with sharp intelligence, studied both Francie and Sam as they spoke. She treated them with politeness and respect, but did not hesitate to ask hard questions. What if the system suffered a breakdown? What if the computerized records were somehow lost due to a power failure or other natural disaster? What guarantees could CompuTel provide that it would make good any loss to Discount Drugs under these and other circumstances?

Francie was impressed by Irene Saperstein, and easily understood why she was so important to her husband's business. As the dinner progressed she became convinced that the respect she felt for Irene was returned.

At the end of the meal Irene took Francie aside in order to compliment her on her appearance as well as her work.

"It's nice to see a young lady who knows her stuff, and can compete in a man's world," she said. "By the way, do you mind my asking what cologne that is you're wearing?"

"Not at all," Francie smiled. "It's Le Bonheur. I bought it at Discount Drugs. It saved me two and a half dollars over your nearest competitor."

"Two dollars and sixty-one cents," Irene corrected. "And the nearest competitor is Phil Potamkin and his Potamkin Pharmacies. He'll never compete with us unless and until it's over my dead body."

Francie nodded admiring assent to these sentiments, adding that she bought all her makeup, as well as her cologne, at Discount Drugs.

Francie and Sam left the dinner in high hopes that its result would be CompuTel's first account.

"They both loved you," Sam said. "Sol was on our side already, but I was worried about Irene until I saw the way she looked at you. I think you brought out her maternal instincts. It's in the bag, Francie."

Francie simply smiled.

Time will tell, she was thinking.

Three days later the bad news came.

Sam took the call, and reported the unpleasant surprise to Francie.

"That was Sol Saperstein," he said. "He said he was sorry, but they don't feel they can take the risk. The competition is too fierce for him to get involved in something that could burn up his records in the event of a mishap. I'm sorry, Francie. It looks as though Sol was more set in his ways than I thought."

Francie merely nodded.

She knew the real reason for CompuTel's failure to sell Discount Drugs on its service.

It was Irene Saperstein.

From their first moments together Francie's woman's intuition told her that Irene was a jealous, possessive wife. Behind her motherly, cordial exterior Irene was very suspicious of her husband's enthusiasm for the scheme proposed by this youthful and attractive girl. Francie's expertise in her field had indeed impressed the wary wife, but not enough to outweigh her concern for her husband's wandering eye.

Perhaps, Francie thought, if she herself had kept out of the deal entirely, Sam alone might have made the sale.

On the other hand, Sam alone might not have succeeded in attracting the interest of Sol Saperstein. For that, Francie's youth and beauty had been necessary.

Francie was learning her first important lesson about success in business. The very weapon which gains precious ground in the beginning may turn out to be the stumbling block which blows an entire deal. In order to carry the day with Discount Drugs a sharp salesman would have had to figure a way around both Sol and Irene. She and Sam had failed to do that.

But Francie did not feel despair at the bad news relayed by Sam. As a matter of fact, she had one more card up her sleeve. Her already bright business mind had been sharpened by her bitter experience with Magnus Industries, and in her new enterprise she was ready for any challenge.

"Cheer up," she told Sam. "Something will turn up. I'm almost sure of it."

Little did Sam realize that Francie had not been talking in optimistic abstractions when she told him good news was just around the corner.

Less than a week after the loss of the Saperstein account Francie walked breezily into the storefront and placed a document on the desk where Sam was sitting disconsolately.

"Surprise," she said.

Sam looked at the document. It was a contract engaging the services of CompuTel for a six-month period for the entire chain of Potamkin Pharmacies throughout Manhattan and the other metropolitan boroughs.

The contract had already been signed by Philip Potamkin, President of Potamkin Pharmacies, and by Francie herself.

"Sign alongside my name," she said, placing a pen in Sam's hand.

Sam was staring at her in disbelief.

"Is this a joke?" he asked.

"No joke," Francie said. "Phil Potamkin is waiting for us to join him for lunch at Sardi's to celebrate the deal. He's anxious to meet you. I've told him a lot about you."

In a daze Sam signed the contract and accompanied Francie to the famed West 44th Street restaurant, where she introduced him to Philip Potamkin, a tall, tanned man in his late fifties.

"Delighted to make your acquaintance, Sam," Mr. Potamkin said with an expansive grin. "This little lady has told me all about you and your computer 9292. I don't mind telling you I was a tough sale, but she managed to convince me that you people can get the job done for my chain, and help me catch up to Sol and Irene. I've been chasing Discount Drugs for fifteen years, and I'm going to match their sales if I have to climb the Empire State Building myself to do it."

Sam looked from Philip Potamkin to Francie. An inkling of the truth glimmered at the back of his mind, but he had to wait until the end of their cordial lunch to find out just what had happened.

As soon as he and Francie were alone he asked the question that had been on his mind all day.

"How did you do it?"

Francie smiled.

"Just plain business sense," she said. "In any market a smart business-man looks at the competition. Discount Drugs has been battling to stay ahead of Potamkin Pharmacies for a long time. It occurred to me that, if Sol and Irene weren't willing to use us in order to stay ahead of the competition, Phil Potamkin might take the plunge in order to catch up with them. I approached him last week, gave him our pitch—and got lucky."

Sam shook his head in wonderment.

"I knew you were smart," he said. "But I didn't know you were that smart. Was this plan in your mind the whole time we were wining and dining the Sapersteins?"

Francie shrugged her assent.

"Well, congratulations," Sam said, giving her a quick, warm hug. "You're one hell of a poker player, I'll say that for you."

"Thanks for the compliment," she said. "Would you like to guess what my hole card was?"

Sam looked at her quizzically. "I give up," he said. "Tell me."

Francie looked into his eyes.

"Phil Potamkin has no wife," she said. "He's a widower."

Sam raised an eyebrow. In that instant he realized not only the crucial role Irene Saperstein had played in ruining CompuTel's chances with Discount Drugs, but also how far ahead Francie had been thinking all along.

"I'd better keep an eye on you," he said. "You're more devious than I thought."

For an answer she simply smiled. Her eyes were full of friendship and impish triumph, but behind them there was something faraway and complicated which filled Sam with a combination of admiration and alarm.

Decidedly, in Francie Bollinger he had found a woman to be reckoned with.

===== 26 =====

New York, April 10, 1957

Julie Magnus was at a benefit being given by the Junior League at the Waldorf-Astoria.

She was bored to tears, and wished she was anywhere else. The ballroom was hot and filled with stultified silence as Mrs. Chillingworth, the founder of the annual event, went through her interminable speech about underprivileged children and the responsibility of wealthy people to help the community.

Julie was sipping absently at her tea and looking for a way to get out of the affair early when a bellman from the hotel silently gave her a message.

"A Mr. Marrante to see you, Miss," he said. "In the lobby."

Julie looked at the message. Anger clouded her eyes.

Johnny, you bastard, she mused. *What a nerve.*

"It's a mistake," she told the bellman firmly. "I know no one by that name."

"Very good, Miss," he said, and disappeared.

Julie shook her head in private irritation. *This ought to teach you a lesson, stud,* she thought bitterly.

Nevertheless she was worried by the message. It had never occurred to her that Johnny might have the cheek to accost her on her home ground.

She listened absently as Mrs. Chillingworth droned on. The speech was mercifully coming to its close. Soon Julie would be out of here.

The bellman returned just as the applause was ringing out at the speech's end.

"Mr. Marrante insists," he said. "Shall I have someone from the hotel speak to him?"

In accordance with his training the bellman was protecting Julie against someone he and she both deemed to be unsavory. He was prepared to have her caller thrown out of the hotel.

But something made Julie change her mind.

"I'll take care of this," she said.

She excused herself and moved somewhat furtively to the lobby.

Despite herself she felt her breath come short as she saw Johnny.

Dressed in a sport coat which suited his athletic body perfectly while in no way concealing his class, he stood smiling at her from his position in the middle of the carpeted room. He was wearing a dark shirt and light tie, and a pair of tight slacks which advertised his manhood in a particularly outrageous way. When her eyes met his he gave her a little salute.

She looked behind her to see Mrs. Lydecker, Mrs. Bishop, and the others moving toward the double doors of the ballroom. They would all spill into the lobby in another moment. She had to move fast.

She hurried to Johnny's side.

"How did you find me here?" she asked.

He smiled. "You weren't hard to find," he said. "A lot of people know you, Cinderella."

Julie looked around her anxiously. She could not afford to be seen in the company of a man like Johnny in a place like this.

"Come this way," she said, pulling him behind a pillar across the lobby from the ballroom.

When they were out of sight of her friends she frowned at him. "What are you doing here?"

"I got to missing you," he said. "It seems that Cinderella forgot her handsome prince. Was it just because of that little tiff we had?"

Julie felt her nerves tingle at his nearness, here in this forbidden place. His sudden appearance had shocked her.

But it was her pride that spoke next.

"Get out of here," she said. "Don't ever bother me in a place like this again. I know where to find you when I want you. Stay where you belong."

He caught her arm in an iron grip. The look in his eyes terrified her. It bespoke a smoldering anger as powerful as the sensual knowledge that clouded his dark irises.

"How would your society ladies like to meet the kind of company you keep at night?" he asked. "I'm not shy, Cinderella."

She turned pale. He was in earnest. She believed him entirely capable of dragging her across this lobby and into the ballroom to introduce himself to her friends. Julie had done many wild things in her time, but always with boys of the best background. She could not see herself being dragged by Johnny Marrante into the ballroom at the Waldorf.

Desperately she looked for a way to get him out of here.

"If I promise to meet you at Ophelia's tonight, will you go away?" she pleaded.

He looked at her for a long moment, suspicion vying with the knowing irony in his expression.

Then, slowly, he released her arm.

"Nine-thirty," he said. "Don't be late, Princess."

She gulped, nodding her assent. He smiled as he drew back from her. His finger touched her lips. In an outrageous way he looked amazingly handsome. Despite herself Julie felt a twinge of desire mingle with the alarm in her nerves.

He must have sensed her feelings with his sharp intuition, for he grasped her hand. Looking past her to scan the room, he guided the slender fingers between his thighs. Julie turned red as a beet when she felt the hard length of his sex straining under his tight slacks.

"Johnny!" she hissed in terror.

"See you at the witching hour." He grinned, releasing her.

Feeling weak in the knees, she turned away from him and hurried back to the ladies.

"Julie!" exclaimed Mrs. Bishop. "I've been looking all over for you. Where have you been hiding?"

"I . . . just powdering my nose." Julie smiled uneasily, not daring to take the last backward glance that would perhaps allow her to see Johnny one more time.

"Come on," said the older woman. "There's someone I want you to meet."

With a sigh, Julie followed her on unsteady legs.

Seven hours later Julie was in Johnny's arms again.

The shadowed walls of his apartment, with their sensual nude paintings, hovered around her, as did the familiar aroma of the place, which mingled the smells of cigarettes, beer, and whiskey with household dirt and the scent of his naked body, close to hers.

The sheets were soft, the feel of his muscled arm around her neck was bewitching as ever, and the warm kiss of his lips on her nipple sent tremors of expectation through her.

"Sorry I had to barge in on you that way today, babe," he murmured, his tongue darting over the silken skin of her breast.

"Forget it," she sighed, holding him close. She realized how much her body had missed him since the night of their fight. Part of her felt this strange, tacky apartment was a sort of safe haven for her emotions, just as his magnificent body was a delight for her senses. With Johnny she could let her hair down in a way she never had before.

She was almost glad he had shown up the way he did today. Only an open threat such as he had posed at the Waldorf could have triumphed over her pride and brought her back here tonight.

"Don't ever hide from me again, babe," he whispered. "I need you too much for that."

"I won't," she promised.

The lips began to explore her more boldly now, and his powerful hands to caress her naked limbs. Thought began to turn to pleasure inside her mind.

Thus she forgot herself in his lovemaking. She could not know what he was thinking as he caressed her.

Johnny had not made bold to show his face at the Waldorf out of mere bravado.

He had done it because his own need for Julie was at the boiling point. And because the strange ache in his heart at being separated from her by anger was too much for him to bear.

Little could she know that barely concealed under his surface of arrogance this afternoon was an entreaty he dared not acknowledge. When he had seen her emerge from that ballroom, so tiny and beautiful in her crisp skirt and blouse, she seemed to bring with her an entire world to which he would have wished to belong at any price, in order to be with her.

But it was her world, not his. And even in emerging from it, her lovely features contorted by anger and embarrassment, she was shutting him out. She was a forbidden princess looking daggers at him across an unbridgeable gulf of her own making. This knowledge, slashing at his heart in the split second when she appeared, had restored to him his burning resentment, and given him the courage to act out his scene of masculine domination in the lobby of the Waldorf.

But even now, as he held her in his arms, it was not easy to play the part of the master seducer who toyed teasingly with her flesh. For great waves of relief were thrilling through his senses at the renewal of their intimacy.

Johnny wondered how he had endured for so long without her, and wondered whether he could ever do it again.

But these feelings of need meshed poorly with his own hard pride. He himself had not relished the thought of parading himself before a bunch of society ladies like an underclass curiosity. The idea of their raised eyebrows and condescending glances as they looked at him, identifying him as Julie's lowlife companion, hardly appealed to him. He had felt distinctly uncomfortable and even inadequate in the Waldorf's elegant lobby rooms full of immaculately dressed guests.

But he had ventured outside his own world for Julie. He had done it because he knew he could not approach her at home, and because she would not knowingly let him approach her anywhere else.

Humiliation burned inside him at the thought of his having gone out on a limb that way to get her back.

But she was back now. And he intended to enjoy that fact, and to make her enjoy it, too—until she begged for what he alone could give her.

"Come on, Princess," he murmured, spreading her legs with a soft touch. "Let's let bygones be bygones, and have ourselves some fun."

He heard the moan of her capitulation as his fingers touched at her secret places. He moved to place himself above her, and very slowly, inch by sensual inch, slipped himself to the hilt inside her.

He looked down and saw the gasp of sudden orgasm contort her features. Her eyes were closed, her hands placed luxuriantly on his haunches. He knew now how deeply she had missed him during their separation.

But was it him she needed? Was it Johnny, the man, or only the impersonal bravura of his flesh? The pleasure illuminating her face gave no clue.

At this thought he ground deeper inside her, anger and frustration giving his stroke an urgency that made her moan once more. And at the sound of that moan his own pleasure, so long bottled up, came quickly to meet hers.

And so they gripped each other harder, both driven by a need never before experienced, but each blind to what the other was feeling.

Yet each knew that in the other someone crucial had come along. And this knowledge, experienced separately rather than shared, drove them to heights of passion they had never known before.

Johnny felt himself begin to come. He pushed deeper into her with a last hot spasm. His features were distorted by rapture. He gasped to feel so much of himself go out to a woman. A sense of dark fate overcame him.

Julie arched her back to receive him. Her tiny body shuddered in his grasp. The pleasure she was feeling seemed to come from another world. For a long moment she forgot where she was. Only the male body possessing her existed.

Then, as ecstasy abated, the real world came back to assert its claims. As her lover stroked her naked flesh with his knowing fingers and covered her brow with soft kisses, she pondered the bed she had made for herself, and began to wonder whether she would be able to get out of it as easily as she had got in.

27

When it rains, it pours, Francie told Sam.

A week after Francie closed the deal with Phil Potamkin of Potamkin Pharmacies, Sol and Irene Saperstein began to feel that they had given away precious ground to their hated adversary. The result, surprisingly, was that Discount Drugs became CompuTel's second customer only two weeks after having been its first great failure.

Almost overnight Francie had accepted the task of computerizing the two biggest drugstore chains in New York City.

It was a considerable challenge at so early a stage in the computer era. But Francie was equal to it. She personally supervised every aspect of the inventory reporting and ordering procedures she had devised for both firms. The programs she had devised worked without a hitch. Having already been burned once by her initial failure to make the Magnus European operation work, Francie had since done her homework, and understood exactly what pitfalls to avoid in programming this sort of job.

As for 9292, Sam Carpenter's homemade computer, it functioned perfectly, using only a tiny fraction of its enormous memory to do the work required.

Within weeks the operation was a complete success for both drug firms. Though the competition between Potamkin Pharmacies and Discount Drugs grew even more fierce now that each company had less overhead to worry about, both were highly vocal proselytes for the expert and affordable service provided by CompuTel.

Thanks no doubt to the word of mouth started by the Sapersteins and Phil Potamkin, new clients came Francie's way. Before long a chain of shoe stores and a large New York dairy had become CompuTel clients.

Francie did not stop there. She had bigger plans. Soon she and Sam were running their feet off to sales interviews with prospective customers. As time passed they both learned to perfect their sales pitch in order to show off their success for Discount Drugs, Potamkin Pharmacies, and their other clients to new prospects who were intrigued by the idea of computerization but still wary of the unknown.

They played off each other brilliantly. Where Sam's low-key friendliness did not succeed in carrying the day, Francie's beauty and sharp display of computer expertise usually did.

And Francie and Sam had learned a valuable lesson from the struggle for supremacy between the Sapersteins and Phil Potamkin. When they approached a successful businessman, they made sure to hint that computerizing his enterprise would facilitate victory over his nearest competitor. More often than not the businessman retained CompuTel out of fear that if he did not, his competitor would do so first.

The combination of clever salesmanship, dependable service, and word-of-mouth was soon paying off. An important chain of dress shops joined the CompuTel fold. Then a large appliance store followed suit. A multi-million-dollar wholesaler of electronic equipment came next.

Then a crucial coup was brought about by Sam. He happened to mention the nature of his business to a vice-president of CompuTel's own bank, First Federal of Manhattan. The vice-president, aware of the rapid growth of CompuTel's account, saw a chance to impress his superiors with his own initiative, and with Sam's help drew up a prospectus on how CompuTel could computerize the bank's entire accounting system, saving hundreds of thousands of dollars in accountants' fees.

A month later, after multiple consultations between the bank's Board of directors and Sam and Francie, the deal was struck. CompuTel was now the official accounting arm of First Federal and all its branches. Before winter was out three other banks in Manhattan had contacted Francie and Sam, asking for the same service as soon as possible.

Business was mushrooming. Overnight CompuTel had risen from obscurity and become a force to be reckoned with in the Manhattan business world.

Francie had long strategic talks with Sam about how to handle the sudden growth facing the company. Its clients were getting wealthier, its work load greater every day. More and more money and responsibility were flowing through CompuTel, which now employed a dozen reporters and operators to help handle the rising flow of information.

The first step was to lease two new IBM computers in Manhattan. The expense was a great one, greater than Francie could have imagined six months before. But 9292 alone could not handle the work load. More hardware was needed. CompuTel had to overextend itself financially to afford the new computers, but Francie and Sam both realized this was the only way to build the company effectively.

At Sam's suggestion CompuTel moved from the storefront to a bright new office on Cedar Street, not far from Wall Street. Francie and Sam had the place decorated to look modern, sleek, and exciting. There were carpeted floors, colorful paintings on the walls, small offices for the staff to keep in phone contact with the major accounts, and a larger conference room for meetings with current clients and new prospects.

In its new location CompuTel looked more like what it in fact was: a rising young company with a great future.

The work load on Francie and Sam was enormous, since they alone were responsible for creating all the programs tailored to the various businesses CompuTel serviced. Each program was different, and programming was still a new art whose rules were not clear.

Oddly enough, Francie came to know Sam better through his programming. They would often work separately on different areas of a program, and then share their work for the final product. Through Sam's work she came to know something about his mind and personality. It was a beautifully logical mind, but not an aggressive one. Instead of cutting through the Gordian knots with quick anxious slashes the way Francie did, Sam patiently found ways to untie them. He had a gentle way of solving problems, a willingness to go with the flow of numbers and equations, that Francie lacked. Francie attacked a problem head-on, shook it like a dog with a bone, and worried it until a solution came to her.

This inner stillness of Sam's also helped Francie to endure the daily tension of building a company from nothing. He recognized that her long hours at CompuTel were threatening to drive her into overwork. So he brought her to his loft at night or on weekends and had her sit and watch while he tinkered with 9292. He fine-tuned the ungainly computer's already powerful functioning, while shrinking the monstrous machine ever further by replacing its heavy vacuum-tube circuitry with solid-state transistor boards. 9292 grew smaller and more powerful—if not more beautiful—every week.

It relaxed Francie to watch Sam, for she could not bear to leave work entirely behind at the end of the day, and would have been much more restless at home alone.

They would chat while he worked—not about CompuTel, but about her youth in Pennsylvania, her mother and father, and his own relatives in upstate New York. Sam seemed to be an essentially happy young man who had been loved and wanted by his parents as a child. He was not driven toward success like Francie, but apparently divided between a healthy thirst for adventure and the deeper desire for a home and family of his own, sheltered from the world.

For this reason, Francie mused, the darkest shadow over Sam's life was the blow of having returned from Korea to a ruined marriage. She guessed that the greatest happiness he could conceive for himself would be a loving wife and the chance to be a father to his own children. This would mean much more to him than any professional success.

She enjoyed learning more about him, and telling him about herself. Their friendship deepened and grew more complex as their work brought them closer.

She came to love watching him as he worked coolly at 9292 in his dirty T-shirt while a cigarette burned in the ashtray on the floor beside him. Soft music played on the radio, echoing through the dark recesses of the loft. Sam's presence was like a hearth, bringing the warmth of home to this impersonal place.

Sometimes on Sundays he took her fishing in a rented boat on Long Island. It amused him to see that she was not cut out for this pastime at all. She lacked the patience to sit and wait for the fish to bite in their own time. She chafed to make things happen through her own initiative.

"You're what my father used to call a doer." He smiled, lazing in the boat as the cool breezes of spring caressed them. "You'll do great things, Francie. But there are some things that only come when you've learned how to wait. I think it's my job to teach you to be a fisherman."

He sighed contentedly. "Back where I come from," he said, "there's a tiny lake called Firefly Lake. It's so small you can call out to someone in the middle from the shore to tell him to come in for lunch. I'll bet I know half the fish in that lake. Most of them are too smart to be caught. And when you do catch them, you don't have the heart to eat them, so you end up throwing them back. When I got back from the war I went out there every day for a month. I would sit on the water for seven hours, and then go home and listen to the radio with my parents. I learned a lot from that lake."

Francie was mystified by his words. She wondered what a man could learn about the real world from the silence of a lake in the woods. But she knew Sam well enough now to respect his considerable intelligence. She would hear more before dismissing his words out of hand.

"Maybe I'll see that lake some day," she said.

"Maybe you will," he nodded.

She smiled at him. She could feel the natural relaxation of his personality doing its best to infect her, and never quite succeeding.

But she enjoyed seeing him try. And she was pleased to wake up each morning and remember that CompuTel was not hers alone, but Sam's as well. If the essence of her was a sort of high-wire act, defying the world to make her fall, then Sam was the steady balance that linked her to the earth's gravity and thus allowed her to press onward.

Thus Francie valued Sam Carpenter a bit more every day, in new and surprising ways.

Happy as they both were with the vertiginous growth of CompuTel, they had to admit that they could not keep up with it themselves. The task of working on new programs and monitoring the three main computers was too great a strain on them.

At this point, just as the work load was threatening to overwhelm them, a piece of luck came their way.

Francie was hard at work one Thursday morning when she received a surprise visit from Dana Salinger, her old roommate and closest friend from the University of Pennsylvania. A slim, quiet girl who hid her very attractive looks behind her glasses and her absorption in mathematics and science, Dana had not changed a bit. She was still as willowy and reflective as ever.

She was only dropping in to say hello, because she had seen CompuTel's ad in the business press, noticed the words "Frances Bollinger, President," and wondered if it was her old friend. She and Francie had lunch at a nearby restaurant and talked over old times. Francie told as much of her own story as she could without dwelling on the unpleasant Magnus episode. Dana, in her usual laconic way, explained that she had finished her curriculum at Penn and done graduate work at MIT before joining a consulting firm in Connecticut.

"We're engineering consultants," she told Francie. "Mostly electronics. I concentrate on mathematical models for applications. It's not too bad. But I miss computers. You're lucky to be in the thick of things."

Francie remembered that Dana had been a great whiz at computers at Penn. Together they had spent many an evening working with the Moore School's professors on problems in high-level analyzing.

Dana did not look a day older, or at all different. She still had the same soft brown hair, the same milky complexion with its touch of natural tan, the same slim figure and quiet brown eyes behind her glasses.

"No boyfriends?" Francie asked.

"Nothing worth talking about," Dana smiled.

Dana had not changed, Francie mused. She had always been so absorbed in scientific work that despite her beauty she never got into serious romantic relationships. She seemed to hide something crucial of herself behind those studious wire-rimmed glasses and that introspective manner. At Penn Francie had wondered whether Dana was afraid of men,

— 198 —

or simply did not take them seriously. She herself had never got quite close enough to Dana to know the answer.

"How about you, Francie?" Dana asked. "You seem happy. Is there someone special in your life?"

It was not like Dana to ask so personal a question, but Francie had invited it.

"No, I'm afraid," she said, hoping that her neutral expression hid the truth about the adventure her heart had undergone since she last saw Dana, and the scars left by it.

The conversation changed to other topics. As the two young women chatted Francie got the clear impression that Dana was not fulfilled by her current work. This, combined with the knowledge that Dana was unattached romantically, decided Francie to make a bold suggestion.

"Dana," she said, "Sam and I really need help with CompuTel. High-level help, I mean. We've both been working ourselves to a frazzle to keep up with the new business. It's a struggle. We're the only programmers, and it's hard for us to be managers too. And Sam has to keep 9292 running, and worry about the other computers at the same time. Listen: I know this is sudden, but what would you think about leaving your job and joining us?"

Dana looked at Francie without showing any sign of surprise. This was typical of her, as Francie knew from rooming with her at Penn. She never showed emotion. Even in a personal crisis she was almost uncannily controlled.

Francie reflected that it was precisely that cool, steadfast quality she needed now, as well as Dana's tremendous skill with computers.

Dana seemed to hesitate.

"Let me think about it for a few days," she said.

"Enough said." Francie smiled, not adding anything or trying to cajole, for Dana was a girl of few words, but one who meant everything she said.

As things turned out, Francie was in luck.

Exactly one week after their meeting Dana called from Connecticut.

"If you still want me, Francie," she said, "I can be available in ten days. I need to finish up a project here, but then I'm free."

"Hooray!" Francie cried over the phone. "I can hardly wait, Dana. It will be like old times. And you'll love Sam."

Within a fortnight Dana had joined the team, and was deeply involved in writing and implementing the programs for CompuTel's growing list of clients. Dana was thrilled to be back in the computer field she had missed so much, and threw herself enthusiastically into the unusual challenge of tailoring a program to a specific business. Francie breathed a sigh of relief each day she came to work, for now she knew she had a trusted associate who could take one-third of the work off her own shoulders.

Dana never complained or showed the slightest sign of being disoriented in her new job. When she had difficulties she came to Francie or to Sam—with whom she had quickly developed a cordial working relationship—and asked what to do. With her sharp mind she seized upon the advice given, and went back to work without another word. Francie was delighted with the immaculate care and intelligence Dana had brought to her job. Thanks to her, CompuTel could continue to expand at its dizzying rate without exhausting its officers to the point of prostration.

It seemed that with Dana another piece of good luck had come to CompuTel just when it was most needed. For the first time in nearly two years, Francie truly felt surrounded by friends. More yet, she began to experience an emotion that had long since been covered over by the private mission behind her hard work.

Francie was happy.

28

August 27, 1957

Belinda Magnus watched the clock.

It was, alas, an all too familiar pastime for her these days.

It was nine-thirty at night. Jack was at the office, working late as usual. He worked long hours. Hard, obsessive hours.

She knew enough about the Magnus Corporation to know that Jack was in charge of a lot of people, and a lot of complex and sensitive projects. She also knew that the day was inevitably approaching when he would assume responsibility for the entire conglomerate. But that alone did not explain his overwork. Another man would have delegated as much responsibility as he liked to underlings, the more so because, as the boss's son and the man due to inherit the business, he did not have to prove himself each and every day on the job.

But Jack worked like a dog. He knew every nook and cranny of the company, and not just the part under his direct control. Those around him were awed by his energy and dismayed by the humorlessness with which he pursued the challenges he had set for himself. He was always several steps ahead of everyone, testing concepts, making contacts, revising old ideas, generating new ones. He acted as though he were carrying the whole corporation on his shoulders.

Belinda knew that Jack was not a happy man in his work. It was not the satisfaction of a job well done that drove him to ever greater efforts. Something else, something invisible and unspoken, was behind his long hours at Magnus.

Nor was he a happily married man—though he gave a magnificent performance of being one.

Jack was an attentive husband. He showered Belinda with hugs, friendly kisses, little gifts, a thousand signs of tenderness and consideration that any wife would envy. He joked with her, read the morning papers with her, helped her make dinner on the cook's night off. He took her on all his business trips, and on weekend vacations skiing in the Adirondacks or swimming in the Bahamas whenever his huge work load allowed it.

But Belinda alone knew how false this display was.

Whenever it was time for them to be together, to have a good time as husband and wife, Jack made sure somehow that other people were involved. He managed to include other people in their leisure-time activities, apparently as an afterthought. Their weekend vacations always seemed to end up being spent on dinners and lunches with company friends or social acquaintances who happened to be in the neighborhood.

Cleverly, even brilliantly, Jack arranged things so that he was hardly ever alone with his own wife.

And during their few moments of real solitude he managed to steer the conversation subtly so that they skirted the issues which might have had the deepest and most intimate meaning to them: their own relationship, their private thoughts about life and each other, and most of all the possibility of children.

Jack had asked Belinda to wait for children until he had had a chance to consolidate his understanding of the corporation, which would take about three years. At first she had agreed, because she wanted to get to know her new husband better before starting a family. But she would never have agreed had she known in advance what an empty shell this marriage was going to turn out to be.

Not that it wasn't a pretty shell. Belinda's life was an easy and leisurely one. Jack was a handsome man, a perfect husband—and a wonderful lover.

Jack was tender and considerate in bed. His caresses were expert, always finding the pleasure points he had come to know in his wife's soft body. But his very expertise at playing her like a harp seemed to show that somehow his heart wasn't in it.

And when he gave her his seed, entering her with the long hard length of himself and driving her with slow strokes to spasms of excitement, it was as though even his excitement were a mask, a wall between them. He became a pure male animal at those moments, with no heart behind his breathless movements.

He was not the Jack she thought she loved. Not the Jack she had coveted and waited for all those years. He was a stranger.

But Belinda did not blame him alone for this. After all, how could he be anything but a stranger? Since the day he found out she had been chosen for him by others, he had seen her as little as possible and shown no interest in learning anything more about her. How, then, could she have come to know him the way a bride knows the young man who has courted her, shared himself with her, poured out his longings and dreams to her?

Yes, Jack was a stranger. But that was the fault of fate, not of Jack himself.

There is no greater torture for a young wife than to be unloved by the husband who owns her heart and does not want it. Belinda lingered over this torture alone at home while Jack was at work, and struggled with it during long wakeful nights as she watched him sleep beside her.

Belinda was an intelligent young woman. She had suspected from the very moment of Jack's sudden proposal to her a year ago that something was wrong. Despite the sincerity and even the passion of his proposal, she knew it made no sense for him to seek her out now, after having avoided her for so many years. It was as though a secret timetable of which she knew nothing had decreed that now was the moment for him to choose her.

Part of Belinda had feared the worst from that very moment. But the rest of her loved Jack too much to say no to him, loved him enough to accept him on any terms, hoping against hope that their marriage would be a success.

And now, in the eyes of the outside world, it was in fact a success.

Early in their marriage, when Belinda felt the screen slowly coming down between her and her husband, she had spoken to Jack about it. She had told him she felt a distance between herself and him.

"I'm sorry, darling," he had said. "It's work. I'm overdoing it. Don't let me."

And he had taken her in his arms and silenced her with kisses so enticing that anyone else would have thought them tokens of the deepest love.

A month later, when she had dared to bring up the subject again, he had been more serious in his answer.

"Perhaps I have more of the Magnuses in me than I'd care to admit," he said. "We're not demonstrative people, Belinda. Just understand that I love you, that I want you. Sometimes I can't express myself the way I'd like. But believe me, I love you."

And there had been just the hint of finality in his tone when he closed the subject, enough so that she had been afraid to bring it up again.

Since then things had gone on as before.

Anton Magnus and his wife were getting on in years now, and had given over many of the corporate and social party-giving responsibilities to Jack and Belinda. Jack took on the job dutifully, for he knew that one day it would be his alone, and he might as well cement good relations with the Magnus people now.

The onus was on Belinda to be a perfect wife and hostess, and she shouldered it with the instincts of her social class, instincts honed and refined through five generations at the finest finishing schools in Europe.

She would not have minded the duty at all had her marriage been real.

Under the circumstances which only she knew, it was the worst torture she could endure.

Belinda lived on the razor's edge between two contradictory views of herself. Part of her felt like the lowest creature ever invented by God to make an innocent man unhappy. She cursed her own cowardice in allowing her father and Anton Magnus to force her on Jack when he did not want her. She felt like an empty vessel, and a poor substitute for the sort of woman Jack really wanted.

On the other hand, Belinda was hurt and angry. She was not without pride. She knew she was intelligent, and creative. She had a lot to give to others. The stern backbone of her personality reminded her of her own worth, and gave her a healthy resentment at being a pawn in a game she had not chosen. She owed it to herself not to let her predicament with Jack destroy her morale. She did not intend to allow her life to descend into tragedy, if she could help it.

So she kept active. She read, and took courses toward her advanced degree in literature. She taught reading and writing as a volunteer at a school for handicapped children. She even found enough self-respect and ambition to write short stories and an occasional poem which she kept in a private notebook locked away in her library. She kept all the obligatory social appointments required by her position as Jack's wife, but she never took them seriously, or allowed their shallowness to infect her.

She clung to her self-respect and tried her best to nurture it, as though aware that it was the quality most imperiled by her present life.

But it was not an easy task, for each day, try as she might to reverse the trend, she felt a bit more hollow, a bit more helpless, a bit more bereft of hope in the future.

She wondered what life would have been like if she had been born into a normal American family, a bourgeois family unburdened by great wealth and social position.

Tears welled in Belinda's eyes as she thought of that modest, simple, heavenly fate. For if she had been a normal girl she could have married whomever she chose. He would have been an ordinary man, a man who loved her and whom she could love. They could have lived wherever they liked, and chosen their friends from among their neighbors. She could have gone shopping, wheeling her first child in a stroller, and bought new curtains for the kitchen, inexpensive curtains, but curtains that she would choose herself. Curtains not meant to impress her society friends, but meant simply to look pretty. Curtains to make a home with.

A normal, happy life! How foolish ordinary people are to take such happiness for granted, and to imagine that the idle rich have something better, something to be desired! If they only knew what it was to be forced into marriage by two wealthy families, and to spend one's life playing a role that had no substance. It was a cruel game in which the only real winner might be the price of certain stocks on the Exchange, a price won at the expense of two human hearts.

Belinda would have dropped the whole sick charade long ago, and gone gratefully back to her lonely life, were it not for the paralyzing fact that she loved Jack.

This was the rub, the fatal irony that sapped her of her strength to change her situation or escape it.

So Belinda tried to be the best wife she could. She covered her shame and hurt with humor, affection, and attentiveness, for the sake of her husband. She forced herself to be a clever and active lover. She did all the little things a good wife does to let her husband know she wants him and depends on him.

She accepted what she had of him, and waited to see if time would bring her more of him.

She prayed that he would eventually learn to want her. Perhaps some day the unseen core behind his perfect imitation of love would warm to her.

For this she was willing to work, and to wait.

And, like many a society wife before her, she had him watched.

Of course she knew his reputation as a ladies' man. Oddly, though, it was not this that concerned her as she had his movements monitored by discreet detectives.

Belinda's feminine radar had not failed to alert her that there was an attraction between Jack and the girl named Francie Bollinger the night the two had met at the Magnuses' party for Gretchen. The involuntary light in Jack's eyes when he looked at Francie had left no doubt of that. And Jack had been just close-mouthed enough about his trips to Paris while Francie was working there to confirm Belinda's suspicions.

Belinda had never been able to get Francie out of her mind. Francie was so fresh, so beautiful, and she and Jack made such a perfect couple. More yet, she combined a terrific intelligence with an unspoiled, natural personality that it was impossible not to like.

In meeting her one could only be impressed by Jack's good taste. This thought scarred Belinda's memory to this day.

And Belinda was clever enough to suspect that if Jack had married her against his will, he must still be seeing the other girl.

Surprisingly, this was not the case.

The detective agency reported that Jack was seeing no one. His late hours at the office were spent on hard, backbreaking work. The exhaustion on his face when he came home at night was from work, not from play.

On the surface this was a good sign. Jack was not unfaithful. But underneath, it could mean something much more sinister. Perhaps Jack, as part of his plan to be a model husband and model corporate executive, would even add fidelity to his wife as a means to an end.

This was what troubled Belinda. Jack's perfect imitation of a happy marriage had no flaws. No outward flaws, that is.

There was no solution to this riddle, except time. Belinda had a strong will, but she was imprisoned by the laws of the society to which she belonged, and by her own love.

So she waited, and loved, and hoped.

Jack returned at ten. He kissed his wife, poured a drink, and sat on the couch with his arm around her.

Though he was smiling, he seemed tired. His eyes were red from overwork.

"Hard day?" she asked.

"No more than usual," he said. "Maybe I'm out of shape. I should exercise more."

There was a silence as Belinda pondered this evasion. Then Jack brightened.

"We finished the Colombian plans today," he said. "They should be in operation by the first of the year. If you play your cards right, you'll have a nice vacation south of the border."

"Wonderful." Belinda tried to sound sincere, but she knew by now what those working vacations were like. She would barely see Jack, and would spend each day planning how to entertain or be entertained by his colleagues at night. With the language barrier it would be worse.

But she knew how proud he was of the new Colombian subsidiary. He had planned it himself, executed it from top to bottom with no help from anyone in the corporation he had not hired himself. It proved his initiative, his expertise, and his independence from his father.

But all this was small comfort for Belinda.

"Hey," he said suddenly. "What are we just sitting here for? Why don't we celebrate? It isn't every day a man creates a new company."

He pulled her to him and kissed her, surprisingly hard. She thought she felt the distant tremor of his male need behind that kiss. She curled up in his lap, pulled him closer, and ran her hand through his hair.

It was late. Perhaps they could make love, have a late supper, and enjoy a quiet time alone, perhaps even talk into the wee hours as they had done once, during their honeymoon.

Belinda began to feel better.

"Sounds great," she said.

He released her.

"Why don't you call the Billingtons?" he asked, smiling. "I know it's late, but I'll bet they're not doing anything. I'm famished. Maybe they could meet us at the Plaza for something to eat. How does that sound?"

Belinda did her best to hide her crestfallen look behind a brave smile.

"All right, Jack," she said. "I'll call the Billingtons."

≡ 29 ≡

Julie Magnus had promised to be on her best behavior.

The party was being given at a venerable Fifth Avenue duplex by her mother's cousins in honor of their sister, Eunice Childs, who was very ill with a degenerative nerve disease, and who was celebrating her fiftieth birthday. The doctors and the family thought it might be her last.

Julie had always liked Eunice. As a girl she had gone on visits to the Childs' estate on Hilton Head Island, and been taken to see the alligators and the hanging moss and the ocean birds. Eunice had had heart-to-heart talks with Julie as they explored the wide flat beaches in search of buried sand dollars. It had all been very tropical and romantic, and Eunice and her husband Geoff lived like natives, spending long hours playing cards and putting together jigsaw puzzles on the veranda of their quaint old house.

The visits had ended when Geoff died of a heart attack ten years ago, and Eunice turned in on herself, no longer entertaining guests. But she remained a faithful correspondent, and Julie looked back fondly on her Hilton Head memories, for her times with Geoff and Eunice had been a refuge from home.

So she greeted Eunice, who did not look at all ill except for the companion who stayed by her side in the event of a sudden weakness, and the two spent a pleasant hour together before Julie took her leave. Eunice was as friendly and humorous as ever, though she could not hide the look of worry that hovered in her eyes when she looked at Julie. She, like everyone else, had heard the many rumors about Julie's wild life, and knew that some of them, at least, must be true.

Julie was preparing to leave the party when she encountered a once-familiar face which she had not seen in nearly twenty years.

His name was Scott Monteagle. His family were the Monteagles of Philadelphia, a once-sought-after name in society which had disappeared from view after the father lost everything in the Depression and jumped out a window over Broad Street.

As a tiny girl Julie had met Scott—Scotty, he was called then—on a family visit, and conceived a schoolgirl crush on him instantly. Scotty was a sensitive, rather delicate boy, and Julie had found his diffident attentions charming. They had been very thick for two or three family gatherings, become pen pals for a while when Scott's mother and sisters took him back to England, the family's original home, and then lost touch with each other.

Julie still remembered a curious occasion when she and the little boy had been alone on the huge lawn of a Monteagle relative's country estate during a garden party, and had snuggled up together in the shadow of an old chestnut tree to hug and kiss like big children. It was she who had led him into it, for she was precocious. But he had been fascinated by her wispy blonde beauty, and the occasion had really been very romantic. She had never forgotten it.

Today, at the party for Eunice, she did not recognize Scott at first. Too much time had elapsed since their last meeting. Strangely, though, she needed no more than three minutes' conversation with him to know that he also remembered their one tryst together. His knowledge was evident in his eyes and in the tender decorum he showed her.

He had grown up into a well-mannered and quite handsome young man. He bore an English accent from his years abroad, but the more he talked the more Julie recognized the dreamy, shy little boy she had had such a crush on in her youth. His family's adversity appeared to have done him good. He seemed happy with his modest position in the world—he was a barrister in London—and full of a charming good humor that made her feel at ease in his company.

Julie found herself enjoying her conversation with him, and stayed to talk with him for over an hour. They told each other about their respective lives. Scott had two sisters, the older one married and the younger a student whose education he was helping to finance, and a mother who worked full-time as an executive secretary in London and lived in a modest suburban flat. His account was brief, clear, and unexciting, but it was fascinating to Julie, because it was such a clean life, so full of honorable motives, courage, and modest expectations.

Oddly enough, as she listened to him talk Julie began to feel the same girlish attraction to him that she had felt as a child. This made her shy. In talking about herself she steered well away from the truth about her life-style, for she did not want him to think ill of her. She felt an impulse to be the girl he had known so long ago.

This was a new experience for Julie, since she had made a point of her bravado throughout her life. But her own embarrassment filled her with a strange and pleasant languor. The attentive, respectful look in Scott's eyes, tinged with the secret memory of their childhood romance, warmed her deep inside. She did not want to break the spell.

At the end of the conversation he surprised her by expressing an interest in seeing her again.

"Won't you have dinner with me?" he asked. "I'd love to talk over old times, and to get to know you better."

Julie was unsure how to respond to this proposal. Scott was a nice young man, obviously very thoughtful and sincere. She sensed that his intentions toward her were serious, as well. He really wanted to make a try at a relationship with her.

Thrown off balance by this unexpected turn of events, Julie hesitated before managing a stammered yes, but smiled when she saw his eyes light up at her acceptance. He promised to pick her up for dinner tomorrow night.

He asked permission to take her home, and she agreed. She took her leave of Eunice with a brief inner pang. Eunice was not of this world for much longer. Perhaps this was their last meeting. But Eunice had noticed her talking to Scott, and there was a matchmaker's gleam in her tired eyes. This made Julie feel better.

Julie's dinner date with Scott Monteagle was both fascinating and unsettling. He picked her up in his hired car—hardly a limousine—and took her to an attractive, modest restaurant in the Village which someone of her blood would never patronize, but which, oddly enough, she had visited several times on her drunken nights out with boyfriends in the past.

The place was so transformed by Scott as to seem unrecognizable. He was a man so cut off from her society, by poverty as well as the Atlantic Ocean, that being with him was like taking a transversal track straight out of the world she knew.

He told her of life in England, which he cheerfully described as dull—"football, the underground, and the BBC"—but which sounded oddly romantic, coming off his handsome lips.

She studied his face and body. He was slender, but athletic-looking. Not a man's man, but clearly a strong man and a strong person. In answer to her inquiries he told her he played cricket, and went riding when he could afford to rent a horse.

He had gray eyes, soft brown hair with a touch of red in it, and a clean white complexion which glowed alabaster in the dim light of the restaurant. His voice charmed her, for it stirred certain far-off memories which were too dim for her to place, but which touched her all the more for their vagueness. He had gentle, delicate hands, and he wore an inexpensive old wristwatch which nevertheless had the minimal elegance required of a lawyer.

There was a proud shabbiness about him that charmed Julie perhaps more than all the rest. A quiet poverty not at all embarrassed by itself, but almost happy.

He tried to learn more about her, but her shame made her turn aside his questions, not very adroitly. He did not press her. Surely he must have heard the many rumors about her. But he did not seem to care. He treated her exactly as though the twenty years since their lawn party together had never happened. He had the same candor, the same boyish attentiveness to her, now as then. Julie was fascinated by his sweet personality and its effect on her.

When he took her home he had the driver wait, and walked her to her door. In the shadows of the vestibule he took her in his arms and kissed her.

"I've been wanting to do that for twenty years," he said.

She looked at him through eyes wide with surprise, and managed a weak smile.

"You don't look different," he said. "Touching you, being with you, I can still smell the grass of that lawn in Connecticut. I can still hear the silverware on those lawn tables, and hear my mother's voice calling to us."

Julie caught her breath. She remembered, too. They had been embracing, actually kissing, she in her party dress and the handsome little boy in his suit and sweater, when the voice of his mother had rung out across the lawn, *Scotty! Where has he got to now?*

The old afternoon stirred inside her. And as it did, so did the evening that came after. Her return home, her bedroom, her childish thoughts about Scotty. Jack and Gretchen still at home in their own rooms. And Mother and Father.

Father . . .

Julie had closed her eyes. When she opened them she saw Scott looking deep into them. He put his hands on her shoulders and drew her to him.

Their bodies touched. A prohibited fire leapt under her clothes at the feel of his limbs against hers. Her hands moved to touch him, hesitated, and fell to her sides. He felt her tense in his embrace, and let her go.

"Have I insulted you?" he asked.

She shook her head in the shadows. "Not at all, Scott."

It's I who have insulted you.

The words formed themselves inside her mind with cruel sharpness, but she said nothing.

"May I see you again?" he asked.

Her answer came in a whisper.

"Of course—Scotty."

"I'll call, then. If I may?"

"Please do. Anytime."

She stood alone inside the vestibule, every sinew in her body trembling, as she watched him go down the marble steps and get into his car. She tried to hide her disarray as she waved to him.

After he was gone she moved weakly to a chair in the downstairs salon and sat in it. She closed her eyes. She felt dizzy, as though trapped on the edge of an abyss and afraid to look down.

Then she went upstairs, took off the pretty green dress she had worn to be with Scott, and stood alone in her stockings and underwear. On an impulse she opened the full-length mirror, removed her stockings, bra, and panties, and stood looking at herself naked. Behind her she could see the room she had lived in since she was a child, the room in which her dreams had turned into nightmares.

She studied the image in the mirror. So this was the flesh Scott had felt in his embrace, the flesh that had not disgusted him.

Everyone said Julie was pretty. The creamy white limbs, the fine slender ankles and wrists, the long doelike neck, the silken hair—it all combined to make up what the world called a lovely young girl.

To Julie it looked like raw carnage, offal, crowbait. Her body was as horrible to her as the scabby flesh of a leper.

Yet only she could see this reality. Like the Emperor's New Clothes, the horror of being herself was invisible to the outside world.

She looked at the eyes, so full of pain and loathing. How she hated those eyes! How she hated her pain, and her futile efforts to dampen it with whatever excesses she could find.

To think that Scott Monteagle had turned back the clock, seen in her a fresh, guiltless little girl, and set out to contact that little girl. He was blind to all the intervening years, blind to the rotting, the humiliation, the horror.

He still liked her.

A great shudder went through Julie as she thought of her hideous past and the strange, quiet determination on the part of handsome Scott Monteagle to turn back the clock and wipe away her shame.

She felt as though these two forces were tearing her apart. In another minute the earth must open to swallow her up unless she fled this place and these thoughts.

She went down the hall to the library, found the bottle of aged bourbon and took a long, deep drink which scalded her throat. Then she returned to the bedroom and put on another dress, this one low-cut and sexy. She found shoes to match it, let her hair down, and applied a touch of makeup to her eyes.

The liquor was warming her insides as she tiptoed down the stairs, got her coat and let herself out.

The night closed its arms around her like tendrils of evil, horrible in themselves, but old companions, the friends who knew her when.

Trembling slightly, she went off down the street to hail a cab.

She had to see Johnny.

═══ 30 ═══

The Wall Street Journal, *May 9, 1958*

CompuTel, Inc. of New York today became a public company, offering stock for sale at a price of $14.12 per share.

The computer consulting firm has grown by 600% in its last three quarters. It has opened branches in Atlanta, San Francisco, Los Angeles, and Chicago, and plans more locations in key cities to be opened within the next six months. The firm's clients now include several dozen banks and investment firms as well as retail chains and large wholesaling outlets.

Frances Bollinger, Chairman and CEO of the dynamic young company, announced the stock offering at a special meeting of CompuTel's managers in San Francisco this morning.

The copy of The Wall Street Journal lay on the floor beside Francie. She was sitting on the ancient couch in Sam Carpenter's loft, watching Sam work on 9292.

Francie was so tired that she could hardly keep her eyes open. Yet the sight of Sam, patiently tinkering with his beloved machine, dressed as always in jeans and a T-shirt, a cigarette burning in the ashtray on the floor beside him, was so welcome and comforting that she could not take her eyes off it in order to let them close.

She had arrived home from San Francisco at five. Sam had been at LaGuardia to pick her up. He had intended to take her out to dinner, but on an impulse she had begged him to let her come here and help him make a little supper as they had done in the old days. They had cooked spaghetti and made a salad, and now he had retired to his old occupation, aware somehow that this was what she wanted him to do.

It was no wonder, she mused, that she was in a mood to bring back old times. The last eight months had constituted a revolution in her life, one that left no time for reflection or even emotion.

CompuTel was growing out of control, its new customers exceeding the capacities of its work force. Since the company had such a brilliant record of success, and since it had no real competitors, the demand for its services was greater than it could keep up with. Businesses in such far-flung cities as San Francisco, Atlanta, Detroit, Chicago, and Los Angeles were deluging CompuTel with requests for its service. These eager new customers had long-standing inventory and bookkeeping problems, and had come to see the wisdom of computerization as a time- and money-saving procedure.

CompuTel had to expand. On the advice of company attorney Lee Nugent Francie had agreed to go public with a stock offering. As a privately held company CompuTel simply lacked the financial resources to keep up with its own amazing growth.

Francie was a full-time executive now. She barely had time for programming, and had to leave most of that work for Sam and Dana and the programmers she had hired from colleges and technical institutes around the country. She was away from New York more than half the time, either starting up new CompuTel branches in other cities or visiting the existing branches to make sure her hand-picked managers had their many accounts under control.

The growth of CompuTel was as exhausting as it was stimulating. It was wonderful to see the company succeed so quickly, but Francie could not escape the feeling that she was on a roller coaster running out of control. When she had started the company as a one-woman operation, she had had vague dreams of eventual success, and had pictured it as a situation of stability and happiness. She never realized success could be this mad rush to keep up with a snowballing operation whose growth was always a step ahead of her efforts to control it.

The job was taking its toll. She was too thin, too tired most of the time, and could not seem to find the leisure to relax anymore. Success was a harsh master.

No wonder, then, that tonight, at her wits' end, she had turned to Sam. When he opened the door to the loft after their brief stop at the grocery store down the block, the place looked like an old friend to her. She had not seen it for three months. Its dark recesses were like a pleasant womb, and 9292, with its circuit boards and dim lights, had a hearthlike quality that calmed Francie's nerves.

But the old days of their quiet intimacy in the loft, when 9292 was CompuTel's only computer, and Francie and Sam the company's only employees, were gone now. Indeed, 9292 was no longer an active part of the operation, having been replaced by two spanking new IBMs leased in the last six months. And Francie never came to the loft any more, for her evenings were spent in her new Riverside Drive apartment making long-distance calls to CompuTel's far-flung executives and biggest customers.

Francie was surprised to see that 9292 had now shrunk to less than half of its former size. Since the machine's services were no longer needed by CompuTel, Sam had been stepping up his experiments with substituting integrated circuits for its thousands of vacuum tubes. An expert on hardware, Sam had been keeping up with the new technology in microcircuitry, and was always telling Francie how deeply he believed that miniaturization was the wave of the future for computers.

"Even today," he would say, "there are microchips the size of your fingernail that can do the work that ENIAC did in 1945. The future is unlimited."

Only now, in seeing how small 9292 had become without losing any of its computing or analyzing power, did Francie realize how right Sam had been. As she studied the computer, which now looked about the size of five or six dishwashers lined up in a row instead of ten or twelve as of old, it occurred to her that the day might come when a computer would be no larger than, say, a refrigerator. How simple things would be then for computer operators, and for everyone who needed the services of a computer.

But that was a long way off.

After dinner Francie's exhaustion made it almost impossible for her to speak. Sam respected her silence, and put her on the couch with a cup of coffee beside her, to watch him work. He looked up occasionally and smiled, but said little. She had always found it easy to be silent with him. Something about his relaxed nature took away all pressure to make small talk.

As she looked at him now he reached to put out his cigarette, which had burned down forgotten in the ashtray. The twisting of his torso pulled the T-shirt out from the waist of his jeans. Francie smiled. He looked like a young boy in that split second, with the skin of his midriff peeking out from the faded fabrics of the shirt and jeans.

But Sam was no boy. He was all man, as Francie had learned by working side by side with him for nearly a year and a half.

Only by knowing Sam's inner strength and confidence could one begin to appreciate the masculine presence of his body. The husky limbs, with their blond dusting of hair, the attractive face with its languid brown eyes, the freckled complexion, the strong arms and hands—it was all a picture of handsomeness which differed radically from what one saw in contemporary movie stars or in advertisements depicting desirable men. Yet it was entrancing in its own peculiar way, because Francie knew how strong a man Sam really was behind his modesty and his relaxed way of accepting the world.

He looked up at her now from his position on the floor, and smiled. She smiled back, blushing a bit in the shadows, for she had unwittingly been studying him with a fascination that unsettled her.

"Tired?" he asked. "Shall I take you home?"

She shook her head. "I'm fine." This was where she wanted to be tonight, and she did not care how tired she was. She did not want to be alone.

Sam went back to his work. Francie was glad he had stopped looking at her, for she felt embarrassed to meet his eyes. Perhaps it was her exhaustion, or something else that had been building in her these past weeks without her knowledge. Sam's hug at LaGuardia had made her feel not only the warmth of home, but also the accumulated pain of having been away. She had wanted to curl up in his embrace like a little girl and forget her troubles.

With this thought her eyes began to close. Dream images began to throng her mind, banishing reflection. She was no longer here in the loft, a dozen paces from Sam, but in his arms, as he hugged her hello at the airport. His embrace was familiar, but also intoxicating, like a drug that lifted her out of herself and made her fly dizzily toward strange places.

Yet she was not at the airport after all. They were at his lake, the lake she had never seen, Firefly Lake, and they were going fishing. She could hear the quiet sounds of the forest birds echoing across the water, and feel the sun of early morning on her cheeks. There was the smell of coffee, and of fresh water, and of the pine needles covering the paths, dropped by the thick stands of trees which embraced the lake like a lover's arms.

And Sam was holding her close. The sweet morning sun had seduced them both into a sudden mood of tenderness, and he had taken her into his embrace, pulling her close and telling her everything was going to be all right. She saw her hair fall across his shoulder. She smelled his clean natural scent mingling with the aromas of morning.

And then, somehow, she was kissing him, her own arms pulling him closer. She was worried that he would be shocked, would pull away, and tell her she was out of line. But no: his tenderness blended easily into her passion, and his lips were opening to return her kiss. The strong male hands were about the small of her back, soothing and caressing. And a terrible prohibited yielding shot through all her senses, a hot surrender confessing itself at last . . .

Francie was fast asleep.

Sam heard her soft, regular breathing and looked up. Francie was curled up on the couch, her head resting against the cushions, her eyes closed.

He had been afraid this would happen. At the airport she had seemed completely exhausted, and at least fifteen pounds underweight. His heart had gone out to her, for she looked lonely and bereft as a little girl when she came through the gate.

He would have insisted she go straight home to bed, but there was something so touching about her entreaty to come here that he had given in for her sake. She had been on the road too long, and needed to regain a sense of belonging.

Over dinner she had looked drained to the point of prostration, but so happy that he did not have the heart to suggest he take her home early. And now, predictably, she had fallen asleep while she watched him work.

He got up silently and went to her side. He touched her cheek softly. She purred in her slumber.

There was no point in waking her to take her home. It would be too cruel. Sam went into the bedroom, made up his own double bed for her, and hunted up an old comforter for himself. He would sleep on the couch after putting her to bed.

He returned to the living room, slipped an arm around her neck and another beneath her knees, and picked her up as gently as he could. She was so light! It made him both proud and sad to think of the terrific brain behind that sleeping face, and the stubborn will inside this frail body. She worked much too hard. She drove herself so relentlessly. He had often wondered why, and never really figured it out.

He carried her to the bedroom and placed her carefully on the bed. Her arms had curled around his neck as he bore her through the shadows, and now she did not let go. Still asleep, she clung to him, a strange little moan in her throat. He smelled the unique sweetness of her flesh, a complex scent that never failed to entrance him.

He tried to extricate himself from her embrace, but she would not let him. It seemed that even in sleep her mood of desperate loneliness had not left her.

Her face was close to his now. Embarrassed, he smiled and patted her shoulder. He felt absurd, bent over her that way in the darkness, imprisoned by her arms and by the dreams that were making her embrace him.

"Mmm," he heard her murmur, her mind invisible behind her closed eyes, but her body clinging all too intimately to his.

Sam tried to make her let go of him. But his own defenses against her beauty were not strong, and he felt himself being pulled closer to her. Her lips brushed his cheek, a warm touch that made his body feel weak. The fragrant hollow of her neck touched his own lips, and he felt a tremor inside him.

A twinge of fear seized Sam. This was dangerous play. Francie was the only friend in the world he valued, and he had respected her separate existence at considerable cost to himself all this time. He had hidden from his real feelings about her as from a curse which could ruin their friendly relationship forever if revealed only once.

And now she was in his bed, holding him close in her sleep, and not letting him go. He could not resist her much longer.

"Francie . . . ," he murmured. "It's all right. Go to sleep now."

But she did not hear him. Her lips were finding their way unerringly to his, and softly seeking to part them.

"Honey," he pleaded. "This isn't what you want."

She silenced him with a kiss that was at once so candid and so daring that it left his body on fire. The whole slim length of her was in his arms. He could feel the small breasts against his chest, the long beautiful thighs grazing his hips. And, from nowhere, her hands had found their way to the bare flesh of his ribcage, where his T-shirt had pulled out of his pants.

He had long since given up all resistance to Francie's beauty in his mind. Her image had owned his dreams since the first week he met her. But now that magnificent body was offering itself to him, and his man's instincts were clamoring overpoweringly to give in to it.

He must not, he thought. She was asleep. She did not know what she was doing.

"Francie," he said, "don't. Please . . ."

Her kiss became more gentle, but somehow all the more seductive. The hands on his bare skin came to rest on his hips.

"Don't say no," she murmured.

And he realized she was awake enough to know exactly what she was doing.

With that knowledge Sam's last defenses crumbled. He held her closer, felt a long supple thigh slip between his legs as her tongue once more came into his mouth, and heard the sweet sigh in her throat as his manhood rose eagerly to meet her.

"Oh," she moaned, holding him with slender arms grown suddenly wise and strong. "Oh . . ."

And Sam gave up the struggle.

Two hours later Sam Carpenter lay awake on the bed beside Francie, supporting his head with a tired palm and watching her sleep.

He felt an uncanny thrill, somewhere between dread and exultation, as his eyes traveled over the soft body whose secret places he now knew. Francie had never looked so beautiful before, or so natural, or so heartbreakingly innocent.

She had the body of a goddess, all sleek curves and nubile contours, with straight girlish hips, flat stomach, firm breasts, and a face made more bewitching than ever by repose.

Sam studied her, thinking back over all the months he had devoted to helping her achieve her dream, and wondering at the fact that it had all led to this. Though every sinew of his man's body sang with the joy of having possessed her, he could not help feeling like a thief who had stolen something from her which she was not truly ready to give.

He thought of their working relationship, and of their friendship. They had been close as colleagues. But they had never been really intimate as people. This was perhaps Sam's doing more than anything else. He had known almost from the beginning that his heart could not resist Francie, and so he had used the best of his willpower to keep his distance from her, and to respect her privacy.

And Francie had done the rest. She seemed to want precisely the friendship he offered, and nothing more. His own distance seemed to make it easier for her to trust him. And, inside himself, he had allowed this trust to substitute for the deeper feeling his fantasies demanded of her.

It had not been easy staying on his side of that invisible line all these months, but he had done it for her sake. And he had been sure he was right.

But now, just like that, all his efforts were undone.

He wondered what he would say to her tomorrow. Would there be apologies? Promises that it would never happen again? Or perhaps the silence that sometimes descends between two people who have taken a step they both regret?

Would she feel the same way about him as before? That was the most important question. Would she trust him?

Sam did not dare think about this. The pain it caused was as terrible as the pleasure she had given him tonight had been beautiful.

But even as he worried about safeguarding the relationship he already had with Francie, a prohibited voice inside him was asking whether a new era had dawned between them tonight. Could she feel about him as he had felt about her, so painfully and gloriously, from the beginning? Could she have been hiding it all this time, as he himself had?

This notion destroyed the last of Sam's resistance. His heart beat madly inside his chest. Exultation took his breath away.

He sat gazing at Francie, wanting a cigarette but not having the courage to tear himself away from the sight of her long enough to get it. He was hypnotized by her, and by the hopes swelling inside him.

As he watched, she stirred in her sleep, and a frown furrowed her brow. A word escaped her lips, muffled and alien as sleep talk usually is. She looked as sweet as a child in her slumber. His heart went out to her.

Then she repeated the word, in a garbled sleepy moan. And this time, to his eternal chagrin, he understood it.

"Jack . . ."

The sound was like a knife plunged into Sam's flesh at its weakest point. A coldness knotted hard inside his stomach, filling him with shame.

"Jack . . ." The word came out again, barely stirring her lips. Mumbled though it was, it sent a sharp echo through Sam's heart, the knell of a reality worse than he had feared, and of a punishment more total than he had dared to dread.

For he knew who she meant.

Then she turned on her side and drifted away into the remoteness of dreams in which he had no part. Sam watched in silence, feeling as though she were leaving him forever.

Now all his questions were answered.

══ 31 ══

*Frances Bollinger, Chairman and CEO of the dynamic young company,
announced the stock offering at a special meeting of CompuTel's managers
in San Francisco this morning. . . .*

Jack Magnus sat at his breakfast table, reading *The Wall Street Journal*.

He could feel Belinda's eyes on him from across the table. She was
dressed in an attractive morning outfit, looking sunny and feminine.
Belinda always dressed beautifully for him.

She was silent. She respected his need to read through the *Journal*
carefully. Only when he put it aside did she converse with him about the
day's plans.

But now Jack was not thinking about Belinda at all.

He was looking at the *Journal*'s article about CompuTel, the successful
young computer consulting company which had just gone public.

And he was looking at the small but devastatingly beautiful photograph
of Francie Bollinger that accompanied the article.

Jack hoped his hands were not shaking as he looked at the photo. He
wondered if Belinda, silent across the table, could feel his emotion.

He was unprepared for the effect of the picture on him, and of the news
about Francie and her successful new life.

He had thought he had things under control. He had done what was
necessary, at a considerable price to himself.

He had had to marry Belinda because the marriage was part of his
master plan. He knew his father would not accept any other choice. It was
Belinda or nothing. If Jack had tried to keep Francie, his whole future
would have been out the window.

It had been the most difficult choice of Jack's life, but he had made it,
and was determined to live with it.

Even when he had first met Francie Bollinger, and fell under the
complicated spell of her smile, her honesty, and her great brain, he
realized that the larger game plan could not include her.

But that did not mean he could resist her.

The first time she kissed him, high above his father's assembled guests at Gretchen's party, something strange and exciting had come alive inside him, a thing he had thought no woman could ever give him. And once tasted, it was forbidden fruit he could not live without.

He had gone to seek her out in Paris because the memory of that first kiss had driven him almost crazy with desire. He had used every wile he knew to get her to give in to him, and when she did—oh! what a night that had been!—he did the only thing he knew that would make this upright and honest girl agree to remain his lover. He had promised marriage.

At that time he was too dazzled by her body and her charms to think far ahead. He only wanted to continue his affair with her as long as possible. So he had convinced her to make a secret of their marriage plans, and to let things ride until her computer system was finished. He had reasoned that he would figure out an arrangement later, bring Francie back to the States as his lover, and gradually accustom her to the idea that they could not marry after all.

Of course he had known that Francie would not dream of becoming his mistress while he married someone else. She was far too proud for that sort of capitulation.

But she was deeply attached to him. The look in her eyes when they were alone together made that perfectly clear. And the way she made love . . . It was obvious that Jack had found his way to her heart. This gave him hope of holding on to her somehow.

So he had tried to string her along until he could figure out a solution. Then his father had stepped in.

Anton Magnus had had a talk with Jack, and made it forcefully clear that the moment had come to stop stalling and marry Belinda. The old man meant business this time, there was no doubt of it. What was more, the peculiar gleam in his dark eyes suggested that he knew something about Jack's feelings for Francie—enough to know that it would be a major sacrifice for Jack to give her up. This was a classic Anton Magnus action. He never felt sure of people until he had forced them to give up something they cared deeply about. Only then was he certain of their loyalty to him and their obedience.

So Jack had given in. There was no choice.

And when he learned that Francie was to be fired as part of the bargain—another typical Anton Magnus gesture of pouring salt in the wound, of taking no prisoners—he had not protested. He must let his father have his way, no matter how much it hurt.

But in doing so he had been thinking of the future. For someday Jack himself would control Magnus Industries.

Everything must be sacrificed to the master plan. As long as Anton Magnus remained at the head of the empire he had created, Jack's own life was incomplete.

It was a waiting game. And Jack had learned everything he knew about gamesmanship from Anton Magnus. As of today Anton had the power.

But Jack's hole card was time itself. Not even Anton Magnus could cheat Mother Nature. Clever though he might be, and diabolical as no man Jack had ever met, Anton could not hold back the march of time. Sooner or later he would have to turn over the corporation he had spent his life building—to his son.

And when Jack had the power, things would be different. He would be free to do things his way, to think about his own happiness, perhaps to reevaluate his marriage to Belinda and make a change if he wished.

He had had to sacrifice Francie to this larger cause. Losing her had nearly killed him, but he had lived through the agony, because there was no other way. Had he married Francie he would have lost everything.

And his plan had worked. As he sat here today with Belinda, his dutiful and attractive wife, he was within a hair's breadth of the prize he had sought all these years. Father was seventy-two years old. Soon he would have to retire. Jack would control everything.

But now this little article in the *Journal* had come along to remind Jack of the single weak link in his entire scheme, a weak link he had tried manfully to forget all this time.

He could not live without Francie.

Though Jack normally wasted little time in considering his own emotions, this time he must do so. For the need shaking him as he looked at the photograph of Francie was like a tidal wave. It was as though she were the center of the earth, exerting a magnetic attraction infinitely more powerful than his will.

His days with her in Paris came back to his mind. Though he had had many women in his time, he had never experienced anything sexually that could be compared to the thrill of possessing Francie. There was a sweetness about her, and a sensual womanly complexity, that made her irresistible.

He had tried to forget those days. But their image had haunted him, owning his fantasies every time he made love to Belinda.

He had tried to combat them by not thinking about sex, by throwing himself into his job, and making work the devouring energy of his life.

And he thought he had succeeded.

But now he had seen Francie's picture. He realized she had not simply disappeared when he married Belinda. She had gone on with her life. And now she was out in the world, more beautiful than ever, independent, following her own initiative, making a success of her work, living in her own place somewhere, wearing her simple, lovely clothes, gracing those around her with her smile, perhaps her laughter.

The thought blinded Jack with wanting. All these months he had lived by pretending that Francie had ceased to exist. Now he knew she was still in the world.

And he must have her.

But how? That was the question.

Jack knew he could not sacrifice everything he had, everything he had worked for and was still working for, just for the sake of his need.

Or even his love, if that was the word for it.

No. The mission of his life was clear. Magnus Industries was being handed to him on a silver platter, and with it perhaps the greatest power any one man could possess in the world of business. What Anton Magnus had already made of that power was enormous. What Jack could do with it in another ten or twenty years was incalculable. He could control presidents, make his mark upon the entire world, influence the course of history itself.

He could not give that up.

On the other hand, as he now realized with an aching hunger that almost made him feel faint, he could not live without Francie.

This created an interesting dilemma. A problem almost as complex as the chess problems which so fascinated Anton Magnus, and which Anton used to explain to his son in years past.

How to gain Francie, but not to lose the prize for which he had already sacrificed so much.

He could not oppose his father. Not at this point. They had struck their deal, and he must go along with it. Anton Magnus was not a man who took betrayal lightly.

There was no way to get around the old man. He was too clever, and too willful.

But one might, if one was cautious enough about it, make a bargain with Anton Magnus.

The prize would have to be a valuable one. Anton Magnus never settled for anything less than total victory—or what he thought was total victory.

It would be a hard bargain, the most dangerous move in the game. Jack would have to think far ahead, and foresee all the possibilities, before taking action.

But even now, as he studied the picture of Francie, he thought he saw a way.

He lowered the newspaper and looked at Belinda. She smiled as she met his eyes.

He felt sorry for her. She was the real loser in all this. But that could not be helped. Women like Belinda were pawns. They were always the losers.

Jack had work to do.

Time was on his side. If he used that fact carefully, he could pick up all the marbles.

And Jack was his father's son. It was all or nothing. A Magnus never settles for second best.

* * *

Had Jack not been so wrapped up in his own amorous thoughts about Francie, and the dilemma facing his own life, he might have mused that other eyes than his own could well be interested by the *Journal* article. And he might have suspected that events were about to push his long-range plans aside, at least for a while.

As it happened, at that very moment, over coffee in his bedroom in the Park Avenue house, Anton Magnus was reading the article about CompuTel and its overnight success.

His conclusions differed considerably from those of his son.

After perusing the article carefully he picked up the phone and called his executive secretary, who was already in the office.

"Vera," he said, "I want you to tell Mr. Decker of the legal department to be in my office at ten this morning. I have something I want to show him."

=== 32 ===

It was the first of June, a week before the first CompuTel stockholders' meeting, which was to be held in San Diego, site of the newest CompuTel branch office. It was a summery morning. The world looked balmy and welcoming through the windows of Sam's loft.

Francie had awakened first. She sat for a long moment watching Sam sleep, and then got up to make the coffee and bring in the newspapers.

She moved through the main room of the loft, where 9292, now shrunken even further than it had been a month ago, looked forlorn and emaciated compared to its former bulk. Francie smiled, for she knew that the computer, despite its pitiful appearance, could do many times the work it used to do. Such was the miracle of microprocessing, combined with Sam's great technical talent.

She could not help glancing behind her to the bedroom where Sam still slept. He was breathing calmly, his thick arm thrown across the bed where she had lain only a moment ago. His body was redolent of her own passion, and as she moved through the loft, using his shirt as a makeshift nightgown, her own senses were full of the pungent masculine aroma of him.

She looked back on the weeks since their first night together. After that initial tryst Francie had been in a state of shock. She could not believe what she had done. What had possessed her?

She did not know. She had been half-asleep when it happened, and crazed by months of overwork. But she did not use this as an excuse. Even if only in her body and her desire, she had known what she was doing. Sam had tried manfully to resist her, and she had overpowered him with the same need that was overpowering her.

Where that need had come from, and what it really meant, was the real enigma. She knew she trusted Sam, respected him, and depended on him a great deal. But did she love him?

Now that she had committed the act of love with him, her upbringing forced her to ask the question. But she could not answer it, and this troubled her. She knew that she did not feel complete without Sam. He brought a sense of home, of warmth and happiness, to her life, that did not seem to be there without him. Yet it was not her feeling for Sam that was driving her toward greater and greater ambition. The unspoken impulse relentlessly pushing her forward in life was separate from the friendship she bore him.

When Sam awoke, that first morning, she had apologized to him for what she had done, and assured him that it would not happen again. She hated to sound so rigid and old-fashioned in her behavior toward him, but she could not help it. Her ideas about sex were deep-seated and strict. More yet, she had already learned to her chagrin how deadly a sexual relationship without genuine love and commitment can be.

Sam had assured her that she had nothing to be sorry for, while promising that their one night together did not give him ideas about his relationship with her. Nothing, he said, was changed. He would continue to be her friend and dedicated colleague, as before.

Yet she could see that Sam himself was troubled by what they had done together. He seemed consumed by guilt, and very unhappy. Touched by this, she had put her arms around him, kissed his cheek warmly, and asked him to help her let bygones be bygones. After all, they had a company to run, and a busy future to worry about.

That very day they went back to work together, and did not mention what had happened. But both of them felt uncomfortable about it. It had upset their sense of their own friendship. In the days that followed they seemed to circle each other nervously, as though afraid to get too close to each other.

Then it happened again.

One evening at the office Francie was going over the day's business with Sam and Dana, and her eyes met Sam's for a brief instant which was like an earthquake to her. She knew she had to be with him again.

She went home, filled with shame. She prowled her apartment like a caged animal, tried to forget Sam by doing some late work, and finally, beside herself, called him to ask if she could drop over for a moment.

When he opened the door of the loft she almost threw herself into his arms. She had never felt so overwhelming a physical need.

To her surprise, Sam seemed to be as much in the grip of that outburst of passion as she. Their lovemaking was more beautiful for the fact that they had both tried to resist each other for so long. Francie's sighs of ecstasy were also sighs of relief at having returned to the closeness she had missed in her long, futile attempt to stay away from Sam.

Since then they had been lovers many times. Neither said a word about the underlying meaning of their relationship. But neither seemed able to resist the pull of their shared desire. There was no talk of love, or of the future. But the bond between them deepened disturbingly. The situation did not grow any easier with the passage of the weeks.

Francie did not know what to make of this. Sam was not the man she had dreamed of as a girl. He was much more down-to-earth, modest, and even rumpled than the man of her fantasies.

The emotion she had felt for Jack Magnus had been an entirely different matter. It was an obsession, a wild feeling of losing herself. What Sam made her feel was not this at all. It was a sweet, welcoming warmth that only gradually increased its heat, leading her naturally from affection to desire.

Francie was still an old-fashioned girl, despite what she was doing with Sam. She worried about it, and she feared that it was leading her into trouble. But such was her need for Sam that she could not resist him. And the strange, seductive feeling of being at home with Sam, of being herself only with him, grew more compelling to her. His attractiveness came not only from the heat of his caresses, but from the belonging she felt in his arms.

Thus Francie walked an uneasy tightrope between a friendship she valued more highly than anything else, and an unexpected sexual relationship which seemed to threaten the very friendship from which it had grown.

This confused jumble of feelings was in Francie's mind this morning as she turned on the coffee pot and opened the door to get the morning paper.

To her surprise she saw an official-looking letter resting on top of the newspaper. It was addressed to Samuel G. Carpenter, Vice-President of CompuTel, Inc. The letter was from a large New York law firm named Coster, Coster and Whitehouse, of which Francie had vaguely heard.

Francie took the letter into the kitchen and put it on the table. She could almost smell the menace coming from it. As she made herself a cup of coffee she felt an extraordinary temptation to open the letter. But she could not. It was addressed to Sam.

She was sitting at the table in Sam's shirt, nervously sipping at her coffee, when a voice rang out, almost making her jump.

"What's the matter? I thought I heard a noise." It was Sam.

Francie leaped to her feet and embraced him. Then she pointed to the letter.

"I may be crazy," she said, "but it's making me nervous. Open it, Sam, please."

Sleepily Sam opened the letter. His expression darkened as he took in its contents. Then he handed it to Francie. She read it through quickly, and then had to start again, so shocked was she by what was in it.

> *Coster, Coster & Whitehouse*
> *Attorneys for*
> *Magnus Industries, Inc.*

May 30, 1958

CompuTel, Inc.
Samuel G. Carpenter, Vice-President
435 Cedar Street
New York, N.Y.

NOTIFICATION OF PATENT INFRINGEMENT

Dear Sirs:

You are hereby informed of a suit being brought against you by us on behalf of Magnus Industries, Inc. for patent infringement in the matter of U.S. Patent #3647576857 relating to Computer Systems, the patent held by Magnus Industries, Inc. It has come to our client's attention that certain computer programs being used by you in your professional consulting work embody technical materials on which our client holds a patent. Permission to copy these materials not having been duly requested by you, our client demands that you cease and desist from all such activity pending a decision of the Federal Court.

Sincerely yours,
Graham S. Coster, President

cc: Frances M. Bollinger, President
Martin W. Decker, Legal Dept., Magnus Industries

Francie had turned pale.

"What does it mean?" she asked Sam.

He shook his head. "Damned if I know," he said. "I don't have a clue as to what they're talking about."

Francie had grasped his hand in her distress. She felt him put his arm around her.

"I have a bad feeling about this," she said. "I think we'd better call Lee Nugent right away."

Sam nodded. Lee, CompuTel's attorney, would know what the letter meant.

Nervously, Francie let go of Sam's hand and hurried to the bedroom to shower and get dressed.

The news was worse than either Francie or Sam had expected.

Lee Nugent, a medium-sized man with blond thinning hair and friendly eyes, welcomed Francie and Sam to his office with a decorum which masked his own concern.

"Francie, Sam, I want you to meet someone," he said, pointing to a distinguished-looking middle-aged man who stood up to offer his hand to Francie. "This is Oliver Meinen, of Briggs, Lotman and Meinen, a prominent Manhattan law firm. Oliver's specialty is patent law. He's here to help us out with some advice."

They shook hands all around and sat down at Lee's conference table.

"I've had a chat with Graham Coster over the phone," Lee said. "Here's the deal. Apparently Magnus Industries holds a patent on a particular type of computer system, a system which handles inventory, overhead, and productivity for businesses. I understand, Francie, that you worked with this material when you were at Magnus. Well, to make a long story short, Magnus and their attorneys seem to think that the programs you're using for your present CompuTel clients contain enough elements of the Magnus original to make the whole thing actionable."

Francie had turned white with anger.

"Lee," she said, "I invented the system they're talking about. Me, personally, I mean. I did it single-handedly. I set up their whole European system for them, and worked all the bugs out of the master program. I was on the verge of implementing it myself when they . . . fired me."

Lee was listening calmly.

"Then what happened?" he asked.

"Well," Francie said, "I started CompuTel, found Sam and his computer, and began devising programs on a much smaller scale to service businessmen who needed to lower their overhead by computerizing their financial records, billing, and so on. That's all there is to it."

Lee cleared his throat. "Would you say, as a computer expert," he asked, "that your new programs contain elements which were originally devised for the Magnus system?"

Francie frowned. "Well, I suppose so," she said. "They have logical elements in common. Of course. I just naturally used my own invention in modified form to create the CompuTel programs."

Lee raised an eyebrow.

"You don't hold a patent of your own on your original program, I take it," he said.

Francie looked at him in surprise. "Well, no," she said. "It never occurred to me."

"It did occur to Magnus Industries," Lee said. "They applied for a patent on that procedure on—let me see—on August 24th, 1956."

Francie turned pale. "That was the week I left," she said in a small voice.

"The patent was applied for and eventually accepted," Lee said. "They hold a patent on the entire logical procedure behind the program. Now, if they can prove that what you've been doing at CompuTel uses the same concept you used at Magnus, then you're in patent infringement. You'll have to pay damages, and perhaps desist from using the programs."

Francie felt her fingers trembling. She could not believe her ears.

"Lee, you've got to believe me," she said. "I invented the prototype they patented. They stole it from me, you see, when they fired me."

"Didn't it ever occur to you at the time to sue them, or to patent the prototype yourself?" Lee asked.

Francie shook her head. "I just thought of it as work," she said. "Not as inventing. It never occurred to me that you could patent a thing such as I had done. I guess I didn't know enough about patents."

"Well, they did," Lee said. "I don't suppose you have any materials on the invention itself which could prove that it was yours in the first place? Some sort of daily records of your work . . . ?"

Francie thought of her time at Magnus, both in New York and in Europe. She had lost nearly all her records, for they had been inside the company when she was locked out the week she was fired. As for her earliest records of her computer idea, such as the prospectus she had given Jack Magnus and read before the Magnus board of directors, she had thrown those away in her disgust and anger after she was fired.

She could only shake her head now. "Nothing, Lee. It's all lost," she said.

"Were there people at Magnus who could testify to the role you played in creating the original programs?" Lee asked.

Francie thought of Jack Magnus, of the board of directors, of Roland de Leaumes, and of her colleagues at Magnus-France.

"Everybody knew it was my responsibility and my invention," she said. "That's why I had to suffer the embarrassment when it didn't work the first time. But as to there being proof of my role . . . I just don't know, Lee."

Lee turned to Oliver Meinen.

"Ollie, what do you think of all this?" he asked.

"In a case like this," Oliver Meinen said, "all the weight of the law is behind the patent holder. If there was a question as to who had a right to the patent, that should have been litigated two years ago, when Magnus applied for the patent. Even then you would have had to have hard evidence of your role in the invention, and it probably would have been a tough fight, Miss Bollinger, given that you were an employee of Magnus Industries when you did the work. Magnus would have claimed that they were entitled to the patent, since your work had been done for them."

"Could I have won?" Francie asked.

The attorney shrugged. "You might have made a fight of it," he said. "But cases like that tend to drag on for years. I just don't know."

Francie smiled bitterly. She thought of her early days at Magnus, and of her work for Raymond Wilbur. Her very first experience at Magnus had been of having the credit for her work taken from her. Now things had come full circle.

She turned to Lee. "What do we do now?" she asked. "Pay them their patent royalty? We can afford it, can't we? It can't be that much."

Lee frowned. "I'm afraid that won't work," he said. "Their attorneys are claiming that under federal law you have usurped Magnus's right to exploit the patent for profit. So they're suing you for lost profits. And they're insisting that you immediately cease and desist from all profit-making activity based on this system."

Francie could hardly believe her ears.

"You mean," she asked, glancing at Sam, "they're trying to put us out of business?"

Lee looked pained. "I'm afraid that's what it amounts to," he said.

There was a silence. Francie cast a sidelong glance at Sam. She was overcome by a dizzying combination of guilt and rage. Guilt, because she felt she had enticed Sam into a venture which, because of her, had come to nothing. Rage, because she knew perfectly well that malice, an infinite malice, was behind the legal action on the part of Magnus Industries.

Lee tried to muster a semblance of encouragement.

"We can fight this, of course, in the courts," he said. "There are clear records of your part in the invention of the concept. We can subpoena the Magnus employees who worked under you, or had contact with you at the time. Of course, what they'll say we can't be sure. And we must assume that Magnus will bring forward people who will tell a different story. Finally, there is still the problem that you were a Magnus employee when you did the work. That's our weakest point, I'm afraid. Magnus will claim a right to the patent and the profits on that basis alone."

Francie looked from Sam to the two lawyers before her. She thought of Magnus Industries' awesome power.

"We wouldn't win, would we?" she asked Lee.

He smiled ruefully. "Against their high-priced law firm, with the weight of the law on their side?" he asked. "Not a chance, Francie. You can't fight them. They're just too big. Half the time they make the rules. The other half they break them and get away with it. That's big business. I'm sorry."

Francie sat for a long moment, as though lost in thought. The silence in the room became unbearable.

At last she stood up and shook hands with Oliver Meinen. "Thank you for your advice," she said. "And thanks, Lee, for handling this."

She turned to leave.

"What will you do now?" Lee asked.

She looked at him with a sad smile.

"I don't know," she said. "I really don't."

$$=== 33 ===$$

That night Sam did not see Francie.

She did not answer her phone at her apartment. Sam went to see if she was there, but there was no answer.

He went back to the loft to wait to hear from her. There were many details to discuss. Lee Nugent was planning to open talks with the Magnus Corporation about a settlement. Someone had to decide how to handle the termination of CompuTel's current clients. There was the question of bankruptcy.

There was a lot to be done.

Sam was worried about Francie. He had seen a dark look come over her in Lee's office, a look unlike any he had ever seen on her beautiful face before. It was a look of anger, and of something beyond anger.

He needed to find her. For the first time since he had known her, he was truly worried that she was not all right.

Francie spent the night in a downtown hotel. She had walked in with no luggage, not even a toothbrush, and had taken a room. She sat up all night without sleeping.

The first hours she spent trying to overcome her disbelief at what had happened. Never in her life had she imagined such power, or such malice, as the Magnus corporation had displayed in putting her out of business for using the system she herself had invented. A system Magnus itself only possessed by outright theft!

At first Francie felt only horror at the thought that the Magnus monster had come out of nowhere to pursue her this way, and to use its ill-gotten patent to do her out of the small but growing business she had built from nothing. The agony of her helplessness in the face of such an injustice blinded her to all else.

Then it occurred to her with a strange satisfaction that Magnus Industries, in all its enormous power and its remoteness, had not been able to go its separate way and forget Francie. Goliath had not been secure enough in his power to forget David. He had come back to pursue her, as though not confident of his dominion over her.

This thought intrigued Francie, and filled her mind with strange new ideas.

She began to think over her past. She thought about Magnus Industries, about Raymond Wilbur, about Roland de Leaumes, about Jack Magnus, and his father. Gradually a kind of clarity she had never known before came to illuminate her thinking. She understood that the rage she had been feeling since she saw the letter from Magnus's lawyers was futile, and a weakness on her part.

Anger would do her no good now.

Something else was necessary.

The next morning, not having slept a wink, she went home to shower and dress, brushed her hair carefully, fixed her makeup, and took a cab to Magnus Industries' Sixth Avenue headquarters.

It was not until she reached the lobby that she remembered she could not get past the security guards into the building.

She stood looking at the directory.

MAGNUS, ANTON. 6511
MAGNUS, J. 6134

Fighting the fatigue in her nerves, Francie wondered why she had come here. As she studied the two names before her, she suddenly understood. The complex shifting of her thoughts throughout her long night alone had led to one question. It was time to find out the answer.

She went to the bank of public phones in the lobby and dialed the number of Magnus Industries.

"Magnus Industries, can I help you?" came the receptionist's voice.

Only at this instant did Francie decide which Magnus she was going to ask for.

"Anton Magnus's office, please," she said.

"One moment, please."

There was a lengthy delay. Then another secretary came on the line.

"Mr. Magnus's office, Miss Ober speaking," she said. "Can I help you?"

"Yes," Francie said. "This is Mr. Coster's office. Graham Coster, of Coster, Coster and Whitehead. We're handling a litigation for Mr. Magnus, concerning a computer firm called CompuTel. I have an urgent call from Mr. Coster for Mr. Magnus."

"One moment, please."

Again there was a delay.

Now a third voice came on the line.

"Mr. Magnus's office," it said. "Who may I say is calling?"

Francie smiled. It made sense that a caller starting with the outside company number would have to get through several levels of the Magnus monolith to reach Anton Magnus's own executive secretary.

Francie repeated her bogus message.

"Mr. Coster says it will only take a moment," she said. "It's in reference to their last conversation."

"One moment, please. He's on another line, but I think I can get you through."

Francie crossed her fingers, hoping that Anton Magnus's secretary would not put her off with a promise to call Mr. Coster back in a few minutes.

But she was in luck.

After a delay of only another minute a familiar, deep voice came on the line.

"Graham, what can I do for you?" said Anton Magnus.

Francie said nothing. She listened to the silence over the line.

"Graham, hello?" said Magnus. "Are you there?"

Again Francie said nothing. She listened carefully to the voice.

Now the pause was longer. Anton Magnus must be getting impatient. Francie wondered if he could hear her breathing over the line.

But somehow he did not hang up. He waited. Perhaps he had an inkling of who was on the line.

"Mr. Magnus," Francie said slowly.

"Yes, who is this? Hello? Who . . ." The voice trailed off. The silence was pregnant now on both sides. Francie could feel Anton Magnus wondering who was calling him. She followed the course of his own thoughts as he pondered his secretary's message, thought of his law firm and the CompuTel litigation, and sought to recognize the female voice that had said only two words to him.

The silence grew deeper. Francie could actually feel Anton Magnus's will poised on the other end of the line. She knew she had him, amazingly, on the defensive. He ought to have hung up by now if he was entirely sure of himself and his world. But he was intrigued, interested, concerned about who was calling him.

She could hear human vulnerability in his silence, flushed out like a prey from behind its fortress of power.

He did not say "hello" anymore. Only the silence linked them.

Very slowly Francie hung up the phone.

She looked out the phone booth at the passersby in the lobby. By now, sixty-five floors above her, Anton Magnus was querying his secretary about the call, and asking her to call Mr. Coster back and see what the mix-up was. In a few minutes the secretary would inform Anton Magnus that Mr. Coster had not called.

Then Anton Magnus would be confirmed in the thoughts that had been racing through his mind.

The Magnus castle keep, then, was not so impregnable as all that. Deep within its walls was a mere human being, with nerves and instincts and perhaps fears, like anyone else. At the heart of the labyrinth, the minotaur was only a man.

As for Francie, she had the answer she had been looking for when she had walked into the Magnus lobby and been stopped by the two names in the directory. Anton and Jack. Father and son.

Nothing is what it seems. The words of Jack Magnus came back to her from the most painful depths of her memory. They had an entirely new ring now. It occurred to Francie that yesterday's truths can be changed by time into utterly new and unexpected truths tomorrow.

"You can't fight them," Lee Nugent had said. "They're just too big."

His words had the undeniable ring of truth. Yet Francie's quick brain had seen something Lee Nugent could not see last night, and had it confirmed on the phone just now.

Somehow she did not feel helpless at all anymore.

She did not go home. Instead, she took the subway downtown and walked to Sam's loft. She let herself in and waited, watching the afternoon slowly go by.

The phone rang a couple of times, but she did not answer it.

At five-thirty Sam came in. He had spent the day at CompuTel's headquarters, waiting vainly for her to call.

Without a word he crossed the room and took her in his arms.

"Francie," he said, kissing her cheek. "I was so worried about you."

She said nothing. But her arm curled about his waist and pulled him closer. She touched his chin with a finger and managed a smile.

"Doing some thinking, were you?" he asked.

She nodded ambiguously. There was a faraway look in her eyes, unsettling but very beautiful.

They sat together for a long while, neither saying anything. The light grew dim around them. Somehow the pain filling Francie's whole body gave way slowly to the warmth of being close to Sam. Though he could not know her thoughts at this extraordinary moment, his affection meant more to her than understanding. All at once Sam's existence seemed the most crucial support in the world to her.

He went on holding her close as the shadows lengthened. When it was dark he held her out at arm's length and looked at her.

"I'm a lucky man," he said. "Who was the genie who made me cross your path that first day?"

Francie said nothing. But her smile told him how she felt.

"I've got an idea," he said. "For old time's sake, why don't we go to the Automat on Forty-second for dinner? It will bring back happy memories."

She nodded. "I'd go anywhere with you," she said.

He held her close and pointed to 9292, who had now shrunk to about the size of two Coke machines strung together by hundreds of wires.

"Well," Sam said, "we may be ragged and funny, like 9292 here, but we still know our business. I have a feeling that what happened yesterday is not the end of Francie Bollinger."

Francie looked at the computer which had shared their fortunes from the beginning. She understood Sam's words. 9292 did not look like much, but its capabilities had increased tenfold as its size decreased.

Francie felt like 9292. She was smaller than she once was, and battered by hard experience, but she still could do a job. And she could think a lot more clearly now than before.

With this thought she looked more closely at the computer. It was really much smaller than she had realized. She had been so busy these last months that she had not seen how much progress Sam was making.

"Before long it'll be no bigger than a refrigerator," she said.

"Smaller than that, maybe," Sam said. "There's no limit. Believe me, I know."

Suddenly Francie sat up. She looked from the computer to Sam.

"How long do you think it would take to make 9292 that small?" she asked.

Sam looked at her, surprised.

"I don't know," he said. "Probably not long. A year. Maybe less. Why do you ask?"

"Would it cost a lot?" she asked.

Sam raised an eyebrow.

"I don't know," he said. "I do it all by myself, you know, picking up circuit boards here and there and just tinkering . . . What are you getting at, anyway?"

Francie patted his cheek. "How about that dinner?" she asked. "You and I have some things to talk about."

"Let's go."

He took her hand and led her toward the door. As he helped her on with her coat he could feel the electric charge of her initiative inside her slim body. Decidedly, nothing could stop her. He had suspected it before, but now he was sure.

Sam was beginning to realize that in joining his fate to Francie's he had hitched his wagon to a star.

══ 34 ══

June 12, 1958

Scott Monteagle held Julie Magnus in his arms.

They were seated in the back of a carriage driving through Central Park. A warm woolen blanket was thrown over their legs. The night was chilly, and they had snuggled close together as their ride progressed.

Julie's eyes were closed in pleasure. She felt warm and protected in Scott's embrace. His cheek was pressed to her forehead. She felt like a schoolgirl with her beau.

It had been eight months since Scott's first visit to New York. Though he lacked the financial resources to return on his own, he had managed to maneuver his way into being assigned another business trip by his London law firm. In the interim he had written Julie at least once a week.

His letters were eloquently descriptive of every aspect of his life. Through them she came to know a great deal about his thoughts and his personality. But more than anything else his letters proved how deeply he cared for Julie, and how much it was hurting him to be separated from her.

Over time, this message had increased the spell cast over Julie by her few days with Scott last fall. And now that he had returned, she realized that he had come to occupy a place in her heart which had not existed before he entered her life.

Even now, as his physical presence rejoined the mental image she had been carrying of him for the past six months, and the personality which had come alive in his letters, she was awed by the strange way he made her feel.

All her life she had been dead inside, and content to walk the earth like the ghost of an aborted human being. But Scott Monteagle believed in her with a faith so strong, so unquestioning, that he succeeded somehow in bringing her back to life. This was a feat quite beyond her comprehension, as though a magical physician had penetrated the thick scar tissue over her wounds and cleansed them, so that they could truly heal at last.

Yet Julie feared the rawness of that unprotected flesh.

But she knew Scott felt her terror, and was not swayed by it from his purpose.

Scott seemed to have known a Julie from before Julie herself, an unspoiled and innocent young girl who had somehow remained intact under the Julie that Anton Magnus and the world had made out of her. A Julie she herself had long since given up on. But Scott believed in her, and, what was more, he could contact her, could hold out his hand and bring her out with his gentle ways.

Though it was frightening to witness the battle his affection wrought against such incredible odds, it was also exciting, and it gave Julie strange feelings which were not so indistinguishable from the most prohibited of all—hope.

The carriage was making its way toward the park's 59th Street entrance. Scott held Julie closer, and she felt the soft kiss of his lips against her brow.

She cuddled up to him like a child.

"You feel good," she said.

"So do you." His murmur soothed her like an exotic drug.

In the last week she had come to feel closer and closer to Scott's body, for now the rich fabric of his many letters had added itself to the physical form she remembered from six months ago. She dared to let herself luxuriate in the warmth of him, and to covet him with a girlish hunger that made her think of the adolescent impulses of normal girls, clean dreamy yearnings she herself had never felt until now.

Their embrace must have struck a new chord inside their bodies, for their lips met suddenly in a kiss which sent a tremor through Julie's senses. Scott held her tighter, and she could feel his need aroused by her own.

Despite all the new and wonderful feelings he had brought her this past week, she shrank from this upsurge of desire. Not that she wanted to. Her movement was as reflexive as the tensing of a claustrophobic who enters an elevator. It happened before she could stop herself.

Scott felt it, and relaxed his grip. Ashamed of the false signal that had forced him to release her, Julie tried to snuggle closer to him, as though to explain with her body the tortured ambivalence of her heart. Her performance seemed both laughable and tragic to her. She felt herself the lowest of liars, and the least desirable of women.

But Scott did not seem disconcerted by what had happened. He held her close, but chastely, and she felt the prohibited heat relax into the softness of his affection for her.

She felt safe in his arms once more. In one gentle movement he had acknowledged her upset, accepted it, and was giving her plenty of room.

Julie was grateful for his understanding, so much so that she could almost forgive herself for her unworthiness.

"Saturday will be my last day," he said.

She murmured her assent.

"I don't want to go." His voice sounded very young as he said this.

Julie looked into his eyes. He was so handsome! Now that she had had a chance to study his face, with its gentle eyes and fine manly features, she realized that she had never entirely stopped dreaming about it since her childhood, though he had only been a little boy when she had spent her secret afternoon with him.

Now his grown-up face seemed to have completed the fantasy and given it life. The gruesome years she had spent without him seemed banished. Scott was as real to her as anyone she had ever known. And he opened the door to a part of herself that was new to her, because it seemed to exist only for him.

When she reported a thought, a feeling, a memory to Scott, it was already different than it had felt before she told him. He made it more interesting, more human and natural, by his very attentiveness to it, and by his respect for her. She surprised herself constantly in conversation with him, for she said things of which she would have thought herself incapable. They just popped out, new and sparkling and unexpected, as though he had made her a different person.

A good person . . .

Nevertheless the ocean of her shame lurked behind these tentative openings to him, and threatened to engulf her at every moment. And she would have been torn unbearably by walking this tightrope were it not for Scott himself, who seemed to sense the depth of her predicament and to soothe it away whenever it rose to attack her.

Being with him was like a beautiful dream. Or, better still, a sunlit reality that made her previous life seem like a bad dream.

Which of the two was real? Was Scott Monteagle too good to be true? Julie's shame and fear made her wonder. But the look in his eyes and the touch of his hand on hers gave her courage to go on believing in this precious new adventure that had opened before her just when she thought it was too late for her to feel anything ever again.

The carriage was bearing them toward the edge of the park, and the end of their evening.

"What am I going to do without you?" Scott asked.

"Well," she smiled, "you'll go back to work, and finish building your mother's cabinet, and babysit for Lucy's little girl, and go to the movies, and read your Shakespeare and your Thoreau and your Dr. Johnson . . ."

"My God," he said. "You know as much about my routine as I do. I feel ashamed to have told you so much."

She laughed. "On the contrary," she said. "It's the most wonderful information I've put inside my head in twenty years."

He looked down into her eyes.

"And what will you do after I'm gone?" he asked.

She paused, thoughtful.

"When you're gone," she said, "I'll look at my watch and add five hours to the time, and think about where you are and what you're doing. When I wake up in the morning I'll think about you having your lunch, and seeing your clients. When I go to school"—Julie had decided to go back to college as a commuter at NYU and finish her degree—"I'll think about you finishing your afternoon. When I have lunch, I'll pretend I'm having dinner with you. And when the weekend comes, I'll think about your cottage at the farm, and wish I was there with you."

She was too wrapped up in what she was saying to think about the sexual and other excesses she might indulge in after his departure. She was so lulled by her closeness to him that she forgot to be ashamed of her life. She was thinking only of him.

His hand grasped her wrist. "Don't go on," he said with sudden emotion. "It hurts too much."

"It hurts?" she asked, surprised.

"I don't want to be gone," he said. "I don't want to be three thousand miles from you. I don't want the old routine, just as it was. Not now. Not now that I know you're here, that you've grown up just as I thought you would, into a beautiful young woman. Not when I know you're thinking about me . . . It hurts too much."

She looked long and hard into his eyes. What she saw there melted the coldest ice within her. She touched her lips to his. Their kiss was soft and chaste at first, then more intimate. She felt the desire in his body, and felt him holding it back for her sake. She touched his face with both hands and released him.

"Scotty," she said.

She tried to suppress the words that were coming to her lips, but it was impossible. She cared too much for him to hide what was on her mind.

"We've talked about so many things," she said. "But not about me. Never about me. That isn't fair to you. You don't know anything about me."

He looked at her with genuine surprise.

"Is there anything I don't know," he asked, "that I need to know in order to make you happy?"

Julie's eyes widened. There was an undeniable logic to his words. She could think of no answer.

Perhaps misinterpreting her silence, Scott smiled.

"I know all I need to know," he said. "When you believe that, you'll understand that nothing can keep us apart."

Julie looked into his eyes. For the first time she was aware of the strength behind his quiet exterior. But she could not forget the obstacles facing him.

"I'm not the girl I seem to be," she said.

"You don't seem to be anything," he corrected. "You're you. You're my Julie. I've waited for you all my life, and now you're here, in flesh and blood, close enough for me to touch. Close enough for me to love. What else is there to say?"

His words made her flesh tingle. For an answer she kissed him again. It was not easy being on this brink, feeling him draw her stubbornly back to life when death had seemed her only refuge.

He reached into his breast pocket and pulled out a small envelope.

"I almost forgot," he said. "I have something here that's going to surprise you."

He handed her the envelope. She could see that it was very old. It was a letter, apparently sent and received many years ago. To judge from the soft feel of the envelope, it had been carried about in someone's pocket for a long time.

She had already reached inside and opened the letter before the chill in her bones told her who it was from.

She began to read the childish handwriting.

Dear Scotty,

Your letter arrived on Saturday, just before we went to East Hampton to go riding with Auntie. You were a naughty boy to take so long in answering me, but now I forgive you because you are nice in your letter.

Mommy says I must spend the whole afternoon in my room and clean up my school things. I hate school because the other girls are mean, and the boys are stupid. You must tell me if you hate school too. If you do, we will sneak away together to Canada or Australia and never go to school again.

Will you never come to America again? Please tell your Mommy to bring you back at once, so we can play checkers and Old Maid as we did at your cousins' home.

Today Gretchen is going out with Mommy to buy clothes for her debut. I will be alone to clean up my school things—UGH!—until Jack comes back. Then Daddy will come home, and we'll have dinner. I hope Nanny doesn't make me eat my peas tonight. I hate peas. Do you like them, you naughty boy?

The childish handwriting had blurred before Julie's eyes. She felt her own tears moisten the old writing paper, which bore her initials and a printed silhouette of a little girl's profile.

Sobs shook her suddenly as she held the letter to her breast. Her whole life was coiled around her, a dark tunnel in which the innocent little girl of her youth had been lost for so long.

And now, heartrendingly, that child had been brought back by Scott.

"Did I upset you?" he was asking, concern in his voice. "I'm sorry, Julie. I thought it would amuse you, after all these years. Please forgive me."

"It's not your fault." She shook her head in frustration, unable to find words to describe what she was feeling. She seemed truly shaken as she gave the letter back to him.

"Strange," he said. "I've read this letter a hundred times. It would never have occurred to me that one day it would be stained by your tears. The tears of the lovely young woman who grew from that little girl. Time plays such odd tricks . . ."

Sobbing, Julie pulled him close. Suddenly he seemed her only chance.

"Oh, Scotty," she said. "Don't go. Please don't—"

He petted her softly, making a soft shushing sound to soothe her.

"Don't worry," he said. "I have to go, but it isn't the same anymore. If twenty years couldn't keep us apart, the Atlantic Ocean certainly won't. Not for long, anyway."

She nodded, her arms curled about his neck.

"Say you'll come to visit at Christmas," he said. "Promise me."

"I'll come to visit," she promised.

He held her close. "I'm going to miss you so much . . ."

She nodded against his cheek, unable to find words.

Now it was time to go home. They left the carriage and he drove her to the Park Avenue house. It was silent. Only the wing where Father and Mother lived was lit. Her own end of the house was in darkness.

She felt herself tense at the sight of the house. He sensed her emotion, and held her closer.

"Will you see me off at Idlewild Saturday?" he asked. "I want your face to be the last thing I see in America before I get on that plane."

"Yes," Julie said. "I'll be there."

He took her to her door and kissed her. Her small body was warm and soft against his own, and he felt her open herself to him, a bit more than before, just as it had been each night of this charmed visit. With every passing day he had the thrill of knowing her a bit better, of wanting her a bit more, of feeling her light him up inside a bit brighter.

Yet in her regret at leaving him now, still tinged by her grief over the letter, there was also an element of fear at having to enter her own house. This was all too clear to him.

"Good night, then," he murmured. "See you tomorrow."

He watched her disappear into the house. There was something furtive about her movements, almost as though she were entering a castle where a sleeping ogre would awaken to gobble her up unless she was quiet as a mouse. In that split second she was not the Julie he knew at all, but a stranger disappearing into an incomprehensible existence.

He walked back to the car and stood looking up at the dark house. It seemed crouched upon itself, massive and sinister in the moonlight.

He felt the letter in his pocket, stained by Julie's tears.

What did they do to you? he wondered silently. *What in the world did they do to you?*

35

At the gate at Idlewild Airport, Julie stood with her hand in that of Scott Monteagle.

They were both sad, but also excited. Though they must part now, they knew they would see each other again soon. The past week had brought their relationship to a new intimacy which filled them with anticipation for the future.

Tears were welling in Julie's eyes as she looked at the young man who had become so important to her in so short a time.

Scott was looking down at her, an expression of admiration and tenderness in his gray irises.

"How beautiful you are," he said. "Do I really have to go back home and see that face only in my dreams?"

She leaned forward and put her head against his chest. She held both his hands in hers.

"I wish you were staying." Her voice had a little-girl quality which she had never heard in it before.

"Don't say it," he said, touching his cheek to her hair. "Don't make me weaker than I already am. I'll end up staying here after all. Then I'll lose my job, and we'll all be in a fix."

She smiled at his humor. But the pain of separation made her pale.

"I don't want to be here alone without you," she said. "It's wrong. I want to be where you are."

"But you're coming at Christmas." He had not really understood her, understood the depth of her crisis. But his words had the desired effect. They calmed her.

"Yes," she said. "I'll see you at Christmas."

The announcer was calling out his flight. Scott looked into her eyes, and his expression grew more serious.

"Don't worry," he said. "All things are possible. Haven't we proved that, this last week?"

She nodded.

He hugged her close. "Six months ago I was just an ordinary man pursuing an ordinary life, with nothing much to look forward to except a lifetime of work, and perhaps some day an ordinary woman. Now look at me. I feel like the Connecticut Yankee in King Arthur's Court. You've made me into a prince."

You're already a prince, Julie thought, her tears glistening on her cheeks.

"I hope to see the day when I can dry those tears instead of causing them," he said.

"Oh, Scotty." She hugged him with all her might. She could never begin to tell him how wonderful those tears felt, and how precious was the pain of leaving him, when she knew he wanted to see her again, and would wait for her.

They kissed. It was a long, passionate kiss, deeper than any they had had before now. A delicious warmth stole through her body, a warmth that was a cessation of pain before it was a pleasure, a warmth that made her safe before it made her excited.

At last, unwillingly, he released her.

"I'll write every day," he said.

"I'll wait for the mailman." She smiled. "I never did that before, until I met you."

"Be happy," he said, withdrawing from her.

Thanks to you, she thought, waving to him through her tears.

She kept waving as he went through the gate.

Her mind was so fixed on the receding form of Scott Monteagle that she never thought to look behind her. Had she done so she would have seen, watchful behind a pillar in the terminal, Johnny Marrante, his own black eyes fixed on her with dark intensity.

=== 36 ===

August 11, 1958

Summer was at its hottest in New York.

Gathered in Sam Carpenter's loft on this hazy evening were Francie, Sam, Dana, and a handful of other people invited here by Francie.

Among them were Barbara Bettinger, who had been Dana's chief programming assistant before the disaster that had befallen CompuTel, and Joel Gregg, who had been CompuTel's head of sales. Joel was an expert manager and sales executive who knew everything there was to know about the financing and management of young companies.

Francie had decided against the obvious course of bankruptcy for CompuTel. She had instructed Lee Nugent to make a show of fighting the Magnus Industries lawsuit, using every strategy he knew to delay the process in the courts. The company was in a twilight state as it slowly dismantled its accounts for its various disappointed customers. Francie had decided to keep the CompuTel name alive, for her own reasons. Reasons she was to share only tonight.

Barbara and Joel were understandably looking for new jobs as they supervised the caretaking of CompuTel's accounts. The same went for Dana, who had renewed contact with her Connecticut research firm, but who was sticking by Francie as long as she was needed. As for Sam, he, like Francie, was out in the cold. But the look on his face did not express dismay. Instead it was, for him, a look of quiet excitement.

There were also two new people who were unknown to the rest.

Francie introduced them.

"I want you all to meet Terry Gelman and Quinn Metzler," she said. "They're specialists in computer hardware who were asked to come here tonight by Sam. Quinn was with Sam in Korea. Terry currently works with Quinn in New Jersey."

Francie had served coffee. Everyone was looking at her expectantly.

"I know you're all wondering why I asked you to come here tonight," she said. "Well, I'm going to give you the answer. Let's start with a couple of comments about CompuTel."

She paused, looking from one face to the other. They were all gathered on the couch, the old armchairs, and some cushions on the floor, looking more like guests at a bohemian wine party than the business and technological experts they were.

"For legal reasons," Francie said, "CompuTel has been forced to cease active operations. Naturally we wish this hadn't happened, because we were doing very well. Nevertheless, we can't dwell on the past. Tonight I want to talk about the future."

Everyone looked surprised. Since CompuTel had no future, they wondered what Francie could possibly be talking about.

"CompuTel," Francie said, "was a fine experiment in how to bring computer technology to business. We were able, in a short period of time, to allow medium- and large-sized companies to afford to computerize their inventory and finance, and thus to cut hundreds of man-hours from their overhead. Our effort was a success, and this is probably one reason why we ran into legal trouble with a conglomerate which thought it had a patent on our own initiative."

There was not a trace of bitterness in Francie's voice. Instead, she was all business. In fact, there was an impressive, steely coldness about her presentation.

"Despite CompuTel's success," she said, "the company always suffered from a weakness which was built into its structure. That weakness was twofold. In the first place, hardware is expensive. The buying or leasing of mainframe computers added substantially to the price we had to charge for our consultations."

Francie paused. "In the second place," she went on, "since the computer consultant—that is, CompuTel—had the hardware, the client had to report his figures to us, and then wait for results, without being able to do his own computations based on a program he himself could operate. In other words, the client still felt uncomfortable with computers, because the computers remained in the hands of the consultant. In the event of problems, the client could only throw himself on the mercy of the consultant for help. To sum up, we never really brought the businessman face to face with the computer."

Those listening to Francie seemed puzzled. It was Dana who spoke up.

"But Francie," she said, "our customers were very happy with the service we provided. Since we understood the hardware and wrote the programs, we were a consultant just like any other. If we got results, which we did, the clients were satisfied."

"You're right, Dana," Francie said. "But only insofar as you're speaking of today's business world. In a few short years computer technology will have advanced sufficiently for the client to be dissatisfied with the type of service we provided. The client will no longer want to farm out his figures to strangers and wait for them to analyze and solve his problems. He'll want to use computer technology directly, to solve the problems himself."

Dana was silent. Her quick mind had already seen where Francie was leading.

Lee Nugent, an attorney with only the most limited understanding of computers, spoke next.

"But Francie," he said, "I don't get it. The whole point of CompuTel was to bring the analyzing power of computers to customers who wouldn't have access to it otherwise. You succeeded in that. You charged a modest fee, and you got results. Your customers loved you. What can be better than that? After all, the customer can't afford his own hardware . . ."

Francie smiled. "That's what we're going to change, Lee," she said.

Lee looked perplexed. "What do you mean?" he asked.

"We're going to bring the customer a computer he can afford to operate himself," she replied coolly.

There was an audible intake of breath in the room.

"I don't quite follow," said Joel Gregg. "Do you mean a mainframe computer the customer can lease?"

"No," Francie said. "I mean a computer the customer can own."

Joel smiled disbelievingly. "With all due respect, Francie, don't you think you're a couple of decades ahead of your time?" he asked. "Computers cost a lot of money, don't they?"

"They do, but they don't have to," Francie said.

She turned to gesture to the loft around them.

"Those of you who know Sam and this loft," she said, "have probably noticed that something is different here tonight."

Dana and Joel nodded. The loft's main room seemed empty. What was missing was 9292, the mainframe computer at which Sam had been tinkering for four years.

"Where's 9292?" Joel asked.

"If you'll all follow me," Francie said, "Sam has something he wants to show you."

Sam led the group to a corner of the loft where an item about the size of a refrigerator was covered with a sheet.

Sam grinned. "I won't pull the sheet off yet," he said, "because I don't want to prejudice you. What's under there is not pretty. Not yet, anyway. But I want you to notice the size."

He scanned the faces of the group. They were all interested. "Over the past couple of years," he said, "I've been progressively replacing 9292's vacuum tube circuitry with solid-state boards. As some of you know, the first transistors were invented way back in 1947. But transistor technology in computers is still a new art. However, there are small research firms around the country that manufacture silicon chips called semiconductors, which have terrific computing capacity, and which are getting less expensive almost by the hour, because they're easy to mass-produce once the prototypes have been perfected."

He gestured to the boxlike form under the sheet. "This is what's left of 9292," he said. "He's approximately one-twentieth his former size. But his computing and analyzing capacity is now about ten times what it was before. All this is thanks to solid-state circuitry and the silicon microchip."

He paused to let his words sink in.

"I have to thank Quinn here, and Terry, for helping me accelerate the process in the last couple of months," he said. "We used some influence to get our hands on the solid-state circuitry without having to pay the market price," he said. "And we made some new friends in the transistor business. Friends we're going to need in the next year. I talked this over with Francie, and we all came to pretty much the same conclusion."

He turned to Francie and gestured to her to continue for him.

"To make a long story short," Francie said, "Sam and I think that with the right technology we can produce a mini-computer, small in size and in price, that can be afforded by the same companies that were CompuTel's clients—banks, insurance companies, retailers, investment firms, and so on."

There was a pause. Joel Gregg, always the businessman, spoke next. "How soon do you think this could be done?"

"That's the sixty-four-dollar question," Francie replied. "We know it can be done soon. What we don't know is whether we'll be able to lay our hands on enough investment capital to finance the operation and keep it solvent until we deliver the product to the marketplace. That's the gamble we face. The reason you're all here tonight is so we can ask you whether you want to take this risk with us. It will mean a great deal of work, and rock-bottom wages, for the duration. We'll all be working for something that may or may not pan out. I'd like you to know that right now, and to think about it."

Francie looked at the faces before her.

"There's one other thing that has to be mentioned," she said. "The reason you're here, and nobody else, is that the people in this room are the only people Sam and I feel we can trust completely. This entire operation is going to be under top security. Sam, Quinn, and Terry will be in charge of the research and development. The rest of us will be collectively working on programming, packaging, sales, insurance, patenting—in short, everything that goes to make a company from nothing. No one else will be in on the project unless that person is cleared by all of us."

She smiled. "If any of you have ever harbored an urge for a cloak-and-dagger adventure, this is your chance."

She sat back down in her chair. "I'm finished," she said. "If anyone has any questions, feel free to speak up."

To her surprise there was complete silence in the room.

Francie raised an eyebrow. "Do you want to decide right now?" she asked.

What she could not know was that the people in the room were not looking at her and her project as unknown quantities. They already knew what she had done with CompuTel. And they knew Sam.

"Well, then," she said, "how many of you are in?"

Every hand in the room was raised.

Francie smiled. "All right," she said, "it looks like we have ourselves a team. If the ship sinks, we'll all go down together. If it floats, we're going to have ourselves a heck of a journey together."

An hour later the details had been ironed out. Everyone present would quit his or her current job and come to work for CompuTel. There would be no formal payroll. Everything would be done in complete secrecy. A warehouse had been rented in Brooklyn for the project ahead. CompuTel's office on Cedar Street would remain open as a sort of decoy, signaling impotence and inactivity. As far as the outside world was concerned, CompuTel would be a moribund company, a ghost.

Francie, Sam, and Dana would pour all the resources they had gained from their time at CompuTel into the new project. It was not much money, but it was enough to keep the Cedar Street office open and to rent the warehouse.

As for the real financing for the new project, Francie intended to approach venture capitalists once the prototype of her new product was complete. She had total confidence that she would be able to attract sufficient funding to bring the product to market.

The session ended at one o'clock in the morning. When everyone had left, Francie and Sam were alone with the shrunken version of 9292. Francie sat back against the cushions of the old couch and sighed.

Sam was gazing at her.

"You're beautiful when you're mad," he said.

She raised an eyebrow, genuinely surprised. "Do I look mad?"

"Mad isn't a strong enough word," he said. "I'd hate to meet you in a dark alley when you look like this."

Francie smiled and looked up at him.

"Well, I'm not mad at you, Sam," she said softly.

She got up and came to his arms. As their bodies touched, a sudden throb of desire passed between them. Sam could feel something exciting and dangerous emanating from her, like the quiet hum of millions of volts of electricity inside an innocent-looking wire.

He pulled her closer, wondering how such a soft female body could contain so much concentrated power. Then her lips touched his own, and thought turned dizzyingly to pleasure inside his mind.

The girl in his arms was more of a mystery to him than ever. But whoever she was and wherever she was going, she was his for tonight.

Her hand curled gently about his waist as he turned her toward the bedroom.

=== 37 ===

September 28, 1958

It was two o'clock in the morning.

The apartment was illuminated only by the glow of the Upper East Side thirty stories below.

The distant sounds of traffic mingled with the soft music playing in the apartment. The furniture and wall hangings seemed to loom furtively in the shadows like pagan religious icons accompanying a mysterious rite.

The only other sounds in the room were the sighs coming from the bed, sighs which could have only one meaning.

The girl was naked. She had stripped off her clothes moments ago, as the light from the now-extinguished lamp glowed golden on her soft skin. He had watched her hungrily, for she knew how to remove her clothes in a

ELIZABETH GAGE

uniquely provocative way, touching gently at the panties as they worked their way down her thighs, then at the hook of her bra, making it come loose in a languid caress of slow fingers.

And she smoothed the clothes over her flesh before taking them off, so sensually that it almost seemed she was making love to herself with them. Her hands made little circles over her skin with the silken panties before she dropped them, her loins stirring in the shadows like beckoning fingers.

She had made him take his clothes off first so she could watch the reaction of his own flesh to her dance. Her eyes slid over him, admiring his hard physique, but always coming back to focus in fascination on the penis, stiff and throbbing in rhythm to the coy seductions of her body.

By the time she was completely naked he needed her so badly he would have pulled her onto him by force, had he not understood that this slow approach was what excited her. And he wanted her to be pleased as well as himself.

She reached to turn out the light and came to him at last, a slender sylph offering her soft limbs to his embrace like a gift.

"Baby," she murmured.

She was a girl of few words. With familiarity he had learned this about her. But those few words were so redolent of pure sex that one could hardly listen to them without feeling the first tremors of orgasm deep inside one's loins.

She crouched atop him and kissed him slowly, a long slippery tongue entering his mouth to taste and explore. Her fingers touched softly at his shoulders, and down his pectorals to his stomach, near enough to the penis to excite it, but not yet making bold to touch.

He could feel her sex suspended above the straining shaft, waiting coyly in the warm air of the bedroom as her knees straddled his hips. Only the caressing tongue linked her to him, and the soft hands on his hips.

"Mmm," she cooed. "I like you this way."

And now her body, so light and slim, lowered itself to caress him with its entire length. He felt his sex hot and urgent against her stomach as she undulated subtly against him. She kissed his eyes, his cheeks, and ran her fingers through his hair, smiling coolly as she rubbed herself with catlike sinews against him.

"Mmm," she purred, slipping her tongue into his mouth again as the hard penis stirred against her. They were both excited now, and ready for love, but she wanted to tease him with herself a bit longer. She seemed to know what a powerful weapon her body was. When she was in her clothes it hid cleverly under her cool personality. She seemed introspective and even vulnerable. One had no idea what kind of woman she was until one knew her this way, naked and provocative and triumphant in her sensuality.

Now she straightened up so that she was squatting over him. Still the pretty sex kept its minimal distance, but now her hands found the stiff penis and began to caress it. He heard her murmur, a throaty purr of satisfaction as her fingers curled around the hard shaft.

And now, he realized confusedly—for the pleasure she was giving him made his eyes close—she was bringing him to the core of her. The tender flesh toying with his penis was not only her fingers, but the sweet center between her legs as well. She was putting him in, half an inch, then an inch, with wise fingers, withdrawing him, kneading smoothly at the tip of him, slipping him back into her a bit deeper, teasing him with her expert play, so that it was impossible to tell which were fingers and which was woman's sex.

"Uh-oh," she murmured as excitement made him grind against her. He could feel the smile on her lips. "Not so fast."

She went on that way, teasing him, cooing her provocations, letting him inside her always a little deeper, taunting him with a flesh that owned him while withholding itself, until he could stand it no longer.

He grasped her with urgent hands, held her by her wrists, and let his eager sex thrust deep inside her on its own. She let out a little cry, filled with feigned alarm and obvious pleasure. This also was part of her game, and she knew it excited him.

The penis was buried to its hilt, working quickly in the core of her. She responded with moans and cries always stifled by her mysterious sense of restraint—she was really a very silent girl—but the more sensual for that, for they were like guilty, intimate whispers, meant to penetrate to the source of his need and heat him to the boiling point.

It was hard not to come with her right away. Her delight in exciting him was so perverse that the semen strained to give itself immediately to those hungry loins trembling all around him. He had to think of other things, to distract himself so he could enjoy her.

This was not so difficult for him. He had many ideas, many plans, each of them almost as exciting, in its way, as a woman. The world was a place waiting for him to conquer it, but it did not give itself as easily and willingly as this sensual girl. It withheld its prize, and the battle to attain it was more subtle and difficult than the immediate pleasure of screwing her.

But she was part of it. That was the beauty of it. Her body, her whispers, her caresses, were all part of that larger challenge.

He thought about this as long as he could. But her hands were all over him, finding pleasure points with unerring instinct, not only those she had found in him the last few times, but new ones, ones he himself had not been dimly aware of until she touched them now.

A soft hand moved slowly along the inside of his thigh, shyly cradling the moving balls before it stole away along his hips to his stomach and touched at his navel, sending a huge surprising tremor through him. The sly voice was still cooing its encouragement.

"Come on . . . A little more . . . Oh! Baby . . ."

He heard a moan, not without a perverse little giggle of delight, as he thrust harder into her. He could see the soft breasts stirring in the shadows as she reared up over him, and the lovely contours of her crouched thighs. Her wispy hair, undone, danced over her shoulders and down her back as her pretty head moved back and forth. She was in her element now, her every instinct joining in the symphony of intercourse. She lived for it.

"Mmm . . . oh! Wait . . . More . . ."

She wanted more, wanted it all, wanted to keep him hard all night long. But this was the end. The last wave was coming, starting hot and tickly deep inside him, and he knew there was no stopping it now. There was just too much of her nakedness, of her love talk, her fingers, her lips, of the sweet working of her sex.

He held her by the hips and pushed as deep as he could inside her. A huge spasm shook him, and she trembled like a leaf, gasping as the sperm erupted into her in long hot waves. Her fingers fluttered against his shoulders, her loins trembled, she moaned in low purring whispers her delight in receiving him.

When it was over she crouched down against his chest and rested there as he remained deep inside her. He felt her buttocks, her hips, his fingertips enjoying the pearly smoothness of the flesh against his own hard body.

They stayed that way for a few charmed minutes. Then, as he began to recede from her, she herself began to withdraw into herself, to resume her cool, quiet exterior. She patted him to thank him for her pleasure, but she did not caress him endearingly or possessively. She was separate again, independent, concerned only for herself. The elaborate game she had played before was only to excite him. There was no affection behind it. Only desire, and perhaps something colder than desire.

He watched her disappear into the bathroom. The light went on. He heard the water run. When she came back she was still naked, but no longer were her movements so sensual. They were natural, smooth, brisk.

She sat on the edge of the bed, pulling on her stockings. When she stood up to look for her panties, the sight of the stockings against her naked flesh almost made him excited enough to pull her back down beside him.

She pulled up the panties, then the tiny bra. She did not look at him, not once. She was absorbed in herself, probably thinking about where she was going, the work she had to do tonight and tomorrow. She was terribly busy nowadays. It was hard for her to get away even at night to see him.

She found her slip, put it on, then the dress she had worn, a pretty shift in a pale color. She felt her hair for bobby pins, returned to the bathroom, and stood before the mirror, touching up her makeup, tying back the hair, applying lipstick with a critical look at herself.

She came to his side. She sat on the edge of the bed. She had not remarked on his languid nakedness, for she knew he enjoyed watching her get dressed.

She smiled down at him.

"When will I hear from you?" he asked.

"When I have something for you."

"Not earlier?" He raised an eyebrow.

"Perhaps. If you're a good boy."

There was a moment's silence. She touched a soft finger to his nose, then his chin, then down to his nipple. It traced a circle there before gliding along the surface of his skin to the penis. She was about to take hold of it when he stopped her.

"I wish you were a little clearer about things," he said.

"About what things?" The small hand still wanted his penis. The wrist strained softly in his grasp.

"About when," he said. "How long."

"It's hard," she said. She smiled. Her double entendre was intentional, referring both to her mission and to the penis which was already coming erect at the proximity of her hand.

"I know." He backed off. There was no use in pressuring her.

"I can't do more than I'm doing," she said. "Everything is up in the air. Things change so fast—from day to day. And I'm not privy to everything."

He wondered whether to believe her.

"She's smart, isn't she?" he asked.

"Yes," she sighed. "She is that."

"Call me on Tuesday," he said. "Whether you have news or not." He smiled. "I like hearing from you."

She nodded, silent.

She gazed with a sort of nostalgia at his penis. Then, with a brisk female sigh, she got up.

"Remember," he warned. "Never call me at work. Never."

She shrugged her contempt at the question. As if he did not know by now that he could trust her implicitly.

She picked up her purse and took the glasses out. They were always the first thing she took off, and the last thing she put on. With them on she retreated definitively behind the cool, emotionless mask which stood her in good stead through her busy days in the world.

"Good night," she said.

He nodded, loath to see her go so soon, but aware that she could not be away from her work for too long. A single unexplained absence could be her undoing—and his.

"Good night, Mata Hari," he said.

With a little smile at his joke, she picked up her coat and left the apartment.

=== 38 ===

March 5, 1959

Francie woke up with a start.

At first she did not know where she was. Her eyes, dulled by sleep, gazed at the shadowed walls hovering around her without recognizing them.

For a moment she thought she was back home in her bedroom in Pennsylvania. She forgot the passage of time, and thought she heard her mother's quiet voice in the kitchen, talking with her father.

Her eyes half-closed, Francie felt the old life come to embrace her softly. She felt the security of home. The sleepy sinews of her body were filled with their own memory of where the old walls had been, and the window which looked out on the yard where her bicycle lay on its side near the swing set she had played on as a child. She drifted back toward dreams, secure in the knowledge that when she awoke the smells of coffee and breakfast would be in the kitchen, and Mother waiting for her with her half-smile and her soft hands.

But sleep receded another pace, and Francie remembered where she was.

She looked at the walls of the bedroom. Gone were the framed pictures and teddy bears of her youth. These walls were bare. Gone was the desk where she had done her homework as a girl. In this room there was only a closet and a filing cabinet.

She turned to see Sam asleep beside her. Her disorientation had upset her, for it made her straddle two worlds that were so far apart. She longed to reach out and touch him, perhaps gather him to her breast. But she did not want to disturb his sleep, so she sat looking at him for a moment, and then slipped out of the bed and padded to the living room.

Neither of them could afford to lose sleep, for it was a precious commodity that they and their co-workers lacked. Everyone was surviving on five hours' sleep per night at the most, and working at a fevered pace all day long.

And no one worked harder than Francie.

She had been forced by necessity to turn over most of the business end of the new project to Joel Gregg. Sam was in charge of the computer itself, from circuitry to housing and controls. As for Francie, she had dropped everything in order to create the master program which would allow the machine to understand instructions and process information.

The program had required the greatest intellectual effort of her life. Its enormous subtlety of detail and execution would remain entirely hidden from the computer's eventual operator, an ordinary individual who would be trained in a few short hours to use the machine in his daily work.

Sam and Dana, expert programmers themselves, frankly told Francie that her program was a work of genius, an innovation that would make her world-famous. But Francie had no time to praise herself for what she had already accomplished. There was still a lot to be done. She must have the program fine-tuned and ready to go by the time the computer was finished, a date that drew closer every day.

The work on the computer was a seven-day-a-week project. No one took days off. But on Sundays the team did not show up at the warehouse until around noon. This meant that everyone could enjoy a relatively normal Saturday night's relaxation—starting, that is, at six o'clock, when work ended.

Francie spent all her nights with Sam. They returned to his loft together from work, had a quiet supper together, and spent the evening making love and lying silently in each other's arms.

They would fall into exhausted sleep early. An instant later, or so it seemed to Francie, she was awake again, her dreams dissipating quickly as she realized that night was gone already and the alarm clock was about to ring. She would rise before Sam and put the coffee on, emerging from her hasty shower to put on her clothes as fast as she could. She was all business again, strung tight as a wire, ready for the mad race of the day ahead.

And the female creature who had snuggled in Sam's strong arms was forgotten now, nonexistent. She would not appear until another day of backbreaking work was behind Francie, a day in which her quest would have taken giant strides toward completion.

Such was the life Francie led. She never thought to question its terrible demands or its secret rewards. Work devoured her days, and pleasure her few moments of rest.

Tonight something important had awakened her. She could feel it. She was a sound sleeper normally, and would not have awakened unless something was on her mind. Though she could not afford to lose sleep, she sat in the living room wondering what it was.

She looked at the old battered hulk of what had been called 9292, sitting in its corner, a large box with wires and circuit boards coming out of it like the stuffing out of a broken doll. The poor thing had been plundered shamelessly in order to complete the prototype of the still-unnamed computer they were manufacturing.

And now Francie understood why she was awake.

The product she and her colleagues were working themselves into prostration to create still had no name.

At the back of her mind, underneath her crowded days, she had been wondering over and over what to call the product. She had discussed the question with Sam, Dana, Lee, Joel, and the others, to no avail. Everyone kept suggesting numerical names like the ERA 1103, or acronyms like UNIVAC. But Francie had a gut feeling that such names were wrong in principle. She was convinced they would prevent the product from selling rather than help it.

But she could think of no alternative.

She sat now in the darkness, searching her mind for the thousandth time. What should the computer be called? It must be something unscientific, something down-to-earth and friendly. Businessmen were terrified enough of computer technology as it was. Names like ENIAC and IBM Type 702 only scared them the more, and made them think of huge expense and daunting technology.

Francie thought for a long moment, feeling sleep abandon her limbs while the tension of work invaded her again. But no name would come.

She lay back on Sam's couch in the darkness and tried to clear her mind. Still somnolent, she suddenly remembered her days at home with Mother and Dad in Pennsylvania, which had been at the forefront of her consciousness when she awoke just now.

She smiled to think that something about being with Sam had made her recall those days. The sense of security and belonging that Sam brought her had been reflected in her memory of her childhood, a time when she felt that the world was like a sweet mother waiting to welcome her to its arms when she awoke each day, threw on her jeans and T-shirt, and went out to play or to help Dad in his workshop.

Yes, it had been a happy and carefree time. And it was light-years away from the crazy, high-tension world she now lived in. How had she come so far? What had she lost along the way? When had the peace and quiet of the old life abandoned her for good?

She thought of the awful days before her mother had died. Helen Bollinger had suffered a long illness, but had never complained. Francie remembered her sitting silent in her chair in the living room, reading or talking to Dad, who hid his anguish so well that Francie at the time was hardly aware of what he was going through.

They had both got used to the idea that their life with Mother was slipping away. And Francie had followed her father's lead in enduring the inevitable while not talking about it. The silent agony they were all living bound them together, and it seemed a struggle they could go on with forever, even as they all grew thinner and weaker and more desperate.

Then one day, just like that, Mother was gone. The ambulance came, then the funeral director. Friends and family were called, the pastor gave a eulogy, they went to the graveyard, and then Francie and Dad returned home alone to face the empty house.

Only then did grief strike them with its full force. Now that the artificial excitement of funeral arrangements, guests, and memorial services had died down, they were alone with the void left by Mother. For several weeks they lived in a ghastly silence which Francie would never forget. The pain that bound them together was the worst she had ever experienced. It seemed that life was impossible.

Then, as luck would have it, someone came to their rescue.

Some farmer neighbors, the Maguires, had a widowed aunt who had recently emigrated from Ireland and was on her own in America with nothing to do. She had been a housewife, and had no trade. Her children were grown and married, living in far-flung places. She was named Mollie, and she was chafing at her inactivity on the Maguires' farm.

It was suggested that she come and live with Francie and her father as housekeeper and cook. Since she had her husband's insurance and some savings of her own, she could live on the paltry wages that Mac Bollinger could afford to pay her. She enjoyed Mac's taciturn ways, and she quickly warmed to Francie's bright personality.

Mollie was a natural complainer, full of grievances about America, her relatives, her advancing age, and everything else she could think of. But underneath her complaints—which were expressed in a marvelously poetic Irish accent, and with a phraseology all her own—she was a woman of great strength and resilience. She came to offer the only replacement of Helen Bollinger that could have cheered Francie and Dad.

The whole house came to life again under Mollie's aegis. She worked in the garden, knitted sweaters for Francie and Mac, and afghans with designs from the old country. She cooked corned beef and cabbage and Irish stew, and kept the kitchen sparkling clean. She learned Helen's trick of shaking Mac out of his lethargy and putting him to work on useful projects. Though she could not help Francie with her homework, being barely literate herself, she did not need to, for Francie's straight A's were a fact of life. But she could and did help Francie improve her appearance, and helped her to grow from a gangly fourteen-year-old into a beautiful and well-dressed high school girl.

In a subtle way Mollie had filled a huge gap in the lives of two grief-stricken and confused people. Her humor, her hard work, and her understanding of their problems made her an indispensable addition to their lives. And, though she never would admit it, her own grief over the loss of her husband and her distance from her children was eased by her relationship with Mac and Francie.

Francie at one time toyed with the idea of playing matchmaker, and getting her father to marry Mollie. But she was too young to understand their relationship. Mac carried a torch for Helen which consumed his entire life, and he could never dream of marrying another woman. Mollie, understanding this within an hour of meeting him, had assumed a sisterly role which she knew would do more to salve his agony than anything else.

After Francie went to college Mollie moved out of the house, for propriety's sake, and back in with her relatives the Maguires. But she still came every day to clean, cook, and make clothes for Mac. They read Francie's letters from college together, and once when Mac was driving to Philadelphia to see Francie, Mollie went with him. They made an odd couple, Mac dressed in a suit which Mollie had found for him at a bargain price, and Mollie wearing a fancy outfit which shocked Francie, who had never seen her in anything but an apron before.

Francie was glad her father had Mollie. Now that she herself was away from home, Mollie kept Mac Bollinger connected to life. Often it was

Mollie who picked up the phone when Francie called long distance from Penn. The crisp Irish voice was a beloved sound, a sound of home.

Then Mollie died.

The event was made the more foreign by the fact that Dad told Francie about it from hundreds of miles away. Mollie had suffered for many years from a serious form of diabetes, and had never told Francie or Mac about it. Her end had been mercifully sudden, but Francie learned that she had suffered great pain all those years.

Now Francie understood the real reason for Mollie's constant lyrical complaints. She was letting off steam over the real agony of her life.

Since Mollie's death Mac had been on his own, employing a local woman to clean for him, but handling his own cooking and buying his own clothes. Though he never showed it, he truly grieved for Mollie now as he still did for his dead wife. When Francie visited him they often talked about Mollie, and both were thankful for the precious years she had given them.

Francie sat now in the living room, smiling to think of the many days that had been brightened by Mollie's humor, her sharp tongue, and her steadfast loyalty to Mac and his daughter. It was more than worth the pain of thinking about Mollie's death to remember the bright, brave way she had entered their life and held it together when the loss of Helen might have darkened it irretrievably.

At last somnolence stole back through Francie's limbs, and she got up to go back to bed. She padded into the bedroom and got into the bed next to Sam. Though she was no closer to a solution of her problems, her thoughts about Mollie and Dad and home had made her feel less lonely.

When Sam felt the bed stir he sleepily held out an arm and pulled Francie to him. Francie felt a pang of gratitude and relief, for being with Sam was warm in the same way her memories were. Though her day-to-day life with him was frantic and rushed as her old life had never been, there was something calm and steady about him that contained, like a secret crystal, the trees and pastures of her childhood, just as somewhere inside his own breast was the memory of his youth in upstate New York, with his woods and his precious lake.

Francie was about to fall asleep in his arms when all at once she saw the secret weave of her thoughts. Mollie Maguire had not come to her mind entirely by accident. She had been thinking about the computer, and how to sell it to businessmen who had preconceived notions of computers as impersonal electronic brains which took the humanity out of everything they touched.

Francie thought of the computer Sam had devised, a humble workhorse destined to make the businessman's life easier without forcing him to become a computer technician in order to use it. This would be a machine that the buyer could think of with familiarity and even a touch of humor, like a friendly and domestic part of his working life.

And now the two trains of thought which had been struggling to find each other came together in Francie's mind. She saw the computer, and also saw the name she would give it. It was the least expected name in the world, but also the most affectionate and human.

"Mollie . . . ," she thought dreamily as she fell asleep in Sam's arms.

═══ 39 ═══

The name Mollie seemed to be the final spark that launched CompuTel's new computer toward a brilliant future. Everyone who heard the name fell in love with it, from Francie's own co-workers to the shrewd and skeptical venture capitalists she and Joel Gregg had been trying to interest in the new project for months now.

A group of investment bankers who had been sitting on the fence since winter at last took the plunge and invested over three million dollars in Mollie and CompuTel, in return for stock options and a place on the company's board. Almost overnight an important mutual fund followed suit, and then another.

Throughout the summer, work on Mollie advanced by leaps and bounds. On September 8th Sam gave a stunning demonstration of Mollie's computing powers and ease of operation to a small gathering of private investors, with the result that four additional commitments of a million dollars each were made.

On their way back from a celebration lunch at the Four Seasons with their new investors, Francie congratulated Sam.

"You're the hero today," she said. "If Mollie hadn't performed so well for their experts, we might have come up completely empty."

"Don't thank me," Sam said. "I'm just a cog in the wheel. You're the prime mover, Francie."

She smiled tiredly. She knew as well as Sam did that they were a long way from the finish line. They would need twice as much investment capital as they now had if they were to launch Mollie nationwide in a convincing manner. It seemed that with every step forward in their campaign the gamble they were taking assumed greater proportions. More and more money was involved, more and more people were waiting for the moment of truth.

And worst of all, not a single penny was being made by CompuTel, because the company's product had not reached the marketplace, and never would unless even more financing became available. Meanwhile the top-secret aspect of the whole campaign made it that much more difficult to attract investors. Managers of mutual funds and other venture capitalists were hardly likely to be able to convince their boards to pour large blocks of funds into a product whose very existence was a secret.

Francie now understood how the producers of lavish Broadway musicals felt after having poured millions of dollars and whole teams of actors and crews into a brilliant musical, then having to live with the fear that the show would close on opening night and be a total financial loss to all concerned.

Despite herself Francie was getting stage fright. She had come too far with Mollie to turn back now. And all the people she had involved in her project were her responsibility. If her ship sank, they would all go down with it.

But there was neither time nor energy now for second thoughts. Forward was the only direction left to go.

An hour after their lunch in Manhattan Francie and Sam were back at the warehouse, which was divided into sections where the various teams worked on their separate projects—the designers, the hardware specialists, the technical writers, the marketing people.

Sam went back to work with Quinn and Terry on the latest problem in Mollie's circuitry. He smiled to think of his beloved 9292, on which he had tinkered for so long, and on its new avatar which, if Francie had her way, would change the way business was done in America and around the world.

He soon became so absorbed in his work that he did not realize Francie had slipped out of the warehouse.

No one knew she was gone. Francie had planned it that way. She took the subway into Manhattan, hailed a cab, and gave the driver a midtown address.

A few minutes later she was inside a nondescript second-floor office, across a desk from a young man in a sweater and slacks, whose informal appearance suited the nature of his business.

His name was Kevin Still, and he owned and operated the electronics supply store beneath this office. His real business, too sensitive to advertise, was electronic surveillance.

Francie had hired him two months ago, and heard from him every week since. So far he had had nothing to report. As of last week he had told her he thought she was wasting her money.

But this morning he had called the warehouse to leave her a cryptic message which meant, in the code they had agreed on, that something had come up at last. This was why she was here.

"What do you have for me?" she asked.

"What you've been looking for, I think," he said. "Here, put on these headphones and listen with me."

They both put on headphones and listened to a reel-to-reel tape played on a sophisticated noise-reducing tape recorder.

Francie heard the sounds of a telephone transmission. Then a man's voice came on the line.

"*Something new?*" he asked.

"*Yes,*" replied a woman's voice. "*It looks as though Aronsen is going to come through. For a million. They saw the latest prototype, and that sold them.*"

Francie recognized the name of one of the investors she had lunched with today.

"*How did it work?*" the man's voice asked.

"*Perfectly,*" the girl responded. "*It was even better than we expected.*"

"*What's your current schedule?*" he asked.

"*No one knows for sure,*" she replied. "*But we're all hoping for early summer. There will be a lot of advertising, a big marketing campaign.*"

"*No technical problems, then?*" asked the man's voice.

"*None to speak of. Sam is working on the RAM. The program Francie wrote is really powerful. I wish I had done it myself.*"

There was a pause.

"*You'll bring it over?*" the man asked.

"*As soon as I have time to copy it,*" the girl replied. "*We're awfully busy.*"

"*All right. Good work. Bring it to me at home.*"

The line went dead.

Francie took off her earphones. She looked pale, but not entirely surprised.

"Did you hear what you wanted to hear?" Kevin Still asked.

Francie smiled. "Not what I wanted to hear, no," she said. "But I found out what I needed to know. Thank you, Kevin."

"Shall I keep my men on the job?" he asked.

"Of course," she said. "And thank you."

"Do you know who the man on the phone was?" he asked, standing up.

Francie seemed to pause for a second before answering.

"That's not important now," she said.

"The girl, though . . . ," Kevin said.

"Oh, the girl, yes," Francie said. "There's no doubt about that."

She thanked him and left. When she was out on the street she looked around her and took a deep breath of the city air. It was not particularly clean, but under the circumstances it was bracing.

And that applied to the chess game she was playing, she thought. It was not particularly clean, and the things one learned were not very appetizing. But one must play it to the end, and play to win.

Dana, she mused. *I never thought it would be you.*

====== 40 ======

The next afternoon Francie called an urgent meeting of her top staff, including Sam, Joel, Barbara, Terry, Quinn, and Lee Nugent.

A question from Quinn preempted the announcement Francie was going to make.

"Where's Dana?" he asked.

"I fired Dana this morning," Francie said. "She won't be with us anymore. Barbara, this is going to put some extra responsibility on your shoulders. You and I will be in charge of the programming. I hope you feel you can handle it."

There was a shocked pause in the room. Everyone knew Dana well, and had counted on her energy and expertise in more ways than one. She would be sorely missed. Mollie was being produced by a rock-bottom group of specialists as it was. The loss of any one of them was a severe blow.

"Can you tell us why Dana had to go?" Terry asked.

"I'd rather not, just now," Francie said. "But I want you all to remember in the coming weeks that security is a top priority around here. The greatest dangers to Mollie are no longer technical. They're strategic. Is that clear?"

There was a silence. Everyone was awed by the cool, controlled tone in Francie's voice, and by the chilling effect of her calm smile. To look at her, one would never imagine she had just been betrayed by one of her closest friends. She looked like a boss who has just announced a new day for the company picnic. She was businesslike and uncannily composed.

When the meeting broke up Sam took her aside.

"How did you find out?" he asked simply.

Francie thought for a moment before answering.

"I had her phone tapped," she said.

Sam looked pained. He had never been close to Dana personally, but had worked with her on a hundred technical issues in the last two years, and thought he knew her rather well.

"What made you suspect her?" he asked.

"Nothing," Francie answered.

"Nothing?" Sam asked, raising an eyebrow.

"I had all your phones tapped," Francie said. The look in her eyes was bereft of all emotion.

Sam looked at her in surprise. He seemed distressed by her words, as though they denoted a level of suspicion that was unhealthy. Yet he could not deny that Francie's action had brought results.

"Just tell me one thing," he asked. "Who bought her? Was it Magnus?"

Francie hesitated before answering.

"Sam," she said, "that sharp mind of yours is needed for more important work right now than worrying about Dana and what happened. I want you to let me handle it. When it's all over, your questions will be answered. All right?"

Sam looked deep into her eyes. Now he saw the hurt in them. She had hidden it from the others, but she was too close to him to keep it from him entirely.

He touched her arm gently.

"I'm sorry, Francie," he said.

She smiled.

"All's fair in love and war," she said. "Let's get back to work."

A moment later Sam was back with Quinn working on the prototype, and Francie was in the tiny cubicle she used for an office in a corner of the warehouse.

She allowed herself a final thought for Dana. Dana was the last person she would have expected to betray her. But now she was glad for the knowledge. It showed her that she still had lessons to learn about human nature—and not much more time in which to learn them.

But the visceral confidence that had seen her through these last hectic months came to her rescue once again. She closed her eyes and focused her mind on the job ahead.

Now it's your move, Mr. Magnus, she thought.

=== 41 ===

During the weeks that followed no one said a word about Dana.

As for Sam, he found time to think about what had happened, and to wonder what it might mean to Francie.

He knew Francie and Dana had once been roommates, and were close friends. A hundred times he had come into CompuTel, or the new warehouse, and seen them working together, a silent intimacy joining them, almost as if they were sisters.

And now, just like that, Dana was gone.

And Francie was not changed. Or rather, she was the same quietly relentless young woman who had emerged from nowhere the day that the campaign for Mollie was first announced. From that first day Sam had realized that Francie had crossed an invisible line that had forced her to re-create herself for the challenge ahead.

The Francie he knew nowadays almost frightened Sam, because she was so deep within herself and so mysterious. She was not the Francie he had first met and come to know two and a half years ago. The Francie he invited to the Automat that first night had seemed a girl who had been hurt, but essentially a normal, healthy person, vulnerable and kind. When he joined her in forming CompuTel he knew he was helping her at a painful time of her life, and helping himself by joining hands with her.

As he became her friend he drew slowly closer to the invisible hurt inside her and the obsession driving her toward success. He did not consider this an obstacle between Francie and himself, because he knew that he and 9292 were helping her toward her goal. There was no contradiction between his friendship and her private life.

Then his punishment came.

On the very first night that their affection, so fragile and delicate a force, had at last brought them to bed together, and they had crossed the forbidden line to become lovers, chance had chosen that moment to give him a fatal glimpse of what was at the back of her mind all this time.

"Jack . . ."

The word on her lips, spoken in slumber, had been like the open door to a nightmare that had haunted Sam ever since, awake or asleep. A thousand times he had tormented himself with the notion that in giving herself to him that way, when she was exhausted, not responsible for her actions, she had had the other man in her fantasies all along.

Sam had suffered atrocious agonies because of that one little word. He had watched Francie sleep a hundred times since then, observing her almost obsessively as she dreamed—but never once had the name come out again.

Yet once was enough.

Sam wondered if he was taking advantage of her, cheating both her and himself, in allowing himself to sleep with her when deep inside she was carrying a torch for someone else. He thought over his relationship with her. He knew she trusted him and depended on him for his friendship as well as for his hard work at her side.

But was there anything in her heart to join the willingness of her body when she made love to him?

Sam had to face this question each and every time Francie was intimate with him. Thus the greatest pain of his life joined the most irresistible pleasure in an amalgam that left him dazed.

Making love to her was like jumping off the edge of the world. So enormous was the tension inside her body from her continual overwork that when it relaxed at last it was like the explosion of a thunderstorm after an afternoon of gathering clouds. The nudity of her flesh was a miracle, glowing ghostlike and sensual in the shadows as her legs caressed his own, and her sweet firm breasts grazed his chest.

She made love with a touching naturalness, her knees upraised to brush his hips, her hands on his shoulders as she welcomed him into the heart of her with a sigh. Yet her caresses, warm and gentle though they might be, were never without that strange inner intensity that was driving her in her working life. An intensity that seemed at once to devour Sam and to bypass him, as though it were not meant for him alone.

This schizoid feeling of being so close to this complex girl, and yet so far, brought Sam straight back to the murmured name he had heard on her lips.

He had known from the day he met her that the Magnus Corporation had hurt her deeply. He also knew that Jack Magnus had left a mark on her which was obscurely linked to her struggles against his company. When the Magnus octopus brought suit against CompuTel, it was as though the final gauntlet of Francie's life had been thrown down. She would not breathe, she would not live, until she had finished her last battle for a success which, Sam suspected, had more of revenge in it than of accomplishment.

Yet, today as two years ago, she would not talk about Magnus Industries. She kept her eyes fixed on Mollie and the future, insisting that what was past was past.

So profound was her silence that Sam sometimes had the strange feeling there was something she was not telling him about Mollie, and about the entire project they were working on. This was of course impossible, since Sam knew every circuit and relay of the new machine, and every inch of the operation. But the feeling haunted him nonetheless. It was as though since he did not know all of Francie, he could not know all her plans and intentions, either.

More yet, this silence of Francie's was the sharper edge of his punishment for having allowed himself to become intimate with her when he had no real evidence that her heart was behind her caresses.

It was a cruel punishment, and its sting grew more agonizing with each week of work, and with each charmed tryst, as he needed her more and became less capable of imagining a life without her.

"Jack . . ." The word still hung over Sam's life like an evil talisman, corrupting every corner of his intimacy with Francie. It seemed that the Magnus empire, and its scion, Jack Magnus, was a web ensnaring her and taking her away from him at every turn. Sam had to wonder whether he himself was only a small cog in a machine fueled by Francie's hatred for a man who owned more of her than Sam would ever own, and whose dominion was proved by the very force of her antagonism.

Sam did not relish being the pawn of her anger and hatred, a hatred directed at another man whom she perhaps had loved, perhaps still loved.

On the other hand, Sam felt convinced that this hell-bent crusade of hers, and the hard, determined woman she had become, were not natural parts of her. They were like character traits from another person, grafted onto her personality almost by a mistake of fate and circumstance.

When he looked at the Francie of today he could still see the gentle girl he had fallen in love with at the Automat—a high-strung, energetic person, no doubt, but a person made for happiness rather than mere success. And behind this image he could almost see the innocent child she had been not so many years before, a bright and mischievous little girl devoted to her family and eager to explore the world around her. A girl who had survived her mother's death and gone on to a happy college career.

This was the Francie who owned Sam's heart. She must be real, he thought. He could not have been mistaken in sensing her presence, especially since he had held her in his arms so many times since, and felt her innocence and her sweetness as she gave herself to him.

Yet now that childlike creature was joined to something infinitely more dangerous in Francie's personality. It seemed that when he made love to Francie there were two women in his embrace, one a sweet and trusting girl with whom he ached to spend the rest of his life, the other a relentless crusader whose obsession was directed at a target outside himself.

He had to know which was real.

In the time since Dana's firing he had made his decision. He would wait until Mollie was finished before asking Francie point-blank where he stood with her. Once the results of her anguished battle were in, for good or ill, she would be able to decide where her feelings lay, and what she wanted to do with her life.

Sam could wait that long. But not a moment longer. He was too proud a man to go on giving his heart so completely to a woman who did not belong to him with all of herself. Not even the love he felt for Francie could bear that.

It was time to find out who she really was—though he dreaded her answer almost as much as he yearned for it.

═══ **42** ═══

December 15, 1959

Julie Magnus lay in Scott Monteagle's arms.

They were in the small bedroom of the cottage his family owned in Surrey. The cottage had been in the family for five generations. It had belonged to the caretaker on the large estate owned by Scott's ancestors, and had survived the loss of all the family wealth during the Depression.

Since he finished law school Scott had been occupied in taking care of his mother and sisters and trying to salvage the damage to the family's finances. He had succeeded in setting his mother up in an attractive flat in London, near her own relatives. He had helped finance his sisters' education, and had personally given away the older girl in marriage.

Scott had saved every penny he had made as a barrister, and managed to buy a small tract of farmland not far from the old family estate. He had hired a tenant farmer, a friendly young man named Ned Templer, who had a family of his own. The two men were friends now, and were working hard to harvest enough potatoes and sugar beets to make the little farm a profitable operation.

With the exception of the cottage, a relic of the distant past, the tiny farm was all the Monteagles owned. Scott's own flat in London was rented, like his mother's, and Moira roomed with three other girls in Bloomsbury, near her University.

The Monteagles were light-years removed from the era of their family's great wealth. But they were solvent, if financially pressured, middle-class Englishmen. And Scott had plans for improvements in the family's lot. He was a brilliant and hardworking barrister, and his work on corporate and international law was gaining him recognition in his firm. He could expect to be a partner in another few years if things went well.

But Scott did not let work devour his life. He had a sense of humor about his family's financial straits, and bore with gentle fortitude his mantle as head of the family and main provider. He joked easily with

— 271 —

Julie about his work. She got the feeling that he actually enjoyed his down-to-earth life-style, and was relieved to be free of the burdens of great wealth which had brought so little happiness to his father's generation.

This combined attitude of sober seriousness and breezy indifference to the vicissitudes of life charmed Julie. There was an independence about Scott, an honest way of dealing fairly and squarely with life, which was completely foreign to her, for she had grown up in a hothouse world in which her family's wealth and social position were as suffocating as was the inhuman power of her father.

Upon her arrival in London Scott had taken her to meet his family—his mother, a tired but attractive woman in her sixties who seemed to depend on Scott for her own smiles, but who welcomed Julie warmly; his older sister Lucy, who was married to a stockbroker and had a new baby; and Moira, a bright, pretty university student who took an immediate liking to Julie.

Moira was very full of herself intellectually—she was majoring in history and international relations—and had left-wing, feminist opinions which sometimes put her at odds with her brother.

"You're so *staid*, Scott," she would say. "You've got to wake up to the truth about women in Britain. Until women get their rights, none of the other downtrodden groups will, either."

Scott smiled, for he admired his sister even when she pointed the dart of her opinions against him.

"It's not that I disagree with you," he said. "It's just that I don't think any political opinion is worth—well, getting so worked up over. We have to live in this world, with all its failings. I have no quarrel with working for change. But we can't hold our breath until change comes. We have to live today, and take care of each other as best we can."

"That's exactly my point," proclaimed pretty Moira in triumph, her dark eyes flashing against her chestnut hair. "Taking care of each other. We can't put off that moral responsibility until the world gets easier for us, Scotty. We have to do it now. Waiting never did anybody any good. Isn't that true, Julie?" She turned to Julie with a smile. "Help me out, now. Make him see reason."

Julie stammered a tactful response sympathetic to both parties. She could not tell Moira how astonished she was simply to have been asked for her opinion, and how grateful to have been included in this moment of a happy family's friendly argument. She saw Scott's family as the luckiest people in the world, people who were allowed by their circumstances to be human and to love each other. And, what was more, they were accepting her.

Scott showed her all around London, and she tried to downplay the fact that she had seen it all before, several times, in her family's travels. But this was not so difficult, for Scott's London was the London of the noisy Portobello Market, Kensington Gardens, and the modest tea shops of Soho, while the London the Magnuses had frequented had been the London of Sotheby's and Savile Row and Claridge's and Wimbledon.

Scott showed Julie a working-class London, a battered city recovering from the war years with effort, but with the stubborn pride of a historic people whose traditions were as strong as ever.

"The country is like us Monteagles," he said. "It's lost its empire and its swagger, but the old ways still offer comfort."

Julie had never enjoyed herself so thoroughly. Every quiet moment with Scott and his family was like Christmas morning to her, filled with a brisk, wintry freshness that braced and invigorated her. The clammy London fog did nothing to dampen her spirits. She wanted to see everything through Scott's eyes.

After they had explored the city Scott showed her around the Surrey countryside. He held her hand as they took strolls in the meadows where he had played as a youth. He took her for drives through charming villages like Shere and Friday Street, and showed her the old family burying ground at Abinger Common, with Monteagle graves dating back to the sixteenth century.

"You see, we've returned to our roots," he told her. "Perhaps great wealth didn't suit us. Perhaps providence had another plan for us. I find that thought somehow appealing."

It certainly appealed to Julie. With each moment she spent with him, she became more aware of how closed and fetid her family's New York world was, and how joyously real were the other alternatives offered by life.

A week after her arrival in England Scott showed Julie the cottage. It was a charming little place, with a coal-burning stove, two tiny bedrooms, and a living room with a big stone fireplace and overstuffed chairs. Some ancient portraits hung on the walls, and landscapes painted by Scott's father in his youth. It was cozy in the extreme, once the stove had spread welcome heat through the cold rooms.

Scott showed Julie where to find the tea things, and watched her with pride as she prepared a pot of tea.

"Perhaps we could have dinner here," he said. There was a touch of diffidence in his voice.

She understood the meaning behind his invitation. It never occurred to her to refuse.

They took a long tramp through the surrounding countryside before dinner, then made a fire in the old fireplace. They heard the old country wind blowing outside, and the flutter of birds' wings and the scurry of field mice, and Julie snuggled close to Scott under the quilt.

She felt his soft kisses on her brow, and his fingers stroking her hair. A prohibited warmth began to steal under her skin. Only a few months ago that sensation would have filled her with such shame at herself that she would not have dared allow it to continue for fear of contaminating Scott with her own guilt. But now, having seen him in his own country, having met his family, and knowing as she did how he felt about her, she could try the impossible: to leave her past behind her, and dare to be herself as a woman with him. It was scary, but it was a good, healthy sort of fear.

When his hand hesitated at her breast, she dared to guide it to the hard nipple under her blouse. There was something simple and honest about the way he caressed her, and before long she began to feel poignant tremors of excitement under her skin.

She knew he was excited, too. She sensed it in his kisses, and in the urgency of his caress.

She knew they were on the brink of the final discovery about each other. And now, despite herself, she got cold feet.

She pulled back in his embrace, just enough to look into his eyes. She caressed his cheek and let him see her pain.

"Julie," he said softly. "What's the matter? Aren't you sure?"

She smiled sadly. "Of you, yes. I just can't help wondering whether I'll be good enough. I don't want to lose you."

He pulled her to him and closed her eyes with his kisses.

"You're a beautiful girl," he said. "A fine and honest person—inside and out. And I love you. I've been dreaming of you all my life, and now I've found you. I won't let you go."

Julie trembled in his embrace. She had never dreamed she could hear such words. They were like a door opened to another world.

He kissed her, slowly and sweetly. Then, from nowhere, he produced a small box.

"Open it," he said.

She opened it to see a lovely garnet ring in an intricately modeled gold setting.

"It was my grandmother's," he said. "This was the ring she married my grandfather with. It came from somewhere in the family, too far back for any of us to know. Long before the Monteagles became wealthy, in any case. Now that we're normal folk again, the ring is a link with the past. I want you to wear it for me."

He paused.

"I want you to marry me, Julie."

She looked at the ring, and into his eyes. He was absolutely sincere. There was no doubt he loved her. Like the ring that linked him to a time beyond his own memory, Scott himself was the link to a time from before her shame, a time when she was still unspoiled. He had known her then, and he was offering her a return to her own lost self.

For a terrible moment Julie hovered over the chasm of her past, and the hopelessness which had been her only world for so long. Scott Monteagle was holding out a lifeline for her, the only one that could allow her to leap over this miasma without being devoured by it. He might never hold it out again. Fate was giving her one chance to save herself.

She smiled. The knife twisting inside her seemed to withdraw for the first time in her memory.

"Yes, Scotty," she said. "I'll marry you."

She put the ring on her finger and looked into his eyes. Then, as he watched, she took off her blouse, unhooked her bra, and placed both his hands on her breasts. Astonished at the golden beauty of her body, he gazed at her in admiration. Then he bent his face to hers and kissed her.

They made love on the old couch before the crackling fire. Scott was a tender and solicitous lover, almost too gentle in his treatment of her. But he could not know how precious his respect was to Julie. Giving him her body was as holy to her as wearing his ring for the first time.

When it was over she held him in her arms and hugged him close.

"Don't ever leave me," she whispered in his ear. "Promise?"

"I promise," he murmured. "Not until death parts us."

Julie tried to convince Scott to elope with her. She knew there were grave obstacles facing her marriage to him. She was sure her father would never approve of it, because the Monteagles were a family without money or stature, a family disgraced by its own poverty. Scott Monteagle had absolutely no plans to become rich or to recapture his family's glory. All he wanted was a simple life—with Julie.

Scott resisted her arguments that they marry in secret right away. He did not want to offend his mother in her old-fashioned concern for the proprieties. More importantly, he wanted to bring Julie into his family officially, in the traditional manner. The family had taken an instant liking to her, and would want to welcome her with the proper ceremony.

Scott announced his engagement at an intimate party at his mother's flat. The wedding was scheduled for June. It would be a simple affair, but Scott's closest friends would attend, as well as the extended Monteagle family.

Unbeknownst to the Monteagles, Julie had not told her family of her betrothal. She wanted to savor her separate future for a while before sharing it with the Magnuses. She simply cabled home that she was staying an extra ten days in London.

But there was one thing she had to discuss with Scott right away. It was the question of her inheritance.

"My father will disinherit me as soon as he hears of this marriage," she told Scott. "He has plans for me, just as he did for my sister and Jack. My father never takes no for an answer. You must understand, Scotty. From the day he hears about this, I'll be on my own. Besides, I wouldn't take his money even if he offered it. I hope you can accept that."

To her surprise Scott was delighted by this news.

"That's a load off my mind," he said. "I was planning to provide for you myself. I've rather got out of the habit of possessing great amounts of money. I don't think I'd like it. I had wondered how to convince you to live like a poor Englishwoman instead of a New York millionairess."

"Oh, I love you!" she cried, taking him in her arms.

He smiled as she kissed him. "That's the first time a woman has ever thanked me for separating her from a great fortune," he said. "I suspect it's a healthy sign for our life together."

For the first time in her life Julie Magnus felt like the mistress of her own fate. Scott stood like a rampart between her and her private demons. She could already feel the Monteagles gathering around her like a new family, to protect her from her past. And now that she had renounced Anton Magnus's money, what could he do to stop her?

Things would work out, Julie thought. They simply had to. The Lord in His wisdom could only reserve a certain amount of misfortune for two little people. Scott had had his, and she hers. Together they would be happy.

Things *had* to turn out.

On the night of her engagement party at Mrs. Monteagle's flat, Julie suddenly felt that her heart would burst with her good news if she did not tell it to someone. But she had no friends. She could only confide in someone who would keep her secret from her parents.

She thought of Gretchen. There was a bond between the two sisters which had allowed them to keep many secrets for each other over the years. Julie knew Gretchen would tell no one of her good news.

She called her long distance. Since it was five hours earlier in New York, she caught Gretchen in mid-afternoon. Gretchen, home alone with her baby, was delighted to hear from her sister.

She was even more delighted when she heard Julie's news.

"Oh, honey, I'm so thrilled for you," she said. "When is the wedding?"

"In June. I hope you can be there, Gretch," Julie said, excitement coloring her voice.

"I'll be there with bells on. But listen, Julie. There's news on this end. You're not going to believe it."

"What is it?" Julie asked.

"It's Jack. He and Belinda have split up. It came as a complete surprise to everyone. They kept it a secret until a few days ago. No one could believe it at first."

Julie was taken aback. She had thought she knew her brother well enough to know that such a step was out of the question for him.

"Well, he's certainly got balls, I'll say that for him," she said, inadvertently reverting to the crude language she used back home. "I didn't know he had it in him."

"But there's more," Gretchen said. "Brace yourself: he's getting married again."

"Again?" Julie exclaimed. "Already? I can't believe it."

"And you'll never guess in a million years," Gretchen said, "who he's marrying."

$$=== 43 ===$$

December 21, 1959

Mollie was no more than six months away.

Excitement was running high at CompuTel. In its last four demonstrations the computer had performed brilliantly, impressing its inventors and financial supporters alike with its combined computing power and ease of operation.

The latter feature, as everyone knew, was due to the machine's master program, which had now been fine-tuned by Francie to an almost unbelievable level of efficiency. Those around her were frankly amazed by what she had done, the more so because nowadays she seemed a bit more possessive and secretive about the program, retreating into deliberate vagueness when questioned about its innermost workings and technical specifications.

The greatest challenge facing the CompuTel team now was Mollie's retail price. It was essential that the finished computer be well within the price range of the average midsized company, and that the service warranty accompanying the machine be very liberal, so that the crucial first wave of customers would not feel they were risking too much in purchasing the new product.

This difficult problem was solved by the herculean sacrifice of all those involved in developing and marketing Mollie. CompuTel's top officers were earning rock-bottom salaries, and pouring their own money into the shoestring operation. They all had stock options in the company, so they knew their eventual financial gain from the work they were doing depended on how deeply committed they were to Mollie right now.

Because of this Francie was able to show her investors a retail price for Mollie that could be afforded by any reasonably successful business, and to assure them that the price would not go up between now and the day of Mollie's distribution. The nation was ready for computerization, she told them. Every company in the country was laboring under old-fashioned accounting and inventory techniques. All that was needed was to get the message of easy-to-use computing across to the nation's businessmen in an effective and convincing manner. Their own self-interest and profit motive would do the rest.

The investors were convinced. They put more hundreds of thousands of dollars into the development of Mollie. They kept their fingers crossed as the date for marketing drew nearer. The gamble they were taking was a big one, but it looked better every day.

In the meantime the pace of work at CompuTel had intensified. Everyone was exhausted all the time. But they worked all the harder. Like soldiers in battle, they ceased to care for their personal condition and pressed forward on automatic pilot. Emaciated, pale, almost unable to smile hello to each other in the morning, they worked on, eighteen and twenty hours a day, forgetting their fatigue as they saw the great day of Mollie's unveiling coming closer.

It was in the midst of this siege situation that, one crisp evening the week before Christmas, Francie was returning home after a long day at work. Her steps were slow as she approached the apartment building. She no longer had the strength to walk at her usual fast pace. All her movements were measured by her need to control her fatigue and prevent it from overwhelming her. She was in a constant daze, barely aware of what was going on around her, but inwardly attuned to Mollie and the future.

Her key was in the door to the building when a deep voice rang out behind her.

"Can you spare me a minute?"

She turned to see Jack Magnus standing before her.

Despite herself she caught her breath. Jack Magnus belonged to the darkest and most hidden part of her past. She had not expected to see him again in this life.

Perhaps it was for this reason that he seemed so handsome. He had never looked so princely, so elegant. He was wearing slacks and a sweater under his raincoat. His informality only increased his air of almost superhuman grace.

Upon closer examination she could see that he also looked tired and overworked. But he still had that hard, vibrant air that was his essence. And his eyes were glowing like coals about to burst into flame as he looked at her. His emotion was obvious. She knew hers was, too.

With an effort of will she managed to control the shaking in her voice and speak clearly and authoritatively to him.

"Jack, I don't want you here," she said. "We have nothing to say to each other."

"Just stand there a minute," he said, his voice dry and urgent. "Just do me the favor of waiting one minute to open that door until I've told you three things."

She hesitated. She looked into his eyes, and saw the entire world of the Magnuses reflected in them. She knew that if she listened to him, treated him as a human being, she was lost.

Yet all at once she recalled the note he had sent her three years ago, a note whose contents were still graven on her heart.

Nothing is what it seems.

What has happened is not real. Not as we were and are real.

I love you more than myself, more than my life.

Francie stood still, her keys in her hand.

"You have ten seconds," she said.

"I'm separated from Belinda," he said. "The divorce decree will go through in six weeks. I no longer work for Magnus Industries. I quit a month ago. I'm cut off from the family forever. Disinherited. I'm free, Francie. Those are the three things."

She looked long and hard into his eyes. She had never seen a look of such intensity. Pleading was mixed with something unbearably angry in his expression. But she knew the anger was not against her.

"You'd better come inside," she told him.

He followed her inside. They rode up in the elevator in silence. She let him into the apartment. He did not take off his coat, but sat down in the chair by the couch when she pointed it out to him.

She took off her coat and put down her briefcase. She moved slowly, trying to use this time to think.

"Would you like a drink?" she asked.

"Whatever you're having."

She made coffee, her mind working quickly as she moved about the kitchen. There was no sound from the living room. She could feel that he was giving her time to evaluate what he had said.

Without excusing herself she went to the bathroom to powder her nose. The eyes in the mirror frightened her, for they bore a composite expression she could not fathom. She almost did not recognize herself.

At length she returned to the living room with coffee on a tray. She put it down before him and sat on the edge of a chair.

"Why do you tell me these things?" she asked. "What does it have to do with me? You and I were through a long time ago, Jack. I'm happy for you if you think you've made the right decisions for yourself, but it's no business of mine. I have my own life, you see."

She saw the effect of her words. He looked as though she had stabbed him in his gut. In that split second she understood he was wondering whether she was in love with someone else.

Then he recovered himself. He spoke in measured tones.

"My divorce is amicable," he said. "I never loved Belinda. You know that, of course. Belinda knew it, too. We didn't marry by choice. We made an effort to play the farce through, but before long we both realized it would only ruin both of us. Oddly enough, we only became friends when we decided together to end it. We both paid the price for giving it up. More than you can know."

Francie was studying him, a cold, appraising look in her eyes.

"What kind of people marry without choice, without love?" she asked.

"We did it—*I* did it—for survival," Jack said. "It's not easy to explain to someone from a normal background, like you, what powers we were up against. I don't expect you to forgive me. I only want you to try to see it from my point of view. To understand."

Francie looked into his eyes. She saw genuine torment there. Her own balance began to falter, not only because of her extreme fatigue, but because of his odd logic. Today she knew more of the world of the Magnuses than she had three years ago. She knew how merciless that world was in devouring its victims.

But she held firm.

"No, I don't understand," she said.

A brief flare erupted inside his dark irises. He knew she was shutting him out, and he knew he deserved it.

"Look at yourself," he said. "You're young, you're beautiful, you're free. You have your intellect, your ability, and your own future. You can do anything you want."

He hesitated, as though searching for the right words. Francie cut him off. What she said took her by surprise.

"Am I supposed to thank your father for that?" she asked. "He stole my work, and fired me for having done my job well. Then, when I thought I was well rid of him—and of you—he sued me for having used my own invention. He ruined the company I had built from nothing. Am I supposed to be grateful for that?"

Jack sat forward suddenly.

"Listen, Francie," he said. "Try to understand. If I hadn't done what he wanted two years ago, things might have been much worse. For you, and for me."

She laughed contemptuously. "How could they be worse?"

Jack shook his head.

"You don't know him," he said. "You don't know what he's capable of. You don't know the things he can make happen. There is no limit to his power. Believe me, you were lucky to get away from him with only the scars you bear. For those of us who had to live with him, it wasn't so easy."

Francie withdrew into herself, trying to see him across a greater distance in order to achieve a clearer vision. His words were confusing her. She knew there was truth in what he said about Anton Magnus's power, and about his infinite malice. But these truths did not excuse Jack. Quite the contrary. She knew she must hold on to this fact, and never lose sight of it.

"Anyway," he said, "it's over. Belinda has her own future. She'll be all right. And as for me, I'm a lot poorer, but I'm free. I had been saving for this moment for years. I have enough money to start my own company. It won't be much, perhaps, but it will be mine."

He paused. He gazed upon Francie with an agonized tenderness.

"I want you back, Francie," he said. "I love you. You're all I've ever wanted."

There was a silence. Francie was staring at him through narrowed eyes.

When she spoke at last, the hatred in her voice surprised her.

"You bastard," she said.

She could see the effect of her words on him. He looked as though he had been slapped.

"Don't call me that," he said quietly.

"You bastard," she repeated. "You think you've come here as innocent as the driven snow, to claim what is rightfully yours. I suppose that makes sense to you. But you've said one thing that's true, Jack—I am a free woman. No man has enough power over me to change that. Not your father, and certainly not you. Now get out of here."

"You don't understand," he said. "I've given up everything for you. Just as I said in my note to you the day—the day he fired you—I couldn't come back to you until I was free. I've left that world behind, Francie. You'll never see it again. We have the whole future ahead of us."

"I told you to get out!" she cried with sudden violence. "You think women are things you use up and then throw away. Well, this is one plaything you can't get back, Jack." She knew her anger was running away with her, she had said too much. But the words tumbled out of their own accord.

All at once he was on his feet. He bounded across the small space between them and seized her in an iron grip.

"Is that what you think of me?" he hissed into her ear. "After all our times together? That I was playing with you? Because if it is—if that's how you felt in Paris—then I'm finished. Tell the truth. Tell me!"

His voice was charged with anger, but also with an almost pleading urgency. She realized how deeply she could wound him.

Slowly he loosened his grip. She looked at him through eyes filled with pain and frustration.

Very slowly she shook her head. She could not deny that truth. It was not in her to be a mere actress at this terrible moment.

But she had let her guard down. He embraced her suddenly, too suddenly for her to defend herself. And the kiss that had once sparked a thousand fantasies in her girlish mind was upon her again, so intimate, so full of magic and mystery, that it sent its potion of surrender into every corner of her before she could stop it.

With a spasm of resolve she managed to push him away.

"You think this changes something . . . ," she hissed. "It doesn't . . ."

"You're wrong," he said, gripping her hard by her wrists and feeling her squirm against him. "Nothing has changed. Nothing has ever changed between us. I haven't had you out of my mind for one instant in three years. I've felt the memory of you tear me apart when I least expected it, in the middle of work, in the street, at dinner, in my sleep. I've lived with that torture every day. And so have you. I can feel it. Don't try to deny it. Tell me you haven't felt that. Go ahead and try . . ."

He kissed her again before she could answer. She squirmed madly in his grasp, fighting him with every sinew of herself. But her struggles were contaminated by a paroxysm of involuntary excitement, and the harsh protest in her voice was not far from a moan of ecstasy. The feel of her in his arms, frail and angry and aroused, made him breathless with desire.

A groan sounded in his throat as he held her in his grasp. His senses were overwhelmed by the scent of her, by the sweet lips, the wild little tongue responding to him despite her best efforts to go on hating him. He could feel her firm breasts rubbing against his chest, her beautiful long thighs stroking him in their struggles, and he could actually smell her excitement, the magic aroma of female hunger mingled with rage and frustration. It nearly drove him mad. He was afraid he might take her by force, even if it caused him to lose her forever, because the passion she inspired in him was simply too great to resist.

But somehow, despite the riot of desire pulling them together, she managed, in a final paroxysm, to escape him. With surprising strength she broke the bonds of his hands, slipped from his embrace, and leapt up from the couch. She stood looking down at him, tall and supple, her hair awry, her breast heaving from their struggle, her eyes alive with a complex, hypnotic expression. She had never looked so beautiful. In that moment Jack realized that he had his old power over her senses, but also that her power over his heart had increased during the years of their separation.

"I love you," he said. "My God, I love you."

The look in her eyes clouded. She seemed confused. Her anger was unabated, but something else, something equally violent, was making her hesitate.

"Marry me," he asked.

"Get out," she replied. "Get out of my life." But her voice lacked conviction.

"I can't live without you," he said. "Look at me. Can't you see it's true?"

"Go," she said, closing her eyes tightly. "Go! Please . . ."

The note of supplication in her voice gave Jack a desperate idea.

"Listen to me," he said. "My divorce will be final in six weeks. If I promise not to touch you until we're married, will you say yes? Not until we've been married in a church in front of the whole world, until we're free of Magnus forever. Not until then. Will you say yes if I promise that? No more wondering, no more doubts. Be my wife, Francie. I'll give up anything. I'd give up my life for you."

She looked down at him, trembling, shaken by unseen forces powerful as earthquakes.

"You mean that?" she said.

He leaned forward, his passion making him look feral and dangerous as a panther.

"I mean it," he said. "Every word. Say yes, Francie. Please! You've got my life in your hands."

She looked long and hard at him. A thousand emotions seemed to cross her face, kaleidoscopic, dizzying. He could see the toll they were taking on her. They were literally draining her before his eyes. Then all expression left her face, replaced by a distant, thoughtful look, almost cold.

Then, very slowly, something like tenderness shone in her eyes. Tenderness, and acquiescence.

She sank to her knees on the carpet before him. Her hair still awry, her slender body crouched on the floor, she looked up at him like the most beautiful female animal that had ever walked the earth. And she spoke words that made him feel faint.

"All right," she said. "I'll marry you."

He leapt at her words.

"Oh, Francie . . ."

"But your bargain stands," she said. "It will be as you say."

"Anything," he said. "Anything. I'd give up my life for you."

"And there's something I have to finish," she said. "I'll need some time. A few months."

"Anything," he repeated.

"All right, then," she said.

They sat that way, both in a sort of shock, staring into each other's eyes, joined and separated by a thousand agonies and remembered joys, and now by a promise of something that would change their lives, something that would have seemed impossible only a day ago.

Then he pulled her to him and hugged her hard. He hoped she could not hear the tremor of his own halting breaths, or feel the extremity of his need. In the past two years, even as he had found life more and more impossible without her, he had forgotten how irresistible she was.

But tonight, at last, she was in his arms. His heart exulted inside him. *She's mine now*, he thought.

The feel of her body pressed tightly against his own made him drunk with happiness. He could not see her eyes, open wide and clear as she looked over his shoulder, and seeing beyond the shadows of this apartment to a future she had not dared to hope for until this moment.

Book III

CHECK MATE

$$=== 44 ===$$

Scott Monteagle sat across the polished mahogany table from Anton Magnus.

They were in the study of the Park Avenue mansion. They had just enjoyed a somewhat stiff but bearable dinner with Julie and her mother. The two women having retired to the downstairs salon, Anton had brought Scott up here for what was to be their most important conversation.

Julie had been of several minds about having Scott confront Anton Magnus. On one hand she was proud to show Scott off to both her parents. On the other hand she was alarmed and disgusted at the idea of bringing the man she loved into close quarters with her father. Her fear of Anton Magnus was as basic to her as breathing out and breathing in. She did not want Scott to come within his orbit.

So deep was her hatred of the Magnuses that she had tried to persuade Scott to simply wait for her in London. Having accepted the inevitable disinheritance, she would extend the Magnuses a polite invitation to her wedding. If they chose to come, that was their business.

This would have been the easiest way out for Julie herself. But Scott came from the old school, and he wished to formally ask the old man for his daughter's hand in marriage. He had been brought up that way by many generations of Monteagles. Though the family had come down in the world, it still clung to its traditions.

Upon reflection Julie was pleased by Scott's insistence that he face her father directly. She was proud of Scott's courage. Anton Magnus would certainly have wanted a better match for her, and could not possibly approve of a pauper like Scott. But since Scott cared nothing for the Magnus fortune, the approval of her family meant nothing. It gave Julie pleasure to think of her father's discomfiture as his wishes and his powers were ignored.

Also, she knew that Scott's simple honesty and love for her would make the old man's opposition look ridiculous. Scott had a powerful, deceptively slim backbone which made him a match for Anton Magnus. He was impervious to the time-honored Magnus weapon of financial intimidation.

In any case, as she had told Scott, she would marry him come what might. Nothing would stop her. "As long as you want me," she said, "I'm yours."

So it was a no-lose situation, even though for Julie it was an intensely unpleasant one. It seemed sinful somehow to taint Scott by bringing him into Anton Magnus's world, even for the shortest possible time.

Julie had been subdued through dinner, as both her parents queried Scott about his background and his life.

"It's all so sudden," Mother kept saying with a feckless look of pleased alarm, for she liked Scott but knew his poverty could never sit well with her husband. Her behavior was somewhere between that of a giddy matchmaker and a frightened rabbit.

Scott reacted to her bubbling with a politeness in which the warmth of an affectionate son-in-law was already palpable. He complimented her on her taste in all things, inquired about her life, and even found that they had something in common: painting watercolors.

"We'll go out together in Hyde Park," he promised her, "as soon as you come to visit."

"We'll go right here, in Central Park," Mother invited hastily, with a fearful sidelong glance at her husband. "It will be fun. We'll have a nice outing . . ."

Anton Magnus said little through dinner. Clearly the moment of truth was to come afterward. When coffee and brandy had been served mother and daughter remained downstairs, while Scott followed Anton to the dark walnut study which overlooked the back lawn.

The room was surprisingly restrained. Beside the pictures of Anton's family on the bookshelf, only a single signed photograph of the President revealed the grandeur of this room's occupant.

Scott complimented Anton Magnus on his fine house, just as he had his wife. His tone was polite and respectful, if a little impersonal.

Sitting behind his desk, Magnus had assumed the mild, paternal demeanor which was so familiar to his many friends and enemies in business. He looked at Scott appraisingly.

"Do you mind if I ask you a question, Mr. Monteagle?" he asked.

"Certainly not, sir." Scott smiled. "Ask away."

"How did you feel when your father lost his money?" Anton asked.

Scott thought for a moment. "You mean when he killed himself?"

Magnus paused, watching his cigar smoke curl toward the ceiling.

"All right," he said. "How did you feel when he killed himself?"

Scott looked serious. "Sad," he said. "Sad and angry. Sad that I had lost him, and angry that a man could take his life over a thing as unimportant as money."

Scott was satisfied with his answer. His own contempt for money dated from the day he heard about his father's death.

Magnus looked interested. "You don't care much for money, do you?" he asked.

Scott shook his head. "Not much, sir," he said. "Money can't buy happiness."

Magnus looked him in the eye. "The world is full of millions of people who live in the worst possible misery, and who will tell you not to talk to them about happiness, or justice, or truth, until they can put a square meal on their table. Money means something to them. Just as it meant to my ancestors, I might add."

Scott nodded thoughtfully. He saw the distinction the older man was making.

"Those people are starving," he said. "They are victims of injustice and indifference. If they had enough money to eat and be healthy, they would still have to seek happiness, or fulfillment, like the rest of us more fortunate people. And money would not help them then. It's true that without a small amount of money, just as without health, life is impossible. But health is not the meaning of life. Neither is money."

Now it was Anton Magnus's turn to acknowledge the distinction. He could see that Juliet's young man was intelligent.

"How would you feel if Juliet had to give up her inheritance in order to marry you?" he asked.

"Relieved," Scott said. "To be honest, sir, I wouldn't want that amount of money between us. I have a great deal of confidence in my ability to take care of Julie and give her a good life through my own efforts. I don't require more than that, and neither does she. We'd both prefer that you use the money in some more productive way."

Magnus raised an eyebrow. "You're not afraid to speak your mind, are you?" he asked.

Scott smiled. "What's in my mind is very simple," he said. "I love your daughter. I want to spend my life with her."

Magnus smiled in his turn. "So love is that important to you?" he asked.

Scott looked surprised. "Why, yes," he said. "It's the only thing that is, really."

There was a pause. Magnus looked away. Something reflective came over his expression, flickered and was gone. He turned back to Scott.

"What is the worst thing that could happen to you in this world?" Magnus asked.

"To lose Julie," Scott answered without hesitation.

"She means that much to you."

"Yes, sir."

"How much do you know about her?" Magnus asked.

"All I need to know."

"You know she's had a pretty wild youth, don't you?"

"Yes, sir."

"And that doesn't bother you?"

"Why should it bother me?"

Scott met the older man's eyes with some discomfort. Their expression of paternal hospitality was gone. Their depths were opaque, empty as the eyes of a predator. No light of human care, human weakness or vulnerability, shone in them.

Scott knew by an indefinable instinct that something was terribly wrong between Julie and her father. He realized that her wild youth had something to do with the relationship between her and Anton Magnus. One evening in her family's company had made that abundantly clear.

Now was the time to get her away from Anton Magnus forever. Scott was here to accomplish that. And he would not back down. He could feel how dangerous Magnus was. But he felt sure that his love for Julie was equal to whatever was going on behind her father's black eyes.

There was a silence. Magnus seemed to be studying the young man. Scott met the piercing eyes without flinching.

At last Magnus spoke. "Juliet is very dear to me," he said. "In a way I think she is the most special of my three children. I feel a special responsibility to her, Mr. Monteagle. Her life has not been an easy one up to now. I want it to be peaceful and happy from now on."

"I see we want the same thing," Scott said, a confident smile on his face.

There was a long pause. The eyes boring into Scott were hypnotic, unspeakably intense.

Suddenly, jarringly, Magnus smiled and pushed back his chair. He held out his hand across the desk. "Welcome to our family," he said. "I think you'll make a fine son-in-law, and a wonderful husband for Juliet."

The two men shook hands and walked toward the door.

"When were you thinking of getting married?" Magnus asked.

"In June."

"I'm having some minor surgery done at the end of May," Magnus said. "Nothing serious—just an old back injury. But I'll be laid up for a few weeks. I don't suppose you could postpone your wedding for a month or so? I'd hate to miss it."

"I don't see why not," Scott said. "I'll talk to Julie about it. I'm sure she won't mind."

"And, if it isn't too much of a burden," Magnus said, "I think I'm going to go against your wishes where the money is concerned. I feel a deep bond with my daughter. I want her to be comfortable. I wouldn't want to single her out by disinheriting her. I want her to feel she is always part of the family, and close to my heart in particular."

"That's your decision, sir," Scott said. "I hope you understand that Julie and I intended no disrespect in expressing our desire to live on our own resources. It's simply our own preference."

He had anticipated this moment, though he had not discussed it with Julie. They could always leave the Magnus money in a trust fund for their own children. Scott would never touch it with his own hands. He knew Julie did not want to either.

Nevertheless Scott measured Anton Magnus's skill as a negotiator. He had just put the money back on the table, when Scott and Julie had tried to erase it as an issue. And he had managed to get Scott to agree to put their marriage off, albeit for a short time.

Scott recalled Julie's warnings about Anton Magnus. He was a devious man, and a dangerous one.

But he had agreed to their marriage. Perhaps this was because he realized that Scott was impervious to the weapons with which he could easily have daunted other young men. Perhaps, indeed, it was because he saw the power of Scott's love for Julie, and genuinely felt Scott would be the right match for her.

In any case, he had given in.

As they left to give the good news to the ladies, Scott thought he had done well.

Anton Magnus was not as tough as he was cracked up to be.

$=== 45 ===$

The New York Times, *January 21, 1960*

Magnus-Bollinger Engagement Announced

The engagement of Miss Frances M. Bollinger, daughter of Mr. Marcus Bollinger and the late Helen Bollinger, to Mr. Johan F. Magnus of New York is announced. A June wedding is planned.

Miss Bollinger was graduated from the University of Pennsylvania and is currently President of CompuTel, Inc. of New York. Mr. Magnus has degrees from Yale and Harvard Universities and was Vice-President in Charge of International Development at Magnus Industries, Inc. until resigning to pursue other interests earlier this year.

Francie and Jack were locked in an embrace so intense that their bodies were on fire.

They were on the couch in Jack's apartment. It was here that, so long ago, Francie had first detailed to Jack her plan for the computerization of the European subsidiaries of Magnus Industries. How far they had both come from that moment! It seemed like ancient history.

The hard male attraction of Jack's body was never more overpowering than now. His long arms held Francie close, and she could feel the whole length of him tensed against her soft limbs. The taste of his lips was intoxicating. The tongue exploring her own sent shudders of desire through her.

Just as her nipples were beginning to strain against the fabrics separating her from him, she managed to pull herself free.

"Whew," she gasped with a little smile. "Please, Jack. No more."

He was gazing at her with a look somewhere between agony and delight.

"You're hard to resist," he said. "I've never felt less able to control myself."

She smiled into his eyes. "It won't be long."

They both knew the rules. They would not be married for at least five more months. Though Jack's divorce was due to come through in about two weeks, Mollie was still in the final polishing stages, and could not reach the public until June. Francie had made clear to Jack that she would not marry until her great experiment was finished, for good or for ill.

And Jack had accepted this, however unwillingly.

"I'll tell you something, Mrs. Magnus-to-be," he said, running a hand through his hair. "Nobody ever wanted a project to be finished as much as I want this Mollie thing of yours to be finished. Sometimes I think I'll burst before you get that crazy machine to market."

"I'm doing the best I can," Francie said, leaning back to look at him. He admired her long, sinuous body, which was clothed tonight in soft slacks and a sweater which made her seem more warm and embraceable than ever.

"No one knows that better than I do," he said. "You spend eighteen hours a day in that damned warehouse of yours. You're harder to see than Anton Magnus himself."

"But less successful," she joked.

"Not for long," Jack said. "I have a good feeling about the future. You're going places, kid. All my years in business make me sure of it."

Since her work was so consuming that she could not see much of Jack—which was all the better, since their evenings together inevitably ended in these moments of rapturous frustration—Francie had told him enough about Mollie's conception and general design to make him a believer.

Jack had decided to begin his new life in business by opening an investment firm. He had told Francie that Mollie would be an ideal tool for him in his new venture.

"Not only will I personally be your customer," he said, "but I have considerable influence in this town, and around the whole country. I can throw a lot of business your way—and I will."

"I'm sure I'll need all I can get," she said. She had discussed with Jack her fear that Mollie was ahead of its time, and that the cost of the machine and customers' fears of operating a computer themselves would cause the whole plan to misfire.

But Jack encouraged her.

"The key thing is that you're fulfilling a need," he said. "Every company in this country is laboring under outmoded accounting and record-keeping techniques, not to mention billing procedures. The whole business world is crying out for something more efficient to cut down all those wasted man-hours and all that overhead. Mollie is just what the doctor ordered. Naturally it's ahead of its time, but so was the telephone in its time, and the teletype, and the wireless. That's the beauty of what you're doing, Francie: you're on the edge of the future."

She thanked him for his reassurances, and even told him some of the details about Mollie's workings and design. He enjoyed listening, though he admitted that her technical expertise was too far over his head for him to appreciate the complexities of her achievement.

"When we're married, and people ask me what my wife does for a living, I'll say she's a computer expert," he said. "That has a nice ring to it. On the other hand, of course, I could say I'm married to an entrepreneur, the president of her own company. I like that even better."

But whenever the subject of marriage was brought up, he could not help hugging her close and asking, "How much longer? I never waited so long for anything in my life."

And she would reassure him, "It won't be much longer." But the murmur of her voice in his ear, and the proximity of her lips to his own, took away his self-control, and he pulled her to him for another of the bewitching, maddening kisses which excited them both so much.

When they were not talking about Mollie or about Jack's new investment firm, they talked about their marriage. They discussed where they would live, and where they would spend their honeymoon. Jack had found a new apartment on Fifth Avenue with a magnificent view of the Park. Even now they were decorating it together, and learning more about each other's tastes. Both agreed that the place should look modern, sleek and spare. They spent their few free hours together looking in galleries for paintings, and in furniture stores for furnishings.

Their honeymoon would be spent on a cruise to the Virgin Islands, with a lengthy stopover at an island in the Caribbean where Jack had found a villa which would afford him ten days of complete privacy with his new wife.

All they had to do was hold out until Mollie was before the public, and then they would have their long-awaited freedom to be alone together, to be man and wife.

Jack had accepted Francie's conditions gracefully, but the strange fact of being this close to such a beautiful woman without being able to strip the clothes from that magnificent body and possess her, kept him permanently off balance. Beyond this, it seemed to throw him back in time to his adolescence. For that was the time, long since lost for him, when girls were magical things veiled by the fact of their youth and his own virginity. A time when young men idealize girls, and lose themselves in fantasies about them.

He felt that way about Francie now. Though he had once known the pleasures of her body in all their hot intimacy, that time was itself hidden behind a veil. Now she was full of mystery. When at last they were married, and he possessed her, it would be like making love to her for the first time.

The waiting was nearly killing him. Each day his desire for her reached a new and less tolerable level. But her beauty increased in direct proportion, and he congratulated himself on the almost unbelievable fact that this gorgeous, talented, brilliant creature was to be his.

Perhaps it was for this reason that he had not been able to prevent himself from asking her about her love life since their first engagement.

"I know I don't have the right to ask this," he said. "But have there been—I mean, has there been anyone . . . ?"

She had looked him in the eye with a frankness that took him aback.

"I'm a free woman, Jack," she had said.

"You're right. I was out of line. I'm sorry. Forget I mentioned it." Jack spoke softly.

"But to answer your question, no, there has not been anyone." Her words were simple and sincere.

His face lit up.

"After all," she laughed, "with Mollie taking up eighteen hours of my day, when would I have time to play around?"

He hugged her close. The very thought of another man wanting her made her slender body feel strange in his arms, more exotic and mysterious than ever. She was older now, more private than when he had first known her. Even her kisses had a complex component which only made her the more attractive. He knew what she had been through these past years, and he could see how it had matured her.

When he had first known her she was more girl than woman, brilliant and confident, but still innocent. Now she had the deeper, enigmatic charm that came from real womanhood. It made her sensuality ten times more powerful than before, and that much harder to resist.

He told himself he would surely burst from wanting her if her damned computer did not get off the drawing board and into the marketplace soon.

So they waited, and held each other close, separated only by time and by the inevitable gulf that divides the thoughts of any two human beings from each other.

═══ 46 ═══

Belinda Devereaux sat alone at her kitchen table, the announcement of Jack's engagement to Francie in her hands.

She was gazing quietly at the announcement, entirely unaware of the tears running down her cheeks.

Belinda lived alone now. Since her separation from Jack she had found a job teaching English and writing at a private school on the East Side. She had rented an apartment in an attractive old brownstone convenient to the school, and commuted to Columbia, where she was now at work on her Ph.D. dissertation on romantic literature.

She divided her busy days between teaching, research at Columbia's library, and work on her dissertation in the evenings and on weekends.

Belinda did not stop to wonder whether she had made her life so busy in order to avoid thinking about what she had lost. She simply survived from day to day, and allowed the future to take care of itself.

She had not been surprised when Jack asked for the divorce. Their marriage had become so barren that it was almost torture for them both to go on with the charade any longer. Belinda was frankly relieved that her entire life was not to be devoured by this impossible predicament.

Of course, her heart was broken. She had loved Jack since the first moment she saw him, and she loved him still. To lose him was to lose part of herself. But she had long since learned the tragic truth that being married to him was no solution for the fatal malady of loving him. She might as well let him go. One way or another she would have had to learn to live on her own. Better, then, that she make a life for herself without him altogether.

She had been in the midst of this busy, empty enterprise when the announcement caught her eye in this morning's *Times*.

Jack's choice of beautiful Francie Bollinger had not surprised Belinda. Her woman's intuition had told her long ago that Francie had a special place in his heart.

Now, at last, he would be happy. In this, for a woman who loved him as deeply as Belinda, there was a kind of consolation. If she could not have him, then she wanted him to be happy with the woman who could give him what he wanted.

These were the first thoughts that came into Belinda's mind when she saw the news.

But they were not the only ones.

In the last three years she had learned a lot about Jack, about his relationship to his father, and about Magnus Industries. Belinda was an intelligent young woman—far more intelligent than she herself was really aware. She was accustomed to analyzing the sinuous subtexts of the most brilliant novels, and to penetrating the hidden motivations of complex characters.

And now something was telling her that there was more to this engagement than met the eye.

But what?

Belinda recalled meeting the Bollinger girl at Anton Magnus's party for Gretchen and her baby. The most impressive thing about Francie Bollinger was her honesty and self-respect. She was a proud person.

And she had been deeply hurt by Jack, hurt as only a woman can be when a man forsakes her for another—in this case, for Belinda herself.

Francie had been fired by Magnus Industries at the time of Jack's marriage. And since then, Belinda knew, the new company Francie had formed, CompuTel, had been sued by Magnus's high-priced attorneys for patent infringement. Belinda had found out about this not from Jack, but from her careful reading of *The Wall Street Journal*—one of the indirect ways she had kept tabs on her husband's life.

Francie Bollinger could have no more malignant enemy than Magnus Industries, and no grudge more terrible than the one she must hold against Jack Magnus.

Why, then, had she taken Jack back?

That was the question.

With this thought in mind, Belinda put down the newspaper. Later, she knew, she would cut out the engagement notice, and paste it in her personal diary as the final note in her relationship with Jack. For the rest of her life it would stand as a sort of tragic but necessary milestone in her life.

But for now she closed her eyes and let her mind focus on the image of Francie Bollinger, as well as that of Jack.

Belinda had some thinking to do.

47

Sam Carpenter sat alone in his loft.

The enormous living room was empty now. The space that had once been occupied by his pet computer, 9292, was cleared, for the computer had become Mollie, and Sam had finally discarded its ravaged shell.

A shell which had outlived its usefulness—like Sam's own dreams.

He looked at the apartment, and pondered the void which haunted it.

In the medicine cabinet of the bathroom, Francie's few toilet articles—a brush, a vial of cologne, a lipstick—were gone. In the kitchen, the new coffee pot she had bought for him remained, a heartbreaking reminder of all the mornings they had spent here, drinking a quiet cup of coffee after awakening in each other's arms, and then hurrying off to work.

The old chipped table in the living room no longer bore the stack of manuals and computer reports Francie used to look at in her few spare moments. Nothing remained but Sam's ashtray, and the bottle of beer he was drinking now.

The two hangers in the closet that had held Francie's coats, the spring raincoat and the wool winter coat, were bare.

And most of all, the subtle aroma of her presence in the loft was gone. It had lingered for a few days after her departure, almost killing Sam with its sweetness—and then vanished. Now there was nothing but Sam himself, his empty life—and his memories.

Francie had told him the news of her engagement honestly and directly. He had listened in silence, hiding the agony inside him. Then he had congratulated her and helped her pack her few things. They both knew she had spent her last night here, and would never return.

He had asked her if she would prefer him to leave the company. It was his first thought. He wanted to get as far away from her as possible. The idea of seeing her at work when he knew he would never hold her in his arms again was almost beyond what he could bear.

She had asked him to stay.

"You're free to do as you wish, of course," she said. "But please stay until Mollie is finished. She's as much yours as mine. I couldn't stand to see her come out without you beside me."

She saw the look in his eyes, and took his hand. The touch of her palm tore at his heart.

"Just stay a little while longer, Sam," she said. "I know you want to make your own decisions for yourself. I'm not getting married until Mollie comes out, anyway. Let's stick together that long. After that, you can do what you think best."

Sam had agreed.

And so he had to endure the torture of being near her at this terrible time. Each day he had to see her at work, her hair pinned up as she wore her smock over her blouse and jeans, her beautiful hands dirtied by her work on the computer, the pencil stuck behind her pretty ear . . . She was a vision of loveliness almost too withering to behold. And he was reminded at every moment that he had once possessed a part of her, and had now lost it forever.

Naturally he had kept his silence about her engagement. He was convinced she was doing the worst possible thing for herself. He knew enough about Jack Magnus, sight unseen, to know that he was the wrong man for Francie, and no doubt for any woman. And he had already caused Francie incalculable harm, directly and indirectly.

But no man can change a woman's heart. If Francie wanted Jack, she must have him.

Sam looked back on his doubts about Francie, and realized that he had been right all along. Her hatred of the Magnuses, her hell-bent struggle for a business success that could only signify revenge, had always included a stinging inner ember that was not hate, but love. She had never gotten Jack out of her system. And when he came back, free to marry her, Francie had been unable to say no to him.

Perhaps she was making a terrible mistake. But falling in love is a mistake that can never be corrected, an incurable illness. No one understood this better than Sam, whose heart would belong to Francie as long as he lived. Love is forever. One cannot deal with it by reason, or will, or even sanity. Once the heart has given itself, there is no stepping back. The fatal step has been taken.

So Sam himself would be a footnote to Francie's life. He had been her support, her friend, and her sometime lover, during the interval of her life while Jack was out of it. But when Jack came back, her heart could only go back to him like a magnet to the north.

While Sam was forgotten . . .

Nowadays Sam worked harder than ever at the warehouse, staying longer hours, trying by his frantic work on Mollie to forget the knife twisting in his emotions. When he came home at night he drank a couple of quick beers, staring into the shadows of the loft, and fell into bed exhausted. Sleep sometimes came quickly, but left him almost as soon, so that he found himself tossing and turning in the night's darkest hours, tormented by thoughts of Francie and by the excruciating dilemma of continuing to live when his soul was dead.

At five A.M. he dragged himself out of bed and back to work for another long day of oblivion, knowing that at its end was the loneliness of the loft.

He had never imagined a torture so absolute. Each night he wondered if he could go on with it any longer.

But Francie had made him promise to stay.

"Just until Mollie is finished," she had said. "Then you'll be free. Do it for me, Sam. Please . . ."

He would do it for her.

And after it was done he would set about the futile business of trying to forget her.

48

Scott Monteagle left his hotel on Tuesday, January 25th, to meet with a partner of the law firm that was his own firm's correspondent in New York. They intended to go over some international contracts, and to discuss some clients who used both the American and British firms. Afterward Scott was to meet Julie at Rockefeller Plaza for lunch.

Scott had called to ask the doorman at the small hotel to get him a cab. When he descended to the lobby the driver was waiting for him, a tall, muscular fellow with agreeable features and long dark hair.

"Morning," said the driver. "Fifty-fifth and Madison, right?"

Scott nodded. The driver led the way to a yellow cab parked in front of the hotel. The doorman watched impassively as the driver held the door for Scott.

A moment later they were on their way.

There was silence as the driver negotiated the first block of busy Manhattan traffic.

"How about this traffic?" the driver said over his shoulder, looking into the rearview mirror at his passenger. "Gets worse every month, I swear to God."

"You seem to handle it quite well," Scott observed politely, noticing how deftly the driver zipped into and out of the various lanes.

"Well, it's partially from practice, but also from just plain nerve," the driver said. "If you let these bus drivers and cabbies get in your way, you'll be an old man with a gray beard before you get across town."

Again there was a silence. The cabby touched the horn in short, almost inaudible beeps as he nudged his way through the heavy traffic.

"Are you from England?" he asked at length. "I've got a pretty good ear for accents."

"That's right." Scott smiled.

"Just visiting?" the driver asked, glancing again at Scott through the rearview mirror. "Or here on business?"

"Well, business at the moment," Scott said. "I have to meet some American attorneys. But that's incidental, really. I'm here to get engaged to be married."

"Hey, congratulations," the driver said, brightening suddenly. "That's what I call a happy occasion."

"It is for me, at any rate," Scott said, more amused than anything else by the driver's curiosity. He had heard that cab drivers in America were inveterate talkers.

"I'm kind of a romantic at heart," the driver said with a grin. "I've been married myself for nine and a half years. I've got two little girls. Believe me, there's nothing like having a good woman to come home to. Will you be taking your bride back to England?" he asked.

"Yes," Scott said. "We'll be living in London, where my work is."

There was a pause as the driver changed lanes with a lurch and blew his horn at a laundry truck. He began to roll down the window, as though to shout something, and then thought better of the idea.

"Some people think they own the road," he said. "I'll bet they're not this crazy in London."

"That depends on where you're going," smiled Scott. "In the Mayfair district the police keep things on the straight and narrow. But if you venture into Piccadilly in midday, you're taking your life in your hands." He paused. "Of course, I don't drive in London myself. I take the underground."

"Is your fiancée American?" the driver asked.

"Yes, she is," Scott replied.

"Did you meet her here, or over there?"

Seeing Scott pause, the driver shrugged in self-deprecation. "Listen to me," he said. "I oughta mind my own business. Sorry, buddy. It gets lonely in a cab all day."

"Not at all," Scott said. "Actually, we met many years ago, as children." He smiled as he thought of Julie. "Our families were loosely connected socially. Then my family—well, we came down in the world, so to speak, and I didn't see her or hear about her for many years. But I remembered her very well. Then, by chance, we met again a couple of years ago. I introduced myself, reminded her of the past, and we struck up a new relationship. One thing led to another, and—well, now we're going to get married."

"That's a beautiful story," smiled the driver. "I love a story with a happy ending. But, tell me. What does her family think about her leaving the country? Some people, you know, they don't like their kids settling down too far away."

"Well, you know families," Scott said. "I don't imagine they're thrilled by the idea. Her father, most of all. He's used to having her around, and he's accustomed to getting his way. But he's approved of the marriage. I think he's more concerned with his daughter's happiness than with pulling all the strings himself."

"That's nice to hear," said the driver. "I always say you've got to let your kids leave the nest when the time comes. When will you be marrying?"

"In July," Scott said.

"Will the wedding be here or in England?"

"Here." Scott smiled at the driver's curiosity.

"Well, that's a lovely story," came the voice from the front. "You know, I've always wished I could go to England. England being our mother country, and all. It's something you think about if you're American."

"You should come and see it one day," Scott said. "Of course, it's not big and sprawling and exciting the way your country is. But it has a charm all its own. And tradition, of course."

"Tradition, yes," said the driver. "Did your wife's folks come from England originally?"

"Well, she's not my wife yet," Scott laughed. "But thank you for putting it that way. Her ancestors are Swiss on her father's side. But her mother's people, if I'm correct, are English and Irish."

The driver fell suddenly silent. He pulled through traffic to a large office building with a bank of revolving doors.

"Here we are," he said. "Fifty-fifth and Madison."

"Thank you very much," Scott said, handing a small tip over the front seat.

"It's been nice talking to you," said the driver. "Have a pleasant stay. And congratulations on your engagement. I'm sure you'll be very happy."

"Thanks for your good wishes," Scott said, getting out of the car.

As he turned to go into the office building Scott smiled. The driver's high spirits and good wishes were indeed appreciated. All America seemed to gleam and smile with his own good news today.

He went in through the revolving doors.

Outside in the car, Johnny Marrante turned the rearview mirror to look at his own face.

"You're good, pal," he said to himself. "Very good."

It had been easy to bribe the desk clerk and the doorman at the hotel, and to borrow a yellow taxi from a cabdriver friend for this little excursion. Johnny had wanted to get a closer look at Scott Monteagle, having watched him from a distance with Julie numerous times.

He looked at the revolving door of the building.

"Enjoy your stay, brother," he said. "I'll be seeing you."

His lip curled in hatred. He thought contemptuously of the Englishman's slight build, his dark suit, his briefcase. He was precisely the sort of society pansy Johnny had often imagined as the mate Julie's family would pick out for her. Johnny's blood had boiled in his veins when he saw Julie kissing the man.

He was lingering over the murderous energy thrilling through his senses when a policeman began walking toward him to tell him to move the cab along.

With a nod to the officer Johnny pulled away. Better play it safe, he thought. This was no time to have an inquisitive cop checking his chauffeur's license.

He had things to do. And nothing must stand in his way.

═══ 49 ═══

February 18, 1960

Victoria Wetherell Magnus sat in the upstairs salon of her Park Avenue house, watching her husband and daughter.

It was one of the rare occasions in the last eight or nine years that the three of them had spent any time together outside the dinner hour. Most evenings Victoria spent crocheting in her armchair while Anton, if not in his office upstairs, sat reading, listening to music or occasionally watching the television, an amused look on his face.

Julie never graced their evenings with her presence. Though she no longer went out at night for her sinister adventures since she had fallen in love with Scott Monteagle, she closeted herself in her room, excluding the family from her private life as much as ever.

Victoria Magnus had got used to this disintegration of her family, as every mother must. But she was also used to worse.

She remembered the tumultuous days of Gretchen's adolescence, when Gretchen used all her intelligence and guile to outwit her family in the pursuit of her own happiness, and was reduced to a hollow shell when Anton prevented her marriage to the boy she loved in Chicago.

And she remembered long before that, when Gretchen had turned from a healthy if slightly overweight child into a withdrawn, moody, obviously miserable teenager.

And she remembered how Julie, a sprightly and bright baby and little girl, had turned almost overnight into a wild, resolutely self-destructive creature whose life had been going downhill ever since—until Scott Monteagle entered the picture.

Only Jack seemed to have been spared the horrors of those early years. Was it because he was a boy? Or because he and Anton seemed to understand each other so well?

Whatever the reason, Jack had remained intelligent, athletic, and entirely normal as he finished prep school, college, and business school with flying colors, and went into Magnus Industries with a great future before him.

Of course, Jack, too, had had his problems. His marriage to Belinda had not worked out. In fact, it had been doomed from the start, as everyone in the family had suspected long ago. But Anton had wanted the marriage, and so it had come to pass.

Yet now it was over, and Jack seemed happy and excited as a boy again, now that he was engaged to Francie Bollinger.

Victoria Magnus hated to see her son at odds with his father. On the other hand, she had always liked Francie, since their first meeting. Truth to tell, she had preferred her to Belinda, for Francie was a ray of light and happiness, while Belinda had the troubled air which already characterized both Magnus daughters.

Of course, Jack had left the corporation before he got engaged to Francie. And, to all accounts, Anton had disinherited him. Yet there were signs of reconciliation in the air. Anton had suddenly insisted upon giving the wedding. This gave Victoria hope that with the passage of time the wounds would heal, and Anton would accept Jack back into the family with his new wife.

And Anton had magnanimously given his blessing to the marriage between Julie and Scott Monteagle, her impoverished but devoted suitor. This was a move that had surprised everyone. Anton had sent cordial greetings to the Monteagles in England, and seemed delighted with the match.

That was why Julie was sitting here tonight, watching the program that was playing on the television, and opening the book in her lap to read a paragraph when the show bored her. She seemed actually to want to be with her parents, now that she knew Scott Monteagle was soon to take her away from them. She had the freedom she wanted and did not have to hide away in her room.

Victoria looked at her daughter. There was a new innocence, a new freshness in Juliet's face. It was almost as though the clock had been turned back, erasing the mask of bitter cynicism that had covered those lovely features for so many years. It wrung the mother's heart to see the ghost of her daughter's happiness return that way after so long an absence.

Anton was reading *The Wall Street Journal*, and Victoria was looking over her crocheting at her little family.

Part of her wanted to feel happy tonight. After all, Jack would soon be remarried, and to a lovely girl. Juliet had found an ideal young man, a young man who adored her, and who was not in the least daunted by her checkered past. It seemed that a new era was dawning, an era that might bring some happiness and closeness back to the ravaged Magnus family.

In a couple of months two weddings would come to undo the misery of the past.

But Victoria Magnus, Pollyanna though she was and knew herself to be, suspected this was all too good to be true.

She had known Anton Magnus for forty years. Her first experience of him had been when, as a youthful and ruthless entrepreneur, he had managed to outwit and terrify her possessive father into giving her up. No one in society had imagined that a Wetherell could marry a nobody, an immigrant. But Anton, through the awesome power of his will and his cunning, had pulled it off, and all but killed her father in the process.

Since that first ravishing of her person Victoria had preferred to look the other way where her husband's affairs were concerned. She let him do what he wanted, and lived like a bird in a gilded cage under his roof. He was far too strong for her.

But she knew him. Decades of marriage had brought familiarity, and intuition.

And she knew he was not a man to allow his son to divorce the girl he had picked out for him, and to marry a nobody from a small town in Pennsylvania.

Nor was he a man to allow Juliet, his prize, his favorite, to marry an impoverished Englishman who intended to take her out of the country.

Things were not what they seemed.

Victoria Magnus looked down at the troubled daughter she loved so deeply. She had always adored Juliet for her spirit, however reckless it had become. And though she knew Julie held her in contempt, if not in outright hatred, she still loved her.

Jack could take care of himself. But Juliet was like a hurt little bird, scarred so deeply—and Scott Monteagle was her chance for freedom. A freedom Victoria Magnus had lost forty years ago.

So Victoria trembled to think of the future.

If only these next few months were over, and Julie safely married! And Jack . . .

But time could not be hurried. It moved at its own sinuous pace, allowing the initiative of men like Anton Magnus to take its toll on other human beings.

Victoria Magnus was afraid. Not only did she know what Anton Magnus was capable of in the world of men. She also had an idea— however hard she had tried to deny it—of what had gone on under this roof in the past twenty years. Of what had changed her daughters from bright, energetic children into haunted, scarred young women.

She knew how dangerous her husband was.

And she suspected that the final tribute he would ask of his family was yet to come. She dared not think how terrible that might be.

Had she had any personal backbone, now would have been the time for Victoria Magnus to make her own final stand, for the sake of her children. To stand up to Anton.

But she had long since lost the capacity to do that.

So she could only sit and watch fate take its final turn for the family she loved, and wonder how she could do anything about it.

⟹ 50 ⟸

March 6, 1960

It was Sunday morning.

Francie stood with Jack in the huge central room of the Brooklyn warehouse where Mollie was being assembled.

No one else was there. The entire staff was enjoying its Saturday night and Sunday morning vacation, the only vacation it was allowed per week. This afternoon everyone would be back to work—including Francie.

She had spent last evening having dinner with Jack and going to the theater. They had seen *My Fair Lady*. It was the first time Francie had gone to the theater, not to mention the movies, in nearly a year. Work had consumed all her hours ever since.

She had agreed to meet Jack for breakfast this morning, and on her own impulsive suggestion had brought him here.

"You might as well see the monster that's eating up my life," she said.

She used her own key to let them into the empty warehouse. The place was a miracle of controlled chaos. It was full of cubicles, tables, and assembly areas, all of which looked sloppy and unkempt. Yet, as Francie knew, these were work stations manned by experts in their field, experts who were going to bring a polished and efficient product to market within a couple of months.

She showed Jack the final prototype of Mollie, which was located in the midst of a concentric circle of technicians' benches. The machine was housed in an enameled aluminum casing which gave it a modern, rather sleek look. Its shape was, as first predicted by Sam, more or less that of a home refrigerator.

Mollie was equipped with a monitor panel, a magnetic tape input, a printout, and a control keyboard that closely resembled an ordinary typewriter keyboard. The machine looked attractive and somehow domestic.

"We designed it to look friendly rather than intimidating," Francie explained, pointing out some of the major features. "When a businessman buys a Mollie, he'll be able to train one of his employees to operate the computer in hardly more than a day. Then that employee can train others. We'll also provide our own free training course as part of the purchase price. And the manual we're writing will be understandable even to the least technically minded consumer. The whole idea is to take the mystery out of computers."

She showed Jack the promotional materials, the advertising designs, and some of the salesmen's brochures.

"We're trying to work out a deal with two of the major business supply retailers," she told him. "Meanwhile we're going to open our own dealerships and service centers in strategic locations—the bigger cities around the country. It will all be timed to start at the same moment. Naturally, we're all on pins and needles."

"Well, you've got one customer, anyway," Jack smiled. "I can hardly wait to learn how to use Mollie myself."

"Want to get an idea?" she asked.

They sat down before the machine and she showed him some of the more basic functions. She even let him use the keyboard.

"The whole trick to Mollie is the master program," she told Jack. "That's what allows the machine to understand simple commands from the operator. Then we add special secondary programs which will be tailored to the needs of most businesses—inventory, billing, and so on. These are added on to the inner program, and Mollie gets the job done. Want me to explain in more detail?"

"No, thanks," Jack laughed. "Computers are your department. This is way over my head. I just want to be like that rather empty-headed secretary who sits down and pushes the buttons after you've done all the work."

He looked at his watch.

"I'm afraid we have to go," he said. "Time has run out."

He took her in his arms. The passion in his embrace was tinged with sadness, for he knew he would not see her for more than a couple of hours before next weekend.

"I'm so proud of you," he said. "You've done all this by yourself. You have a hell of a backbone under that soft skin of yours."

"Oh, I didn't do it all alone," she smiled. "I had a lot of help."

"That's not what I mean," he said. "For a man like me, achievement is easy. I had all the advantages. The best schools, the best training for what I do. My place was prepared for me at Magnus before I was even out of school. I've only done what was expected of me. But you, Francie—you came from nowhere, and made your own luck. And even the power of Magnus didn't slow you down. You'll never know how I admire you for that."

He hugged her closer and kissed her, hard. She felt herself respond to him. As though from outside herself she watched the smoldering ember of her flesh burst into hot flame at his touch. For the first time in her life she felt that she could contain that flame, and not let it consume her.

Francie was in control now.

"Come on, let's go," Jack said reluctantly. "If I stay here a minute longer, I'll turn into a wild animal. Then we'll make your warehouse more of a mess than it is already."

She took his hand to lead him toward the exit.

She could not see his eyes traveling quickly over the corners of the loft, and noting the lock on the front door as they left.

A moment later they were in the car, on their way back to Manhattan.

51

April 2, 1960

Julie Magnus smiled and pulled the face of Scott Monteagle to her own. She kissed him slowly, with the new familiarity that came from knowing her lover's flesh intimately.

They were in his hired car, stopped before the gates of her father's house. They had just spent a delightful evening together, with dinner at a modest restaurant in the theater district, and a movie which Julie had hardly noticed, so absorbed was she in her closeness with Scott.

Julie was on top of the world. Tonight had been like a hundred nights she could look forward to in the future with her handsome husband. They would enjoy the simple pleasures of the world together, holding hands as they had done tonight. And for the rest of her life she would look into Scott's eyes and see that same look of complete trust and confidence, and feel the protection of his love.

"Mmmm," she murmured as their lips parted. "I wish we could—you know."

He smiled against her cheek. "Me, too," he said. "That goes double, as you Americans say."

"But there will be plenty of time for that soon enough," she said. "I just hate waiting."

"Soon you won't have to wait for anything anymore," he said. "Just a few weeks, darling. Just a few more weeks."

She hugged him close. Even the ache of wanting him made her happy, for she knew she had found a home in his love.

"Until tomorrow, then?" he said, holding both her hands.

"And make it early," she said. "I'll think about you all night."

"Well, do it in your sleep," he said. "I want you to get your rest."

"All right, then. I'll dream about you."

"We'll dream about each other," he said. "I wonder if we could talk to each other through our dreams. Shall we try?"

"Yes, darling. Yes. I'll tell you everything." An involuntary tear welled in her eye as she looked into his face and saw her own happiness there. "Good night, Scotty."

"Good night, Julie."

He watched her open the gate and disappear into the shadows surrounding the house. Then, with a sigh, he told the driver to take him back to his hotel.

Julie entered the house and wandered through the main foyer. It looked dark and uncanny, for the servants had been sent to bed. She always entered with her own key when it was this late, so as not to awaken the house.

She felt an introspective mood come over her, and sat for a moment on the carpeted stair, looking at the silent furniture in the salon. She reflected that this was the front room where she had played as a child, and gotten into mischief long since forgotten now.

Soon she would leave here forever. She would look back on the whole place as a nightmare from which she was lucky to escape with her life. The evil of the Magnus world was indeed sufficient to kill a person, at least in slow motion. Julie had been well on the way to killing herself with alcohol and bad companions before Scott came along.

But now that freedom was in sight she could look back on her life here with something more than mere horror and nausea. Terrible things had been done to her in this house, true. Nevertheless it was here that she had experienced a child's joys in discovery, a girl's adolescent fantasies, a young mind's intellectual growth, and all the other lessons and accidents that make up the life of a creative and bright young person.

And she had survived. The proof of that wonderful fact was that she had found Scotty, and through him a door out of this mire to a real future all her own.

In a way, now that it was over, she would miss home. She would miss the days when Gretchen had been a big sister to her, taking her shopping and dressing her up for the Grosvenor Ball, and when Jack had helped her do jigsaw puzzles, bought her a doll which she had cherished throughout her youth, taken her swimming and riding and taught her to play tennis. And even Mother, who used to read to her, and who once roused herself from her daily headache-ridden siesta to make gingerbread with her in the kitchen.

Yes, life on Park Avenue had been complex, and even beautiful in some ways. It had not been all hell.

It had not been all Father.

With this thought Julie got up and went upstairs. The dark hallways of the house passed her. She avoided the elevator, for she did not want the hum to wake anyone.

She was tired by the time she reached her room on the fourth floor, a floor above everybody else's. It must be well after two o'clock. She could still feel Scott's kiss on her lips. She was in the glow of the special feeling he gave her about herself, clean and young and pretty. She could hardly wait to get into her bed and, like a schoolgirl, covetously enjoy her thoughts of him until sleep took her. Only nine hours separated her from tomorrow morning, when she would see him again. This knowledge was like a blessing, and filled her with an almost religious thanks for her good fortune. The tendrils of the Magnus world were growing weaker around her now. Freedom was beckoning to her.

She opened the door of her room, entered the gloom, closed the door and locked it behind her. She wished she had a latch, but Father had years ago ordered it removed each time she tried to install it. This was for his own purposes, of course. He had used the excuse that since she was so unstable and troubled, he wanted the servants to be able to get into the room in the event of some sort of extravagant behavior on her part.

But Julie was not thinking about her father tonight.

In the glow of the nightlight she took off her dress, her slip, and her bra. Then she reached to turn on the light to find her nightgown.

Before she could touch it a hand came from nowhere to curl around her neck and close over her mouth. The scream that rose in her throat was cut off.

She knew it was Johnny instantly. She knew his feral, pungent smell as well as she knew the sensual aromas of her own passion.

During these last weeks she had tried so hard not to think about him that it had at last become a habit. She had made sure she never went anywhere unaccompanied, and had bribed the secretary to tell a Mr. Marrante, if he called, that Julie was out of the country, in Europe.

In her mind Johnny was in the past. And the closer she came to leaving her own world for Scotty, the sooner Johnny would be separated from her by an ocean and a culture as well as a social class. Thankfully, he was receding into the privacy of memory, where he belonged.

But she had underestimated him. And, she realized too late, he had not forgotten her.

She struggled silently in the darkness, thrashing this way and that. She saw the bell pull for the servants and tried to make for it. But her small body was no match for him. He held her easily with a forearm as powerful as a vice. Surely he could kill her with one wrench of that arm if he liked.

She could not speak. There was no way to communicate her protest to him, except to flail helplessly in his grasp.

He seemed to savor her forced immobility and her silence. She could feel his exultation at being within her own room, deep inside this bastion of Magnus power which she had sneeringly warned him he would never get within a mile of.

She thought of his intelligence, his resourcefulness. No wonder he had managed this. She should have realized he was capable of it. She should have taken more precautions.

Frantically she tried to bite him. But his huge hand was too securely closed over her mouth for her teeth to reach him.

And now, with the sensual subtlety that was so much a part of Johnny, he began to hold her in a faintly different way, so that the bondage of his grip was also a sort of sexual attack. She could feel herself pulled hard against his chest, and once again, as the first time she had been with him, she could feel the hard shaft of his sex poised against the firm globes beneath her waist.

It was a seduction, that bondage and that savage grip. And despite the ironlike fingers over her mouth and her desire to cry out, to get him out of here even if it meant an uproar in the house, she could not help but feel tremors of female yielding under her skin as he pulled her closer and closer. He could feel her terror mingling with her excitement, and a low laugh inside his throat told her how much he was enjoying this.

His left hand had closed around both her wrists. But now it let go, for he had her in the middle of the room where she could not touch anything or knock anything over. His hand closed softly over her stomach and slid upward to caress her breasts, the fingers easily reaching both nipples, for she was small and his hand was very large.

The maleness poised against her backside was more urgent now, more intimate. The harsh proximity of his body had that old subtlety, that special talent Johnny had of measuring her responses almost before she could feel them herself. And now the hand was traveling down her stomach, grazing her navel and flowing further down, finding its way unerringly to the panties that were her last protection against him.

An uncanny immobility came over her. She began to realize that she must get him out of here without rousing the house. She could not afford to let him confront her parents, for she could not predict the results of such a scene.

But Johnny was reading these thoughts even as they occurred to her, and savoring her fear of discovery. The taut power of his embrace softened. His touch became more languid, more sensual.

Now she felt his lips touching soft kisses to her ear, and finding the tender little spot beneath her earlobe that always sent the first chills of passion through her.

And she heard his whispered voice as his tongue licked at that sweet place.

"What's the matter, Cinderella? Did you have a hot date tonight?"

His fingers had slipped inside the panties, and he was caressing the center of her, feeling the response between her legs despite the trembling of her limbs.

"Mmm," he whispered. "That's my girl . . ."

She gasped, and tried spasmodically to struggle again. But it was no use. He was too clever for her. She could not cry out, or jerk loose from him. All she could do was stew in this incredible grip as in a pressure cooker, and feel her temperature rise as he explored her, teased her, taunted her from behind with his awful hard sex, and felt her become ever more helpless in his arms.

Slowly he pulled the panties down around her knees. Still holding her tight, he edged her toward the bed. Inch by inch he lowered her to the spread, pulling her always against his own body, so that his sex squeezed and probed at the center of her.

She could feel her own saliva moistening her cheeks as his hand remained clamped over her mouth. And she remembered the terrible night they had made love with the taste of her blood commingling in their kisses. She thought of Johnny's way of making everything, from tenderness to resentment to violence, and even blood, into sex. This was his genius, and now he was using it on her in the most cruel and triumphant way.

"You thought you'd got rid of me, eh?" he whispered. "It's not that easy, is it, Princess? Johnny has his ways, doesn't he?"

She was on the bed, a tiny nymph in his arms, the panties pulled down about her knees. She felt him loosening his own garments. She could smell the unique male aroma of him, tinged with alcohol, tobacco, and his crude but sensual cologne—all of it overladen now by the musky smell of desire.

And somewhere under all this, still clinging like a remnant from another world, was the sweet clean fragrance of Scott Monteagle, overwhelmed but not entirely banished by the awful animal sexiness of Johnny.

The complexity of it, the contradiction was too much for Julie. She lay in a thrall of frustration and surrender. Helpless, she felt the powerful hands caress her, smoothing and moistening everywhere. She felt her legs parted, felt the strong fingers slide up and down the insides of her thighs, pausing at her knees to measure their tremors. And the male tongue was at her ear, kissing and nuzzling and probing.

"That's my girl," he murmured. "Daddy's girl still knows where her bread is buttered, doesn't she?"

No man on earth knew her body as Johnny did. No man ever would. Even as she had planned a life without him, she never expected another man to know her in that way. And deep inside she knew it was a memory that, perversely, she would cherish and hold close. For every woman, whatever her destiny, is made for a Johnny to know her at some point, to know every recess and corner of her passion, to know her as his slave, to bring those most secret places alive.

So now it made no difference that she was fighting for that other life, fighting to get rid of him. He knew that in this moment and in this way she belonged to him, and always would. Her protests, her struggles, were merely varieties of her surrender to him.

And now, still trapped by his terrible grip, she felt the smooth hard rod of him probe delicately at the portal of her. It paused, unhurried, and then slipped quietly and triumphantly into her, its path prepared by her own passion. She gasped in ecstasy, still fighting him, but no longer with her body.

And he savored that rebellious heart within the pliant, yielding woman's flesh. Slowly he pushed deeper into her, his lips against her ear, his sex working hotter and hotter as forbidden undulations made her squirm with excitement in his grasp. Her body seemed childlike, impaled that way on him, and her passion touchingly innocent, as she gave more of herself with each spasm of struggle.

She could feel his smile of acknowledgment against her cheek. He knew, as always, just how close to orgasm she was, just how excited he had her. And now, as he thrust slowly into her, a bit more knowing and perverse with each stroke, he felt her paroxysms one by one, sweet and feminine and helpless.

And only when he knew that she had no defenses against him, that the barriers were all broken down, only then did he smoothly work himself deeper, upraise her to the final trembling plateau, and let himself come. A frantic little cry escaped her lips. Tears filled her eyes, and rolled down her cheeks to moisten his fingers.

When it was over he was gentle; he could afford to be gentle now. He loosened his grip and held her about her stomach, his fingers caressing her breasts, her collarbones, her shoulders as the tense shaft remained buried inside her.

She made no move to resist or to fight, now. He had made his point. He was inside her house, inside her bedroom, inside her body, all right under the nose of the Magnus palace guard, under the roof of her ineluctable father.

Julie tried to find a measure of calm.

"You've got to go now," she said. "They'll find us."

He shook his head.

"You've avoided me long enough, Princess," he said. "I took a lot of trouble getting in here. I'll leave before dawn. But until then, you've got to pay the piper."

Julie's heart sank. So he expected full tribute for what she had done to him. He wanted to enjoy himself with her, and he wanted her to know the full measure of his dominion over her.

Naked in his arms, she gave up all thought of escape. The awful male thing buried inside her must have its day, then. And Johnny must have the full proof that she belonged to him.

The warm hand patted her hip, and the fingers ran smoothly down her thigh, as her lover held her closer. The clock showed long hours of darkness yet to come.

"Don't worry," Johnny said. "I'll be out long before anyone thinks to worry about you. You see, I can come and go as I like. But I'm not trying to get you into trouble, babe. I'm on your side. You've got to understand that."

Suddenly, violently, he grasped her by her hair and pushed her face down against the pillow, hard.

"*Do* you understand, my sweet?" he asked.

She nodded desperately. Anything to get him out of here without a scene.

"That's good," he said. "We're going to have our little party, and when it's over I'll go. No one will be the wiser."

Again she nodded.

"But there's just one more thing, Princess," he said, his tone darker now.

She looked up at him inquiringly.

"You belong to me," he said. "Not to anyone else. Least of all your little Englishman friend, Monteagle. Least of all him."

He laughed, a low, frightening laugh.

"You're not getting married," he said. "You're not going to England, honey bunch. You're staying right here, where I can have you when I want you. Is that clear?"

Her eyes opened wide in horror. She said nothing. The hand in her hair pulled a bit tighter, shaking her head this way and that.

"You see, babe, you can never get away from me," Johnny said. "I'm your Prince Charming. I'm your Romeo, sweetie. And any man who gets in my way is dead. Understand that?"

Julie was too shocked to think of an answer to this insanity.

"Well?" he asked, pushing her face into the pillow.

She sketched a humble nod, though she could barely move her head.

Too late, much too late, Julie was realizing how much she meant to Johnny, and how dangerous he really was. The world she had seen opening before her was closed off by the huge hands around her small body, and the enormous power of Johnny's will, and perhaps Johnny's love.

Pensive, Julie kept her silence as the hand of her lover caressed her neck.

═══ 52 ═══

April 20, 1960

Francie was seated on the porch across the chessboard from her father.

It was a beautiful spring day. The buds were springing out in the trees, for a spell of unseasonable warmth had settled over the countryside. The air was so balmy that Francie and her father were playing outside instead of indoors in the living room.

She looked up from the board to see that he was gazing at her closely. She smiled.

"Why do you look at me?" she asked.

"Two reasons," he said. "In the first place, you've never looked more beautiful. In the second place, you remind me so much of your mother in this light."

He sighed and puffed at his pipe, which had gone out. Francie noticed the frayed sleeve of his checked flannel shirt, and resolved to buy him a new one. He looked older now, she realized. He was grayer, and the skin around his eyes was more wrinkled. During the last five years she had been too absorbed in the hectic changes occurring in her own life to realize that time was changing Mac Bollinger as well.

"The two of us used to sit out here," he said, "and watch you swing on that swing in the yard. Helen would face me, just as you're doing now, and I'd keep my eye on you. I wish you could see the way she used to look at you . . ."

He fell silent at the memory. His passionate love for his dead wife shone touchingly in his lined face. Francie knew how hot was the torch he had carried for Helen Bollinger, not only before their marriage, but throughout it.

She reached to touch his hand. "Daddy, I love you."

"I love you, too, Frannie," he said.

There was a pause as they looked into each other's eyes. They seemed to measure their understanding of each other, and also the recent events which had somehow come between them.

"You're so thin," he said. "I can't imagine how hard you're working. I never was a man to work that hard. Didn't believe in work. I don't know whether that's a good thing or not. But you've got so much of your mother in you. She was all business, all industry. Never had an idle moment."

The pride in his face as he looked at her was full of memory of his wife. After Helen's death it had fallen to Francie—first alone, then with the help of Mollie Maguire—to keep a watch on Mac's dreamy personality and make sure the practical tasks of his life were taken care of. To this end Francie had mobilized the hardheaded, responsible part of her personality, inherited from her mother, to the fullest.

But as she gazed at him now, seeing how at peace he was with himself and his life, Francie wondered if her hovering had ever really been necessary. Perhaps even Helen Bollinger's protective fussing over Mac had been more for Helen than for Mac himself.

Now his face darkened.

"What you're doing," he asked. "Are you really sure it's what you want?"

She squeezed his hand and nodded. "Yes, Daddy," she assured him. "It's what I want."

They both knew what he was really thinking. Since she had gone to work for Magnus Industries, and suffered the tortures she had kept from her father, Francie was a changed woman. And she could not hide the change from her father, however subtle the web of lies she had woven to keep him from knowing how badly she had been hurt.

She was thinner now, and more intense. It was as though she was devoured by the crusade on which she had embarked—a crusade that was almost over.

He was looking at her closely as he held her hand.

"Your young man—Jack," he said. "When do I get to meet him?"

"Soon, Daddy," she said. "We're both so busy. Jack has his own company to start, and I'm up to my ears in Mollie. It will be soon, I promise."

"I'd sure like to meet him," Dad said. "I feel sort of trapped on the sidelines."

She saw how important this remark was. Dad knew her well enough to know that if she was involved in a serious relationship, one leading to marriage, she would not hesitate to bring the young man home to meet him. It would be, indeed, her first thought.

The fact that she had not brought Jack home dovetailed somehow with the remoteness and fame of the Magnuses and their empire. Mac Bollinger could not help being suspicious of this turn of events. For two years he had watched his daughter get more and more deeply involved in something beyond his world, something technically and financially incomprehensible to him. And now she was to marry the scion of one of the most enormous fortunes on earth—a young man he had never met.

Francie had told him the full story, of course. She had worked happily at Magnus Industries until she decided to start her own company. Since then she had had a certain measure of success, and was on the verge of a great breakthrough in the computer business. Meanwhile she had never forgotten young Jack Magnus, who had worked with her at Magnus Industries. Jack had amicably divorced his first wife, and had asked Francie to marry him. She had accepted.

The story made sense, in a way. It would have made complete sense—if she had brought the young man home.

Mac let go of her hand and sat back looking at her.

"Your friend Sam," he said. "Do you see him anymore?"

"Every day." She smiled briskly. "We see so much of each other in that warehouse that we're sick of the sight of each other."

Her performance was clever, but Mac could feel the nervousness underneath it.

He had met Sam Carpenter once only. Francie had brought him home for a weekend with Mac, the two arriving on Friday night and Mac taking Sam and Francie fishing Saturday. Sam had been a polite young man, down-to-earth, and of course had slept in the guest room. Mac knew how involved Sam had been in all Francie's business activities, and frankly wondered whether their attachment went deeper.

Mac had watched Francie's eyes as she looked at the young man in the boat on the lake. There was a sidelong glimmer in them, a look of amused possessiveness, that reminded Mac of the way Helen used to look at himself.

But he could not know what this meant for Francie.

As for Mac, he had admired the way Sam fished. Sam was a patient young man who knew how to enjoy the lake, the ripple of the water against the boat, and his companions. And it was Sam who had caught their only big fish of the day—perhaps because of his remarkable patience. Mac liked the young man. He found it easy to talk to him.

Mac studied his daughter now. The mention of Sam had thrown her off balance. That was obvious.

He said no more about it. He would not pry into her private affairs.

But he knew Francie well enough to know that, in some secret sense, she was more alone now than she had been that day when she brought Sam to meet him. It was obvious from the quietly determined look in her eyes. She was less herself now. She was strung tight, wary, and fatigued more by her own vigilance than by the sheer load of her work.

"This Mollie business," he said. "You've given so much of yourself to it, honey. When it's over, will you be happy?"

Francie smiled at him. It was a smile full of mystery, part of it intentional perhaps, and part of it built into the complex structure of his daughter's character.

"I've always been happy," she said. "When this is over, I'll be happy, too."

There was a long silence. He studied her beautiful face, so thin now, and looked at the slender hand under her chin as she looked down at the chess board. He heard the rustle of tree limbs. In the distance a train whistle sounded. The smell of spring was in the air. Francie was part of this land, a precious part, and always would be, as far as Mac was concerned.

But now she was slipping away into her own life, further and further. He only hoped it was the right life for her. She was a strong girl, he knew. But was she strong enough to survive in the world of the Magnuses, and of people like them?

His ability to protect her from harm was a thing of the past, gone with her girlhood, and perhaps never really there at all. We can't protect our children from life, he mused. We can only love them.

As he was thinking these thoughts Mac watched her hand drop to the board to move her knight.

"Check," she said.

He smiled.

"I never could beat you," he said. "You've got too good a head on your shoulders."

"There you go," she smiled, as though this observation must calm his fears, if he but heeded his own words. "Now come on inside. I'm going to make you some chowder. I have to leave soon. If I didn't watch out for you, you'd waste away to nothing."

He watched her open the screen door. In that instant she looked like the little girl he had so loved and admired in the old days.

Yet she was a woman now, full of secrets and unseen scars. She was hiding something from him, with all her courage and her newfound maturity.

But what?

Mac Bollinger shook his head. He could not figure her out. She was too good a chess player for him.

53

While Francie was sitting on the front porch with her father in Pennsylvania, Anton Magnus was behind his executive desk in Manhattan, looking into the face of his son.

Jack looked calm and confident. He had matured in the past few years, Anton noticed with satisfaction. Jack was a man to be reckoned with.

There was patience behind those dark eyes. A patience Anton had been born with, and had tried to pass along to his son. A patience that told him when to strike, and when to wait. Jack was using it now.

But there was passion in Jack's eyes as well, try though he might to hide it behind his mask of assurance. Francie Bollinger had put that passion there; Anton had never seen it in Jack before she entered his life.

And it was because of this that Jack, whatever his abilities, was no match for his father today.

Anton concealed this knowledge as he spoke.

"Everything is under control, I presume?" he asked.

Jack Magnus smiled at his father. "Completely. It hasn't been easy, of course. She keeps everything under tight security. But I got a lot from Dana to start with, and my people have worked out the rest. We're keeping an eye on her operation every step of the way. The situation is under control."

"Can we beat her to market?" the father asked.

"Easily." Jack smiled. "I know her timetable. We have ten times her resources. I have people in six factories working on the thing twenty-four hours a day. The advertising agency has the campaign entirely polished. And the sales and service facilities are set to go. All I have to do is push the button."

Anton Magnus's smile was thin, cautious.

"Does she suspect you?" he asked.

"She's going to marry me, isn't she?" Jack laughed. "How much closer can you get than that?" He folded his hands. "As far as she is concerned, Dana was the end of it. When I came along, the subject was romance, not computers. She doesn't even think I work here anymore. She believes Magnus is part of my past."

Anton nodded slowly.

"As to the date of marriage," he asked, "do you still want to marry her before we bring our product to market?" There was something pointed about the question, as though he wished to irritate his son.

Jack raised an eyebrow. "Do you think she'd marry me otherwise?" he asked. "This girl has a backbone of steel. She'd never speak to me again."

"What makes you think she'll stay with you after it's done?" the father asked.

"She won't realize I was involved," Jack said. "I'll blame it all on you. And so will she. You know how she feels about you. I don't think you'll be receiving many family visits from us for a while. But she'll stick by me. Marriage changes women. They need love. Look at Mother. Believe me, Francie will fall into line."

Anton Magnus said, "I'm sure you're right, son."

There was a pause.

"Very well, then," Anton Magnus said. "You've done your part of it. I intend to stick to my end of the bargain. I wanted you to make a better match, but if this is what you want, I won't stand in your way."

Jack nodded. He was pleased with himself. He had realized long ago that his father would never allow him to divorce Belinda and marry Francie without some sort of monstrous reprisal. Anton Magnus had the power to accomplish anything he wanted, no matter how terrible, how perverse. The only way to outwit him was to play ball with him.

So Jack had made this deal. He had promised to deliver Francie's new computer, in return for Francie herself.

He had separated from Belinda, left the corporation, and gone undercover. He had even taken steps to set up his own new company, and severed all his visible financial links to Anton Magnus.

Meanwhile, behind this camouflage, he had worked for Magnus all along, and convinced pretty Dana Salinger to work for him as a spy. Dana was a curious character, her mind full of formulas and equations, her heart full of nothing but hunger for power. He had used her brilliantly, and enjoyed her sensual little body in the process.

Through Dana he had learned the essence of Francie's new computer project—a revolutionary one, to be sure, and worth untold millions of dollars once it was brought to market—and he had followed its progress toward completion, step by step.

When Dana's cover was blown—a danger he ought to have anticipated, but had not—Jack moved in himself, with his story of his newfound freedom and his proposal of marriage to Francie. It had worked like a charm. Francie had accepted him. Now he was close enough to her to know the gaps in her security, and to tell his own people how best to monitor Mollie's specifications. Specifications which would soon be safely built into a sleek new Magnus computer which would hit the marketplace just before Mollie did.

Jack had laid out his plans carefully. He would find a way to explain the theft of the computer to Francie after they were married. He would blame it on a spy, a mole they had not known about. The awesome tentacles of the Magnus Corporation. Anything . . .

CompuTel, Inc. would die a quiet death after Magnus Industries beat Francie to market with the very product she had worked so hard to develop. Jack would comfort her, and commiserate over the evil of his father's corporation. He might even threaten something extravagant, like killing his father. Francie herself would have to restrain him, to convince him to be reasonable and to think of his own happiness first.

He might help her institute a lawsuit against Magnus. That would show her where his loyalties lay.

But she would never win. The Magnus attorneys were too powerful for an upstart like Francie. Jack was surer of that than of anything.

Jack would hold her hand, take care of her, encourage her, and perhaps get her involved in his own new business. Long enough to get her used to the idea of having lost Mollie.

And before long he would get her pregnant. Children meant a lot to women. As soon as she had a baby to love and care for, Francie would no doubt give up the idea of business altogether.

More time would pass. Then, when the moment was right, Jack would return to Magnus Industries. By then Francie would be in the fold, a good wife. She would no longer be in a position to protest. She would go along.

And they would live happily ever after.

This was Jack's plan.

And it was going to work. Because the entire resources of the Magnus Corporation were behind him at this crucial moment, just when he needed them.

As a result of Jack's endeavors Magnus Industries would have a corner on the most revolutionary new product to hit the marketplace since the telephone. Francie's minicomputers would change the face of every aspect of life, not only business. The amount of money involved was incalculable. The amount of power was even greater.

It would all belong to Magnus Industries.

And in a few years Magnus Industries would belong to Jack.

It was impossible to slow the march of time. Eventually Anton Magnus would become too old, too tired, perhaps too sick to stay at the helm of the corporation, and would step down or die. Jack would take over.

As for Francie, she would not stand in the way of her husband's accession to the responsibility which had been waiting for him all his life. She would give in. Her will would be broken.

Jack knew women. The plan would work.

And so he would have defeated his father, in this most sinuous and complex way, by giving him a prize—the computer—in return for Francie.

Jack smiled to think how crude the old man was, how petty. Like a cunning peasant, he was easily satisfied by money. All one had to do was offer him a big enough piece of bait, and one could outwit him.

The prize Jack wanted more than anything he had ever wanted in his life was almost in his grasp: to have a free hand at Magnus, and to be married to the most beautiful woman in the world.

And as for Francie's computer system, it would of course belong to Jack, like everything else, once he took over at Magnus. Jack would pick up all the marbles, just as he had always intended to.

"Well," he said, standing up to leave the office. "I'll be in touch. If there are any last-minute changes, I'll let you know."

"Thank you, son."

Anton saw his son's complacency written all over his handsome features as he left the office.

When he was alone he shook his head in amusement.

What a fool Jack was! He attributed to himself so much brains and so much backbone. He had neither. He was a woman at heart.

Magnus got up and moved to the chessboard beneath the window. He gazed down at the silent men, each so quiet and dignified, but all representing power in its purest and cruelest form.

Anton Magnus smiled. His greatest victory was at hand.

═══ 54 ═══

New York Daily News, *May 2, 1960*

Magnus and Monteagle Will Tie Knot This Summer

Juliet Baker Magnus, long one of the wilder eligible females around town, has reportedly settled down at last. The beau who snared her is Scott Monteagle, a London barrister whose illustrious family has known the Magnuses for decades.

Wedding plans are said to be confirmed for July, after which lovely Julie and her new hubby will live in London. We wish you all the happiness in the world, Julie, but our town will miss your derring-do and joie de vivre . . .

Johnny Marrante had left the item from the *Daily News* sitting on the coffee table in his apartment.

On top of the item sat a snub-nosed .38 revolver, fully loaded.

Johnny gazed at the gun and the folded newspaper, a glass of bourbon in his hand.

It was the third drink he had had already. Though not normally a heavy drinker, Johnny had found that the item in the newspaper did something to his nerves. The cold liquor seemed to make him feel calm and in total control of himself.

He thought of Scott Monteagle. What a faggot, he mused. A mild, decorous Englishman. What a milquetoast. Just the sort of fool he had always imagined Julie marrying.

A sneer of contempt curled his lips at this thought. But his smile faded when he thought of Julie.

He had warned her. He had made it absolutely clear where things stood. And now, as the newspaper testified, she had defied him anyway.

That was why he had needed those three drinks tonight. Because he realized that in Julie's mind she owed him nothing. Not even his performance in her bedroom of a month ago had convinced her. She was a Magnus, and she believed she could do what she wanted.

It was time to prove to her that she couldn't.

Her knock came at the door at nine o'clock.

He smiled bitterly as he got up to answer it. As usual, she came to him after hours, when her society stopped caring about her whereabouts. She came slumming . . . And tonight she was not even here by choice. He had warned her that there would be dire consequences if she did not show up. She was only here to placate him with her obedience.

He opened the door and stood smiling as she entered the apartment.

When the door had closed he slapped her face.

The force of the blow sent her reeling backward into the couch. She sat looking up at him, her palm against her cheek. Then she looked down and saw the *Daily News* item. And the gun.

She looked guilty, frightened.

"So you saw," she said.

"Yes, lover, I *saw*," he hissed through clenched teeth, coming to her side.

Julie did not know what to say. The look in Johnny's eyes was wild. She knew how obsessed he was with her. She had seen the *Daily News* item herself today, and wondered whether he had as well.

Now the sight of the gun on the table, and the look in Johnny's eyes, terrified her. She would have to think fast.

"Listen, Johnny," she said. "We're not going to England. That's just gossip. My father doesn't want me to leave the country. He's going to offer Scott a legal position at Magnus, something too important for him to refuse. Scott is a proud man, he wanted to take me home with him—but he'll come around. He'll have to. My father will make him. So, you see, we'll be right here in New York. I'll be able to see you whenever I want."

She managed a fearful smile. She had rehearsed this moment, and wanted to seem flip and cheerful, delighted to be able to be together with Johnny. But in reality she was so frightened, and so sure that she was in fact going to England, that her act was hard to bring off.

Johnny was looking down at her through eyes filled with cocky, leering skepticism. She could see he had been drinking heavily.

Then, with jarring suddenness, the look in his eyes changed. He was the old Johnny, smiling down at her. The abrupt metamorphosis left her off balance.

"Sure, kid," he said. "Whatever you say. Sorry I flew off the handle. I've been under some strain lately. Business."

He came to her side and kissed her. He held her with unaccustomed tenderness.

"We'll talk later," he said.

He picked her up like a doll and carried her to the bedroom. He placed her on the bed and tenderly undressed her, taking off her dress, then her stockings, and finally her slip and panties, almost like a solicitous parent with a child. He did his work slowly, watching the sweet girlish nudity appear bit by bit before his eyes. He smelled her expensive perfume.

Then he began to caress her. The large dry fingers slid warmly over her body, full of sensuality, but gentle in their passage, as though he was covering and protecting the fragile flesh. She looked up at him, trying to hide her anxiety. But not even the tingling in her nerves could dampen the excitement his touch caused in her. She was trembling with desire by the time he had finished.

She could see the bulge of his own excitement under his tight slacks, and she ran a hand along his thigh to his crotch. He stood up and took off his clothes. She watched the huge penis stand up, proud and alert, as his underpants came off. What a magnificent animal he was! He had a body hewn of sheer male sexuality, a body worthy of a fertility statue.

He bent to kiss her between her legs. She closed her eyes, gasping in ecstasy at his touch. The tongue that knew her so well was taking its pleasure now in the way he alone knew.

Somehow her fear made her sexy. Almost at once she gave him her first orgasm, then another and another. She could feel him respond to her pleasure.

He got up to a crouching position and spread her legs so that he could enter her. She said nothing, but lay back, watching him in awe.

His large hands raised her loins to meet him. The organ came to probe teasingly at the center of her, and then slid to its hilt inside her, inch by inch. Somehow it felt larger than ever before, more dangerous. She gasped despite herself.

Slowly he began to move, his large body pushing her back against the pillows as he thrust into her. Her ecstasy was so intense that her eyes half closed.

"That's right, babe," he murmured.

She was beginning to writhe under him with hot little moans when all at once his hands closed around her throat.

Surprised, she did not react quickly enough. She could not breathe. His grip tightened.

"Not leaving, eh?" he said. "You're not a very good liar, Princess. Your friend Scott is leaving, all right. And you're leaving with him. I found out. Johnny found out. Johnny has his ways. Tell the truth, now, if you want to breathe again. I'm right, aren't I?"

The pressure around her throat was making her faint. A blackness rose before her eyes, blinding her. She was already on the edge of unconsciousness. Desperate, she sketched a nod.

"You were going to run off with him, weren't you?" he asked savagely. "You lied to me, didn't you?"

Again she nodded, her eyes wide in panicked supplication.

"But now I know everything, don't I?" he asked. "Now you know you can't hide from me, don't you, baby? Don't you? Don't you?" He slammed her head rhythmically against the pillow as he repeated his question.

She nodded frantically, her hands fluttering against the sheets. The roaring inside her head made it difficult to hear him.

All at once, as though to express his triumph, the penis inside her erupted, and she felt the hot lick of his semen deep in the quick of her. It was a sting of pure anger, without love, without pleasure.

His grip on her neck relaxed. She began to breathe in halting gasps. He was still staring down at her, but she dared not meet his eyes.

He pulled out of her roughly, the huge sex leaving a painful emptiness inside her. He stood up, still hard, and stalked to the living room. When he came back he carried a large glass of bourbon in one hand and the gun from the coffee table in the other. He seemed a bit unsteady on his feet. She looked up at him in terror.

"What's that for?" she asked in a whisper, her eyes on the gun.

He ignored her question. He said nothing for a moment, and then looked at the glass in his hand.

"Want a drink?" he asked coolly.

It took her a long moment to think of an answer. The sight of the gun paralyzed her.

"Whatever you're having," she replied at last, hoping to gain time.

He went away, still carrying the gun in one hand, and returned with a glass for her. She took a sip. The liquor hurt her throat, but sent a welcome glow through her shaken insides. Still naked in the sheets, she gazed up at him.

The obvious question came to her lips.

"What are you going to do?"

He sipped at his drink ruminatively, and looked down at her. Then he put the gun down on the bedside table and caressed her breasts with his free hand.

"Well, Princess," he said. "That's a tough one. I haven't quite figured that one out. To be honest with you, I like your friend. He's not a bad fellow."

Julie's eyes widened. "You mean . . . you mean you've seen him?"

"Sure," Johnny said. "We had a nice chat. He thinks the world of you, babe. Worships the ground you walk on."

Julie flushed in the shadows. The sudden rage she felt was as great as her fear. Somehow it had never occurred to her that the two separate corridors of her existence could ever intertwine. The very thought of Johnny speaking to Scott Monteagle sent chills of revulsion down her spine.

Johnny saw her reaction and smiled.

"Don't worry," he said. "I didn't tell him about us. I was the soul of tact. I did wonder, though, what his reaction would be if he knew . . ."

"You wouldn't dare." The words had slipped out before she could stop them. She saw rage quicken in his eyes. The hand on her breast squeezed her so suddenly that she cried out.

Then his anger abated, eclipsed once more by drunken bravado. He was grinning down at her.

"It would be a pity to have to kill him," he said.

Julie turned pale. She saw the gun on the table out of the corner of her eye.

"What?" she whispered.

"To kill him," he said. "To rub him out. To grease him. Get it, babe? To make him go away. No more Mr. Monteagle. You follow?"

"You're joking," she said.

He shrugged. "Your father will probably thank me," he said.

She could feel the force of his intelligence coiled behind these words. He was right on the money. Even Julie herself, piously clinging to Anton Magnus's approval of Scott as a son-in-law, had not allowed herself to dwell on what her father's real feelings might be.

But Johnny, drunk and full of rage though he was, understood everything all too well.

Julie fought to think clearly. She knew Johnny, and understood his feelings for her. She must try to reason with him before it was too late.

"Johnny, think what you're saying," she said. "You'd get into trouble. I might never see you again. I wouldn't want that."

She watched her words take effect on him. He was listening carefully, albeit through the haze of his drunkenness and his anger.

"Listen, Johnny," she pleaded. "You've got to understand. You wouldn't want to screw this up if you understood. Scott is the best way. For me . . . for both of us. I'll find a way to stay here. I won't go to England. I can make Scott do what I want. But you've got to believe me, Johnny: Scott is the only solution for me. Of course, he'll never be what you are to me. But he is the only way out—in a way I can't explain. You must believe me. Please . . ."

Johnny was shaking his head.

"That's where you're wrong, babe," he said. "*I* am your only way out. *Johnny* is your only way out. Understand?"

She looked at him. There was no reasoning with him. Hatred and obsession had taken him over completely.

"Do you want to marry me?" she asked on a desperate impulse.

He looked down at her strangely.

"No way, kid," he said with a savage laugh. "I couldn't live with you. You'd cramp my style. You rich broads are all the same."

Her brow furrowed in perplexity.

"Then why can't I marry Scott?" she asked.

He shook his head at her innocence.

"I want you not to be married to anybody else," he explained. "Understand, sweetie pie? Nobody but Johnny is going to enjoy that pretty little pussy of yours. No society faggot is going to put children in there. Not while I'm around."

Now she understood him. He wanted her all to himself.

It didn't matter to him if she never got married, never found love or happiness. He didn't care if New York, under her father's roof, was a living hell for her. He was only thinking of his own pleasure, and of his jealousy.

There was no way to explain to him what Scott Monteagle really meant to her. Scott was her only chance for a human life. Johnny was holding out an indefinite future of horror and degradation with a smile on his face. And, unbeknownst to himself, he was offering a future in which he would share her with Anton Magnus. Johnny could not know he was being cuckolded by Julie's own father.

At this thought something suddenly guided Julie's hand to the gun on the bedside table. She picked it up and pointed it at Johnny's chest.

"You're not going to ruin this for me," she said, her voice dark with warning.

Johnny smiled.

"You spoiled little rich bitch," he hissed. "I'll bet you think you can get away with anything. Go on. Pull the trigger, if you're so smart."

His intelligence was on his side. He was daring her to take the biggest chance of her life. Because of him she had been walking a dangerous tightrope for months. He was daring her to step off it.

"Go on," he said. "Let's see what you're really made of. I'll bet your father would be proud. Go on. I dare you."

He was crouched, leaning closer, pointing his chest at the gun.

"I'm going to make sure your Monteagle boy knows all about us, babe," he said. "All the gory details. I'm going to make sure he knows what kind of girl Cinderella really is. After all, it's to his advantage. How's he going to make you happy unless he knows what turns you on?"

Julie's eyes were open wide. The gun was shaking in her hand.

"And I'll bet your father will thank me . . . ," Johnny added.

At these last words the gun went off, as though with a will of its own. The explosion was loud, but brief, in the quiet apartment. It was quickly lost in the rumble of trucks and horns and sirens in the city outside. But it rang in Julie's mind like a bomb as she stared at Johnny.

He was looking down at her, surprised. Something in his posture told her he was hit badly. But his bravado was keeping him up.

"Well, well, well," he said, raising an eyebrow in acknowledgment of her daring. "I underestimated you. You really are your father's daughter, aren't you, Princess? You're quite the . . ."

A sudden gasp took his breath away. His body tensed in the darkness. Then he coughed. Blood gushed from his mouth, spattering Julie's naked body and the dirty bedsheets.

He pushed himself upright. He was still smiling, but the expression in his eyes was one of terror, almost childlike in its innocence and pain. He looked down at the hole in his chest.

He was trying to say something, but the blood in his throat gurgled, and his eyes glazed. He reached out for her, as though one last touch would prove his point, prove how right he was, how inexcusably she had betrayed him, how richly she needed punishment.

But in that instant death leapt forward in his eyes, canceling all human intention with its emptiness. He fell on his face, his hands twitching, the blood from his mouth inundating the bed and Julie's naked legs.

Julie stared at him. The gun was still in her hand.

My God, I've killed him.

An involuntary sob of grief and horror escaped her lips. Johnny had always been so vibrantly alive. And death leered on the bloody face with a hideousness she had never imagined possible.

She recoiled from the body, curling into the pillows. As she did so she saw the stains of his blood spreading further, painted by her naked legs on the sheets.

At this a sudden impulse of self-protection penetrated her horror, and she took stock of her situation.

She was still holding the gun in her right hand. Her left was clenched against her breast.

Her fingerprints were on the gun, and on the glass on the bedside table. And elsewhere in the apartment, of course.

But they were not in the blood smeared over the bedsheets. Not yet.

And they would not be. Not if she was careful.

Her mind began working quickly.

All she had to do, she mused, was to get out of here, taking the gun with her. The police would find Johnny here after a decent interval. Perhaps days. They would find alcohol in his blood. They would find traces of a woman in the bed. They would assume there had been a quarrel, a drunken fight between a lowlife Brooklyn lothario and one of his women friends. A fight that ended in a shooting.

They would not find the gun.

They would dust the apartment for fingerprints. They would find many. Johnny had brought dozens of women here.

Among the prints would be Julie's.

But Julie's fingerprints were not on any police file. The power of Anton Magnus had seen to that, even though she had been arrested for her various drunken misdemeanors.

No one had seen her come here tonight. There was no doorman, of course. The other tenants in the huge building might have glimpsed her in the past. But no one in this place could have known who she was. They would be unable to separate her from Johnny's dozens of dates.

The police would focus on his other girlfriends. Some of those girls would have been fingerprinted. That stood to reason. The police would find them, interrogate them. They would be the logical suspects.

The police would not be able to find sufficient evidence to make an arrest. They would eventually shrug their shoulders, deciding that a small-time hustler had got his in a drunken brawl with a girlfriend or fellow crook. They lacked the money and resources to make a crusade out of finding the killer, because Johnny was not an important enough victim. They would drop the matter after a few days or weeks.

With all these thoughts in her mind, Julie shrank away from the dead body in the bed. She looked to see whether the prints of her toes were in the blood. They were not.

Slowly, carefully, she got off the bed. She tiptoed into the bathroom to wash the blood off her legs. She took care not to leave her fingerprints on any of the bathroom things.

She returned to the bedroom, took her glass of bourbon from the bedside table, and carried it to the kitchen.

There she saw several dirty glasses on the counter by the sink. This gave her an idea.

Holding the bottle of bourbon with a handkerchief, she poured the liquid into two of the glasses. The rest she left empty, with the residue of whatever had been in them. Holding each glass so as not to smudge the fingerprints its last user had left on it, she took them to the bedroom and living room, leaving them on tables, as though a group of people had been in the apartment.

Now she emptied and cleaned the glass she had used tonight. Taking care to leave no prints on it, she placed it in the cupboard with the other clean glasses and plates.

She went back to the bedroom and surveyed the situation. The sight of Johnny's body made her want to retch, but a cold sense of purpose made her keep control. She picked up the gun and put it in her purse. She put her clothes on carefully, retrieving them from the floor where Johnny had thrown them. Luckily there was no blood on them.

The police would focus on the glasses she had placed around the room. They would look for their owners. The only items that could have revealed who was really here tonight—her bourbon glass, and the gun—were accounted for.

Julie thought of Scott Monteagle. She had done murder for him tonight. She had taken her first step to save their life together, their happiness. Now she had to finish the job.

She looked for a last time at Johnny. He lay like a dead animal, his eyes glazed, his muscled body misshapen on the bed, his legs splayed behind him. In the center of his back was her bullet's exit wound, a hideous ragged gash.

She could still feel his touch all over her. Ten minutes ago he had been a living being, obsessed by his love for her.

Something primitive armed Julie to finish what she had started. With icy calm she surveyed the room for a last time. It was full of traces of her. But the police would never know how to follow those traces, because she came from a world light-years away from this sleazy apartment.

Since she did not belong here, they would never be able to connect her to this place.

She was in the clear.

She began to open the door. As she did so she suddenly stopped short. She was looking at the coffee table, on which the issue of the New York *Daily News* was opened to the item announcing her engagement to Scott Monteagle.

She darted back into the room, scooped up the newspaper, folded it under her arm, and went back to the door.

Cautiously she backed out of the apartment, making sure no one was in the hall. She left no fingerprints on the door or knob. She slipped down the hall and out the front door of the building, seeing no one on the street outside. She walked several blocks, making sure she was not being followed. Then she got on a bus without noticing what its destination was.

She got off a mile or so down the line, and switched to the subway. She took the Lexington Avenue IRT back uptown, and then hailed a cab. She had the driver let her off at the Pierre. Then she walked the last five blocks home.

As she opened her wallet to pay the driver, she felt the gun inside her purse.

Despite the horror inside her, she thought of Scott and stopped the shaking of her hands. She was fighting for him now, fighting for their future together.

She stole upstairs to her room and took a long hot shower. She hid the gun. She crawled between the sheets and lay trembling for a long time.

She was a murderess now. This was what her whole tainted life had brought her to.

But at the end of the dark tunnel before her, Scott Monteagle waited, with his smiles and his love. She would not let anything on earth keep her from him.

With this thought in her mind, Julie Magnus fell into a deep and dreamless sleep.

$$=== 55 ===$$

May 15, 1960

The clock on the wall showed 3:15 A.M.

Francie sat alone at the work table in an inner cubicle of the CompuTel warehouse, studying a schematic of the programmed instructions at the heart of Mollie's memory. A pencil was poised in her hand. So intense was her concentration that she had lost all awareness of her fatigue as well as her surroundings.

Francie was working on the most complex adjustment of a computer program that she had ever attempted. The struggles she had had with her computer link-up of the Magnus-Europe subsidiaries four years ago were child's play compared to the challenge she had set herself now.

More than once she had despaired of her ability to carry the whole thing off. She had made a special trip to Boston to consult with one of the foremost computer experts in the nation, a programming genius named Karl Eccles. And even the great Eccles, sworn to secrecy by Francie as she described her scheme on a hypothetical basis, had been puzzled by it. He had only been able to advise her in the most general terms, and to wish her luck. She had returned home with no blueprint to follow but the one inside her own mind.

Yet Francie was certain that the plan she had in mind would work. And as she had designed it on paper at home in her apartment, and put it into practice element by element here in the laboratory, in the night's darkest hours, she had found that it was more than a merely intellectual concept. It could become a working reality.

The only thing about her endeavor that distressed her and sapped her confidence was her loneliness. She had no one to help her in what she was doing. No Sam, no Dana to listen to her idea, to encourage her, to offer advice.

Francie was completely alone.

Fatigue was coming on her fast now. She sat back, stretched her aching back, and closed her eyes. Almost at once the figures and concepts she had been working with began to whirl inside her brain. With a final effort she jerked herself back to consciousness, turned to the control board of the computer's inner memory and implemented the tiny changes dictated by the schematic she had brought with her.

Then she turned on the computer and ran through some of its most basic functions. She ran routine computations, then more complex analyses which the computer would be asked to perform in its daily work. She checked and double-checked the machine's memory for figures and instructions.

Everything was perfect. Mollie worked without a hitch.

Now Francie's exhaustion overwhelmed her. She got up, turned off the light, left the cubicle, and padded in her stockinged feet to a small bedroom she had improvised in a corner of the warehouse a month ago when she first realized she would have to come here at night. There was a bed with a comforter. She took off her jeans and blouse, put on a cotton nightgown, and slipped between the sheets.

She set the alarm beside the bed for seven. She knew that when she awoke the warehouse would be abuzz with activity as all the CompuTel employees worked in quiet haste at their respective tasks.

None of her colleagues were aware of the change in Francie's routine that had taken place in the last couple of months. They only realized that she came to work at somewhat less regular hours now. One or two—Sam, perhaps, and Quinn—realized that she slept here sometimes. But they naturally assumed it was merely her way of working overtime.

No one suspected the real reason for what she was doing.

Not the head of her security staff, for instance, who had been taken aside by Francie three months ago and given special instructions for surveillance of the building, instructions which were unlike any he had ever received before, and which made him feel more like a spy than a security guard.

Not Kevin Still, the surveillance expert who had helped her expose Dana last fall. Francie had since instructed him to conduct a regular sweep of the warehouse for bugs and other surveillance devices, and to report to her in detail about what he found—but not to remove anything.

Francie's instructions were as precise and firm as they were puzzling. No one around her knew what she had in mind. And no one knew what sort of work she did here alone in the wee hours of the morning.

That was the way Francie wanted it. She had never felt more alone before in her entire life—or so coldly in control.

She lay somnolent now, watching dream images steal over her mind. Some of them were images of Jack, smiling and handsome in his beautiful clothes. Others were of Sam, rumpled and lovable in his T-shirt and jeans, working on the computer years ago as Francie worked on it now. Other images were of her father, looking at her through worried eyes when she visited home a few weeks ago—or of Dad twenty years ago, when she was a tiny child, taking her on rides around the county in his pickup truck, and waving to his Amish friends in their carriages.

The last images were of her mother, sitting quietly in the living room with that odd, faraway look on her face, when the last illness was ravaging her body, and she gazed at Francie through loving, haunted eyes. That silent display of love in the face of destruction comforted Francie now, and she seemed to reach out to Helen Bollinger across the abyss of death itself as sleep began to whirl her on its magic carpet out of this dark warehouse and into a place where no one died, no one was hurt or betrayed, no one was lost.

A few weeks more, Francie mused. A dozen more nights like tonight, a few more adjustments in the heart of Mollie's controls, where no one but herself could see them—and all would be ready.

Then she could rest. Then the roller coaster would stop. Then she would . . .

The thought died with her waking consciousness. Francie was asleep.

══ 56 ══

May 20, 1960

Scott Monteagle was on a plane bound for England.

He was getting ready to put the finishing touches on the new flat he had rented for himself and Julie in London—Julie had refused her father's offer of a luxurious home in Wilton Place as a wedding gift—and to make arrangements for his honeymoon with Julie at a small resort on the English seacoast.

The wedding would be a large one, since Anton Magnus was giving it. It would take place at St. Bartholomew's Church in Manhattan, attended no doubt by everyone who was anyone in international high society and business. This would be Anton Magnus's way of rubbing other people's noses in their own rumors about Julie's unmarriageable, wild personality. Anton seemed truly proud of Scott's stability, and incidentally not displeased by the fact that the Monteagle family name was an old and respected one.

Scott and Julie would go through with this gala for the sake of Julie's parents, because it was the right and the responsibility of the bride's family to give the wedding. But after that Scott would have Julie to himself forever. They would live in London, and see the Magnuses on rare occasions just like any happy young couple with less-favored in-laws, and enjoy their freedom for the rest of their lives.

Anton Magnus's insistence on giving Julie her money did not daunt Scott. He and Julie had discussed it. They both understood that this was Anton's way of trying to exert some influence over their future. They would take the money, but refuse the influence. It would be a simple matter to put it in a trust fund for their children and grandchildren and forget it.

The meaning of this marriage was clear, and very traditional: Julie was leaving the Magnuses to join Scott's family. Not the reverse.

The plane had taken off twenty minutes ago. Below him Scott saw only cold, choppy ocean touched by whitecaps. He could almost feel England approaching, for there was nothing between him and home but this frigid gray water which was the element of the British Isles.

He was putting his seat back to relax and close his eyes when one of the stewardesses approached him, a large envelope in her hands.

"This was given to us back at Idlewild," she said. "A messenger. It got lost in the shuffle. I'm sorry for the delay in giving it to you."

Scott raised an eyebrow in surprise. "Thank you," he said.

The envelope was unmarked, with Scott's name on the front in dark ink. He opened it.

His hands began to tremble before he saw the entire contents.

They were pictures of Julie.

In all of them she was naked. The man she was with was shown from a dozen different angles, but it was clear it was the same fellow. A big man, strong, with a handsome physique, longish dark hair, and, Scott could see, very large sexual equipment.

In the photos he was shown making love to Julie in all sorts of positions. His organ seemed to penetrate her wherever it liked. She coveted it, and him, with an ecstatic look in her eyes. There was something more than mere pleasure in her expression. It was a sort of thrilled humiliation. It was as though she were his slave.

The most eloquent photos showed her lying on her stomach with the man entering her from behind. Her body, dwarfed by his own, was pushed into the bedsheets. Her little fists were clenched, her lovely features distorted by excitement as the man crouched behind her.

Scott had known about Julie's wild life, but he had never imagined anything as grotesque, as nightmarish, as this. It was not so much the physical reality of what she was doing with this lover, a man who came from a society far beneath her own, to judge from the tattoo on his forearm. It was her utter delight, her voluptuous absorption, her abasement before the male flesh that owned her.

For an instant Scott thought the man looked familiar. Then he dismissed the idea. He himself lived worlds away from such a fellow. There was no way they could have crossed paths.

But he would never forget that face now. Not after seeing these photographs.

Scott put the pictures away and closed his eyes. The Julie who had been in his mind all these years, the Julie he had loved and waited for and dreamed of, was disappearing, replaced by this monstrous image of creamy female flesh offered perversely, willingly, to the most concupiscent of males, a rutting animal spilling his sperm into her like the hero of a pornographic movie. And Julie, her eyes half-closed in ecstasy, loving it, delighting in it . . .

Scott looked inside the envelope for a message. He was not surprised when there was none.

The pictures themselves were the message.

Scott forced himself to look at them one last time. For a brief instant he felt a surge of pity for the little girl he had once known on the lawn of his aunt's house on Long Island, the girl whose life had been darkened by forces which Scott himself had luckily escaped in his impoverished existence. He felt a glimmer of understanding for this girl who had somehow been tainted so badly in the heart of her existence that she must take out the most perverse punishment on herself in this awful way.

But Scott's pity was eclipsed by nausea as he saw the look of slavish delight in her eyes. This was not the Julie he had sought out across an ocean and two decades, the Julie in whom he had placed all his hopes. This was a whore. Scott himself could never make love to her again with the memory of these images in his mind.

The plane gained speed, leaving the United States further and further behind. To Scott it seemed that a door was closing forever behind him, a door leading to a happiness which now could never be. In his wildest dreams it had never occurred to him that his dream could be shattered so thoroughly, so violently, in one moment. Yet it was true. What he had seen in the pictures could never be erased from his mind or his memory. And with that poison inside his heart, he could never be a husband to Julie.

Never.

As the black Atlantic yawned beneath him, separating him more and more from Julie, Scott Monteagle wept.

$$=== 57 ===$$

June 5, 1960

The wedding was ten days away.

Francie received an unannounced visit at her apartment. The voice on the intercom was so unexpected that she buzzed the visitor in without thinking twice.

When she answered the knock at her door, she saw Belinda Devereaux standing in the hallway.

Belinda looked thinner than Francie remembered from their long-ago meeting at Gretchen Magnus's party. Thinner and older. But there was something attractively independent about her. She was dressed simply in a skirt and blouse. She carried a raincoat over her arm.

Francie smiled guardedly.

"I hope I didn't catch you at too bad a time," Belinda said. "I may be out of line in presenting myself here, but I couldn't help myself. May I come in?"

Francie stood back to show her guest into the apartment. She was struck by the incongruity of Belinda's presence here.

Perhaps this was because Belinda came from Jack's society. She was the first visitor to come here from that society, beside Jack himself. However simple her attire and her mannerisms, she could not hide the generations of breeding that shone in the way she sat, clasped her hands in her lap, and smiled at Francie. Belinda almost had the sheen of Jack all over her.

Yet it was Belinda he had divorced, and Francie he was to marry. There was an irony to this that was not lost on Francie.

"Would you like something to drink?" Francie asked.

Belinda shook her head. She had kept her raincoat, and now put it on the couch beside her. She clearly did not intend to stay long.

"You're a beautiful girl," she said to Francie. "Even lovelier than when we met. No wonder Jack is crazy about you."

Francie said nothing. Her smile was neutral, without hostility or triumph.

"I feel funny," Belinda said. "You're the one Jack is marrying after I'm gone, but in a way you were there before me, as well. I know all about it, you see. I knew about your . . . romance, at Magnus, before my marriage. I knew, or deduced, something about how you two broke up. I suppose I knew more than I had a right to know. Not that it did me any good."

Francie still said nothing.

"And yet, in another way, I came before you," Belinda went on. "Jack and I were informally engaged for a long time. Of course, it was an engagement he fought against tooth and nail, but it was a relationship of sorts, and through it I learned a lot about him, and about the Magnuses."

There was a pause. Belinda looked thoughtful and composed. Obviously she had come here to say something important, and she wanted to put things in their proper perspective. Nevertheless, a tear appeared from somewhere and rolled down her cheek. She produced a handkerchief and dabbed at it, blushing.

"I'm no prize, I guess," she said. "But I don't want my own bitter experience to benefit only me. You're at the door to the world of Anton Magnus, Francie, and I came here to ask you if you're sure you want to go through it."

"Sure?" Francie asked. "Of course I'm sure, Miss . . ."

"Call me Belinda."

"Belinda. Of course I'm sure. Otherwise I wouldn't be engaged to marry Jack."

"You know your own mind, don't you?" Belinda asked.

Francie nodded slowly. "That's something I've learned one must do," she said.

Belinda sighed.

"I came here to tell you one thing," she said. "It may not sound very noble, and no doubt it shouldn't be coming from me. But when the time comes, I want you to remember that I was here. I want to have done this one thing. Is that clear?"

Francie nodded. "What do you have to say to me?"

"Jack may seem different from his father," Belinda said. "But what makes a man a Magnus goes deeper. They're cut from the same cloth. I want you to know that. I want you to go in with your eyes open."

Belinda blushed. She seemed ashamed of her own words, and yet relieved, as though they had been burning her insides for a long time before she got them out.

Francie looked long and hard at her visitor. So penetrating were the dark eyes on Belinda that her blush turned to pallor.

Then Francie spoke. Her words took Belinda by surprise.

"If I didn't marry Jack," Francie asked slowly, "would you want him back?"

Belinda looked away, and back at Francie. She began to answer, then held her tongue. She thought for a long moment before replying.

"Jack never loved me," she said. "Not the way a husband loves a wife. He was only going through the motions. He did it elegantly, perhaps even generously. But for me it was torture—every minute of it. Would I take him back? It would be crazy. I would be letting myself in for a lifetime of the same agony. Yet, to be completely truthful, yes, perhaps I would. Not because it would be right, but because—well, because love does strange things."

She paused. "But please believe me," she said in a determined voice. "I didn't come here to talk you out of marrying him so I could have him back. He won't come to me again, no matter what. You can count on that."

"Then why did you come?" Francie asked.

Belinda thought for a moment. "For the sake of my own conscience," she said. "Is that honest enough for you?"

Francie smiled. There was sympathy in her smile, and firmness.

"I doubt that there is any reason for you to have trouble with your conscience," she said. "But if it will make you feel better, Belinda, let me say this: I know all I need to know about Jack Magnus." She paused. "Does that clear things up between us?"

Belinda nodded. She was thinking about a folder in her desk at home, which contained photographs taken by her detective agency of Jack Magnus in bed with a young woman named Dana Salinger, who had worked with Francie at CompuTel, and been suddenly discharged under strange circumstances.

Belinda had come within inches of bringing those photos with her tonight, but something had stopped her. She realized now how right she had been to leave them out of her encounter with Francie Bollinger. On one hand it was not her place to be the bearer of such news. On the other hand, more obscurely, she sensed that Francie did not need to hear it, for Francie knew exactly what she was doing.

With an odd smile Belinda got up, moved to the door, and held out her hand.

"I wish you happiness," she said. "I mean it. And if—if you ever need a friend, you have one in me. Don't hesitate to put that to the test. Will you believe that?"

"Yes," Francie said, shaking her hand. "And thank you."

Francie opened the door and watched the other woman go through it.

There was a firmness to Belinda's step, despite her emotion. Somehow Francie could tell that Belinda was closer to getting over Jack than she realized.

As the elevator closed the two women's eyes met once more. Belinda's were full of relief and lingering pain. Francie's were calm, cautious, but not without sympathy.

When the door had closed Francie felt a sudden wave of exhaustion. She went straight to bed and slept eight much-needed hours. In her dreams the tormented image of Belinda appeared again and again, mingling with those of Jack and his father.

The dreams were not pleasant. But when Francie woke up she felt refreshed.

She had much to do.

$=$ 58 $=$

June 11, 1960

It was two o'clock in the morning.

Anton Magnus was sitting on the edge of his daughter's bed.

Julie looked dazed. Her eyes were stained with tears, but no grief showed on her face. Instead there was a look of bleak, infinite hopelessness.

On the bedside table was a brief letter from Scott Monteagle, delivered this afternoon. In it Scott broke off his engagement to Julie, his politeness and sympathy belying the fact that his message was final. She knew she would not see him again.

Anton Magnus was speaking softly.

"When you're older," he said, "you'll understand that I had no choice. I could not allow this marriage, Juliet. It would have been disastrous not only for our family, but for you and Scott as well. Someday you'll realize that."

She said nothing.

"I've always tried to let you have freedom in your choices," her father said. "That's the least a father can do. And, at the risk of sounding pompous, I've paid the price for that in your own behavior. It was that behavior, ultimately, that did you in, Juliet. You have only yourself to blame."

Her eyes were not focused on him. They were staring blankly at the walls.

"It's not too late for you to turn over a new leaf," he said. "Remember, you come from one of the finest families anywhere. There are lots of young men who would be happy to . . ."

Julie leaned forward suddenly and spat in her father's face, cutting off his words.

The gesture took Anton Magnus completely by surprise, the more so since she had seemed so passive since he came into the room.

He pulled out a handkerchief and cleaned his face, slowly and carefully.

When he put it away and looked at her again there was a dangerous glow in his black irises.

"Now listen to me," he said. "The police may not know who killed Mr. Johnny Marrante in his apartment, but I do."

He felt her react to his words. The look of contempt in her eyes became colored by fear.

"Do you think I haven't been keeping an eye on you these past years, in view of your childish and outrageous behavior?" he asked. "A man in my employ was inside that apartment within minutes of your departure. Your pathetic attempts to conceal your presence there were not what saved you from the police. It was the thorough work of my own man at the scene that erased all traces of you."

He could feel her resistance collapsing as he spoke.

"I have the evidence that places you at the scene," Anton Magnus said. "In addition, I have documentation of your entire sordid relationship with the dear departed Mr. Marrante. Though the gun has disappeared, there is enough to hang you, my dear. Lest you imagine yourself doing something silly, I suggest you ponder the alternative of twenty years in prison."

There was a silence.

"I think you'd better tell me what you did with that gun," he said.

Julie said nothing. There was hatred in her eyes, but also surrender.

"Tell me," he said.

She sighed. "I got rid of it."

Anton Magnus looked at her, paternal tenderness coming back into his eyes.

"When will you understand," he asked, "that your father's only concern is your safety and happiness? Everything I do, my dear, is done for you."

He took her hand. She let it rest in his. He felt the triumph of his will over her own. As usual, Anton Magnus held all the cards.

"Now," he said, "I want you to try to pull yourself together. I want you to start getting out with your mother, and seeing people. The right sort of people. I have a young man I want you to meet. He comes from one of the best families in the East, and his people are very anxious for a potential match between you. I've already spoken to him. He's more than willing to overlook the past. He understands what he would gain by marrying you."

He looked down at his daughter. His face softened.

"Give up, Juliet," he said. "Give up trying to fight me. Give up trying to fight against what is inevitable."

She said nothing. He saw a tear run down her face.

"Stop being a little girl," he said. "It's time for you to be a woman."

His hands touched her pajama top, finding their way toward the soft skin he knew so well. No rebellion opposed them. His daughter's will was crushed, just as he had intended it should be.

To Anton Magnus, this was the sweetest foreplay of all.

59

June 13, 1960

The wedding was forty-eight hours away.

St. Bartholomew's Church was prepared for a historic occasion. The ceremony would be covered by journalists from forty countries. The reception would be held at the Waldorf-Astoria. The affair was being designed by Peter Dyson, who had done galas at Buckingham Palace and the Elysée. The décor would be by Henri Descombes, the catering by Jacques Mercier. Jack Magnus's wedding would make history for its style as well as its guest list. Since he was the most eligible unattached man in the nation, his new marriage must be celebrated to the hilt.

In his apartment on East 68th Street Jack was gazing at the Manhattan skyline and trying to control his nerves.

The riot in his senses was worse than anything he had ever felt before. In forty-eight hours Francie Bollinger would be Mrs. Jack Magnus. At last she would belong to him, and the agonizing frustration of being near her, touching her, kissing her these past months would end.

Jack could hardly think straight. He had never wanted anything in his life as desperately as he wanted this beautiful young woman. There had been something about her these last months, something deep and feminine and a little mysterious in her manner, even as she returned his kisses, that drove him mad with desire.

He felt as eager as a schoolboy. It had been difficult to conceal this as he went over the last details with his father in the office today.

After much discussion Jack had convinced Francie to marry him now, rather than after the launching of her new computers. His reasoning was that they should enjoy their honeymoon in the Caribbean before she went to work marketing her computers. Francie, after some initial hesitation, had agreed.

Jack had breathed a private sigh of relief at her acquiescence. The early marriage and honeymoon were essential to his plans, and to those of Anton Magnus.

As soon as Jack and Francie were safely out of the country on their cruise ship, the new Magnus computer designed to steal the market from CompuTel's "Mollie" would be offered to the public.

The Magnus computer was to be called the MC 2000, and it would be launched through an unprecedented nationwide marketing blitz within hours after Jack and Francie departed from New York Harbor.

Within forty-eight hours of that moment, a worldwide revolution in business computing would have begun, engineered by specialists at Magnus under the authority of Anton Magnus himself, but made possible by Jack's crucial advance work since his betrothal to Francie.

On board the cruise ship it would be Jack who would hear the news first. The message would come by cable, and Jack would inform Francie of it a few days after their departure.

Jack would put on the most important act of his life at that moment. He would threaten to kill his father. He would insist on leaving the cruise immediately to return to New York and help Francie cope with the situation.

His emotion would not be difficult to feign, for in fact he hated his father almost as much as Francie did. Nevertheless his performance would have to be subtle, for she would be on her guard.

The ensuing weeks would be unpleasant. Jack would do everything in his power to help Francie fight the Magnus behemoth with her company's frail powers. There would be lawsuits, battles over patents. These would drag on for many months, probably for years. The results were a foregone conclusion, of course. Magnus would win.

But Francie would be by Jack's side all that time.

Everything depended on this initial phase. Once they were safely married, and Jack could claim to be Francie's ally against his father's company, he would be home free.

But he could barely think about all those subtleties now. In forty-eight hours Francie would be in his arms. This thought blinded Jack to everything else.

Upstairs in his office, Anton Magnus was blind to nothing. His mind had never been clearer.

The launch of the MC 2000 would be one of the most important events in the history of American business. Major advertising on television, radio, and in newspapers and magazines would announce to the world the revolutionary new affordable computer for large and small businesses. Sales and service centers for the new product would open immediately, each one announced to its surrounding community by a lavish local advertising campaign.

Two hundred Magnus Research and Development people had been at work on the computer, on Top Priority status, for the last six months. Their managers assured Anton Magnus that the computer was a work of genius, based on the most advanced state of microprocessor technology and an almost unbelievably subtle master program which made the machine easily usable by virtually any employee of average intelligence.

Anton Magnus had used his personal influence with leaders of American business to see that they bought the new machine for themselves and their subsidiaries. Confidential advance orders for the MC 2000 were already in the thousands.

Additionally, Anton Magnus had used his covert power with dozens of newspapers as well as the television networks and wire services to ensure that the revolutionary appearance of the MC 2000 on the scene would be covered in dozens of feature stories everywhere.

An epoch-making event was about to take place, an event which would change the shape of world business overnight—and Anton Magnus had made it happen.

Magnus sat studying his chessboard. The game was the 1937 World Championship between Alekhine and Euwe, but he could not concentrate on it, so consumed was he by his own more masterful game—a game that was not being played on a tiny board with inanimate men, but on a worldwide scale, with thousands of lives and hundreds of millions of dollars at stake.

This was the master stroke of a lifetime, the stroke that would make Magnus Industries the most powerful business entity on the planet.

Anton Magnus was happy tonight. Happier than he had ever been.

Julie, her little adventure with Scott Monteagle ended, was back in the fold where she belonged. She would give no more trouble. Her spirit was obviously broken by what had happened with Scott. Her wild days were behind her now. In due time Anton would arrange a suitable marriage for her.

As for Jack, Anton Magnus had a far subtler plan in mind for his shrewd and willful son.

Within a few weeks Jack's marriage to Francie Bollinger would be just a memory.

Anton would allow the marriage, of course. Jack had done his work well in bringing Magnus the computer system, and so Jack would have his Francie.

But when the time came Anton Magnus would see to it that Francie found out about Jack's role in the stealing of her system.

It would be simple. There was ample documentation of Jack's not-so-subtle spying on CompuTel over the past few months. Documentation which showed how Magnus Industries, thanks to Jack, had progressively monitored the gradual progress of Francie's "Mollie" through each stage of its development, and duplicated the machine's specifications in its own laboratories.

Anton Magnus intended to present Francie with this information himself. He wanted to see the look on her face when she found out her husband was the traitor who had ruined her company and stolen her most brilliant idea.

Once she knew the truth Francie would divorce Jack, no matter what the cost to her in heartbreak or humiliation. Of this Anton Magnus had no moral doubt.

Magnus understood people better than his son. Thus he knew his son's girl better than the son himself, and without the benefit of having savored her lovely body between the sheets. He knew her through the special intimacy of having fought her for four years with all his powers. This Francie was a girl with a will of iron, and an unshakable sense of right and wrong. When she found out Jack had betrayed her she would drop him like a piece of rubbish.

And that would break Jack's heart. For Jack loved her. Anton Magnus was more certain of this than of anything else.

When the first stage of the game was over, Magnus Industries would be the greatest corporation on earth. This fact would begin the second stage, the middle game.

Jack would be unable to resist the lure of so much power. He would lick his wounds for a while, and no doubt hate his father with as much passion as he now loved Francie Bollinger. But eventually he would come crawling back. That was Jack's nature.

Anton would graciously offer him his old position. But as a final quid pro quo, Anton would have another girl picked out for him. Someone from the right family.

And Jack would give in. For if he didn't, he would lose Magnus Industries.

Thus Anton would checkmate his son, once and for all.

It was all as simple and as beautiful as the great matches Anton liked to play over on the marble board in his study at home. But in this game the pawns were Francie Bollinger, with her energy, her intellect, and her ambition—and Jack, with his greed and his passion for Francie.

They were pretty pawns, nice to look at and full of ability. But they were only pieces to be moved by a finer hand. The hand of Anton Magnus.

Soon it would be over.

With that thought Anton Magnus closed the door on his son's image and went back to thinking of other things.

One floor below Anton Magnus sat his wife, alone in her reading room, watching distractedly as a variety show played on television.

Victoria Magnus was on tenterhooks. Since Julie's engagement had been broken Victoria had realized not only that something terrible had happened, but that something perhaps even more terrible was about to happen.

She knew her husband, and what he was capable of. She had known he was not in favor of Julie's marriage to Scott Monteagle. Thus, as night follows day, the marriage had not taken place.

This was a sad event, for Victoria Magnus had genuinely liked Scott, and looked forward to having him for a son-in-law. More yet, she knew that Julie loved the young man. He had been Julie's only real chance for happiness.

But from this sad state of affairs one could deduce more—if one knew Anton Magnus. For Anton was not in favor of Jack's marriage to Francie Bollinger. He never had been. He had prevented it the first time around, and seen to it that Jack married Belinda Devereaux. And now, subtle though Anton was in his apparent acceptance of the match, his wife knew he approved less than ever of Francie Bollinger, a girl he had hurt badly in the past, a girl whose marriage to his son would be a slap in the face to him.

Anton would not allow it.

But how could he prevent it? That was the question. To all intents and purposes, Jack was a free man.

Victoria Magnus was no match for her husband in cunning, not to mention power. She did not know how he would go about things. But he would not admit Frances Bollinger into his family. Of this she was convinced.

And this would destroy Jack's happiness as surely as the loss of Scott Monteagle had destroyed Julie, and as surely as marriage to Elliot Trowbridge had destroyed Gretchen. For Jack was wild about Francie, absolutely mad for her. Everyone could see it.

Anton never seemed satisfied until everyone was under his thumb. And he seemed to prefer that everyone be unhappy, for this proved the extent of his power even more. Not only was he a tyrant, but a sadistic one.

Victoria Magnus wrung her hands. She suspected what her husband was up to, but there was no way to stop him, no way to warn those concerned of the danger they were in.

So Victoria Magnus sat watching the meaningless images on the television screen, and waited for the cataclysm which might destroy what was left of her small world.

Upstairs in her room, Julie Magnus sat quietly in her bed, staring at the gun in her hand.

It was Johnny's gun, the gun she had killed him with. The barrel was pointed at her mouth. She held it without trembling. The tranquilizers she had taken tonight—and each day, in dangerously large doses, since she received the letter from Scott—made her hand steady.

She was glad she had kept the gun. There would be poetic justice in taking her own life with it. It would bring her closer to Johnny, who was, in a perverse way, the only man who had ever really known her inside and out. Too bad she could not be buried beside him. That would be the greatest joke of all.

But the gun would put her out of her misery, and stop her from having to face the fact that each day she lived in a world which separated her from Scott Monteagle.

Her death would be the final embarrassment to her parents. But she would not be around to enjoy it. She was past caring about such insignificant rebellions.

No, she just wanted it to end.

But as she looked down the barrel of the gun, something made her hesitate.

The moment was not right. It was too soon. The coming days were to bring important events to the Magnus family. Jack's whole future was at stake.

Julie wanted to see how things came out.

She would live a while longer, then, for the sake of mere curiosity.

With this thought, and a sour little smile to herself, Julie put the gun back in her lap.

Francie was in her office at the warehouse. The place was nearly empty now, for it was late.

She picked up the phone and dialed a number. There were three rings. Then a man's voice answered.

"Sam Carpenter."

"Sam . . ." For a moment Francie felt weak. Her voice failed her.

"Hello? Who is this?" Sam's voice sounded hollow and irritable.

"It's Francie, Sam. I'm sorry to bother you at home . . ."

"No bother," Sam said. "What can I do for you?"

He spoke in the calm, businesslike tone he had adopted ever since the day Francie's engagement to Jack Magnus was announced. There was not a hint of reproach in his voice. Nor was there sadness. Just a blank neutrality that wrung Francie's heart.

But she had been strong up until now. She had to go on being strong.

"Sam, I just wanted to make sure you're going to be home tomorrow night," she said. "I'm going to have some last-minute details to go over before my . . . before I leave. I don't want to call everyone together for a meeting. If you don't mind, I'd like you to be the one to pass the instructions along."

"No problem," Sam said. "I'll be here."

There was a pause. His words, so cold and brief, hung in the electronic ether joining them across the city. Francie wondered whether he could feel her sadness. She felt his own only too much. It broke her heart.

But today, more than ever, she had to keep her feelings in.

"Thanks, Sam," she said. "I'll talk to you tomorrow, then."

"Right, Francie. Goodbye."

"Goodbye."

Her eyes misted as she hung up the phone. Somehow she felt more alone at this moment than ever before in her life. For so many weeks and months her solitary mission, her plans and her exhausting work, had kept her going even as they consumed her. But tonight she felt like a needful little girl, desperate for love.

She took a deep breath to clear her mind.

Just a little while longer, she told herself. *Hang on. You're going to make it.*

Then she picked up the phone again, forced herself to smile, and dialed Jack's number.

═══ 60 ═══

June 15, 1960

The day of Jack Magnus's wedding dawned propitiously. It was a lush June morning, full of tender new leaves and signs of the fruitful summer to come.

Jack lay in bed for a long time after waking, feeling an almost childlike excitement, as though it were Christmas morning and he was about to rush downstairs to open his presents under the tree.

At length he got up, shaved and groomed himself carefully, dressed in his cutaway jacket and gray waistcoat with dark striped trousers, and had himself driven to his parents' mansion. An atmosphere of quiet excitement reigned in the stately rooms.

Jack went upstairs to see Julie. He was worried about her, for Mother had warned him she might be too upset to go to the wedding.

But Julie seemed calm and even good-humored.

"Wait till you see the present I got you," she said. "It will come in handy on your honeymoon."

The twinkle in her eyes was a trifle wild. He wondered if she was on something, even at this hour of the morning. But she had put on a beautiful dress for the occasion, and assured him she would not misbehave. Something cool and determined in her demeanor reassured him.

Mother was flitting nervously around the house, alarmed by everything and trying to appear pleased. She had already seen her son married once, and was not up to the excitement of going through it a second time. She was in her usual tizzy as she called the church and the director of the reception, making sure everything was ready for an eleven o'clock ceremony with reception to follow an hour later.

Jack knocked at his father's door. Anton Magnus greeted him with a hug and a wink. "Today's the day," Anton Magnus said. He himself seemed surprisingly excited.

Jack wished he could call Francie, but remembered her firm injunction against it.

"It's bad luck to be in touch with me on our wedding day," she had said. "I'll see you at the altar, handsome."

Jack's anticipation rose with each instant. Tonight Francie would be in his arms, aboard a cruise ship bound for the Virgin Islands. The pleasure he had dreamed of all through all these months of rising tension would at last be a reality. He would be the happiest man in the world.

As eleven o'clock drew nearer, minute by frustrating minute, Jack felt he was about to burst.

During the morning, at Magnus International headquarters, a hundred specialists were putting the finishing touches on the biggest marketing blitz in the history of the company. At the distribution facilities in New Jersey, Chicago, and San Diego, hundreds of MC 2000s were boxed and ready for delivery. An army of sales reps were standing by to begin the most important campaign of their careers, and the most secret.

Full-page ads in the *Times,* the *Chicago Tribune,* and the *Los Angeles Times,* not to mention the major business magazines and newspapers, would appear tomorrow morning. Feature articles on the MC 2000 would appear in the upcoming issues of *Time, Newsweek,* and *Look,* announcing the computerization of American business, and analyzing the epoch-making significance of the Magnus innovation. The major international publications would not be far behind.

Within a couple of weeks the whole world would know about the MC 2000. Never before had a product been kept secret for so long, and unveiled with such a splash.

This was the way Anton Magnus wanted it.

The family gathered together in the downstairs salon at ten o'clock. Flanked by two Magnus press secretaries, they went out through the front doors, passed a hundred reporters, got into their Rolls-Royce limousine, and began the slow journey through traffic to St. Bartholomew's.

Little was said in the car. They all knew what was coming. This was Jack's day, the day he had fought for, waited for, and finally won.

Anton Magnus held his wife's hand. Jack held Julie's. Julie sat staring quietly out the window.

* * *

In his loft on Spring Street Sam Carpenter sat with a cup of cold coffee and a stubbed-out cigarette, looking at this morning's copy of the *Times*.

MAGNUS NUPTIALS TODAY, read the headline in the society section, above a lengthy story of the relationship between handsome Jack Magnus and the brilliant, beautiful young woman with whom he had had a storybook romance that was at last leading to matrimony.

Sam looked at the story and the accompanying pictures for the hundredth time.

So today was the day.

He had dreaded it and waited for it all these months, as a patient fighting an incurable disease waits unbelievingly for death. He had tried to tell himself something would come along to stop it, or that Francie would somehow come to her senses. He had never really faced the truth, for the ache in his heart had not allowed him to accept the idea that he would lose Francie forever.

He looked at the loft around him. It had never looked so empty. He recalled the first week he had spent in New York, seven years ago, when his broken marriage was a fresh wound, and he felt completely alone in the world. It was then that he had rented the loft and begun filling it with spare computer parts, the eventual building blocks of Mollie, simply to keep himself from going crazy.

But the grief he had known in those days was as nothing compared to the void inside him now.

Last night Francie had called him to relate the special instructions for CompuTel during her honeymoon. Sam had listened patiently to the somewhat surprising instructions, trying to concentrate on her words rather than on the fact that the next time she spoke to him, she would be a married woman.

He thought of Francie and her new husband, the man who had been there before Sam and after him, the man with whom he had never been able to compete. What kind of man was Jack Magnus? Could he be as evil as Sam's instincts had told him he must be? Or was that impression the result of the most terrible jealousy Sam had ever dreamed possible?

Sam shrugged. It made no difference. He was through tilting at windmills. The game was over.

Be happy, Francie, he thought as he looked at the picture of her in the *Times*.

* * *

The organ was playing quietly in the church, which was packed to the rafters with guests whose illustrious names matched their priceless designer clothes. Everyone Anton Magnus had invited was here; no one had dared refuse. Wedding gifts of incalculable value from presidents, royalty, and the pillars of business and society, were waiting in the reception area. Outside the church a dozen limousines waited, and a crowd of journalists.

The Magnuses were seated at the front. Jack and his best man, a Magnus colleague who had been his roommate at Yale, were waiting to enter the church.

Someone noticed that the space reserved for Francie's father was empty. Mr. Bollinger had not attended the rehearsal four days ago, because of a family illness. None of the Magnuses had met him.

It was ten minutes to eleven. Anton Magnus began to get worried.

"Has anyone spoken to Francie?" he asked his wife.

Victoria Magnus stammered that she knew nothing about it.

"Juliet," Anton asked Julie, "go speak to your brother. See if he's heard from Francie."

Julie excused herself. Jack was nervously waiting in the wings.

"Julie," he said, "you're just the one I want to see. Go find Francie. See what's keeping her."

Julie disappeared. Jack waited, making embarrassed conversation with his best man.

Five minutes later Julie came back. The look on her face was inscrutable.

"She's not here," she said.

Jack turned pale.

"Not here?" he asked. "What the hell do you mean? She has to be here. What's going on?"

Julie shrugged. "I spoke to the rector and the wedding director. She's nowhere to be found. And her maids of honor haven't shown up yet, either."

Jack's lips curled in a tight frown. "Maybe something's happened to her," he said. "Someone should go look for her. This is impossible."

Anton Magnus had appeared from inside the church. Hearing the commotion, he accompanied Jack to the nearest phone. Julie trailed after the two men, a strange, watchful look on her face. Jack called Francie's apartment, waiting nervously as the phone rang and rang on the other end. Julie stood looking into her father's eyes calmly.

At last Jack put down the phone. He dialed a new number. The phone was picked up almost immediately.

"CompuTel, can I help you?"

"This is Jack Magnus calling. I need to speak to, or locate, Frances Bollinger. It's urgent."

"Miss Bollinger is not available," the secretary said in a neutral voice. "I'm sorry."

"For Christ's sake, it's her wedding day!" Jack shouted into the phone. "She's got to be available. This is an emergency. Where can I get in touch with her?"

"Miss Bollinger is not in the office," the secretary said. "Would you like to leave a message, Mr. Magnus?"

Jack's pallor had turned to a hot flush of embarrassment. His hand was shaking as he held the receiver. Behind him he could feel his family watching him. The truth was beginning to dawn on him.

"And you don't know where she is?" he asked in a lower voice.

"Miss Bollinger is out of the city today," responded the implacable voice. "She can't be reached. I'll be happy to give her your message . . ."

Jack slammed down the phone.

When he turned he saw Julie smiling at him.

"Brother dear," she said, "it appears you've been stood up."

She looked at her father.

"Someone had better tell the guests," she said. The triumph in her voice was obvious.

Anton Magnus reddened. Only now did he begin to suspect that he had been monumentally outwitted.

"You and your mother can handle this from here," he said to Jack with a sour curl of his lip. "I'm going to the office."

I'll kill her for this, he mused as he strode out of the church.

He thought how ridiculous he and his son and his family were being made to look in front of the assembled cream of society and business, not to mention the press. In tonight's papers the whole country would be informed that Jack Magnus had been stood up at the altar by a nobody, a girl from an insignificant rural background.

In thirty years at the head of a legendary corporation Anton Magnus had never been so embarrassed. He would get his revenge on the Bollinger girl for this, if it was the last thing he did in this world.

When he arrived in his office at Magnus Headquarters there was a telegram waiting for him.

"I thought you should have this right away," his executive secretary said, holding out the telegram. "It seems—well, perhaps you should look for yourself."

Anton Magnus snatched the telegram and tore it open.

It read:

THE MASTER STROKE

DEAR MR. MAGNUS,

QUEEN TAKES PAWN. I BELIEVE IT IS YOUR MOVE.

The telegram was unsigned.

Anton Magnus crumpled it and threw it on the floor. His secretary stood looking at him, a helpless expression on her face as she admired his formal clothes and his bright red boutonnière.

Anton Magnus did not move to enter his office. He stood gazing out the window at the skyline, the crumpled telegram at his feet, the wheels turning quickly in his mind. He realized he had encountered a determined and damnably intelligent adversary, someone clever enough to have seduced his son and set up this grotesque situation, simply to get at Anton Magnus himself. The quiet triumph in the telegram left no doubt.

But already Anton Magnus was beginning to get control of himself, and to assay his powers. It was Jack who had been jilted, not Anton himself. Young Francie Bollinger, a woman scorned when Jack married Belinda, had taken her revenge. A woman's revenge. So be it.

But tomorrow morning Magnus Industries would take its revenge on little Francie in the only arena that really counted—the marketplace.

Tomorrow we take no prisoners, he said to himself. *Let the game begin.*

Leaving his secretary staring at him open-mouthed, he entered his office and slammed the door.

$$=== 61 ===$$

The morning after Jack Magnus's aborted wedding, the new MC (Magnus Computer) 2000 hit the business world with an enormous splash. So great was the impact of the Magnus-orchestrated publicity that news releases about the new computer appeared on all the wire services simultaneously, and features on its workings and its great future were done on all three television networks. The MC 2000 was the biggest business story since the advent of television. Anton Magnus himself was interviewed on "Meet the

Press," and the Magnus Research and Development staff who had worked on the MC 2000 became overnight celebrities.

In the midst of this storm of publicity few observers noticed that, two weeks after the stunning appearance of the MC 2000, the oddly named "Mollie," a competing product manufactured by tiny CompuTel, Inc. of Brooklyn, New York, made its modest debut in the computer marketplace.

When Anton Magnus was informed of this event he smiled to himself. There was no possibility of Mollie competing with the MC 2000, which was already installed in hundreds of locations and had been ordered by thousands of customers. CompuTel had been beaten to the punch, and with a vengeance.

What puzzled Anton Magnus, though, was that there was no lawsuit by CompuTel alleging that trade secrets or patented material had been stolen by Magnus Industries. This surprised him. It also surprised the Magnus legal department, which had been preparing an elaborate and unbeatable defense against just such a suit for months now.

Anton used his chess master's mind to study the situation. If the Bollinger girl had somehow been wised up to Jack's chicanery, and jilted him for that reason, then why did she not sue Magnus? This was the first move Anton Magnus had expected her to make. After all, a lawsuit was her only chance for financial survival, since her foolishly named "Mollie" could not hope to compete with the powerhouse MC 2000.

What did she have up her sleeve?

Anton Magnus was to find out, to his chagrin. What happened to the Magnus Corporation in the next three months was to become one of the landmarks of American business history.

The marketing of the MC 2000 was a huge success initially. Companies all over the country competed with each other to be the first to computerize their operations with the affordable new computer. It was considered the "modern" way to do business, and no corporate president wanted to be branded as a fuddy-duddy. The MC 2000 came with elaborate training manuals and basic programs, so that a company could use its own operators to man the machine, without having to hire professional programmers.

Within a month after its launch the MC 2000 was working efficiently in over two thousand locations nationwide, with units being shipped to Europe, South America, and Australia as fast as production could proceed. Five thousand units had been sold, and Magnus was rushing to produce another ten thousand to keep up with demand. The corporation stood to show a record profit for the next three quarters, thanks to the MC 2000.

Magnus Industries was being hailed as the greatest office producer in the world, having superseded IBM at a single stroke.

Meanwhile, virtually no one had heard of the modest "Mollie" from CompuTel, Inc.

Then something went wrong.

About six weeks after the introduction of the MC 2000, a small company in Virginia complained to the Magnus service specialists that its computer was hopelessly confusing the company's records and payroll. Since the service policy on the MC 2000 was extremely liberal, Magnus computer specialists rushed to the scene, free of charge, to fix the computer and make good any damage to the company.

But the computer could not be repaired. The specialists worked on it for three days, studying the interior workings and basic operating programs over and over again. They took the machine apart and put it back together again. But they could not find anything wrong with its mechanics or with the programs.

Everything was in order. Yet the results were disastrous.

The Magnus salesmen offered the Virginia company a brand-new machine, which it accepted. The defective model was scrapped, and its performance chalked off to a fluke, a faulty circuit, a burnt-out transistor.

But no sooner had this episode been laid to rest than a complaint came in from a clothing company in Chicago. The problem was the same. The MC 2000 had worked perfectly for several weeks, and then "gone crazy." It was juggling figures uncontrollably, printing out wildly wrong paychecks, and making a nightmare of inventory and sales.

By the time the service people got to Chicago, there were more complaints from companies throughout the country. All the complaints were identical. The MC 2000, after performing in an exemplary manner for several weeks, began to show bugs, problems, peculiarities. Its performance rapidly worsened, and no technician or programmer could fix it.

By the time the complaints reached the flood stage, the companies which had received the first replacement models of the MC 2000—the first complainers—had found that their replacement machines were also defective.

An urgent meeting of the Computer Research and Development Division at Magnus was held. Computer experts were ordered to work around the clock to find the source of the problem. It was not an easy job. The inner workings of the MC 2000 were complex and very subtle. So were the programs that gave the machine its marching orders.

Before the experts could make their report, a bank in Ohio, in a landmark court case, brought suit against Magnus Industries for damages it had incurred in its savings, checking, and investment divisions because of the non-performance of the MC 2000. The bank charged that the claims made for the product by Magnus were deceptive, and that the machine had violated the terms of its sales contract under federal and state law, and had caused the bank severe financial distress.

More companies followed suit. In a whirlwind of nightmarish activity, Magnus was not only forced to take back MC 2000s by the thousands, incurring an enormous financial loss, but the huge corporation saw its legal department fighting a desperate battle against lawsuits amounting to hundreds of millions of dollars.

The MC 2000 was a disaster. By the third month after launch the Computer Division was refunding customers for all the units sold, and Magnus was inundated with lawsuits. Articles were appearing everywhere as the press, smelling blood, jeered at the "Edsel of the computer world." Magnus Industries was becoming a laughingstock. The business press teemed with stories about the giant conglomerate's premature distribution of an insufficiently tested product. Some publications suggested that Magnus had "set back the computer age by twenty years."

But this prediction, surprisingly, turned out to be incorrect.

For slowly, quietly, the humble "Mollie" from little CompuTel of Brooklyn had made inroads into the very marketplace devastated by the Magnus MC 2000.

Despite the disaster of the MC 2000, businessmen, once introduced to computer technology, had realized that it could make their lives much easier. When they were visited by friendly, helpful CompuTel salesmen who explained to them that they could have a Mollie for less than what they had paid for an MC 2000, with unconditional guarantees on the Mollie's performance and free visits by service personnel to make sure of the machine's continuing effective operation, some of them were willing to take a chance.

The Mollie operated perfectly. Not a single Mollie customer was dissatisfied. By the end of the three-month period in which the MC 2000 became a landmark disaster, 7500 Mollie units had been sold, and business was growing every day.

In the scorched earth of the MC 2000's failure, the seeds of Mollie were bearing fruit.

Now that sales justified a major advertising campaign for Mollie, CompuTel placed glossy ads in all the major business publications, under the telling slogan, MOLLIE. THE COMPUTER THAT WORKS.

A cleverly produced television commercial was seen nationwide, showing a crusty but highly competent middle-aged housekeeper who put the affairs of her employers in order. The attractively rumpled woman—a brilliant actress chosen for this crucial role after a lengthy search by Francie and her people—spoke to the camera about the virtues of old-fashioned dependability, and suggested in her no-nonsense voice that the businessman with a good head on his shoulders should buy a Mollie to help him streamline his operation and free his employees from boring record-keeping work.

The campaign was an immediate success. The name Mollie accentuated the non-threatening image of the new product, and humanized the computer age.

CompuTel's stock went up day after day, then split, then went up again. The company's sales skyrocketed.

And now the business press took note of this modest newcomer that was succeeding where the mighty Magnus corporation had failed. Articles began appearing in business magazines on the new company and its efficient, innovative management. CompuTel became a high-profile company overnight.

On September 17th Anton Magnus was informed by his Board of Directors that there was no alternative but to cancel the MC 2000 product line, make costly settlements in the lawsuits pending, and dissolve the entire Computer Division of Magnus Industries at once. The corporation's foray into computers had been a failure. Hundreds of millions of dollars had been lost. Magnus Industries' stock had plummeted, because the disaster of the MC 2000 was reflecting on the company as a whole. It was time to cut the losses.

Reluctantly, Anton Magnus agreed. His capitulation made national and international business news. Anton Magnus read the humiliating articles, some of which appeared alongside large glossy ads for the Mollie, whose sales were reaching higher and higher levels. THE HARDER THEY FALL, read one headline about the Magnus fiasco. ANTON'S FOLLY MAKES HAY FOR MOLLIE, read another.

The battle was lost. There was nothing to do but retire as gracefully as possible, and live to fight again another day. Retreat was not in Anton Magnus's nature, but this time he had no choice.

Anton Magnus realized he had been beaten.

But not how badly he had been outwitted. The worst news was yet to come.

* * *

On October 1st an exclusive interview with Francie Bollinger appeared in *Fortune* magazine. It created such a sensation that abridged versions of it were picked up by the major wire services, and appeared in magazines and newspapers all across the country. Profiles of Francie in *Time, Newsweek,* the *Journal,* and a dozen foreign publications followed.

The interview told an incredible story.

Frances Bollinger, as president and CEO of CompuTel, had invented and developed Mollie with the help of her top staff, the item read. In the course of research and development she had become aware that a major corporate competitor—whom she refused to identify by name in the story—was preparing to steal her design. The latest techniques in corporate spying were involved. The financial resources of the invading conglomerate were beyond little CompuTel's frail defenses.

"So we decided," Francie told the reporter, "to let them dig their own grave. We knew that Mollie still had a few bugs, serious ones, though they weren't visible to any but the most expert eye. So we instituted some special security measures for the final product, and left the earlier prototype more or less unprotected in our warehouse.

"Sure enough," she went on, "the larger corporation stole our work and came out with a product before us. But their machine failed after a few weeks, because of the faults in its design. Luckily for us, customers around the country were still interested enough in computerization to turn to Mollie. In the interim, of course, we had ironed out the bugs and perfected our machine. Luck was on our side and against them. So this was our unusual way of defeating a competitor of superior fiscal power and, of course, dubious business ethics."

Francie could not, of course, tell the entire truth—namely, that she and she alone had intentionally sabotaged Mollie's design so that the computer would work effectively at first, and then deteriorate over time. Her own greatest and most devious accomplishment as a programmer would never see the light of day.

But its effects were already making history.

The interview created a sensation. DAVID BEATS GOLIATH, read one headline. MAGNUS COMPUTER CHICANERY REVEALED, read another. FRANCIE, THE GIANT-KILLER, read a third.

None of the business reporters was fooled as to whom Francie was referring to when she openly accused a competitor of stealing her trade secrets and her patented material. Magnus became known as the monster conglomerate who had tried to eat up its smaller and more honest competitor, and got richly punished for its trouble.

* * *

When Anton Magnus read these articles he saw red.

He called a special meeting of his top legal staff, and of the Board. The legal brain trust was instructed to institute a suit against CompuTel which would force the smaller company to pay all the damages incurred by Magnus through the MC 2000 fiasco, since CompuTel was indirectly responsible for all the losses.

The legal experts shook their heads.

"We can't sue CompuTel for test-developing a defective product with the knowledge that we would steal it," the chief attorney said. "In order to do that we would have to admit that we *did* steal it—and we can't do that."

"Well, then," Anton Magnus asked, "can't we at least sue CompuTel for libel based on this defamatory interview she has given in the press? Our legal people ought to be able to win such a suit."

The chief attorney shook his head.

"Miss Bollinger refuses to name names," he said. "She hasn't directly accused us of anything. And if we try to call her bluff, we'll be admitting to her accusations. She'd beat us in court."

Anton Magnus pointed to one of his executive assistants, who now spoke up.

"Can't we countersue alleging that CompuTel stole *our* product?" the young man asked, looking at the notes in a file folder before him. "It may sound like a tough position to attack from, but we have the strongest legal people anywhere. After all, we beat CompuTel to distribution."

The lawyer shook his head. "On one hand, their machine works, while ours doesn't. Our suit would appear frivolous, and make us look ridiculous. Also, it goes without saying that we lack the research and development records to prove that the idea was ours from the beginning. This," he added, clearing his throat, "is because the idea was not in fact ours."

He sighed. "Frankly, sir, I think we would lose all around. The only thing we can do is to sit it out and wait for the furor to die down. And, I might add, we should be glad CompuTel isn't suing *us* for unfair practices and theft of trade secrets."

Anton Magnus looked angrily around the table.

He had lost.

He dismissed the Board and the legal experts.

The rage burning inside him would never be allowed to spend itself. Little Francie Bollinger, the nobody he had intended to crush like a gnat, had outmaneuvered the entire Magnus Corporation, and Anton Magnus himself.

And, what was even more humiliating, she had used poor foolish Jack as her pawn in this clever game. She had allowed him back into her life, made it easy for him to steal her secrets for Magnus, but cleverly arranged things so that the computer would not work for Magnus, but would work for her. This had required enormous technical intelligence.

But it had also required an incredibly subtle instinct for human weakness, and a relentless concentration on revenge. Francie Bollinger had been a step ahead of everyone all along. She had used the Magnus Corporation to the hilt even as she destroyed its best-laid plans. And today she could watch her new product achieve greater and greater success, and savor the fact that Magnus could do nothing but sit on the sidelines and stew in its own bile.

As a chess player, Anton Magnus had met his match. His greatest strengths had been turned into weaknesses. The ramparts of his power had been turned into a house of cards.

He was not so surprised, then, when a second anonymous telegram arrived soon after the scrapping of the MC 2000 was announced to the business world.

It read:

DEAR MR. MAGNUS,

CHECK—AND MATE.

Now Anton Magnus knew the full measure of his humiliation.
Goliath had been defeated.

═ 62 ═

Sam was alone on the lake.

It was late afternoon, and he had been out all day, but he was loath to go back to shore.

He hadn't caught anything, but he was enjoying the sweet rippling of the water, and the cradling motion of the boat.

Sam was home again. The lake was still the same, and the land around it. The fish under this boat knew him. He could feel it in the way they nibbled at his bait and circled around the boat. There was a kind of permanence to their welcome, as to the lake itself.

For the second time in his life Sam had come back here after having lost the happiness he had tried to make for himself in the other world. The first time he had come back embittered, realizing that his marriage had never been worthy of the name.

This time he was coming back with a deeper wound to heal. For he knew that, where Francie was, there his heart would remain forever.

Sam had never felt emptier or more tired. He wished he could hide in this safe place forever, and never again throw himself into the unequal battles of the world.

But the water underneath him was telling him he was not finished. He would live, somehow. There were still things to learn, challenges to meet.

And carrying around with him the scar Francie had left was in itself a noble torch to bear. It had all been worth it. Giving one's heart to a Francie was a chance so special that even when it lead to loss, one could hardly regret it.

He recalled how fate had made him stumble, nearly four years ago, on that tiny ad in the newspaper—COMPUTEL, INC., COMPUTER CONSULTANTS —and led his steps to the dingy little storefront on 40th Street where Francie looked up at him from her desk as he came through the chipped old door. What an unlikely setting for the greatest encounter of his life! Even now he smiled to remember it.

Sam was musing over this thought when something made him sit up. It was the sound of an oar against the water, and the groan of an oarlock.

He looked up to see a boat approaching him. It was hard to make out the occupant at this distance, particularly in the gathering dusk.

But as the boat came nearer he recognized Francie. She was dressed in jeans and a checked wool shirt, and a fishing hat that did not fit her.

Sam could not believe his eyes. The vision before him took his breath away, and sapped the last of his courage. He could only sit and watch as she came closer.

Francie rowed to his side and extended her oar to pull his boat to hers. Then she held him by the gunwale and smiled.

"Is this where they're biting?" she asked.

Sam gazed at her through the sudden mist clouding his eyes. She had never looked more beautiful. The smile on her face made it clear why she was here.

"They haven't yet," he said. "But I have hopes. It's a long day."

"Of course it is," she said. "We have all the time in the world, you and I. Isn't that right? A good fisherman knows that all things come to him who waits."

Sam nodded. Their heavy boats were held together only by her slender hand, but there was no current to separate them.

He leaned forward and grasped her hand firmly with his own.

"Want to come aboard?" he asked.

"I already am, skipper," she said.

=== 63 ===

The Wall Street Journal, *November 1, 1960*

Magnus Stock Hits Record Low

Troubled Magnus Industries, fighting hundreds of lawsuits over the failure of its vaunted MC 2000 business computer, and under indictment by the U.S. Department of Justice on a variety of unfair trade practice and fraud charges, had its lowest third quarter in twenty years, its stock closing at $77.82 on the Exchange.

The woes of the giant conglomerate are sending ripples through its international network of stockholders, who are selling the formerly blue-chip Magnus shares in large lots. Action on the rapidly falling stock has been tumultuous in the past three weeks.

Spokesmen for the reeling corporation assured stockholders yesterday that the setback suffered in the wake of the MC 2000 is only temporary, and that the company's firm economic base will see it through to a prosperous future. There are rumors, however, of high-level shake-ups within the corporation, and of pressure from the Board to force the retirement of Chairman and CEO Anton Magnus, whose personal imprimatur, according to rumor, was on the MC 2000 project from its outset.

Whether Magnus Industries will bounce back any time soon is any-

one's guess. It seems safe to say that the glory days of the famous
conglomerate are at an end.

A large drop of aged Armagnac fell onto the surface of the newspaper and slowly seeped into the porous newsprint. A somewhat unsteady finger hovered over the stain for a second, touched wistfully at it, and then sank to the desk top.

Anton Magnus was alone in the upstairs study in his mansion.

He was drunk. He had been drinking thirty-year-old Armagnac since early this evening. As he looked down at the newspaper he saw the lines blur before his eyes. He could barely see straight.

Magnus was unaccustomed to drunkenness. It was a weakness he had not allowed himself throughout his long business career. But tonight, after seeing the record-low third quarter earnings of his corporation trumpeted to all the world, something had snapped inside him. He had refused dinner, stormed upstairs with his bottle of brandy, and closeted himself here to think.

But thought would not come. So enormous was his rage that as he sat at the desk, consuming drink after drink, his insides on fire, he did not come one inch closer to the sharp insight that had sustained him all these years.

For the first time in his life, Anton Magnus was out of control.

When he made the effort to analyze his situation, his thoughts only reminded him of the utter defeat he had suffered at the hands of a callow girl he should have destroyed long ago. Never in his worst nightmares had he imagined himself being outwitted by an opponent of such meager powers. Yet it had happened, and all the world knew about it. He was the butt of a thousand bad jokes up and down Wall Street. The countless enemies he had made over the years were all jeering at him today.

Thanks to Frances Bollinger.

Feeling his rage well up inside him, he took another large swallow of the brandy. As he did so he noticed the clock on his desk top. Two A.M. He had been lost in his drunken reverie for seven hours, then.

The house was silent around him. The family, daunted by his display of anger, must have gone to bed without daring to say goodnight.

He picked up the folded newspaper and threw it toward the wastebasket. He missed by a foot, though the receptacle was only inches from him. His rage deepened. Even the most pliant of objects resisted his will.

All at once he thought of Julie.

He had not touched her since the night they had their final conversation about her Englishman. He had wanted to give her time to get over that before he went to her again. Since then Jack's aborted marriage, followed by the horrific turn of events at Magnus, had distracted him. He had been so busy in Board meetings, and working so late to stem the tide of disaster, that he had not had time to think of his daughter.

But he thought of her now.

He got to his feet. He stood leaning against the desk, the glass of Armagnac in one hand, the bottle—now almost empty—in the other. Though he could feel his body sway somewhat in the silence, like a skyscraper in a high wind, he seemed to be in possession of his faculties.

He left the library, shambled down the hall, and took the elevator to the fourth floor. He knew his steps were unsteady, but he managed to be silent so as not to wake up the house.

He reached Julie's door. It was locked. He fumbled for his key, his favorite key, the one that always seemed to symbolize her girlish charms. He had more difficulty in finding it than he had expected. Frustration made him even more angry than before.

He fitted the key into the lock and turned it.

The door opened.

He went in. He closed the door behind him as quietly as possible and turned the knob to lock it. He looked at the bed. The creature in it was invisible in the darkness. There was no nightlight.

"Juliet," he muttered thickly.

There was a movement in the bed.

"Don't come near me," came her voice.

"Juliet, be reasonable." He tried to put on his old cajoling manner.

"Get out of here. I'm warning you . . ."

This rebellion was too much. Anton Magnus saw red. In the last month he had suffered the worst humiliations of his life. This girl would not stand in the way of what he wanted tonight.

He moved toward his daughter.

"Don't play hard to get tonight, young lady," he growled. "One more word out of you and I'll break your little neck."

He sat on the edge of the bed. He reached to caress her. A hand came from nowhere and hit him hard in his face. Aroused, furious, he struck her back. She hit him again. He struck her harder.

Suddenly it seemed as though their final battle had erupted. He could feel the entire force of her hatred in the darkness, and could also feel the full fury of his own madness and frustration. They struck at each other in the charged silence of the room. There was an intimacy to their struggle that fueled his desire and also gave him the odd thought that he loved his daughter very much, after all.

He heard a noise from somewhere, but he was no longer possessed of reason. He attacked Julie with all the force of his rage, tearing at the buttons of her nightgown, pawing at her breasts, mawling furiously at every part of her he could see.

He was excited now, and ready to take her. He began to climb onto the bed. He thought he saw something in her hand. A gun? Impossible. Women of her class didn't own guns.

In that split second he thought of the young man she had killed, the Marrante fellow. She had said she got rid of the gun. Had she lied?

This thought came an instant too late.

He felt a white-hot explosion somewhere in the middle of his body. In its wake he heard a loud bang.

He went limp. He saw Julie's face, illuminated by a light whose source he could not fathom. Her eyes were open wide in terror and a sort of triumph.

His body was weightless, numb. He slumped atop his daughter.

He looked at her with a last glare of hate. Then he lost consciousness.

Behind him, staring from the doorway across his inert body into her daughter's eyes, stood Victoria Wetherell Magnus.

Epilogue

The bullet that entered Anton Magnus's torso fortunately missed all the crucial internal organs. However, it pierced the spinal cord, and the damage was irreversible. After exploratory surgery, Anton Magnus was pronounced a quadriplegic and confined to a wheelchair.

In view of his crippling injury Anton Magnus was forced to step down from his chairmanship of Magnus Industries. He remained a member of the Board, but his condition prevented his attending meetings or playing an active role in the company he had founded.

Jack Magnus became President and Chief Operating Officer of Magnus Industries. A year after assuming this post he married the former Priscilla Knowlton, of the Knowlton manufacturing family.

Francie Bollinger became Mrs. Sam Carpenter a month after her company, CompuTel, reached the Fortune 500 list. She remained as president of CompuTel, and became one of America's most celebrated businesswomen. CompuTel continued to grow as the foremost computer manufacturing firm in the nation, and eventually opened subsidiaries in fifteen countries.

Anton Magnus remained in seclusion after his accident, spending half the year in his Hilton Head Island house, the other half in New York. He was nursed exclusively by his daughter Juliet, who never married.

No official investigation of Anton Magnus's accident was ever held.

Police officers closest to the case were of the opinion that the wound to Anton Magnus's spine was caused by a revolver fired at point-blank range. The evidence of a struggle in his daughter's bedroom, combined with the bruises found on Juliet Magnus's face and arms, created strong suspicions that a dispute of unknown nature between the father and daughter had brought about the accident.

The gun used in the incident was never found. The investigation was dropped after pressure from influential parties was brought to bear.